Thorns of Truth

Thorns
of
Truth

EILEEN
GOUDGE

PENGUIN BOOKS

PENGUIN BOOKS

Published by the Penguin Group
Penguin Books Ltd, 27 Wrights Lane, London W8 5TZ, England
Penguin Putnam Inc., 375 Hudson Street, New York, New York 10014, USA
Penguin Books Australia Ltd, Ringwood, Victoria, Australia
Penguin Books Canada Ltd, 10 Alcorn Avenue, Toronto, Ontario, Canada M4V 3B2
Penguin Books (NZ) Ltd, Private Bag 102902, NSMC, Auckland, New Zealand

Penguin Books Ltd, Registered Offices: Harmondsworth, Middlesex, England

First published in the United States of America by Viking Penguin 1998
Published in Penguin Books 1999
3 5 7 9 10 8 6 4 2

Set in Adobe Garamond
Printed in England by Clays Ltd, St Ives plc

For Sandy, who showed me what it was all about

Acknowledgments

Over the past decade or so, since the publication of my first novel, *Garden of Lies*, readers from all over the world, and from all walks of life, have uttered the magic words every author wants to hear: "Those characters were so real to me, I keep wondering what might have happened to them." I, too, couldn't stop wondering. And having written the following, in which that question is at last answered—for now, at least—I wish to acknowledge all those who cared enough to ask, as well as every bookseller who believed in and supported me from the start. With particular thanks to the most dedicated and tireless of my supporters, Hermine Lieberman and the gang at Bronx Bookplace.

Truth and roses have thorns about them.

proverb

Thorns of Truth

❧ *July 6, 1996*

My dearest daughter,
Yes, my daughter. *I know what you're thinking, that it isn't fair. How can I claim you as a daughter when no one but the three of us—you, me, Nikos—knows the truth? The reason is simple: I am your mother. In fact, and in my heart, if not in the eyes of the world.*

I'm writing this, not as an apology, but in the hope of shedding some light on that dark place my secret has forced you to occupy. Only God knows how deeply I mourn the life that might have been yours, ours, had I made a different choice all those years ago. I've told you what happened . . . but do you know how often since that day you first came to me, demanding the truth, I've wanted to sit down with you, and simply talk? *Hear your thoughts and feelings . . . and tell you mine. Once, I believed I had all the time in the world. Now, as I sit by my bedroom window overlooking the garden, I see, instead of the roses I spent all morning pruning, only the lengthening of shadows.*

You see, my dear Rose, I am dying. Dr. Choudry tells me it may be only a matter of months; the heart that has been my faithful shepherd these seventy-four years is as worn-out, it appears, as I am. By the time you read this, I'll be gone. Along with, I pray, any bitterness you might still feel toward me.

That is why I'm writing this, the last of so many of letters addressed to you but never sent. I held back at first because they wouldn't have made sense—you wouldn't have known who I was—then, later, because I was afraid. I feared you would see them, not as expressions of love, but as pale substitutes for what I couldn't give you in person. This letter, too, will be put away with the others until after I'm gone. Perhaps then you will understand that I ask nothing of you other than for you to believe that you were dearly loved.

1

For regardless of what you might think, I would not have left you to be raised by another woman had I known how cruel she was. Truly it wasn't a decision I ever imagined I would have to make. Our lives, our future, everything would have turned out differently if not for what happened the night you were born. The fire. Oh, Rose, you can't imagine what it was like! Smoke, sirens, people running crazy in the corridors. I went a little crazy, too, I think. My only clear thought was that I had to find you. Rescue you.

But by the time I reached the hospital nursery, there was only one newborn left to be rescued . . . and it wasn't you. Afterwards, when everyone assumed the baby girl I'd carried to safety was mine, I felt I had no choice but to continue along the path on which fate had placed me. I was so desperate! With your dark eyes, and black hair, my husband, Gerald, would have known at once you weren't his. Any suspicions he'd had about Nikos, your true father, would have been confirmed.

In a moment of madness, I honestly believed the baby I held in my arms, with her fair skin and blue eyes, was the answer to my prayers. Who was I to question what was so clearly God's plan? It was as if I were being given one last chance to save myself . . . and save you. Yes, as crazy as I know it must seem to you, I truly believed you would be better off.

It didn't take long for me to realize how wrong I'd been. What a ghastly mistake I'd made. But by then, it was too late. Not only would it have cost me my marriage, but it would have meant giving up Rachel, whom I'd already grown to love dearly. I'm sorry if it hurts you to know this, my darling Rose, but otherwise, would any of it make sense? If not for Rachel, there would have been no need for secrecy after Gerald died. No need to protect anyone.

Don't think I'm unaware of what this has cost you. And how have I repaid you? Instead of acknowledging you openly, I made you promise to keep my secret. I've robbed you not only of a mother . . . but of a grandmother to your sons. And why? So that Rachel, the daughter you must think of as unfairly favored, won't be robbed of her peace of mind?

I wish it were as simple as that. But the situation, as you know, is far more complicated. Who was it that said, where one lie is planted, a thousand more will grow? Now, after all these years, it's not only Rachel I must think of . . . but her daughter. What would it do to Iris to learn that everything she's come to believe in, to trust, is nothing more than an elaborate deception? If she were a stronger person, she might not need protecting. But you know as well as I do, perhaps even better, how fragile Iris is. How easily something like this could push her over the edge.

And so I must leave you as I left you once before: with regret. I'm sorry. Not only to have let you down . . . but for raking all this up at what must seem the worst possible time. I know what it's like to lose a beloved husband. With Max, you had the rarest kind of love—passion coupled with friendship. Though we never married, that is what I've found with Nikos. Look after him. It will be hard for him without me. And don't blame him. None of this was his fault. He kept quiet all those years out of loyalty to me . . . not from any lack of love for you, his only child.

Try not to blame Rachel, either. Believe it or not, in some ways she envies you. Your wisdom. Your courage. You see, where adversity has made you strong, Rachel, I fear, tends to be headstrong. She rushes in where angels fear to tread, and is often so determined to save the world she doesn't notice when she herself needs saving.

But your greatest gift, my dear Rose, is also your greatest burden: compassion. If not for the goodness of your heart, you would have turned your back on me years ago. And who knows? Perhaps your life would have been the better for it.

All I can say for certain is that mine has been far richer for you being in it. The miracle is that we survived, somehow, you and I. And, I hope, grew closer along the way. For love, once planted, can thrive in the harshest soil. Given half a chance, it can even flower.

Trust in the power of love, Rose. Don't be afraid to open your heart to its possibilities when they come your way, which I promise they will. It won't mean you didn't cherish your husband. Quite the opposite. It will be a tribute to all that you and Max shared.

I must go now. If I don't hurry and get dressed, I'll be late for the party in Brian's honor. No one but Nikos knows how ill I am, so I must put on my best face. You will be there, too. I will smile, and make small talk. And hope that one day you'll see it as I do—that, in life, certain choices are like dying. Final, with no hope of ever turning back. You simply have to get through it with as much grace as you can muster.

Love always,

Sylvie

July

The old woman lived peacefully and happily with her children for many years. She took the two rose trees with her, and they stood before her window, and every year bore the most beautiful roses, white and red.

Grimm's Fairy Tales

Chapter 1

❧ "Mom, what would you think about Drew and me getting married?"

Rachel Rosenthal McClanahan didn't so much hear as *feel* her daughter's question: like a sharp tap between her shoulder blades. She'd been struggling with the clasp on the pearl choker Brian had given her last Hanukkah, and now stood frozen before the round mirror above her Art Deco vanity, arms upraised like wings, her reflection stark as an exclamation point in her fitted black dress.

Letting one end of the necklace slip from her fingers, cool as running water, she lowered her arms as slowly and carefully as if she'd been a patient at her clinic submitting to an exam. She'd been looking forward to this evening, to the party in her husband's honor . . . but what she now felt was something closer to dread, as if probing fingers had found a lump that might turn out to be malignant. The kind of low-grade dread she used to feel with Iris years ago, before—

Her mind slammed shut on that thought as effectively as a film director's clapper on a scene that wasn't going quite right. *Before she started seeing Dr. Eisenger,* Rachel finished on a safer note.

She turned slowly. Her lovely daughter, wearing only a slip, stood in front of Rachel's open closet, rooting for a jacket she'd asked to borrow. In her bare feet, Iris was just over five feet, her hair—the dark gold of alfalfa honey—falling in loose, slippery waves to the small of her back. Her delicate cameo of a face, with its rounded chin and forehead that somehow gave her a sweetly old-fashioned appearance, was flushed pink, and her brown eyes sparkled.

Rachel remained perfectly still, hardly daring to breathe, her arms and legs heavy with a cold, spreading numbness. The only thing

7

stirring was her heart—as it dropped into the pit of her stomach with the swiftness of a precariously balanced stone.

I must have misunderstood, she thought.

Yesterday. What Rose had confided to her over lunch—about Drew wanting to break things off with Iris. Rose had said he loved her as much as ever, couldn't imagine life without her. But it was slowly killing him . . . never knowing, from one minute to the next, what Iris might do. What kind of mood she'd be in. What she might accuse him of.

Rachel had been too stunned to reply.

Drew without Iris? That would be like the moon without the stars. When she tried to picture one apart from the other, all she could see in her mind was the two of them, like snapshots in a family album: Drew pulling Iris about in her red wagon while she shrieked with delight. Drew and Iris blowing out the candles on the cake they insisted on sharing, though their birthdays were a week apart and, technically, though bigger, Drew—who'd skipped a grade—was a year younger. At the cabin on Lake George that Rose and Max had rented every summer, Iris trotting after Drew like a puppy everywhere he went, even far out into the lake, where, on previous visits, she'd screamed and flailed when Rachel tried to teach her how to swim.

Then, in high school, after Iris . . . when she was so *sick* . . . there was Drew, stopping by every afternoon to sit with her in her room, careful to leave the door open so Rachel wouldn't wonder what they were up to. Telling her what had happened in school, or which of their friends had asked after her. Reminding Iris with every smile, the lightness of his voice, his touch, that she wasn't crazy, that she would get better. Drew had given her what neither Rachel nor Brian—both too shaken by the episode—were able to provide back then: reassurance that she was normal.

Going to separate colleges had only left them more fused at the hip, their combined phone bills alone amounting to a third-world dowry. Drew at Yale. Iris at Bryn Mawr. Weekends, they were like bird dogs on opposite trails, following the same scent—Drew riding the train down from New Haven, and Iris taking the bus from Philly. The two of them arriving here with their backpacks slung over opposite shoulders, so they could walk as closely as possible without bumping against one another. Laughing and talking a mile a minute, their faces aglow and their hair wild from kissing.

Now here they were . . . home for good. Iris getting ready for Parson's in the fall. Drew working to earn extra money before med school at NYU. He'd rented a tiny studio in the Village, where Iris spent every minute that she wasn't at her easel, or Drew at the computer store where he worked. Marriage? Rachel had always assumed they would get married. Someday. When they were older. When Drew finished his residency, and Iris was . . . when she was more stable.

What could suddenly have gone so wrong?

And if Rose *was* right, why was Iris standing here now lit up like Times Square on New Year's Eve?

Shaping her mouth into a smile, Rachel replied lightly, "Is there something I should know?" She hoped her voice sounded upbeat, that of a mother whose heart wasn't drowning in worry.

Iris smiled mysteriously. "Not yet. But Drew said we needed to talk. Tonight. After the party." Her dark-lashed eyes, the color of old Egyptian amber, seemed to hold a buried history of their own.

"What makes you think it has to do with marriage?" Rachel asked.

"Something Drew said—about needing to make some decisions about the future. What else could he have meant?" Iris' smile faltered then, but only slightly—as if it had only just then occurred to her that things might not be quite as rosy as she'd imagined.

"Oh . . . I don't know," Rachel ventured. "It could be anything. Every couple has wrinkles to iron out."

Iris shot her an odd look, as if she sensed Rachel was keeping something from her. Then, with a sigh, she confessed, "You heard about the fight we had, right? From Rose? Okay. But it was no big deal. I think Drew and I are still recovering from being apart for so long. But now that we'll be at graduate schools that are practically next door to one another, why not make it official?" She laughed. "Stop looking so panicked, Mom. We're still a few years from a wedding. But if we got engaged . . ." Her voice trailed off.

Rachel waited a moment before asking, "Do you two fight a lot?"

Iris frowned. "Mom . . . you're not *listening*. Of course we fight—that's the whole point. If we were together more, we wouldn't be so stressed out."

Rachel, poised before the mirrored vanity, peered closely at the necklace puddled in her palm. She remembered when Brian had given it to her, how the pearls in their velvet box had glowed in the soft light of the sterling menorah that had been her great-grandmother's. What would it be like, she wondered with a pang, to have no sense of where she'd come from?

"A diamond ring isn't always the answer," she said.

"It's not like that with us." Iris sounded a little irritated at Rachel for not getting what was so obvious. "It's never been a question of *if*, only a matter of *when*. As far back as I can remember, Drew and I have talked about what it would be like when we were married, how many kids we'd have."

"You know how your father and I feel about Drew. We'd like nothing better than for him to be our son-in-law," Rachel replied cautiously.

"Then why are you acting this way? Like . . . oh, I don't know, like I just told you I was pregnant or something?"

Rachel felt a dart of alarm. "Are you?"

"God. You're such a Jewish mother!" Iris threw her arms up . . . and with an exaggerated sigh toppled backwards onto the bed. Blowing away the wisps of hair spread over her face like fine lace, she smiled dreamily up at Rachel. "I just want to spend the rest of my life with Drew. That's all."

Rose's words at lunch echoed in Rachel's mind. *He loves her, honestly he does. . . . Maybe that's part of the problem. When you love someone that much, it hurts to see them suffer. . . .*

She fought to keep from darting a furtive glance at her daughter's bare arms with their exposed wrists flung out on either side of her on the woven blue spread. *Don't,* a voice in her head warned. *Don't look.* But she couldn't help herself. And, yes, oh God, there they were: pale raised scars like the thinnest of silver bracelets circling each wrist. Hardly visible . . . unless you knew to look for them.

But Iris wasn't suffering now. She looked happy. Nearly ecstatic, in fact. Except Rachel knew how abruptly her daughter's mood could change—like a tropical storm sweeping down out of a clear blue sky, blacking out the sun, and flattening everyone around her.

Gently, Rachel dropped her choker onto the vanity, next to the crystal perfume bottle that had been her mother's. The pearls made a soft slithery sound against the polished surface, a sound that for some reason set her teeth on edge. What now? Where were the written instructions on how to repair a damaged child? How had she arrived at this point in her life, with the ground she'd always thought of as rock-solid melting from under her feet?

A glance in the mirror showed a reasonably attractive middle-aged woman with shoulder-length blond hair going gently silver, who only vaguely resembled the image of a much younger self Rachel carried about in her head like an outdated wallet photo: the idealistic resident in hippie clogs and poncho who'd traveled halfway around the world to minister to the injured and dying in a village no one had ever heard of, in a zone of hell otherwise known as Vietnam.

Not that she was so old, Rachel was quick to remind herself. She could still get the zipper up on most of her size eights, and the squarish jaw that made her look stubborn, even when she wasn't butting her head against a brick wall, had turned out to be a blessing: it refused to sag. Even the fine lines that radiated from the corners of her eyes worked to her advantage; they softened the stark blue that had so often caused people to squirm.

She'd been as good a mother as she knew how to be. One thing for certain: if Iris had been her own flesh-and-blood child, Rachel couldn't have loved her more. That's what made it so damn frustrating, this battle against demons she'd had no hand in making. Against the woman who'd given birth to Iris, and who, eighteen years ago, had excused herself to use the restroom in McDonald's . . . leaving her three-year-old waiting in a booth, like an empty wrapper or a dirty tray, for someone else to find.

Rachel sank down on the bed beside Iris. "Oh, sweetie, I only want what's best for you," she said. "Whatever happens."

Iris must have caught something in her voice, for she suddenly grew very still, and her expression darkened. "Drew would never, *ever* leave me, if that's what you're implying. He wouldn't. He just wouldn't. And if he ever did—" She stopped.

"You'd talk it over. Straighten out whatever was wrong," Rachel supplied briskly in her doctor's voice, using it to cover her own rising panic.

Iris looked right through her then, eerily, her gaze fixed on some vanishing point only she could see. In a voice as matter-of-fact as the weatherman reporting that tomorrow it would rain, Iris said, "I'd kill myself."

The ground that had been melting under Rachel suddenly dropped away altogether. All at once she was flying backwards down the slippery slope she'd spent the last seven years scaling, that ghastly day jolting past in vivid splashes of color, and bursts of memory out of sequence. She saw blood. Everywhere. Staining the bathwater a deep rust, and soaking the pink mat next to the tub; dappled over the wall tiles in feathery patterns, oddly—it had struck Rachel in the first moment of glassy shock—like the ones Iris had made in kindergarten, using fern fronds dipped in poster paint.

She had seen Iris, floating pale and still as a fish gone belly-up in all that shocking redness. Her face partly submerged, so that the lower half appeared distorted, shimmering grotesquely below the clouded surface. Her gaping wrists seeming to grin up at Rachel.

Towels. So many towels. Swaddling Iris like a large infant as she was carried out to wait for the ambulance. Leaving pink, glistening trails of watery blood on the hallway's parquet tiles. Rachel had left the towels piled on the floor by the front door, where to this day—never mind that the entire vestibule had twice been refinished since then—a faint cloudiness marked the spot on the old oak floorboards.

As a reminder.

Rachel was jolted back to the present with a suddenness that caused her to bite down on the tip of her tongue. She felt a heated rush of pain, and her mouth filled with the taste of blood.

She stared at her daughter. In fifteen minutes, they were to be dressed and downstairs, ready to meet the car that was picking them up, but Iris might have been a million miles away. Fear, rage, impotence—all of it came surging in on a dirty, foaming tide. Rachel fought it back, reminding herself that Iris was no longer in danger. Dr. Eisenger would have warned them if she'd shown signs of slipping back into that abyss.

"You wouldn't do anything of the sort," Rachel scolded with the gentle force of a doctor applying pressure to a wound—not a mother who felt as if she herself were bleeding. "No matter what happens, you have me and Daddy. And Grandma."

At the mention of her grandmother, Iris brightened, her mouth flickering in a brief smile. She adored Sylvie—more, in some ways, Rachel thought with a twinge, than she did her own mother. From the very first instant, the two had taken to one another like parched grass to rain. As if forming a silent pact of some kind—one that didn't include Rachel.

Abruptly, Iris sat up. "Will Grandma be at the party?"

"She said she'd try her best to make it. If she's up to it." Rachel sighed, smoothing one of her daughter's fallen slip-straps back into place. She didn't want to think about her mother's fading health right now.

Iris shot her a sharp look. "You'd tell me, wouldn't you? If she were *really* sick, I mean. She's always saying she's fine, just a little tired . . . but I don't know."

"I'd feel better if she got a second opinion," Rachel admitted. "But you know how stubborn Grandma is."

"She says she gets it from you." Iris allowed a grin to surface.

Rachel, seated on the bed, had to smile, too, in spite of the dread weighing heavily on her heart.

"Your dad has another name for it, which I won't repeat," she joked. "I think he misses the old me, who used to deliver babies for a living. Administrators have to be tough as nails."

"Do you ever miss it?" Iris asked. "All the blood and guts?"

Rachel sighed again, thinking, *How can I explain it?* All those feelings too complex to be contained in a single sentence? If she'd had to, she would have summed it up as an overdose of adrenaline in those early years—the madness of Vietnam, followed by her residency in obstetrics at Beth Israel, then the battle to establish her free clinic. Except the truth was that in a perverse way she'd loved it all, deep inside where logic held no sway.

Before Rachel could explain—that her place now was at the helm of the East Side Women's Health Center, along with Kay—Iris was jumping off the bed, exclaiming, "God, look at the time. It's after seven! If Daddy sees me like this, he'll have a fit."

Watching her dash for the door, Rachel smiled. Brian would make the usual disgruntled noises, for sure, but he was much too besotted with their daughter ever to get truly angry with her.

Her husband strode into the bedroom as Rachel was dabbing perfume behind her ears. She could see his reflection in the mirror as he walked toward her—a long ramble of a man who moved with the loose-limbed ease of someone more accustomed to jeans than to black tie. He was wearing the dark-blue suit custom tailored for him during his trip to London last year to promote the British edition of *Twelve Degrees North*. Now, though, the jacket fit more loosely than she remembered. Had he gotten thinner?

If he had, he'd lost none of his appeal. Brian, she reflected, had the kind of looks that other men never thought much of, but that women seemed to find irresistible. Like the lady standing in line at a book signing in Cincinnati, who'd whispered loud enough for Rachel to hear that she'd like to run her fingers through his hair—hair still as long and full as it had been in his twenties, its light brown now brushed with silver at the temples. His bookish face, with its slightly irregular features, always made him appear to be listening intently to everything you said, while his thoughtful gray eyes seemed to say, *Yes, I know just what you mean.*

The damnedest thing, Rachel thought, was that he usually *did* know. It was what made him such a fine writer.

Tonight's party, thrown by Brian's publisher, was in honor of Brian's having won the National Book Critics' Circle Award for *Dawn's Early Light*. A hundred guests, ranging from print and television *mochers* to book publishing heavyweights, all coming together at Avery Hammersmith's Riverside Drive penthouse to pay tribute to her husband. Yet here Rachel stood, wishing they could sneak off somewhere, just the two of them. Somewhere quiet where they could talk. Or make love.

Lately, they hadn't done enough of either.

She retrieved the pearl choker from her vanity and held the hair off the back of her neck while Brian fastened it around her throat. The warm pressure of his fingers as he fumbled with the clasp soothed her, but at the same time sent a light chill trickling down her spine. She hadn't told him about her conversations with Rose and Iris; that would only have made her fears more real somehow. And what would have been the point of getting Brian all worked up over something that might turn out to be, as her mother would have said, nothing with nothing?

Now wasn't the time. She mustn't let anything ruin this evening for Brian. Tomorrow she would tell him.

"I heard the intercom a minute ago. Was that our car?" she asked, feeling edgy all of a sudden.

"Take your time," he soothed, patting her shoulder. "I told the driver we'd be a few minutes." If she had to pick one thing she loved best about her husband, Rachel thought, it was that he always seemed to know when something was bothering her. Like now, asking softly, "Want to talk about it?"

"It can wait," she told him.

"That's what you said the last time."

She realized then, with a guilty pang, that he was reminding her of how busy she'd been lately . . . and how distracted. These past months, when her husband reached for her in bed at night she was usually too tired for more than a drugged kiss. Then up at the crack of dawn, her mind filled with lists of things to do at the clinic for which there were never enough hours in the day.

"We'll have all weekend. Well, most of it anyway," she added, remembering her meeting with the technician from Pure Logic, scheduled for Saturday morning—the only time the clinic's computers weren't in use, when the new software they'd ordered could be installed. "We could drive up to Lake Waramaug on Sunday."

"Sunday evening you're speaking at the Brandeis Women's Committee banquet," he reminded her. "We'd have to make it early to beat the traffic."

"How about a picnic lunch in the park instead? Saturday or Sunday—your choice."

"Sandwiched between appointments, so to speak?" he teased, but she could hear the barb buried there. "Actually, it's supposed to rain all weekend. I'd suggest something indoors . . . if I thought I could talk you into shutting off the phone."

"We'll come up with something," she told him.

Rachel felt an abrupt coolness as his hand fell away from her neck. The double strand of pearls dropped into place against her collarbone with a soft tick. In the little hollow at the base of her throat where they lay nestled, she was aware of a pulse leaping.

She watched him cross over to the window, where he stood gazing out at Gramercy Park three stories below, a shadowy island where flower beds bloomed like bright nosegays beneath the glow of cast-iron streetlamps. She felt a sharp pinch of anxiety. How had they come to this? Jockeying for stolen moments, negotiating hours like commodities on the stock exchange. Brian had always been the solid reef against which her days swirled. Except when he was on tour, he was usually here, in his office, hammering away at his keyboard. She could call him in the middle of the day to let off steam about the empty suits in the mayor's office, or the stuffed shirts at Community Health. And in the evening, when she dragged home so late that dinner was out of the question, he never berated her—he just poured her a brandy, and put his arm around her while she talked.

Except these days, Brian wasn't quite so available anymore. Sometimes he didn't surface from his den until after she'd gone to bed. And when she called home, more often than not she got his machine.

She thought back to another time . . . a time when every choice had seemed as clear-cut as a road heading in only one direction. In her mind, she was seeing a dying soldier on a stretcher, covered in blood, a hole the size of her fist blown in his belly by a land mine. She hadn't stopped to think then. She'd acted swiftly, decisively, insisting, over the objections of her superior, that they operate at once.

That young sergeant was Brian.

Two months later, they were exchanging vows in the back room of a dingy bar in Da Nang. Rachel remembered every moment as if it were etched in crystal—the hibiscus Brian had picked for her, the beaded curtain tinkling like chimes, the *chong sam* she wore in place of a wedding gown. And, most of all, the face of her bridegroom, gaunt and ravaged, yet suffused with love. A man still recovering from his wounds, who hadn't hesitated to go back into that jungle to rescue her from behind enemy lines.

Rachel felt her chest constrict.

What had become of those two people? That fiercely idealistic girl with her heart on fire . . . and the young soldier who risked his life for her? Oh sure, they'd had their ups and downs, particularly in the beginning, but . . . how had they come to this? A middle-aged couple on their way to a party, with most of what there was to say to one another left unspoken.

As Brian turned away from the window, she longed to go to him, to smooth back the curls springing loose from the damp comb tracks over his temples. Did he know how much she loved him? How much she wished, sometimes, that she could just walk away from it all—the East Side Center, and all its demands—and just *be*. To enjoy the simple pleasures of having coffee with her husband in the morning . . . and falling asleep at night in his arms.

With his back to her, Brian remarked casually, "Avery offered us his place in Amagansett for the last two weeks in August. I was thinking I might take him up on it."

"Oh, Bri, I don't see how I can get away then." Rachel almost hated him for dangling in front of her the very thing she craved. But he couldn't have chosen a worse time—her grant proposal for the Sitwell Foundation was due to be submitted the week before Labor Day.

He shrugged, and somehow that hurt more than if he'd protested. "Either way, I could use the time to finish this draft before I go on tour in October. If you change your mind, you can always join me."

"If it were up to me—" But she stopped when he didn't turn around. What would be the point? He'd heard it all before.

Minutes later, gliding up Park Avenue in their hired limousine, Rachel wished she could grab hold of her husband and daughter, seated on either side of her, and never let go. She felt as if they were caught on a rock at high tide and at any moment a huge wave might sweep one of them away.

And if that happened to Iris, it could very well be for good.

Rachel shivered in the air conditioning that, in the enclosed back seat, surrounded her like a capsule of ice.

Then she remembered: Rose would be at the party. Someone with whom Rachel could share her concerns; someone who always seemed to know the right thing to do. Wasn't it Rose who'd brought Iris to them in the first place, all those years ago? Besides, she had children of her own. She knew what it was like. Rachel wouldn't have to explain to Rose what it was like to be a mother fearing the unthinkable.

The taxi was pulling to a stop at the corner of Eighty-sixth and Riverside when Rose Griffin leaned toward the front seat and ordered crisply, "Drive around the block, please." She didn't feel any need to explain to the cabbie why she wasn't quite ready to get out. Who cared if he thought she was crazy?

The Pakistani cabbie shot her a look over his shoulder that said she *must* be crazy . . . but then shrugged. She was probably no worse than three-quarters of the city's population. The hell with it, Rose thought. The meter was already into quadruple digits, thanks to a traffic jam on Eighth Avenue that had felt more like a wagon train crossing the Great Plains. What was another dollar or so? The few extra minutes of peace were worth the price.

The truth was, if she spent all night gearing up for it, she'd be no more ready to face the crowd at that banquet. It was only out of affection for Brian that she'd accepted the invitation in the first place. Now she wished she'd sent her regrets instead. What on earth could she have been thinking?

For one thing, she hated big parties. To her mind, they were nothing more than an excuse for avoiding *real* conversations: the social equivalent of the hors d'oeuvres that passed interchangeably from one function to the next—seldom as tasty as they looked, and not the least bit nourishing. It was Max who had made them tolerable, even fun. Just when she thought she'd rather have bamboo shoved under her fingernails than listen to another minute of some self-satisfied idiot droning in her ear, she'd catch her husband winking at her across the room. Or, fighting her way through the gridlock at the bar, she'd find Max, a fresh drink for her already in hand. Then the taxi ride home, slumped against him with her head on his shoulder while they giggled over Mr. Zweillerbach's toupee, or the rumor that Myra Kennedy was having an affair with her doorman.

This evening's event, with its inevitable onslaught of unfamiliar faces and names Rose wouldn't remember—not to mention the yawn-inducing speeches that were sure to follow like wet towels in the wake of a pool party—would be no different from a hundred others like it. Except for one thing: Max wouldn't be there.

On her way out the door tonight, her son Jason had gaped at her, commenting, "Wow, Mom, is that you? For a second, I thought you were Madonna." A sixteen-year-old's ass-backward idea of a compliment, she supposed. And he was right. Hadn't she chosen the red crepe Dolce & Gabbana exactly for that reason? A crimson banner to be waved in the face of all those who might feel sorry for her. At the last minute, she'd been half tempted to tuck a rose behind one ear. Max, she knew, would have loved it. She'd have spent the evening flirting with him, and then gone home both delighted and amused at having seduced her own husband.

But tonight, as she had for the last three hundred twenty-seven nights, Rose would be sleeping alone.

The thought made her yearn to tell the cabbie she'd changed her mind altogether, would he please just turn around and take her home. She could think of a dozen things she'd rather be doing. Like, say, answering the stack of letters on her desk, mostly condolence notes that continued to trickle in, nearly a year after Max's death. Or preparing her notes for yet another motion hearing in the Esposito case, which, God willing, would go to trial next month. Even cleaning out Mr. Chips' cage seemed a reasonable alternative.

She cringed at the prospect of having to smile and nod in response to murmurs of sympathy offered by those who'd known Max. Then having to assure people she barely knew that she was getting on with her life. Yes, her husband's passing had been a blow to the firm, but with time and some reorganization—did they know her stepdaughter, Mandy, just made full partner?—things were back on track. And, no, her youngest wasn't going away to Deerfield as planned. Jason's decision, not hers. She had no patience for grieving widows who clung to their children as if to life preservers; she believed in doing what was best for her sons. Take Jackie Onassis, she'd say. Nobody had had to tell that woman, "Get a life," and look how well *her* kids turned out.

It was all a big fat lie.

Rose hated every single minute spent walking this earth without Max. She was furious at everyone from God to Mr. Mandelbaum, the hapless client Max had been on the phone with when he suffered his fatal heart attack. Something as innocent as driving to Port Washington for a Saturday visit with her eldest sister Marie was enough to trigger an attack of rage so profound it left her shattered and trembling. At toll booths, in stalled traffic on the LIE, all those couples and families in Range Rovers and Jeep Cherokees, talking animatedly, jostling each other, their heads thrown back in unheard laughter. How unfair! How wicked and wrong that those people were allowed to live—people with bumper stickers that read, "I Brake for Deer Hunters" and "Don't Honk, Get Even"—while *her* husband, who twice had argued cases before the United States Supreme Court, who always remembered to fill the Volvo's gas tank even when she forgot, and who never walked out the door without kissing her and telling her he loved her, was gone forever.

The only thing Rose had gotten over was her desire to be dead as well. Sometimes, she missed even that. Amazing, she thought, how many idle, aching hours it had filled, fantasizing about ways she might kill herself. A gunshot to the head? Quick and easy, but too messy. Slitting her wrists was equally unthinkable—Rachel and Brian, my God, how awful for them, after what they'd gone through with Iris. A barbiturate cocktail would be the cleanest, she'd supposed, but think of the trouble getting such a prescription filled, and what if it didn't work?

Killing herself would merely have been taking a stand against the quiet little suicide of each day without her husband, the bit-by-bit crumbling of a heart gone stale and dry as old toast, the little throb in the back of her throat when she caught his scent on a sweater she'd forgotten to donate to the Goodwill, or came across his handwriting in a file at the office.

Rose blinked against the tears that had made a country-western ballad of an innocent evening out. Traffic lights wheeled and flashed overhead. She caught a glimpse of a homeless woman in a knit cap huddled over a steam grate, a sight that didn't strike her as all that strange until she remembered it was the beginning of July. Wasn't it just last week she'd been scurrying past Valentine's Day displays in drugstores? Just yesterday that she'd noticed the first crocuses pushing up in the flower beds along Park Avenue?

As her taxi, for the second time that evening, pulled up in front of Avery Hammersmith's building—its address discreetly displayed in brass letters over plate-glass doors thick as a vault's—Rose offered up a little prayer: *Please, God, let me get through this in one piece.* One bad night could cost her days, send her spinning back to the time when the color blue made her think Gillette, and Guns n' Roses was more than just a rock group her sons listened to.

And, God, while You're at it, spare me from being seated next to some well-meaning hostess's idea of a swell blind date. Or, if there was no avoiding it, at least let him be a decent guy—someone who wouldn't ask if she'd be interested in a Hamptons summer share . . . or a Broadway show for which he just happened to have tickets.

The penthouse owned by Brian's publisher occupied the entire eighteenth floor of the prewar building, which overlooked the Hudson and Riverside Park. As Rose stepped from the elevator into a paneled foyer as spacious as her own living room, she felt oddly soothed. Places like this, she thought, were impervious to ordinary human woes. The only mayhem likely to slip past these solid walnut doors came tidily packaged in the *Times*, which no doubt was delivered each morning by a white-gloved doorman.

Even the elderly retainer from Central Casting who'd ushered her in spoke as softly as if they were in church. And in some ways, it *did* remind her of a church—the polished old wood giving off a faint scent of lemon oil, the towering floral arrangements, the crystal chandelier twinkling like a hundred penny candles.

When asked what she'd like to drink, Rose answered without hesitation, "Water. A glass of water will be fine." When the time came, she'd lift the requisite flute of champagne to Brian . . . but only because it was easier than having to explain to a lot of busybodies that booze made her weepy and, worst of all, sorry for herself.

Rose passed through a set of double doors into what at one time must have been the ballroom—a vast arena with a walk-in marble fireplace, and a row of French doors that opened onto a wrap-around terrace. The view of the river, with the George Washington Bridge straddling it like a diamond tiara, literally took her breath away. For a moment, she hardly noticed the guests clustered about the candlelit tables—at least seventy, all of them chatting as comfortably as if they'd known each other all their lives.

Dear God, just how late *was* she? For a flustered moment, Rose couldn't remember if the invitation had said seven-thirty or eight.

Then Avery Hammersmith, a florid-faced man in his fifties with thinning white hair as artfully arranged as the decor, was hurrying over to escort her to her seat—steering her past the marble griffins carved on either side of the fireplace, and through the thicket of tables ringed with animated faces glowing in the soft light—none of which she recognized. Seeing she was at Brian's table, Rose went weak with gratitude.

As she sank into her chair, she found herself blessedly surrounded by friends and family. Across from her were Drew and Iris, flanked on either side by Rachel and Brian. Next to Brian, Avery Hammersmith was settling back with the sigh of a contented host. Only the man seated on Rose's right was a stranger.

She'd barely glanced at him when Sylvie, on her left, greeted her with, "Rose! Thank heavens. I was beginning to worry you wouldn't make it." Her expression was warm and lively—not at all that of an elderly woman with a heart condition, Rose thought, remembering with a flicker of concern how pale and tired Sylvie had looked the last time she'd visited her.

Tonight, Sylvie was as elegant as ever, dressed in a pale-green dress with flowing sleeves that disguised how thin she'd gotten, her silver pageboy shining like polished sterling in the candlelight. Her only jewelry was a pair of discreet pearl earrings, and the emerald ring that matched her eyes—a ring given to her years ago by Nikos.

And just where *was* Nikos? Rose was so used to seeing him at Sylvie's side, it was a moment before she thought to scan the room, where she caught a glimpse of him at one of the other tables. It struck her as a bit odd, until she realized *why* he'd been seated elsewhere. So there would be an extra place for—

The thought was cut off when Sylvie leaned forward to introduce Rose to the man on Rose's right, where Nikos should have been sitting. "Dear, I'd like you to meet Eric . . . Sandstrom, isn't it?" To Eric, she explained, "Rose lived upstairs from Brian when they were growing up. She's now a dear friend of our family."

Dear friend. Rose felt a throb in her gut. But how else could Sylvie have introduced her? Not as a daughter, though she was that. Not when Sylvie refused to acknowledge Rose as her own, except in private. And surely not with Rachel listening. The only person in this entire room who knew the truth, besides Rose and Sylvie, was Nikos.

For an instant, Rose had trouble focusing on the man holding out his hand to her. He looked vaguely familiar. Had they met at some other party? Early forties, she thought. With that schoolboy's thatch of sandy hair, she might have guessed him to be even younger, except for the hint of hard living in his stone-washed blue eyes, and the deep lines carved on either side of his mouth. He regarded her intently from under pale lashes that almost made him appear to be staring—and suddenly she wanted to look down, look away, look anywhere but at him. Damn, she thought, heat crawling up into her cheeks. Rose didn't know whose idea it had been . . . but any fool could see it was no accident she'd been seated next to Eric Sandstrom.

But was that so terrible? He looked nice enough. What saved him, really, was those eyes—the eyes of someone who wouldn't have been shocked were she to confess she'd once spent an entire hour searching her apartment for a light fixture sturdy enough to hang herself from.

"A pleasure," she murmured, allowing her hand to be squeezed briefly before turning to address the table at large. "Sorry I didn't get here sooner. The traffic was murder."

"Mom's almost never late," Drew piped up, in her defense. "It's really a thing with her. Dad used to say—" He stopped, and an awkward silence settled over the table.

"That I'd rather be known as the *late* Rose Griffin than be late for an appointment," Rose supplied, the brave widow demonstrating that she hadn't lost her sense of humor.

Everyone laughed a bit too heartily, and Drew flashed her a relieved grin. Oh, that smile of his, so like Max's. It broke her heart a little each time. Drew's rebellious dark hair and brown eyes were hers, but in every other way he was his father's son. The angle at which his head was tilted just now, and the way he hunched his shoulders as he leaned forward onto his elbows. What struck her most, though, was his sweetness. In Drew's open face she hoped she would never stop seeing the twelve-year-old boy who'd read aloud to his little brother that time Jason was so sick with mumps, and whose room had been a zoo of cages housing everything from gerbils to an albino gopher snake—pets his less tenderhearted friends had grown tired of caring for.

She watched him lean sideways as Iris whispered something in his ear. Drew looked uncomfortable, almost *pained.* Rose felt a pulse of worry. The other day, when Drew had come to her, nearly in tears, her first concern had been for Iris. Rose didn't even want to *think* what she might do if Drew broke up with her.

It wasn't just that she was fond of Iris; in a way, Rose felt some-how responsible for her, too. It had been *her* doing, all those years ago, begging her buddy, Lieutenant O'Neill, to hold off calling Social Services on that little girl found abandoned in a McDonald's. Her string-pulling, too, that had made foster parents of Rachel and Brian practically overnight. And, months later, when Iris' mother was picked up on a drug charge, who was it that had been called down to the station in the middle of the night? Upon hearing the woman's nearly incoherent tale of woe—a fire, it seemed, had left the woman homeless—Rose had believed, with all her heart, that she was doing the right thing in convincing her that Iris would be better off where she was. With Rachel and Brian, too, hadn't she glossed things over, keeping certain bits to herself—parts of the story that would only have alarmed them unnecessarily? Never could Rose have imagined that one day it would be her own son who would pay the price.

For, in the end, it all boiled down to one thing: blood was thicker than water. A lesson Rose hadn't learned from her own mother, but was determined to apply to her sons.

And, certainly, there was no denying Iris could be temperamental. Trouble seemed to follow her like mud tracked indoors on a rainy day. Who could forget the Christmas Eve she'd flown out the door in the middle of a snowstorm, wearing nothing more than a silk jacket? When she didn't turn up, both families—Max and the boys, as well as Brian and Rachel—spent half the night searching for her out in the freezing cold. They were all relieved, of course, when she turned up, safe and sound, in a coffee shop on Lexington Avenue . . . but they were bewildered as well. What had happened? Iris had seemed fine one minute, happily wrapping presents, and then, all at once, something Rachel said had caused her to snap. Where had it come from, that sudden tempest? How could they prevent it from happening again? For as long as Rose could remember, Drew had been the only one capable of soothing Iris . . . and now even *he* was close to giving up on her.

If only she weren't so heartbreakingly beautiful, Rose thought with dismay. Look at her now, leaning into Drew, one hand resting on the sleeve of his jacket as delicately as a fallen rose petal. In her purple charmeuse dress that made her glow like a pale sliver of moon against deepening twilight, Iris was an enchantress straight out of a Hans Christian Andersen tale. And if Drew didn't watch out, the spell she cast would be on him—maybe forever. . . .

"May I pour you some wine?"

Rose was jarred from her thoughts by the easy voice of the man seated next to her, low and smoky, like an alto sax.

She turned toward him. "None for me. I don't drink." She added with a laugh, "I must be getting old. One glass, and I feel it the next morning. More than one, it's like tunneling out from an avalanche."

Eric's mouth twitched in a small, knowing smile. "Been through that tunnel myself a few times."

She noticed he wasn't drinking, either. She almost remarked on the coincidence, but something stopped her. It wasn't to avoid putting him on the spot but because she sensed it might involve a story of some kind—about how he'd battled alcoholism, or some other hardship. And she didn't want to know, not any of it. She'd piled up too much misery of her own to risk upsetting the apple cart with someone else's sad tale.

Instead, she asked, "Haven't we met before, at one of Brian's publication parties?" He could be Brian's editor, for all she knew.

"I don't think so. I would have remembered." He flashed her an easy, we're-in-this-together smile, leaving her certain that this was indeed what it appeared: a fix-up. Except Eric was nothing like the stodgy types who had been foisted on her at other functions. She noticed the silver bracelet peeking incongruously from under the cuff of his dinner jacket. It looked vaguely Southwestern, and very old. What *was* this guy's story? Rose found herself leaning forward with interest when Eric said, "But you might have heard me on the radio. I host a talk show on WQNA. That's how I got to know Brian— when he was promoting his last book."

"I don't listen to the radio much," she apologized, "but I could have *sworn* I've seen you somewhere."

"I used to be on TV. Years ago." He shrugged, clearly not wishing to elaborate. Was he just being modest? "Actually, I prefer radio. For one thing, it gives me more freedom."

"Are you one of those talk-show hosts who go out of their way to embarrass guests?" she asked jokingly.

Eric shook his head, smiling. "I don't go for the cheap shots. But I *do* love controversy. If I don't get at least one irate caller, I don't feel I'm fulfilling my vocation as worthy opponent of the politically corrupt, morally bankrupt, and terminally complacent."

Rose found herself smiling, too. "I guess that puts you somewhat to the left of Rush Limbaugh."

He laughed. "Yeah . . . but he makes a lot more money."

"I've handled my share of *pro bono* cases," she told him. "But I know what you mean—it doesn't pay the rent."

Eric cocked his head, eyeing her with interest as he smoothed a callused thumb down the stem of his empty wineglass. "A lawyer, huh? I wouldn't have guessed it."

Rose felt herself bristling. She'd been getting this reaction since law school—people making assumptions about her wild hair and exotic coloring, the way she dressed, the little bit of Brooklyn in her voice . . . even the fact that she liked rock music, the louder the better.

But so what? Better simply to roll with it, she thought.

"Trees aren't the only thing that grow in Brooklyn," she replied archly. "My grandmother figured I'd wind up pregnant and barefoot at eighteen, like my older sister. Mainly, I just wanted to prove her wrong. Law school made as much sense as anything at the time."

She thought of the years of juggling night classes with her day job as a secretary, working for Max. Then, when they were married, and partners in their own firm, how hard she'd had to fight just to be taken seriously by their mostly corporate clientele. And now here she was, fighting just as hard to hang on to her very sanity, to fashion some sort of existence from the rubble that was all that remained of the life she'd shared with her husband.

Rose found herself wishing she could be like the Italian widows in her old neighborhood—women from the old country who wore black right up to the day of their own funerals, and who felt no need to pretend that their lives would ever be the same after their husbands died.

Suddenly Eric surprised her by saying, "Brooklyn? I lived in Park Slope until I was eight, when my dad got transferred."

"That explains it," she said.

"Explains what?"

"What happened to your Brooklyn accent."

He shot her a wicked grin. "Minnesota is what happened. In Maplewood, they'd run you out of town for wearing a green shirt when everyone else is wearing blue. In the end, though, it was what kept me from ever wandering off to the right—all those flag-waving solid citizens who believed the war in Vietnam was rescuing the free world from Communism, and that the people protesting it must be Commies themselves. It wasn't long before I was out there waving a sign, and yelling at the top of my lungs. I'd have burned my draft card, too, if I'd had one." His grin widened. "I was fourteen."

"I don't have many good memories of those days." Rose was mildly taken aback to realize she still felt a tiny grain of resentment for what the war had taken from her. Specifically, Brian, with whom she'd been desperately in love at the time, and for many months after his return . . . as a married man. But, even more, Vietnam had robbed her of her innocence, too; her belief that good people, in the end, got what they deserved. Wearily, she recalled, "What I remember most was that while everyone my age had time to march in the streets and smoke pot I was knocking myself out to pay the rent."

Eric shot her a keen, measuring look as he sampled the salad that had been set in front of them—something with Belgian endive, and bits of shredded radicchio. "You don't mince words, do you?"

"Not much." She gave a short laugh. "My husband and I lived in

L.A. for a couple of years when we were first married, and you know what I missed most? The chance to mouth off on a regular basis. That, and Avenue J bagels." She tore a chunk off her sourdough roll.

"Is that why you came back?"

"Partly. Our oldest boy"—she nodded in Drew's direction—"was walking already. And we wanted to start our own firm. As far as my husband was concerned there's only one place on earth to sink roots. Max is—*was*"—she corrected herself—"a born and bred New Yorker." Seeing the question in Eric's face, she added softly, "He passed away last year."

She braced herself for the usual sympathetic murmurs, but Eric just looked her in the eye and said, "That must have been hard."

"It still is." She swallowed against the lump forming in her throat.

"Any other kids?"

"I have a sixteen-year-old still living at home, but Jay would rather sit through two hours of *Masterpiece Theatre* than come to something like this."

He laughed knowingly. Once again she was struck by the odd dissonance of his youthful looks and exuberant laugh with the sadness she sensed underneath. "I'm familiar with the territory. I volunteer two mornings a week at a shelter for teen runaways."

Whoever had thought to seat her next to Eric was no dope, Rose thought. She was intrigued, if not exactly rushing to sign up for twelve easy installments.

"Do you have children of your own?" she asked.

He shook his head. "No wife, either. Not even an *ex*." Rose waited for the usual bullshit disclaimers she'd heard from a hundred die-hard bachelors—guys who acted as if their single status were some sort of prize for being smarter than the average zhlub. But Eric didn't elaborate. He seemed neither bitter nor particularly pleased with himself—just matter-of-fact.

"I was married for nearly twenty-one years," she told him, more bluntly than she'd intended. "My husband was the kindest person I ever knew. I can't imagine ever being with another man."

He smiled—a little wistfully, she thought. "You're luckier than most."

Lucky? What an odd thing to say. Rose couldn't remember when she'd last felt blessed in any way. But he was right. She *had* been lucky. How many women had even *one* year, much less twenty, with a man as wonderful as Max?

Suddenly she remembered where she'd seen Eric before. "You co-hosted *A.M. America*. About five years ago, wasn't it? You and Ginny Gregson. It was terrible, what happened to her."

"Yes," he agreed mildly, but in the instant before his gaze cut away she caught a glint of something dark and fierce. "I was with her that night. It was my car she was driving." His delivery was flat, that of a reporter merely stating the facts·... but somehow Rose recognized a fellow traveler who'd done his own time in the breakdown lane. When he went on, it was in another voice, softer, but with a vein of iron ore running through it. "I was drunk at the time," he explained. "Ginny was only being a good samaritan—she couldn't see well at night, so she never drove after dark unless she had to." He took a long swallow from his water glass. "I was drunk at her funeral . . . and stayed drunk for about six months afterwards. Then I got sober. End of story." He shook his head as if to clear it, and offered her a vaguely apologetic smile. "I don't know why I'm telling you all this. After what you've been through, the last thing in the world you need is someone else's hard-luck tale."

"I'm sorry," she said, but it came out sounding stiff and insincere.

Rose ducked her head so he wouldn't see how perilously close he'd come to breaching her self-imposed fortress—one more step and she'd be in danger of caring too *much*. Already, he'd stirred up feelings she didn't want or need. Damn him. For making her eyes sting. For causing her heart to pump as if there was real blood in her veins, not just antifreeze.

Just then, fortunately, a waiter appeared to whisk away her un-touched salad, and to ask which entree she'd like. Rose welcomed the distraction, and not just because it took her mind off Eric. She was suddenly hungry. Starved, in fact.

While devouring her salmon, she was exquisitely aware of Eric beside her. His sleeve brushing her bare arm as he reached for the salt shaker. The easy laugh that rolled out of him when Rachel teased Sylvie about a woman at the next table she'd seen flirting with Nikos.

Eric, as if sensing her discomfort, left her alone. Perversely, she al-most wished he *would* do or say something stupid or annoying. Then she could have put him out of her mind as effortlessly as if he'd been the waiter whisking away her now empty plate.

When the table had been cleared, Avery Hammersmith rose to his feet and tapped his glass with a spoon. The rustle of voices around them dwindled, then died.

"I must confess," began their avuncular, white-haired host, "I've been so busy monopolizing our guest of honor that Cynthia"—he glanced affectionately at his wife beaming at him from the next table—"had to remind me that if I didn't hurry up and make my speech you'd all go home wondering why you'd been invited here tonight." He paused, waiting for the chuckles to die down. "But I'm sure that our guest of honor, who you all know and admire, doesn't need much of an introduction. . . ."

He went on to praise Brian's eight novels before congratulating him on winning the prestigious Book Critics' Circle Award for his most recent one, *Dawn's Early Light*. Rose tuned out the rest—a string of encomiums that were no doubt heartfelt, but hardly origi-nal. She knew it all anyway. She remembered even the short stories Brian used to scribble way back in Catholic school. What no one knew was that she had written a few herself, mostly dreadful, in which a character named Brian was always the hero.

Brian, looking somewhat embarrassed by all the extravagant praise, stood up afterwards to offer his thanks and say a few words of his own—and to receive a round of applause that continued even as guests began drifting over to shake his hand. Rachel stood, too, warmly greeting a couple Rose recognized from Brian's last book-signing.

Neither could have seen what Rose, along with everyone still seated, was afforded an unobstructed view of—Iris leaping to her feet, looking tearful and upset. What had Drew said to her?

He rose quickly to soothe her. Rose couldn't hear his murmured words, but in her son's weary, tormented face was mirrored what Rose already knew—that this was more than a minor squabble. He couldn't have meant to disrupt Brian's party; that wasn't like Drew. Iris must have prodded him somehow into letting slip what he'd intended to tell her later on.

Rose squeezed her eyes shut. *Why now, why this, on top of everything else?* When she opened them, she caught Eric Sandstrom looking at her curiously. She didn't care. Why should she? What did it matter if he thought she was crazy? He was nobody, a perfect stranger.

The room's temperature seemed to drop suddenly. She shivered. If only Max were here. Whereas she had a tendency to make a felony out of every misdemeanor, Max had been quick to defuse tense situations. He'd have taken Drew aside, counseled him wisely on what to do.

Instead, Rose sat frozen, watching Iris shake her head violently in response to something Drew had said, then dart off into the crush of people now milling about, with Drew in pursuit. Rose was halfway out of her chair, meaning to go after him, stop him from doing something he might regret—like giving in to Iris—when she felt a cool hand on her arm.

"Leave them be." Rose looked into Sylvie's green eyes, fixed on her with an intensity that held her pinned to her seat. "I doubt there's anything you can say that Drew doesn't already know."

Rose shook her head, impatient. "He's in over his head and I'm supposed to just sit back and let him *drown?*"

Sylvie patted her arm reassuringly. "Heavens, who's talking about drowning? A lover's quarrel isn't the *Titanic* going down. Either they'll work it out, or they won't. Do you honestly think you putting your two cents in will change anything in the long run?"

"I don't know," Rose admitted. "What I *do* know is that my son feels responsible—for things he has no control over." She felt a sudden sense of urgency, though she couldn't put her finger on its exact source.

"The most difficult thing, I've found," Sylvie said slowly, and with the utmost kindness, "is trusting people to look after themselves. They generally do, you know. One way or another. It's only when they take the long way around that we get impatient."

She reached up to brush Rose's cheek, and her gossamer sleeve rippled in a sudden breeze from the open French doors, making her arm appear in that instant to be floating, ghostlike. A smile touched her lips . . . a smile that didn't quite reach the veiled regret in her eyes.

Rose felt a burst of resentment. How dare she! Giving advice, doling out her platitudes and small endearments. Acting as if she were . . .

My mother.

Well, that's what she was, Rose reminded herself.

Not in any way that counts. Not the way she is to Rachel.

Rose tasted something bitter in the back of her throat—the betrayal she'd had to swallow, again and again. Pretending to be no more than Sylvie's good friend when all along . . .

All these years, I've kept quiet, and never asked why. Why Rachel's happiness is more important than mine. In some deep way, she knew it was more complicated than just Rachel—it had to do with Iris as well, the love and concern Sylvie felt for her granddaughter. Concern that apparently outweighed any she might have for Drew, her grandson by blood.

Rose took a breath, and willed herself to grow calm. She couldn't afford such thoughts right now. And Sylvie was certainly right about one thing. What would be the use of trying to reason with Drew *now,* in the middle of this latest crisis with Iris?

She sank back, shivering, rubbing her bare shoulders in an effort to warm them. Since Max had died, it seemed she could never get warm enough, as if the fiery core that had fueled her had been reduced to little more than ash. Yes, she would wait, speak to Drew later on, when they had a moment alone. Whatever the trouble between himself and Iris, it would still be there tomorrow morning. Hadn't she learned, the hard way, that while good times had a habit of going sour overnight, the bad seemed to have an almost limitless shelf life?

The thought was snatched from her head by a sudden commotion across the room. A sound that sent icy fingers skittering up her spine: Drew yelling for help.

🐾 Sylvie Rosenthal heard it, too. Drew's frantic shouts seemed to be coming from the terrace outside. But she couldn't see beyond the knots of alarmed guests now clustered about the open French doors. What on earth—?

Then, all at once, Sylvie was watching Rose bolt past, Brian and Rachel close behind her. She tried to stand up, but her legs wouldn't hold her; she fell weakly back into her chair, her heart pounding. It was as if a huge weight were pressing down on her, making her dizzy and short of breath.

Don't you dare faint, she commanded herself.

Sylvie tried to remember Dr. Choudry's instructions. *Take slow, even breaths. . . . Don't panic.* In her velvet evening bag was a vial with her prescription, just in case. But, really, she was fine. It was her granddaughter Sylvie was worried about.

Drew's shouts could mean only thing: Iris was in some kind of trouble.

Sylvie, now nearly frantic with worry, searched the crowd for the one face sure to bring her comfort, the one shoulder on which she allowed herself to lean. *Nikos . . . where are you?*

Then she spotted him—making his way toward her. Good, dependable Nikos, who seemed not to have aged a day in all these years. While this body of hers had wound down like a finicky old clock, Nikos' only seemed to grow more rugged. His once-black hair was now white, but he had never been more fit, or handsome—a CEO who spent more time out on his construction sites than in his office, with the calluses to show for it.

Now he was bending over her with his hands on her shoulders, and his breath warm against her face. At once her heartbeat grew more steady. Her breathing slowed. She started to get up, but Nikos gently pushed her down.

"What's going on? Is it Iris? Is she hurt?" She clutched at him, her chilled fingers soaking in his blessed warmth.

He hesitated, and she could see the fear in his eyes—for *her* as well as for Iris. As if her own health mattered at a time like this!

"Not hurt, no." In his deep rumble of a voice she could hear Nikos' own tightly reined panic. She saw that he was trembling slightly, and that made her even more alarmed.

"*What,* then?"

His expression turned grim. "It appears she has climbed onto the terrace wall and—Sylvie, are you all right? You are so pale!"

She whispered hoarsely, "Dear God, no, not again."

Sylvie closed her eyes, wanting *not* to remember . . . but unable to keep the images from flooding in. Iris, in a hospital bed, her poor bandaged wrists on the white coverlet turned upward, as if surrendering somehow, like in paintings of the crucified Jesus. And when she'd opened her eyes, oh, the smile that lit her face—grateful to be alive yet, at the same time, oddly resigned. As if, for Iris, merely existing on this earth required a courage others couldn't begin to imagine . . .

Nikos crouched down so that his eyes were level with Sylvie's— the same black eyes that, years ago, had captivated her as the young wife of a much older man. "You must not be afraid. No harm will come to her." His voice remained calm, but in his face, which was like old timber crosshatched with grain, she saw the doubt. He didn't have to say what they both knew—that, if Iris went through with it, this time there would be no rescuing her.

Sylvie felt a pang of guilt—*could* she have prevented this, if she hadn't stopped Rose from going after Drew? Maybe if Rose *had* spoken to the two of them. . . ?

Her heart seemed to thud weakly without really catching, like a car engine that wouldn't start. She thought: *I have to DO something*.

She hauled herself to her feet. This time, when Nikos tried to restrain her, she politely but firmly pushed his hand aside.

"If you stop me," she said in a quiet voice, "you may end up with two souls on your conscience, Nikos Alexandros. I may be old and sick, but I know my granddaughter. She *needs* me."

Nikos studied her for a moment . . . then wordlessly offered his arm. Silently, Sylvie blessed him, for the room suddenly felt as vast as an Arctic tundra. She had to stop several times, to catch her breath and lean into Nikos' shoulder.

Pushing through the crowd, they stepped onto the terrace. It was deep and surprisingly cool for July, dotted with tubs of greenery and patio chairs gleaming like pale skeletons in the light that spilled through the open doors. Sylvie spotted Iris at once: perched perfectly straight on the four-foot ledge, her back to them, her hands in her lap like those of an obedient child. There was nothing between her and the pavement below but eighteen stories of emptiness.

Sylvie couldn't see her face, only her long hair stirring in the faint breeze. It was the absolute correctness of her granddaughter's posture, like the first brave daffodil spears in spring, that wrested a low cry from Sylvie, and caused her to tighten her grip on Nikos' arm.

She caught sight of one of Iris' slingback pumps on the tiles by the low glass table that had been pushed up against the ledge, and it cut her to the quick: the sight of that child-sized shoe stranded there like a discarded toy.

Oh, Iris.

Sylvie fought to control her panic. She could see from the frantic expression on Rachel's face—she stood poised several yards away—that a steady hand was needed on the tiller right now. *God, give me the strength. . . .*

She drew away from Nikos to slip an arm about her daughter. Rachel was shivering violently. A deep shadow, like a gash, angled across the lower half of her face, leaving her blue eyes starkly exposed. Sylvie longed to be able to calm her daughter's fear the way she had when Rachel was a child. How long since this brisk, competent daughter of hers had even let Sylvie hold her?

In a low voice that was almost hysterical, Rachel pleaded, "Brian's calling the fire department, but that won't help. Mama, she won't listen to me . . . or anyone. You've got to do something. Please. She trusts you."

Sylvie felt the pull of responsibility like an ocean current, dragging her down. "I'll do what I can," she whispered.

She walked slowly past Drew, who stood with head bowed, his cheeks polished with tears. Sylvie wanted to console him, too . . . but Iris needed all her time and attention right now.

Cautiously, she stepped over to the ledge where Iris sat gazing out at the distant expanse of the Hudson, glittering with the drowned reflections of brightly lit buildings.

"Iris?" Sylvie spoke softly, as if to keep from frightening away a bird. "It's Gran. Won't you at least look at me?"

Nothing. It was like talking to a statue. Sylvie waited, holding perfectly still. At last she caught a flicker of movement. With aching slowness, Iris turned to look at her—her eyes bright against all that dark emptiness.

Sylvie reached up and lightly stroked the pale fingers gripping the ledge for support. They were like ice.

"Don't," Iris moaned.

"We can go to the house, where it's quiet . . . where we can talk." Sylvie leaned into the rough concrete. Iris had always loved coming to her house, had asked her once, as a child, if it was magic, like the castles in her storybooks. "You could spend the night, and in the morning we'll have breakfast in the garden. You should see how pretty it is now. Remember the Cécile Brunner you helped me plant? It's all covered in pink blossoms. You can't imagine how heavenly it smells."

Sylvie longed to tug her granddaughter into her lap as she had when Iris was younger, soothe her with the motion of the deep padded rocker that had once occupied a corner of Rachel's nursery. As a little girl, her granddaughter had been like a stray kitten, clinging as if for dear life. And no wonder. She'd been abandoned once before, and didn't intend to let it happen again.

The way you abandoned Rose.

Sylvie stole a look at Rose, standing with her arm around Drew, looking anxious and at the same time faintly defiant—as if she'd have spit in the eye of anyone who suggested her son was in any way to blame for this. Dear, brave Rose. Who had been there to protect and comfort *her* as a child?

Iris was saying something now, in a voice so soft Sylvie had to strain to hear her. "It's no use, Gran. I can't pretend anymore."

"I know, dear. But with me you don't have to. Come, let me take you home, where you belong." Sylvie stretched out arms that felt like lead.

Iris shook her head, left to right, with slow deliberateness. A tear slipped down her cheek, and Sylvie, frozen with terror, watched helplessly as she turned away and scooted farther out onto the ledge.

"Iris!" she heard Drew cry. His raw anguish was like icy water dashed over Sylvie.

All at once, she was acutely aware of the agitated murmurs floating around her, and the horrified guests silhouetted against the light, like cattle too stupid to realize their presence might only be making things worse. She was relieved when, out of the corner of her eye, she caught sight of Brian, with Nikos and that nice man, Eric Sandstrom, herding them back inside.

"I don't belong anywhere. Not really," Iris said with an exhausted resignation that tugged at Sylvie more than if she'd wept or gotten hysterical. "And, Gran, I'm too old to be babied."

"Goodness, isn't a grandmother allowed to fuss?" Sylvie, despite her mounting panic, managed a weak chuckle.

"It won't work, Gran. You can't make it better this time." Iris' voice was like a violin string, taut and trembling.

Sylvie felt her control start to crack. Yet she knew that any show of panic could be fatal. Taking a breath, she replied matter-of-factly, "I know. Talking isn't going to change how you feel. But it'll give you a chance to think things over."

"What would be the point?" Iris heaved a defeated sigh.

"Well, for one thing you'd have to be either simpleminded or cowardly to end your life without at least giving it some serious thought. And you're neither." Sylvie spoke briskly, yet she couldn't imagine where it was coming from, this measured strength flowing outward from her core, like ripples on water from a tossed stone.

"I must be crazy then. *Everyone* thinks so, not just Drew."

"Nonsense. You're not crazy."

"How can you say that? You don't *know.*"

"I know enough. I know what it's like to hurt so much you want to die."

There was a long silence in which only the noises of the city could be heard—the hum of traffic, the distant bleating of horns, the sound of a jet overhead that was like a long, exhaled breath.

Iris half-turned, asking in soft amazement, "You do?"

Sylvie straightened with an effort. "I may look like an old lady content to putter about in her garden, but I've had my share of heartaches, darling." She hesitated a moment before adding gently, "Nothing is as bad, though, as the heartache we bring to those we love."

Iris appeared to think this over. Then a shudder passed through her, as visible as a gust of wind blowing the branches of a supple tree. In a tiny voice that Sylvie had to strain to hear, Iris whispered, "It hurts."

Sylvie's eyes filled with tears.

"I know," she said simply, sensing that less was better.

"Does it ever stop?"

"It gets better."

"What if that's not enough?"

Sylvie drew in a deep breath. "Sometimes all it takes is a little faith."

Iris fell silent again, and in that eternity of waiting, the universe seemed to shrink, to become as small and weightless—and finite—as a suspended breath.

Then, all at once, with a sigh, she was swinging around, a bare foot dancing tentatively over the surface of the table below before she slid her weight onto it.

Sylvie sagged with relief, pressing her knuckles to her mouth to stop from crying out. *Oh, dear Lord . . . oh, thank you.*

In the heated commotion that followed—Drew pitching forward to gather Iris in his arms, and Rachel throwing herself against Brian with a strangled sob—Sylvie stood perfectly still, not daring to move, certain that if she took one step she would collapse. With no one to catch her, not even Nikos, who was off inside.

Sylvie felt certain death would come soon. Dr. Choudry, though vague about how much time she might have, had been careful not to raise false hope. Oh yes, there had been X-rays, and EKGs, and every other kind of diagnostic test imaginable. But even with the vast body of medical technology available, what it had all come down to in the end was that her heart was worn out.

She wouldn't be terribly sorry to leave this earth. Like Iris, she was well acquainted with how seductive death could seem, when living became too difficult or painful. It was saying goodbye to those you loved that was hard.

Especially when you had regrets . . .

She glanced over at Rose, standing alone by the ledge, the soggy breeze making her dark hair, with its startling ribbon of white, look even wilder. Her high cheekbones were hollowed with shadow, her black eyes glittering with unshed tears. Watching her from the opposite end of the terrace was Eric Sandstrom. Sylvie couldn't read his face, only his stance—he appeared to be waiting, but it wasn't clear for what, or for whom. Not Rose, surely. They'd only just met. And yet ... there was something in the way he held his arms—bent slightly at the elbows, with the light skimming the knuckles of his loosely cupped hands—as if he were holding something out to her, a promise or a gift.

It reminded Sylvie of how little *she* had given her daughter. A bundle of letters not sent, locked away in a desk drawer? A love that was like some hothouse hybrid, confined to a life behind glass? No wonder she resents me, Sylvie thought bitterly. How could she not?

Yet Rose couldn't know—*no* one could—the circumstances that had led Sylvie to betray her own flesh and blood.

In her sick exhaustion, she found tonight's harrowing experience blending with the memory of another, long-ago ordeal. The shock of going into labor while shopping at Bergdorf's. Then the mad dash to the hospital in the sweltering July heat, where she was met with unfamiliar faces and cold, probing hands. Followed by pain, so excruciating she was certain she would die right then and there. Yet it wasn't until afterwards, while she slept—the fitful sleep of an unfaithful wife who dared not let her husband see the dark child he would never believe was his own—that the fire had broken out, that the *real* nightmare had begun.

They said she looked like me. Tiny Rachel, with her fair hair and blue eyes.

It was fear that made Sylvie go along with the assumption at first—fear that if Gerald ever learned the truth she'd be disgraced, thrown out onto the street without a cent. But what kept her silent in the end was Rachel herself, the love she felt for her changeling daughter—a love that seemed to grow, perversely, in direct proportion to her guilt over her other daughter, her *real* daughter. The child of her lover, who'd grown into the beautiful, strong woman standing before her now.

Fate had blessed her with a second chance, Sylvie thought. All those years ago, Rose seeking her out, demanding the truth. And out of the ruins of lost opportunity, they'd managed to build something seaworthy, if not exactly unsinkable.

Sylvie blinked, and felt a tear slip down her cheek.

The lines from the Robert Frost poem came to mind. *But I have promises to keep . . . and miles to go before I sleep.* She had promises of her own to keep. And people she loved to help keep safe. Iris, buckling under the weight of a past she scarcely remembered. And Rachel, struggling to hold together a marriage, and a family, without knowing where to begin. Rose, too—grieving for Max, and torn between her affection for Iris and wanting what was best for her son.

In her mind, Sylvie was seeing her roses: the climbers sagging under the weight of their blooms, the grass below the shrubs littered with petals now growing withered and brown. Just as her garden needed extra care in summer, this was a time for tending to her family. When winter came, stripping the boughs and spreading its soft blanket of snow over the earth, she could rest . . . and let go.

Until then, she must hang on. If she'd been able to make it this far in life, with all the briar patches she'd had to pick her way through—bruised and bloodied at times, but still managing to put one foot in front of the other—then surely she stood a fighting chance of seeing her loved ones safely home out of the dark.

Chapter 2

❧ The call came the following morning, just after nine, when Rose was in the midst of cleaning Mr. Chips' cage. The gray cockatiel sat with his plumed head cocked, watching from his perch on the back of a kitchen chair, as she dropped the tray she'd been washing into the sink and reached for the phone. Rose saw that her hand, which had dripped soapy water over the counter, was shaking. *Please don't let it be who I think it is. Make it someone I don't know. Some idiot pitching a magazine subscription, or conducting a survey . . .*

"Hi, Mom. You get home okay last night?"

Drew. She felt some of the tension go out of her—and then, surprisingly, the tiniest twinge of regret. But how stupid, she berated herself, to think that Eric would call. Even if she were interested in him—which she wasn't—after that awful scene last night, why on earth would he want to get involved with her? She might no longer be a wife, but she would always be a mother, for better or for worse.

And right now, it was her mother's instinct that was causing the tiny hairs on the back of her neck to stand up. Drew, she sensed, hadn't called to say he'd had it with Iris, once and for all.

"All in one piece," she assured him. "What about you?"

"I called when I got back to my place, to let you know everything was okay. But you weren't home."

In a voice as bright and false as the silk flowers on the windowsill above her—African violets given to her by Rachel after Max's death, when every plant in this apartment had withered from neglect—Rose informed her son, "I shared a cab downtown with Brian's friend—Eric Sandstrom—remember him from our table? We stopped for coffee on the way home."

"Did he hit on you?" Drew wanted to know.

Rose was startled into a nervous laugh. "I hardly know the man!"

"Hey, just asking. Aren't I allowed to worry?"

"If anyone should be worried, it's me." Rose squeezed her eyes shut, and asked, "Drew, what happened last night?"

He sighed and she could picture him unconsciously scrubbing the hair over one ear, making it stand on end—exactly as Max used to. "My fault," he confessed. "I opened my mouth when I should've kept it shut. The thing is, with Iris . . . she feels things more than other people. Yeah, it scares the shit out of me at times, but—Mom, I don't want to lose her." He inhaled sharply. "Right now, I'm probably not making much sense. Iris and I were up all night talking, and I'm a little whacked."

"Go on. I'm listening," she urged.

A beat of silence. Rose could hear drops of water from the faucet pinging onto the birdcage tray. Mr. Chips' low cackling reminded her of an old man on a park bench, muttering under his breath. She looked around the cluttered kitchen, really seeing it for the first time in months—the oak pedestal table strewn with newspapers and magazines, her collection of vintage cookie cutters on the wall over the stove, the antique dresser drawers in which her good silver and linen were stored. The relentless sunniness of it all suddenly made her want to weep.

Then Drew was telling her, "We've decided to move in together." His voice seemed to come from a great distance, from another time zone, where the sun had not yet risen on this late-night decision of his. "Mom, I asked Iris to marry me."

There was a forced upbeat note to his voice, like the music piped into dentists' offices, more numbing than Novocain. But this wasn't going to wear off, Rose knew. Drew was going to spend the rest of his life taking care of Iris. Rescuing her.

Last night, watching helplessly from the curb as Drew shepherded Iris into a cab as gently and carefully as if she were an invalid, Rose had been struck with a terrible realization: her son would never get away now. How could he leave Iris, knowing what it might do to her?

And how could she, Rose, endure to sit back and do nothing while Drew put his own life on hold? Especially when she herself was partly responsible. *If I hadn't played God . . . imagining I could give to some poor child what had been taken from me.* What had she expected? Rebecca of Sunnybrook Farm? How could Iris—or any child—have emerged unscathed from *that?*

"Mom? Are you there?" Drew's anxious voice jarred her from her thoughts.

"I'm here," Rose replied, surprised at how calm she sounded, even though her insides throbbed as if she'd swallowed something burning hot.

"Look," he said, "I don't expect you to be thrilled. Not after last night. But trust me, Mom, I know what I'm doing."

Do you? she longed to cry. *Oh, Drew, have you any idea what you're committing yourself to?* Marriage, for her, had been a joy. With another man, it might have been a life sentence. Even divorce, she thought, was better than being shackled to someone who would only drag you down. But Drew would never divorce Iris. He was too much like his dad, who'd been pushed past the breaking point by his first wife, yes, but who wouldn't have left her, Rose felt sure, had there been one single grain of love between them.

"I have no doubt you *believe* it's for the best. . . ." Rose stopped, arrested by the sight of Mr. Chips, head stretched forward with his beak slightly open, like a very alert pupil. Yes, she *was* lecturing. And it was the last thing Drew needed right now. Instead, she sighed, "Oh, honey, you know me—I want everything tied up with a red ribbon. Why don't we discuss this later, when we're both a little more rested? I don't know about you, but I feel like I've been run over by a truck."

"I could use a couple hours' sleep," Drew admitted. "Why don't I stop by later on? We'll talk then."

"Great." There was so much more she wanted to say, but some

instinct made her hold back. Her son had nearly hung up when Rose said fiercely, "Drew? I love you."

"I love you, too, Mom." He laughed, sounding a little embarrassed.

"You remind me of your dad."

"Yeah. Everybody says I look just like him."

"I don't mean just that. You're . . . true blue." An old-fashioned way of putting it, sure, but so apt. "It's a good thing you decided to become a doctor."

"Why?"

"Because you'd have made a lousy politician." She smiled, thinking that Drew couldn't be deceitful if you put a gun to his head.

"Gee, thanks."

"Don't worry. You have my vote anyway."

"Glad to hear it. Thanks, Mom. Talk to you later, okay? Oh, and if Jay's up tell him it's okay if he uses my bike helmet—the strap's broken, but he can fix it."

No sooner had she hung up than Rose found her younger son poised in the doorway to the kitchen, yawning as if he'd just rolled out of bed. He was wearing a baggy T-shirt and boxers—his idea of pajamas—and stood balanced on one leg, storklike, while absently scratching his ankle with the big toe of his other foot. His dark-brown hair, straight like his grandmother's, stood up in spikes all over his head, making him look like the world's skinniest rooster.

"Was that Drew?" he asked.

She nodded. "He said to tell you—"

Jay broke in. "I heard you talking about the party. How'd it go? Did I miss anything?"

Rose nearly smiled at the innocence of his question. "I'll tell you all about it. After breakfast." She couldn't face it right now, on an empty stomach, with Mr. Chips squawking and fluttering his wings to get Jay's attention.

"You must've gotten in late. It was after midnight when Drew called." Jay shot her the narrow look of a suspicious father.

"I stopped at a diner on my way home. What *is* it with you guys?

Do I have to report back to you every time I have coffee with a friend?"

Jay snorted knowingly. "A guy, just like I figured." He shuffled across the kitchen and pulled a box of Toastie O's from the cupboard over the stove. "Anyone I know?"

"I don't think so. He's a friend of Brian's." Rose saw no point in mentioning that she hadn't noticed what time it was, had been startled when she'd glanced at her watch and seen that a quick cup of coffee had somehow become two hours.

"Mom, you're all red." Jay, on the verge of cramming a handful of Toastie O's into his mouth, stopped short to stare at her. "You must like him."

"Don't be ridiculous." Rose, her face growing even warmer, suddenly became busy lining the birdcage tray with fresh newspaper.

But Jay just stood there, staring. "Wow. You must *really* like him."

Without looking up, she advised briskly, "You'd better get dressed. Aunt Marie is coming over." Her sister was making a special trip into the city, to pick up the old sofa Rose had recently replaced.

"Okay, okay. I can take a hint."

"And for heaven's sake, would you please eat that out of a bowl? You're dropping it all over the floor."

"Jeez. You don't have to bite my head off. It's not *my* fault if you feel guilty for sneaking around behind Dad's—" Jay broke off suddenly. His face, already hectic with acne, flushed a feverish crimson. Clearly, he hadn't meant for that to slip out.

Even so, Rose whirled about, her face tight and hot. *"What did you say?"*

Jay, looking guilty, backed up against the counter, tiny doughnuts of sugar-crusted cereal dribbling from his fist onto the linoleum, crunching under his bare feet. His greenish eyes—Sylvie's eyes—slid to one side, as if he couldn't bear to look at her.

"Sorry. I didn't mean anything." His voice, low and sullen, pricked at her.

"Look." She faced her son squarely. "I am not going behind anyone's back here. Your father . . ." She swallowed hard against the rising lump in her throat. "He wouldn't have wanted me to just sit home every night." There, she'd said it. Even if she didn't exactly *feel* it.

"I *said* I was sorry," Jay flung back at her.

"You sound as if you have a problem with it. Do you?" She wasn't going to let him wriggle out from under this one, no sir.

"Not with this *guy*, whoever he is." Jay's eyes blazed with a hostility that seemed to come out of nowhere. "Anyway, it's not my opinion that counts."

"Who are we talking about, then?"

The minute the words were out, she knew she'd walked into a trap. She could feel it closing about her, cold and unforgiving as steel. Even before Jay answered with a tight little shrug, "You *know* who. Dad."

"Your father is dead," she reminded him.

"Yeah, but it's still always about him, isn't it? Everything. Even the new sofa—you said it was what *he* would have picked. Like he's ever gonna see it. Like it friggin' *matters*." Seeing her son looking so grave, with those roosterish tufts all over his head, Rose would have smiled if she hadn't been so close to tears. He shook his head as solemnly as a professor and said, "Mom, don't take this the wrong way, but you need to get a life. One that's not about Dad. You want to see this guy? So *see* him. Don't go around acting like he's some kind of friend."

"I have a life, thank you very much," she snapped. "And right now it's about all I can handle." She slid the tray into its slot in the birdcage with a loud clang.

Was she overreacting? Probably. But she was so upset she could hardly see straight. As she stood—her back to Jay, leaning into her fists on the counter—Rose found herself remembering last night. The calm oasis of that little coffee shop on Third Avenue, the simple pleasure of another adult seated across from her. Someone who passed the sugar without her having to ask, who seemed to know intuitively what she needed: conversation that had nothing to do with what had happened at the party.

Instead, they'd talked about Eric's volunteer work at Haven House . . . and her big case, *Esposito* v. *St. Bartholomew's Hospital*, for which she had a preliminary trial date set for August, after more than three years of collecting affidavits and evidence, not to mention a seemingly endless string of evidentiary and motion hearings. He told her about his lifelong love of aviation, confessed that when he was down in the dumps he sometimes took a drive out to the airport. Nothing seemed too impossible, he'd observed with a laugh, watching those big jets lift off.

Eric had once flown in a B-17 bomber, for a TV segment he'd done on a former World War II fighter pilot who'd restored one of the old planes. "If you want to know what it's like to *really* fly," he told her, "take a ride in one of those suckers. The noise alone is enough to knock the wind out of you."

"I prefer taking my chances on the ground," she'd said, shuddering as she remembered Iris' close call out on the terrace.

Eric had shrugged. "Win or lose, it's all a gamble. The way I look at it, the only thing you can be sure of is that unless you're willing to take some risks, you wind up with nothing."

As she'd listened to him then, it had all seemed so simple . . . a perfectly acceptable risk. Dinner next time, maybe a movie. Or even a drive out to an airfield to watch the planes take off. What could be the harm?

Yet, meeting Eric's gaze, she knew it wasn't as simple as that. Nothing about Eric, she suspected, would be uncomplicated. Even the way he was sitting—loose-jointed, with a hand curled about his coffee mug, measuring its warmth, yet at the same time seeming in no hurry for it to cool—suggested a man of many textures and facets. Some rough, others worn smooth as volcanic glass.

Until now, she hadn't dared to *really* look at him, to take in the whole of him. What if she liked what she saw a little too much? But now she allowed herself the small, guilty pleasure, noting his long fingers and unusually large wrists; the crease of an old scar over one eyebrow, and the way his shoulders seemed to cant at a slight angle. He'd loosened his bow tie, and unbuttoned his dinner jacket, which gave him the vaguely rakish look she associated with old Cary Grant movies. Yet there was nothing studied about his appearance. She noticed a darker patch of jawline to the left of his Adam's apple that he'd missed while shaving, and smiled. Max was always doing that, she remembered. His "blind spot," he'd called it.

Rose, instead of the usual tears, was flooded with an unexpected warmth. She felt a sudden urge to reach across the table, and wrap her fingers about Eric's. But how could she, without giving him the wrong message? For the truth was, no matter how interesting this man, how *desirable* even, she just wasn't ready for anything more than this: sharing a late-night conversation, and cup of coffee, with a friend.

Jay is right, she thought now, in the warm safety of her kitchen. *I should get a life.* The question was, what kind? What could another man possibly offer that her own husband hadn't already given her, a hundred times over? Isn't that what disturbed her most about Drew and Iris? That her son, if he married for the wrong reasons, would never know the kind of happiness she and Max had shared?

Slowly, she turned to face Jay, who'd loved his father, too . . . and who was still angry at Max for leaving them. She could see it in his jaw, cocked at an angle, and in his long arms, poised tensely at his sides. Somehow, she'd let him down. Drew, too. She'd allowed her own grief to swallow up everything in sight.

And now there was nothing left to say, nothing that would make a difference. She watched as Jay abruptly turned, and began rummaging in the cupboard where the bowls and plates were stacked. With his back to her, she sneaked a hasty swipe at her eyes.

"I forgot to buy milk," she told him, wanting to say more, to explain—but nothing she could say would make things better, ease his pain . . . or bring Max back. "I'll call Marie, and ask her to pick up a carton on the way."

🎗 "Drew better watch himself. That girl will push *him* over the edge, I'm telling you." Marie shook her head.

She sat across from Rose at the kitchen table, facing the window that looked out over the stone well of a garden, where a rare shaft of sunlight was being served up like a slice of some exotic fruit. Rose's sister didn't seem to notice, or care. Her thin face was pinched, and the nails on the fingers clasped about the mug in front of her were more bitten-looking than usual.

"Iris doesn't *mean* to hurt anyone," Rose felt compelled to argue in Iris' defense. She already regretted having succumbed to the impulse to tell Marie what had happened last night. Her eldest sister, who wasn't exactly the forgiving sort, would only underline what Rose herself was thinking.

"People like her, they never do," Marie stated with flat authority. "They're like a walk at night in a bad neighborhood—you may get mugged, but it's nothing personal. I ought to know. I made the same mistake marrying Pete." She peered into the sugar bowl, wrinkling her nose. "Hey, you got anything besides this Sweet 'n Low crap?"

Marie, who as a teenager could eat anything and never gain an ounce, wasn't so much skinny nowadays as downright scrawny. In her mid-fifties, she looked a good ten years older. Her face was hard and lined with too many disappointments, her once-brown hair dyed an unflattering shoe-polish black.

"In the cupboard to the right of the stove." Watching her sister rummage among the boxes and jars, Rose had to avert her gaze from the sight of Marie's spine running like a lumpy seam up the back of her cheap polyester blouse. She asked, "Would it have made a difference if I'd tried talking you out of it?" Marie had been nineteen and pregnant, but, still . . .

Marie shrugged, settling back into her chair. "You're talking ancient history. Who the hell knows? For one thing, with Nonnie breathing down my neck twenty-four hours a day, I'd probably have run off with the Son of Sam if he'd asked. The only thing I regretted at the time was leaving you alone with that old bat."

"I had Clare, remember?"

At the mention of her younger sister, Marie snorted. "For whatever it was worth. Saying all those rosaries might've put her one step closer to heaven, but let's face it, living with Miss Goody Two-Shoes was hell." Roughly, she shook a teaspoon of sugar into her mug straight from the box, then sat back and lit a cigarette. She was the only person Rose allowed to smoke in her home. "Anyway, Pete was okay when he wasn't drinking."

Rose idly stirred her coffee. What did you say to a woman who'd been beaten for years, until she finally got fed up enough to walk out? A woman who was hospitalized once with a ruptured kidney, and whose nose had been broken more times than a prizefighter's? At the time, Rose had had plenty to say. But now . . .

If Marie had little sympathy for others, she had none for herself. And if her tiny apartment in Port Washington, which was all she could afford on her salary as a Macy's clerk, wasn't exactly what she'd wanted out of life, Marie was far too proud to show it.

"But if it was *your* son, Bobby or Gabe?" Rose persisted.

Marie set her mug down with a decisive clunk. In the stark morning light, with the smoke from her cigarette drifting in lazy wreaths about her head, her eyes were a queer shade of milky blue that Rose associated with burned-out lightbulbs.

"I'd do whatever I could to save him," she said in a voice as hard and tight as the look on her face. "Get rid of the girl myself, if I had to."

❧ Monday morning, Rose sat at the desk in her office, feeling vaguely let down. She couldn't put her finger on what was missing . . . until she remembered that this month was when she and

Max had planned to take that trip to Nepal they'd always talked about—he'd wanted to go hiking in the Himalayas at least once before he died, he'd told her.

Two months after sending in the deposit, he was in a mahogany casket being lowered into the ground.

And now his widow sat with her back to a breathtaking view of Park Avenue and Fifty-second from the twenty-fourth floor that another executive would have forfeited several years' worth of vacations to be gazing out on.

With a sigh, Rose leaned back in her swivel chair, staring at the accordion file in front of her, bulging with filings, briefs, affidavits, rulings—and that was only the last few months' worth. There was a whole file drawer in the outer office dedicated to *Esposito* v. *St. Bartholomew's Hospital*. And now, finally, it was going to trial. Max would have been pleased, she thought. Though it was technically her case—via Rachel, who was affiliated with St. Bart's—from day one, Rose and Max had worked side by side on it, compiling and documenting. Hadn't it initially been Max who'd argued in favor of their representing the hospital, and thus taking on what had all the markings of a lost cause? He'd pointed out that however sympathetic a jury might feel, the plaintiff—a seventy-five-year-old woman who'd suffered a stroke on the operating table while having her gallbladder removed—had been chronically ill to begin with, and that there had been no clear negligence on the part of her doctors.

Max. God, how she wished he were here. While she tended to sift doggedly through mountains of discovery material, piecing together a case bit by bit, Max usually spied the one piece of evidence so obvious that everyone else had missed it. Like with *Ackerman* v. *Brushrite Industries*—Max pinpointing the source of his client's lead poisoning by having not only the paint currently manufactured by Brushrite tested, but the layers of Brushrite paint on the factory's *walls,* some of which dated back to the time of Ackerman's claim.

But if there was a magic bullet buried somewhere in *Esposito* v. *St.*

Bartholomew's, she had yet to find it. Against the team of ambulance chasers representing Mrs. Esposito, a half-paralyzed old lady in a wheelchair, Rose would have to come up with an argument so compelling it would make a multi-million-dollar institution look like the underdog. . . .

She was going over the anesthesiologist's deposition—fifty pages of truly numbing transcript, no pun intended—when her intercom beeped. "Rose? I have that file you wanted Xeroxed. You asked me to give it to Mandy . . . but she's not in her office yet." She sounded apologetic, but it wasn't *her* fault Mandy wasn't in. Hell, she probably felt guilty for failing to cover for her.

Rose tapped her pencil against the desktop in annoyance. Her stepdaughter had promised to go over next year's proposed budget before their partners' meeting at eleven. Rose needed the figures on Mandy's department. It would have been helpful, too, to get some overall feedback on the firm. Like her father, Mandy had always been good at spotting places where they could trim back a bit; and since she was generally the first to show up in the morning, and the last to leave at night, she had a pretty good perspective on things.

Except, lately, Mandy hadn't been quite as available as usual.

Come to think of it, Rose wondered, when *had* she last seen her stepdaughter? Whenever she buzzed Mandy at her desk, or stopped by her office, Rose was informed that Mandy was either in a meeting, or in court, or having lunch with a client. Was family law such a booming enterprise these days? Or was Mandy simply avoiding her?

Rose made a mental note to invite her stepdaughter over for dinner one night next week. For hadn't she been avoiding Mandy, too? When was the last time she'd suggested even a cup of coffee? Mandy was also grieving, she reminded herself. Maybe that was why they'd been subconsciously keeping one another at arm's length: each was for the other too painful a reminder of the husband and father they'd lost.

It wasn't that Rose didn't care; she just didn't feel she could handle more than what was on her own plate. When the simple act of weeding out a closet seems like the excavation of Troy, you don't have a lot left over for your family, she acknowledged ruefully.

"Ask her to stop by my office when she gets in," Rose directed her secretary—a bright-eyed Sarah Lawrence graduate whose anal doggedness secretly drove her a little nuts. "And—Mallory?—what is this on my calendar about a speech I'm supposed to give tomorrow afternoon?"

"The Chelsea Tenants Association," Mallory reminded her. "Something to do with legal rights in landlord disputes, I think." She added nervously, "You spoke to the woman in charge, remember?"

"Of course. It's coming back to me now," Rose lied.

"Do you want me to see if I can reschedule it?"

"No ... I'm sure it's in their bulletin already. I'll squeeze it in somehow." Running around like a chicken with its head cut off was better than having too much time to think, she'd found.

"Oh, and one other thing," Mallory remembered to tell her. "Before, when you were on the phone with Judge Henry's office, there was a call. Some man—he said he was a friend."

Rose felt herself grow warm. Eric? Like an uninvited guest, he'd been on her mind since Saturday night. When he didn't call on Sunday, she'd figured that was the end of it. She should have been relieved ... but, instead, she'd been secretly disappointed. Now, perversely, what she felt was pure panic.

"Did he leave a number?" Unconsciously, she'd brought a hand to her throat, where a pulse leaped. Rose quickly dropped her hand into her lap.

"He said he'd call back."

"Next time, be sure and get his name." Better not to arouse her secretary's suspicion, Rose thought.

The intercom clicked off.

Rose returned to the paperwork on her desk, but found she couldn't concentrate. Even the simple task of flipping through her

Rolodex—looking for a name she couldn't find at first, because she couldn't remember if the "P"s came before the "R"s—left her feeling muddled and irritable.

She stared at the framed portrait on the wall above the ecru sofa, a charcoal sketch of Max done by a sidewalk artist. Not particularly skillful, but somehow it captured his essence. That hint of irony in his crinkled eyes, and the angle of his head—chin tucked low, as if he were a boxer squaring off for a punch.

She thought of Max in bed; his hands, which had known her body so well, all the places she liked to be touched. The rhythms of their lovemaking like a familiar song she never got tired of hearing. How, even after they'd both come, he'd stay inside her another minute or so, not moving . . . as if withdrawing would shatter something precious.

Now, in her head, she could hear him, as if he were whispering in her ear. *I know you loved me, Rosie. Don't you realize that nothing could ever cancel that out?*

Mentally, yes. But her heart . . . ah, that was a different matter. It was made of more resistant stuff. Probably she was capable of sleeping with another man, but Rose couldn't imagine sharing a bathroom sink with anyone other than Max. Or a closet. Or in airports, on long layovers between flights, falling asleep with her head nestled in a lap that wasn't his . . .

She was halfway through the pile on her desk when the intercom buzzed once more. "It's *him* again, and this time I got his name," a conspiratorial voice announced. Another thing that annoyed Rose about her secretary—Mallory's assumption that, like herself, every single woman over the age of thirty was at all times actively seeking a husband. "Eric Sandstrom. Line two."

Rose, suddenly furious that she'd been placed in this position, punched the blinking button. "Rose Griffin," she announced crisply.

"Am I catching you at a bad time?"

Eric's voice, like no other—faintly husky and at the same time resonant—caused her face and scalp to prickle, and the skin on the back of her neck to grow tight. Well, of course, she thought, feeling impatient with herself. Didn't he make a living as a host on the radio?

"I have a meeting in half an hour, so I *am* a little rushed," she told him.

"This will only take a minute."

"What can I help you with?"

There was a pause, and she heard the bemusement in Eric's voice when he said, "You sounded so businesslike just then."

"This *is* my office," she reminded him.

"Well, I won't keep you then." He became suddenly businesslike himself, leaving her feeling the tiniest bit guilty. "I need a legal expert for a show I'm doing next week. You interested?"

Rose immediately felt foolish. What could she have been thinking? That any guy over forty would succumb to the charms of a middle-aged woman with two grown boys, and more gray hairs than there were papers on her desk?

"Depends. What's the topic?" she asked, more brusquely than she might have had her heart not been pounding.

"Domestic violence. My main guest is a former battered wife, who just published a book about her experience. I've lined up the director of a local shelter, too, along with one of the residents."

"Sounds interesting, but I'm afraid it's not up my alley," she told him. "Why don't I have my stepdaughter give you a call? She specializes in family law."

"I don't need an expert witness—nobody is on trial here." He chuckled. "You ever done any radio or TV? I have a feeling you'd be good at it. Frankly, that's why I thought of you."

Rose hesitated, uncertain how to respond. She'd been so busy putting up barriers against a romantic interest Eric didn't appear to have, his simple directness threw her off guard. It might be fun, being a guest on his show. Certainly it would be a change of pace.

"What the heck, why not?" she relented with a laugh.

"How about Tuesday? One-thirty, you're out by two-fifteen."

"You got it." Grabbing an envelope, she scribbled the address. In SoHo, West Broadway. That would be cutting it close, but unless she got stuck in traffic she'd make it back in time for her three o'clock.

She was on the verge of saying goodbye when Eric remarked, "By the way, I spoke to Brian this morning. He told me Iris and Drew had gotten engaged."

He had the good sense, at least, not to congratulate her. On the other hand, he didn't sound troubled, either. Why should he? It wasn't Eric's son about to ruin his life.

She said cautiously, "Drew seems to think they can work it out. In any case, there's not much I can do about it. He didn't exactly consult me ahead of time."

"And if he had?"

"I'd have told him to wait until he was absolutely sure. Like the song says, only fools rush in."

" '. . . but I can't help falling in love with you,' " he finished the refrain.

In the beat of silence that followed, Rose felt suddenly, frighteningly vulnerable—as if he'd somehow stripped away her executive veneer and could see how desperately lonely she was. But she sensed Eric wasn't mocking her.

"Something like that." Rose closed her eyes, pressing the heel of one hand to her aching chest.

"You've never felt that way yourself—like you'd die if you had to wait a single more minute for something you wanted?" Eric's voice, low and soothing, seemed to tug at her like a gentle tide.

"If I ever did, it's been so long I can't remember," she lied.

"Or would just as soon forget," he countered, with the wry lightness of someone who must tread cautiously himself, or risk opening old wounds.

Rose thought of Brian, how desperately in love she'd been at Drew's age. What had it earned her besides a broken heart? If Max hadn't come along then, she might not have found the courage to love again. It was Max who'd made her believe in second chances . . .

who'd shown her that even a heart that seemed damaged beyond repair can be mended. . . .

She felt a sudden need to get away from this man, as fast and far as possible. There were no sappy love songs for women who read *The Wall Street Journal*, and moisturized with Night Repair. No encores, either.

And that was just fine with her. She needed to concentrate now on what was important: her children, and her work. With *Esposito* v. *St. Bartholomew's* looming, she'd be lucky if she found the time to do her nails, and grab a half hour in the morning on the Stairmaster. Sex? Yeah, she dimly remembered what that was. But right now, the idea of even getting to know Eric—much less actually *sleeping* with him—seemed as remote and unlikely as a cruise to the Fiji Islands on a private yacht.

"I'd better go," she told Eric. "I'll see you next week."

🌹 Tuesday of next week, at precisely one-thirty, Rose was stepping out of the elevator on the tenth floor of the West Broadway office building in which WQNA was located. She was buzzed through a set of plate-glass doors into a reception area paneled in pale oak, then escorted by a punk-haired blonde in a black miniskirt along a corridor lined with office cubicles the size of post-office boxes, each crammed to the ceiling with electronic equipment and snaking cables.

At last, Rose was ushered into a recording studio walled with carpet and tucked behind the Plexiglas-walled engineer's booth. The room was small, just large enough to accommodate a table, two swivel chairs, and a pair of mikes mounted on flexible metal arms suspended over either end of the table. Eric, seated before one of the mikes, stood to greet her.

"Sorry it's so cramped," he apologized. "I feel like the old charlatan hiding behind the curtain in *Wizard of Oz*. Most of my guests expect a glitzier setup."

"That's the *last* thing I need," she said, laughing. "I spent the whole morning in court, and right now all I want is to take off this jacket and kick back." She felt ridiculously overdressed in her Isaac Mizrahi suit and pearls, like someone who'd wandered into the wrong hotel banquet room.

Eric himself looked the part of the relaxed radio personality, in navy corduroys and blue pinstriped shirt with the sleeves rolled up. Yet it was obvious he knew how to dress. Eric's family was well off—he'd told her he'd gone to prep school, then Princeton. Only someone who'd been raised with money, she thought, would dare kick around in crew socks and scuffed Gucci loafers. Plus that hair of his—mussed, as if he'd just rolled out of bed, a dozen shades of blond and brown and gold all tossed together . . . It made her think of running barefoot over a sand dune on a warm summer evening.

At the same time, there was that edge she'd picked up on the other night. A vague restlessness just below the surface—as if he'd just come from somewhere and already couldn't wait to leave. His blue eyes, on the other hand—given an almost naked look by the paleness of his brows and lashes—were disturbingly intense.

Rose gradually became aware that Eric was speaking to her.

"Liz Aikens and Shirley Cunnigham, my other two guests, will be patched in via phone," he was explaining. "You'll be able to hear them through your headphones. And when you talk into the microphone, they'll be able to hear you."

As he was adjusting her mike, she had a sudden urge to slip a finger under the little wave of hair that curled over his collar. The skin on the back of his neck would be soft, she thought. As soft as—

She dropped her gaze, a flash of heat scalding her cheeks.

Mother of God. What rock had *that* crawled out from under? She hadn't thought about making love to a man, *any* man, since Max died.

Seated across from Eric, with the mikes open and the tape rolling, Rose did her best to concentrate, to sound articulate and well informed. But, annoyingly, uncontrollably, her eyes would cut over to Eric, cataloguing and storing away the frayed Band-aid around one thumb; his top lip, which dipped in a cupid's bow and made his bottom lip seem even fuller; a front tooth that slightly overlapped the one next to it. There was a tiny ink stain on his front pocket, like a period at the end of a sentence, where he'd absently stuck an uncapped pen . . . and in her mind she was once again seeing him in that coffee shop, scribbling her phone number on a napkin. Half-hoping he would call . . . and at the same time dreading what he'd say if he did.

Jesus, Rose, get a grip.

She leaned into the mike, bringing a hand to the headphones, which felt large and clumsy over her ears. "The laws *are* changing . . . but I agree with Liz: they're not changing fast enough." The words flowed easily, and Rose was surprised by how cool and collected she sounded. This wasn't much different, really, from presenting a case in court. "Basically, it's still a problem of perception. If the police officers responding to domestic calls don't take them seriously, more wives like the one you just described will grab for a gun instead of the phone, and their abusive husbands will end up in the morgue . . . instead of behind bars, where they belong."

"I wish mine *was* dead," spoke a hard voice—the battered wife currently in hiding at the shelter run by Liz Aikens. What was her name again? Shirley. Yes, that was it.

"Believe me, Shirley, you wouldn't want that." Rose felt her professional veneer slipping, and heard the slight tremble in her voice. "Death is . . . well, there's no turning back from it."

"Yeah? That's good. No more tiptoeing around the house wondering which bone he's gonna break this time," the woman replied with a harshness that was like biting down on tinfoil.

"Shirley, what are you feeling right now?" Eric moved in quickly, as adept as an orchestra conductor. "What do you want to say to those women out there who have no idea what it's like?"

A brief pause, then: "It's scary."

"Scary in what way?" he pressed.

"Just . . . scary. Not only when he's bein' mean. What's scary is how you get used to living like that. After a while, it seems almost *normal.*"

In her mind, Rose was seeing Marie's bruised and swollen face, and remembering the times she'd visited her sister in the hospital. Nothing she could say ever seemed to get through to Marie, then one day she'd simply had enough—and walked out.

"Let's talk a little bit about the role of alcohol in all this." Eric switched to another tack. "Liz, in your experience, are abusive husbands often under the influence when they beat their wives?"

Bingo. He'd hit the nail on the head, launching the author into a diatribe on what was obviously her pet cause—getting judges to remand abusive husbands to rehab facilities in lieu of overcrowded jails. For the next ten minutes, Rose barely got a word in. Then, out of the corner of her eye, she caught sight of the burly redheaded engineer signaling to Eric from inside his Plexiglas booth—holding up two fingers. Only two minutes left. Rose blinked in surprise. Where had the hour gone?

When they were off the air, Eric swung aside the flexible metal arm on which his microphone was mounted, and leaned back in his chair with a knowing grin. "It felt more like five minutes, right? Most people have that reaction. Being on the air is like pedaling a bike downhill—unless you're the one running the show."

"You make it look so natural," she said, genuinely impressed.

He shrugged. "I've had a lot of practice faking it." Glancing at his wristwatch—Swiss Army, its leather band darkened with age—he asked, "Can I tempt you with a late lunch? I never eat before I go on the air."

Rose realized she was starving. But there was no time, not even for a quick bite on the run. She had to be back in her office in fifteen minutes for her three o'clock.

"Can I take a raincheck? I'm running late as it is." Rose felt both relieved and a little regretful. "In fact, I should call my secretary and let her know. Mind if I use your phone?"

But when she got through to her office, Mallory informed her that Mark Cannizzaro—of Cannizzaro, Palmer, and D'Amico, the firm representing Mrs. Esposito—had canceled. Damn. That would mean yet another delay, and might result in their trial date's getting bumped ahead another week . . . or month.

At the same time, her empty stomach was demanding to be fed. And Eric . . . smiling at her, with those blue eyes of his that seemed to know more about her than he had any business knowing. Slouched against the door with one scuffed loafer crossed over the other, and a hand resting lightly on the knob—as if he'd known all along she'd have lunch with him.

He took her to a funky outdoor café, which turned out to be just what she was in the mood for. The weather was perfect: bright and clear, but not too hot. Under the shade of their Cinzano umbrella, with the sunlight winking off the wet rim of her iced-tea glass, Rose, for the first time in months, felt something close to contentment.

"You were great on the show," Eric praised her. "Not just a lawyer giving legal advice—a woman reacting to another woman's pain."

Rose smiled grimly. "It *does* make me mad. My older sister was married to a guy like that. Her ex-husband would get smashed, then smash *her*. Pete finally stopped drinking—after serving ninety days for hospitalizing her with a ruptured kidney."

Eric grimaced. "I guess your ex-brother-in-law won't be getting any Christmas cards from you."

"I never liked him in the first place. And after what he did to Marie . . . I give him credit for getting sober, but that doesn't mean I'll ever forgive him." Rose was surprised by the bitterness she still felt, after all these years. Maybe it was because Marie, when they were growing up, in her own stingy, hardbitten way, had been the only one to look out for *her*. Even that time Marie had stolen from her—sneaking money from the secret bank account set up by Sylvie in Rose's name—couldn't erase that deep bond.

"If it makes you feel any better, we're even harder on ourselves."

It took a moment for the meaning of his words to sink in. Then Rose remembered: Eric was a recovering alcoholic.

For some reason, it didn't disgust her. Quite the opposite. There was something . . . well . . . *dignified* about him. As if he'd had his own hell to pay, but made excuses to no one. And she couldn't imagine him ever hitting a woman, even if he was drunk.

"How long have you been sober?" she asked.

"Five years." His tone was matter-of-fact, with only the faintest suggestion of what it must have cost him.

"I'm sure it wasn't easy."

"It never is."

"You don't like talking about it, do you?"

"Talk's cheap. Takes money to buy whiskey." He smiled at his own joke—the kind of gallows humor Rose could appreciate—but his face, under the shade of the umbrella, was pensive.

She sat back with a sigh, playing with the straw from her iced tea. "I know what you mean. After my husband died, I got sick of listening to myself carry on. After a while, so did most of my friends. A woman in my grief group turned to me at one point and said, 'Talking isn't going to make it go away, you know.' And she was right." Rose crumpled the straw in her fist. "After that, I kept my mouth shut . . . and thought about ways to kill myself instead."

She averted her eyes, feeling oddly naked, and imagined he could see right through her, down to where her heart thumped in heavy, hot dismay. Why had she told him that? After that scary scene with Iris, followed by Drew's proposal, Eric would think their whole family was certifiable.

Rose glanced around her. The sidewalk in front of the restaurant, deep enough for at least a dozen tables, was fenced with high wooden planters spilling geraniums and bright impatiens. Lively reggae music pumped from overhead speakers. Yet the SoHo gallery types lunching with their black-clad artists in nose rings, however offbeat, couldn't have begun to imagine the dark universe she occasionally inhabited.

"I used to think about killing myself, too." Eric's words were an echo coming back at her from the chilly cave of her thoughts—reassuring her that she was neither lost nor alone. Rose had to turn and look at him to be sure she'd heard correctly. Eric looked back at her, his gaze serious . . . and blessedly sane. "Every single day for the first year and a half," he recalled with a small, mirthless smile. "Ironically, it was the only thing that kept me going."

"How do you mean?" She leaned forward in fascination.

"My obituary," he explained. "Knowing I wouldn't be more than a paragraph buried at the bottom of the page. After I'd pissed away my entire career, it's ironic, isn't it, that in the end what saved me was my big fat ego?"

"My sister Clare, the nun, would see it differently. She'd say that God was saving you for something special."

Eric nodded thoughtfully, and said, "I don't know about God . . . but it's amazing what can happen when you let go and stop believing it's all up to you. When you finally realize it's got nothing whatsoever to do with willpower."

"That doesn't make sense," the lawyer in her objected. "If it's not about free will and choice, how would anyone ever get sober?"

"Choice? Sure." He leaned on his elbows; the light filtering through the canvas was grainy and golden on his face. "The choice is in letting go of the notion that you're alone in all this. Embracing . . . a higher power, if you want to call it that. Not God necessarily, but the simplest form of faith. Trusting that, if you let go, someone or something will catch you." He sat back. "Am I making any sense? Sometimes I get carried away."

"I was brought up Catholic, the whole nine yards," she confided. "Before I'd really learned how to read, I thought 'sacred heart' was '*scared* heart.' It's good to be reminded sometimes what religion is *supposed* to be about."

When their sandwiches came, Rose found she was as content eating with Eric in silence as she had been talking to him. There was none of the discomfort she usually felt with other people. Even old friends. No need to explain herself, or apologize.

Too soon, their plates were being cleared away, and Eric was picking up the check. Yet the spell, if that's what this was, stubbornly refused to be broken. Staring at the sunstruck hairs on the back of his wrist, oddly muscular for someone who made his living behind a desk, Rose felt something hard and guarded inside her dissolve, sifting downward like loose, hot sand.

Sweet Jesus. This warm heaviness between her legs; this empty socket where her full stomach had been. Familiar feelings, *good* feelings . . . but from another time, another place. The intimacy she'd known with Max—intimacy that had deepened with each passing year—how could she ever share that with another man? What could Eric Sandstrom know of the secret places on her body where she liked to be touched? Or the words of love she needed to hear?

She prayed that he was right, that God would catch her if she fell. Otherwise, it would be a long hard journey just to get back to where she was now—halfway up the precarious slope of her shattered life.

A guilty relief washed through her when Eric glanced at his watch and said, "I'd better hustle; I'm taping a show in half an hour. Come, I'll walk you to the corner." He stood up, and placed a hand lightly against the small of her back to guide her through the maze of tables.

In the sunlight, with the hot blue sky stretched like a freshly ironed sheet between the tall buildings overhead, Rose shivered.

It wasn't until she was in a cab hurtling across town that she was struck by a horrible realization: feeling attracted to Eric hadn't made her miss Max any less. In fact, she missed him more than ever.

Damn this Benedict Arnold body of hers, carrying on like a teenager's; all that adrenaline-shot, moist-between-the-legs nonsense she'd have to take care of, on her own, later on, in the privacy of her bedroom, if she was going to get any sleep at all tonight.

What she needed more than getting laid, Rose thought angrily, was to get a grip. Until she got her own life together, how the hell was she supposed to help her sons, and her stepdaughter, fix theirs?

She recalled Sylvie's words from Brian's party. *People generally figure it out for themselves . . . even when they take the long way around.*

Rose wondered if maybe she was right. But with Drew, could she just sit back and watch him destroy any chance for a normal life? Her son needed to know that marriage wasn't one person carrying everything on his or her shoulders; it was equal partners, each pulling his or her own weight. The way it had been with her and Max.

Sylvie. What if her mother were to talk to Iris? The girl adored her grandmother. Sylvie could explain that marrying Drew wouldn't solve anything, not in the long run.

On impulse, Rose leaned forward, releasing her grip on the strap to which she'd been clinging for dear life as the cab bounced and slalomed its way through the traffic along Houston.

"I've changed my mind, driver. Take me to Riverside and West Seventy-ninth instead," she directed crisply. "And, please . . . try not to kill us on the way."

Chapter 3

Sylvie stood on the path that wound like a ribbon through her rose beds, their bushes heavy with blooms. Her garden, by city standards, was quite large—roughly the size of the one-bedroom apartment on Tremont Avenue where she'd grown up. Though not nearly spacious enough, she observed, for the wealth of vines, flowers, and boughs that crowded and spilled their way down brick walls, up bamboo stakes, and over trellises.

Under the shade of a spreading ginkgo, the maidenhair ferns, in their bronze planters tarnished the green of living things, trailed like drowned Ophelia over the scrolled back of her cherished wrought-iron loveseat—bought years ago at an antique auction in Rhinebeck. What had caught her eye was an unusual detail: a pair of sweet-faced cherubs, their open wings forming the loveseat's arms. She'd instantly fallen in love . . . never dreaming, of course, that those angels might one day feel a bit too close to home for comfort.

Home. Oddly, it was *here*, more than in the house itself, that she felt most at ease—with her roses and peonies and daylilies. As if somehow she could *think* better among all the trees and plants and flowers that had become woven together through the seasons to form a single, glorious tapestry.

The middle of July, and nearly everything was in need of pruning, she noted with a sigh. English ivy cascaded down brick walls beginning to crumble under its weight, the tangled green splashed with bright spots of color—purple clematis and morning glory, along with several varieties of climbing roses. Marigolds, violets, pansies, and sweet William bordered the raised stone patio—and the steps leading down to the path where she stood—like a bright, ruffled hem.

Honeybees stitched invisible patterns around shrubs and climbers and trellised arches—the 'Prosperity' and 'Perpetual', the golden 'Buff Beauty', the 'Madame Pierre Oger' ablaze with roses the delicate pink hue of porcelain.

Oh, the fragrance! As she drew in the mingled scents, Sylvie felt a heightened awareness of life's riches rinse through her, cleansing her somehow. She remembered an incident from her childhood, the time a neighbor had remarked insensitively about the number of times Sylvie's best dress had been let down—just loudly enough for Sylvie's mother to overhear.

"Why, yes," Mama had said, smiling as if no offense had been meant or taken. "Isn't it lovely, how my Sylvie is growing? What a blessing, to have such a tall, healthy daughter."

Sylvie smiled at the memory, and how it had made her feel: special and important. Not poor, with hardly enough to eat, but wealthy beyond measure. Because she and her mama had known what their friends and neighbors—sour-faced women wearing expressions of perpetual dissatisfaction—couldn't begin to fathom: that richness wasn't just something to be bought or sold; it was there for anyone with the courage and imagination to reach out and pluck it. The gold in a sunset, the wildflowers that poked their heads up amid the weeds of vacant lots like scattered gems, the priceless masterpieces on display in museums—like the one Mama worked in—that were freely available to everyone.

Now, her own hands stiff with arthritis, and her floppy straw hat pulled low against the sun that made her age freckles stand out, Sylvie realized with a start that she was a good fifteen years older than her own mother had been when she died. *If Mama could see me now, she wouldn't recognize her own daughter.* She marveled at the strangeness of it. More and more, it seemed to her that life was nothing but a series of small oddities and ironies, all strung together by some yet-to-be-revealed celestial scheme. Like the irony of her two daughters' becoming such good friends. And now, dear heaven, here was Rose's son engaged to Rachel's daughter. . . .

Rachel had phoned last week with the news, sounding more relieved than happy. Drew was so good with Iris, she'd pointed out; he would look after her, make sure nothing bad happened. As if that were any reason to marry! At the same time, Sylvie had heard the anxiety in Rachel's voice, like a stitch pulled tight. She knew how easy it was to fool yourself into thinking that any port in a storm, even a marriage rooted in guilt and fear, was better than none.

Sylvie had wanted to argue how wrongheaded it would be. But she didn't dare. Hadn't she done enough already? All those years ago, turning two innocent lives—Rose's and Rachel's—irreversibly inside out. If it hadn't been for her own arrogance in believing that fate could be twisted, physically *wrenched* like a broken bone being set, none of this would be happening. Rachel might not be losing sleep over a daughter as troubled as she was charmed. And Rose worrying over a son who felt responsible for everyone but himself.

Rose. Sylvie hadn't spoken to her since the party, but guessed that Rose, as fond as she was of Iris, had to be beside herself. Under the circumstances, what mother wouldn't be?

It was all Sylvie could do not to put in her two cents. And this morning, after tossing and turning all night, hadn't she nearly done so? She'd been dialing Rachel's number, in fact, when reason finally got the upper hand. What, after all, could Rachel do? Or Rose? Drew and Iris were old enough to know their own minds, if not their hearts. Either God would guide them onto the right path, or they would stumble onto it themselves. Interfering might, in the end, only make matters worse.

Seeing how nice a day it was turning out to be—sunny, but not too humid—Sylvie had decided to prune her roses instead.

Yet here it was nearly three in the afternoon, and she had only just now set foot outdoors. Where had the time gone? She'd lingered over breakfast, true—eating was such a chore when you had no appetite—then had indulged in a short nap that had somehow stretched into a long one. Before she knew it, Milagros was standing over her bed with a lunch tray, looking as if there would be the devil to pay if Sylvie didn't take at least a spoonful or two of the nice soup she'd fixed.

Poor Milagros, who used to come in three days a week—Nikos had prevailed on her to move in so as to keep an eye on Sylvie while he was at work. Sylvie hated it, of course. Having her housekeeper fuss over her was an affront to her independence and her privacy . . . but most of all, she hated it because it was *necessary.*

The least she could do, Sylvie resolved, was to continue filling the house with the scent of fresh-cut roses.

Stooping with her secateurs to snip a pinkish-gold bloom from the 'Peace' rose that had overtaken the trellis where she stood, Sylvie thought how much easier it was to make a resolution than to keep it. Like her decision—one she'd insisted that both Nikos and Dr. Choudry honor—to shield her family from how *truly* ill she was. It was easy to argue that Rose and Rachel had more than enough of their own worries to handle right now. But at 2:00 A.M., with her chest on fire and her heart racing like the engine of a car stuck in mud, sometimes not even Nikos' loving arms and whispered reassurances were enough. What Sylvie desperately yearned for in those hours was to grab hold of what she could feel slipping away, to hang on tight to her precious loved ones—Nikos, Rose and Rachel, her grandchildren.

Faintly, from deep in the house, Sylvie heard the front door buzz.

Milagros would get it, she thought. Mostly likely it was for Nikos—a set of blueprints being delivered by hand, or some official document from the buildings department too important to risk being lost in the shuffle at his office.

She kept on with her gardening—tying back a runner, picking a Japanese beetle off a leaf riddled like fine lace. The sun settled over her shoulders and the backs of her bare arms like a lovely warm shawl, thawing the ice that had taken up more or less permanent residence in her fingers and toes.

It occurred to Sylvie that, as active as Nikos still was in his business, it had been some time since she'd missed her own. All that delicious excitement and challenge—poring over luscious fabric and wall-covering samples at the D and D building on Third, bidding at auctions, hearing the cries of delight over a room transformed from a raw space into something wonderful and inviting. But maybe she didn't mourn it so much because she'd discovered the greater joy of simply *being*. Of taking the time to marvel at the curve of a rose petal . . . or rejoice that she was still breathing.

Nikos, she smiled to herself, wouldn't know what to do with himself if he were to retire; for him, working *was* being. But if there was a silver lining to this blighted existence of hers, she was seeing it now—in the primroses, snapdragons, and hollyhocks reaching up to touch the afternoon sun that slanted across a brick wall, and in the ladybug trundling across a hosta leaf outlined in red like a valentine. . . .

"Sylvie?"

Startled, she straightened and looked around. At first, all she could see was the sun's reflected light backfiring off the French doors that stood open onto the patio. Then her vision cleared, and she recognized the figure walking toward her. Rose.

Sylvie felt a flicker of anticipation that was followed, as always with Rose, by a tiny throb of regret—the knowledge that, try as she might to compensate in other ways, she would never be the mother Rose wanted, or deserved.

Rose looked as if she'd walked all the way here—her face flushed, and her dark hair sprung loose in wild tendrils, its distinctive white stripe standing out like a feathered plume. But today was Tuesday, Sylvie remembered, and Rose was clearly dressed for the office, in a stylish suit and sensible heels. What was her daughter doing here in the middle of a weekday afternoon?

"Goodness, you startled me!" Sylvie instinctively brought a hand to her heart. "I heard the door, but I had no idea . . ." She wagged an affectionately scolding finger. "You should have called to let me know, I would have put on something nice." She looked down in chagrin at the faded housecoat she was wearing.

Yet a day that brought one of her daughters, or grandchildren, was automatically a good one, no matter how dowdy she looked—or ill she felt. She wouldn't let anything spoil this lovely surprise. She would ask Milagros to bring a pitcher of iced tea out to the patio, where she and Rose could sit and visit. There was even a clump of lemon mint somewhere, if she remembered correctly. . . . Yes, over there, under the Oriental poppies . . .

"I can't stay long," Rose protested as Sylvie bent over to snip some mint. "There's something I need to discuss with you. Do you have a few minutes?"

Discuss? So formal! Sylvie smiled encouragingly.

"Oh, I don't know. You see how busy I am. So busy I can hardly see straight." With a merry laugh, she stepped up onto the patio. But the effort left her winded, as if she *had* been dashing about . . . and suddenly it felt much too warm to remain outside. Gesturing toward the open French doors, she said, "Come, dear, let's go inside, where it's cool . . . and I can put my feet up."

Kissing her daughter's cheek, Sylvie was pleased to see that Rose was wearing the ruby earrings that had once been hers. Old, precious—yet, like so much of what she'd tried to share with Rose, those, too, had been given to her in the most unorthodox fashion— the first earring when Rose was just a little girl, the second not until many years later. . . .

Her mind slipped its groove, and she was seeing Rose again as she had on that long-ago day, standing outside her school—a little girl with olive skin and wild dark hair . . . and the grave eyes of a grown- up. Except for the one glimpse of her daughter just after Rose's birth, Sylvie had not laid eyes on her until that moment. She remembered the shame she'd felt . . . and the longing. She'd yearned to hold her daughter. To give Rose something of herself.

On impulse, Sylvie had snatched the earring from one ear and thrust it into the hand of the child gaping at her in disbelief. A mis- take, of course. She'd realized it at once. What must that astonished little girl have thought? How could she have imagined that the strange lady acting so crazy was the mother she hadn't even known existed?

Yet that lone earring had proved to be the compass that years later had led Rose back to her, to this very spot.

Had her daughter ever regretted seeking her out, finding the truth?

Over the years, their friendship had grown, like the roses in her garden—slowly, and not without its thorns. But they never spoke, except obliquely, of the secrets that had been revealed that cold afternoon.

Now, as she saw the sun flash off the ruby teardrops in her daughter's ears, it struck Sylvie that Rose must have worn them for a reason. And that maybe whatever it was had something to do with why she was here today. . . .

Sylvie shivered, her fingers growing icy again.

Inside, the house felt cooler than usual for this time of day. Sylvie led the way through the sun-splashed morning room, with its chintz-cushioned wicker chairs and forest of potted plants, down the hallway, and into the sitting room just off the parlor.

Sinking onto the velvet sofa, she felt embraced somehow. In this room, unchanged in over half a century—since she'd come here as a young bride—she could honestly believe that the best things in life were the most lasting. Her tired gaze welcomed the sight of her Queen Anne secretary, glowing in the muted sunlight as if freshly polished. And the rich jewel tones of the Berber rug in front of the fireplace, with its ornate lion-headed brass andirons. Even the flowers arranged in the Chinese vase on the marble mantel—a mass of daylilies and gladioli—seemed a part of the lovely timelessness.

She watched Rose lower herself into the easy chair under a pair of framed Audubon prints. "Sorry to sneak up on you like this," she apologized with a nervous little laugh. "You've probably guessed why I'm here." The polite smile slipped from her face. "Rachel, I'm sure, has told you."

"About the engagement? Yes." Sylvie sighed.

Dear Lord, give me the strength to help her. . . .

Rose was frowning, her face clouded. At the same time, Sylvie couldn't help thinking how much lovelier she had become with middle age. The bold features that had once seemed too large for her face softened somewhat by her years. Even the sadness she'd worn since Max died hadn't diminished her beauty. If anything, she was even more haunting. It was hard to take your eyes off Rose—and, in some ways, even harder to look at her.

"Then you must know, too, about the party she's throwing." Her daughter's dark eyes flashed with outrage. "As if this ridiculous engagement was anything to celebrate!"

"Celebrate? Oh no, I don't believe Rachel sees it that way." Sylvie didn't add that Rachel had asked her to help organize the party, for which she'd already set a date—little more than three weeks away. "She wants for Iris to be happy, that's all."

It was the wrong thing to have said, Sylvie realized at once.

"It's what she's always wanted, isn't it?" Rose replied coolly. "A magic bullet to fix whatever's wrong with her daughter. What would surprise me, frankly, is Rachel having any illusions about it being the best thing for my son."

Sylvie, feeling boxed in, was moved to defend Rachel. "I know how fond she is of Drew. Rachel wouldn't want to see *either* of them get hurt. Anyway," she gently pointed out, "it isn't up to Rachel. *Or* you."

"If it *had* been, believe me, I'd have had plenty to say about it," Rose shot back, her face flushed.

Sylvie winced in sympathy. "Oh, my dear . . . I don't blame you. I've had my own doubts."

Rose squeezed her eyes shut, massaging them lightly with her fingertips. "You're right about one thing—Drew isn't interested in what *I* think. But Iris . . . Well, there *is* one person she might listen to. *You.* The two of you have always been so close. She trusts you. You could tell her how crazy this is. How wrong."

Sylvie sat back, flattened by the heated force of Rose's request.

No, not a request. More of a demand—one that Sylvie, for the life of her, couldn't satisfy. Oh, how could she explain it so Rose would understand? It wasn't that she didn't care . . . but that she cared enough to keep her distance.

"If what you say is true," she replied quietly, "then Iris needs to find that out for herself."

"When? After she's ruined Drew's life?" Rose sucked in a breath. "Look, I don't mean to sound heartless. I care about Iris, too. But don't you see? This will be a disaster for *both* of them. Iris needs more than Drew can ever give her. Much more. And you know it."

Sylvie pulled herself up straight, tucking an embroidered pillow against the small of her back, where a cold ache was sinking roots. "Whatever our fears, don't you see how useless it would be to try and prevent them from coming true? Drew and Iris would only resent it and pull away from us. Then, if and when they *really* needed us, they might not let us back in." She wanted so for Rose to see it as *she* did, but Sylvie felt as if she were floundering in the great cold sea of Rose's resentment. Weakly, she added, "We'll just have to pray that the situation will sort itself out in its own time."

"In other words, Drew can sink or swim—without your help." Rose's stare was flat and unwavering.

"I *can't* help him. There's a difference, don't you see?"

"Maybe it's the difference between *me* asking . . . and if it were Rachel."

The room's temperature seem to plunge sharply. Sylvie was left shivering in a shaft of sunlight that angled like a drawn saber across the sofa where she sat. A dull ache bloomed in the hollow just below her rib cage.

"Oh, my dear . . . you can't honestly believe that." Filled with dismay, she simply stared at Rose, unable to say what she was really thinking.

I abandoned her in favor of another baby. Rachel. And years later, when I begged Rose not to reveal my secret, wasn't I looking out for Rachel then, too? She's right. Always Rachel.

Who wouldn't resent that? Sylvie was seeing it now as she must—Rachel growing up in this beautiful house, attending private school, whereas Rose, living in a cramped Brooklyn apartment, had to beg for the few scraps of attention she'd gotten from the hateful woman she'd believed was her grandmother.

And now there was someone else Sylvie had to protect: Iris. However unfair it might be to Rose and her sons, the reality was that Iris simply was not capable of withstanding the blow of learning that her beloved Gran, whom she trusted, had lied to them all. Until she was strong enough to stand on her own, she had to be nurtured—as tenderly as a rosebush in spring. Not with stakes and twine and force-feedings, but with love . . .

Not everyone was like Rose, who, instead of being beaten down by adversity, had only grown stronger. Against all odds, she'd triumphed. If only Rose could know how proud her mother was of her—and how humbled.

But, no, Rose could only see it through her own eyes, which right now were fixed on Sylvie with dark accusation.

"What difference does it make what *I* believe? Or what I want." Rose leaned forward. Her hands, gripping the arms of her chair, were clenched, white-knuckled. "All these years, you never cared. You never once stopped to think what it was like for me, being introduced as your *friend,* having to pretend it was all just so nice, your taking an interest in me and my boys. After all, I'm nothing to you, right? Not your *daughter,* like Rachel."

The ache in Sylvie's chest sharpened into real pain, and she fought to keep from pressing a hand to her heart. *Oh, my Rose, if only you knew . . .*

The letters. Dozens and dozens of them, written over the years but never sent. All the thoughts and feelings she'd wanted to share with her daughter, her Rose, which she could never speak aloud. Each tear she'd shed in private, each milestone she'd celebrated fully, as any proud mother would: Rose's graduation from law school, her marriage, the births of her sons. In words written in secret, she could explain why it was necessary to remain silent even now. Especially now. For with each passing year, hadn't the stakes merely increased? The result was a wrong that had grown in on itself so many times over that the path back to forgiveness was now covered with brambles.

The letters were in a locked drawer in her desk, to which Sylvie had the only key. She'd thought about destroying them, burning them in this fireplace, lest she die before Nikos could get rid of them for her. But something always stopped her. Perhaps it was that the letters were her only real legacy to Rose.

There were no framed photos on her mantel of Rose and her sons, as there were of Rachel and Iris. No snapshots in an album, either, except those taken of their two families as a group. Her bundle of letters was the only history she had of Rose. But not the only legacy she would leave . . .

In that locked desk drawer, along with the letters was a copy of Sylvie's will. After her death, when Rose learned what she'd inherited, maybe then she would know at least some fraction of what she'd meant to her mother.

Now, in this room, all Sylvie could do was what she'd always done: far too little.

Her throat tight with anguish, she confessed, "Every single day for the past fifty years I've wished there was some way of undoing what I did."

"It's not too late to undo another wrong," Rose urged fiercely. "You can at least *try*."

Sylvie shook her head sadly.

Rose stared at her, long and hard. And in that moment Sylvie saw what for all these years she had, for the most part, been spared: the world of pain behind her daughter's dark eyes that until now she'd only glimpsed. The intensity of that pain nearly robbed Sylvie of her breath. She realized that the relationship she and Rose had painstakingly fashioned—the warm exchanges, the thoughtful cards and phone calls, the holidays at which they'd sat across the table from each other—was nothing more than a flimsy structure built on quicksand. Not enough to shelter either of them from the cruel wind of her own cowardice . . . and her daughter's deep-seated resentment.

At last, Rose pulled herself to her feet. She looked more tired now than angry, her shoulders sagging.

Even so, Sylvie felt the need to tread softly. "I won't pretend I've been any kind of a mother to you," she said in a low, halting voice. "I only wish . . ." She had to swallow hard before she could go on. "It . . . it doesn't matter anymore what I wish. And you have every right to be angry with me. You deserved better. But you're wrong about Rachel. If she'd asked me to interfere, I would have told her the same thing."

Rose eyed her for a moment, then, in a voice like frost on a windowpane, said, "In that case, I'm sorry I came." She rose abruptly. Turning from Sylvie, she paused in the doorway, just long enough to cast a glance about the room, as if memorizing it—or seeing it for the first time. "I won't be back. I'm sick of pretending. For what? So you can feel virtuous without taking the risk that anyone might learn the truth?"

Then she was gone, and Sylvie was left staring at the empty sun-lit doorway, in which a storm of dust motes swirled like tiny trapped insects. She closed her eyes, and thought, *How, dear Lord, how has it come to this?* By doing what she'd thought was right, she had succeeded only in making the situation worse.

In her mind, Sylvie heard her mother's firm, sweet voice admonish: *It's not too late. She's still your daughter . . . and she needs you. Don't abandon her a second time.*

With her eyes shut, Sylvie imagined she could hear her heart, each beat like the ponderous ticking of the grandfather clock in the hallway outside. When she was dead, there would be only one person on this earth in whose veins her blood flowed, and in whom her family's history was written: Rose.

Sylvie sat without moving for minutes that stretched unnoticed into hours, until at last she was stirred from her trance by the deepening shadows that caused her to fumble for the switch on the lamp next to her chair. She listened, dry-eyed, to the rustling of the swallows that had foolishly made their nests deep inside the chimney. She had no more tears left—she'd used them all up, years ago. All that remained was a hard stone of regret.

Too late, she told herself. The time to have openly acknowledged her daughter was long past. . . .

Is it? Or is that just what you tell yourself to make it easier? her mother's voice persisted, maddeningly, like the warbling of those swallows, whose babies, when it came time for them to leave their nest, Sylvie knew, would not be strong enough to fly up out of the chimney . . . and would most likely die from the effort.

🌹 By the time Nikos arrived home, Sylvie had summoned the strength to put away her gardening tools and arrange the roses she'd cut in her best Waterford vase. She was setting it down on the lacquered chinoiserie chest in the hall when he walked in.

"You promised Dr. Choudry you would stay off your feet . . . and look at you," he scolded gently, capturing her wrist in a large, callused hand. "Pink from the sun, and dirt under your fingernails."

"Speaking of which, where did all that mud come from?" She frowned down at his filthy boots with mock disapproval. "You're supposed to be *overseeing* construction on that office building, not actually building it with your own hands."

Nikos, she knew, was the kind of boss who simply could not resist demonstrating to any carpenter, welder, mason, and electrician unlucky enough to cross his path that there was a better way to do whatever it was they did. *His* way. Never mind that Anteros Construction had grossed over twelve million last year, and that their CEO ought to have been enjoying the retirement he'd surely earned. When he died, an employee had once joked, Nikos would be digging his own grave.

The days of Nikos' coming in through the back door instead of the front seemed to have belonged to another lifetime. Sylvie had to struggle to remember the handsome young immigrant, like a lesser Greek god, who'd shown up one day to apply for the job of handyman. She'd hired him on the spot—how could she not? And maybe she'd been half in love with him even then. All Sylvie knew was that even her devotion for her husband, Gerald, couldn't keep her from Nikos' bed. She'd hated herself, yes, but had been as powerless against the inevitability of their affair as a barrel hurtling over Niagara Falls. Was it any surprise, really, that in one of those stolen hours in Nikos' tiny basement room Rose had been conceived?

". . . and then there was a problem with one of the mains in the subbasement." Sylvie struggled to focus on what Nikos was saying. "I got it fixed in the end—after I fired the plumbing contractor." He grinned, a flash of white teeth in a face as rugged as the broken-in boots he was now tugging off.

Nikos, padding over in his stockinged feet, drew Sylvie into his arms and kissed her. A lovely warmth spread through her, soothing her . . . as well as reminding her that, even at her age, she was far from immune to his charms.

"Hungry?" she murmured.

"Like a bear." He nuzzled her neck, making her skin tingle and her cheeks grow flushed.

"Milagros left something in the oven," she told him, pushing him away with a good-humored laugh. "I haven't the slightest idea what. Isn't that awful? I used to be so organized, and go over each week's menu with her, but lately . . . oh, Nikos, you're right, I *do* need to sit down."

"Let me get supper on the table, then." The authority in his voice made it clear he wasn't just offering. "You can sit and tell me about your day."

He brought her hand to his mouth, and the warm pressure of his lips against her chilled fingers was like a balm.

"My day? Well, Rose stopped by this afternoon. . . ."

"Sylvie, you're trembling!" The concern in Nikos' face turned to worry.

"I'm all right—it's been a long day, that's all." She took his arm and leaned against him as they made their way toward the kitchen.

A memory leaped into focus: that terrifying day Gerald had surprised her coming up the basement steps, flushed and dewy from her lover's embrace. Her husband had known—Gerald *had* to have known—but was too much a gentleman to confront her. So he'd fired Nikos instead. Sylvie hadn't known it then, but she was already more than a month pregnant.

Nikos, who hadn't known she was expecting, had unwittingly done her a favor by staying away. Even years later, when he learned of Rose's existence, he'd respected Sylvie's wish that he not reveal his identity to their daughter. It wasn't until Gerald had passed away that Nikos had come back into her life . . . and into her bed.

And how had she rewarded him for his patience? By denying him the one thing he still wished for: his only child. It was his love for *her*, nothing more, Sylvie knew, that had kept him from publicly acknowledging Rose.

My darling, you deserve so much more. . . .

In the big, old-fashioned kitchen, Sylvie sank into a chair at the pine trestle table. She remembered how, after Gerald died, it had seemed the most sensible thing in the world to remodel this space—tear out the thirties kitchen cabinets and enamel sinks, replace the original black and white checkerboard tiles with something more modern. But she'd resisted the impulse, and now was glad that she had. For there was comfort in familiarity. Even, she thought, a kind of grace.

Nikos was standing at the stove, ladling something into bowls. "The last time I made us supper was when Rachel and Brian were here for your birthday," he recalled.

"Maybe that's why they haven't been back since."

Nikos laughed boisterously, and Sylvie felt her spirits rise.

She watched him move about, banging open cupboards and drawers, reaching into the oven. At the last minute, he even remembered to set out candlesticks.

"Now," he said when he was finally seated across from her, "will you tell me why it is you look as if the sky has fallen in?"

"Later," she told him. "Let's first enjoy this delicious cassoulet. Who would have guessed it, a Filipina who cooks like Julia Child?"

In the glow of the candlelight, Nikos looked as wonderfully solid as this kitchen, and Sylvie felt secretly grateful that she, not Nikos, would be the first to go. She couldn't have borne life without him. It didn't matter one bit that they'd never married. Her reasons for refusing him—reasons that had seemed perfectly valid when Nikos first proposed to her, all those years ago—were of less importance now than the food in front of her. No wedding vows could ever mean as much as the tenderness she saw in the handsome, work-hewn face of the man seated across from her at this table.

When his empty plate—and her barely touched one—had been pushed aside, Nikos reached across the table and took her hand, urging once more, "Now. Tell me what is making you look so sad."

"Oh, Nikos . . ." Sylvie pulled her hand free and cupped it over her eyes, shielding them from the candlelight that was suddenly too bright. "Rose was so upset with me. You can't imagine! I'd thought she was beyond being angry about the past, but I was wrong. For her, it might as well be yesterday. She hasn't forgiven me, and she never will."

A tiny sob escaped her. And then Nikos' chair was scraping back, and he was stepping around the table to comfort her. "What did she want?" he asked, holding her head pressed to his belly, where she could feel his belt buckle against her cheek, cool and reassuring somehow.

"She seems to think I'm the only one who can convince Iris to break off this engagement," Sylvie told him. "As if I could! As if *any-one* could."

"So you refused." Under the soft cotton of his shirt, Sylvie felt the hard muscles of his belly contract.

"I had no choice!" she cried.

"No wonder she was angry."

"That wasn't all. She accused me of taking sides."

Nikos hesitated before asking, "And is she perhaps right?"

His words seemed to rise from some cavern deep within the mountain against which she rested. Sylvie abruptly pulled away, and looked up at him. "No," she said. "Of course not. There *are* no sides."

Nikos regarded her gravely, the flickering candlelight carving deep creases in his weathered face. When he spoke, his voice was gentle but firm. "In all honesty, can you blame Rose for feeling this way?"

Sylvie jerked to her feet and began stacking plates, gathering cutlery. A fork clattered to the floor, and she stared down at it as if it were the ceiling that had fallen in.

"No," she sighed at last, "I don't blame her. She has every reason to doubt where my loyalties lie."

"Then you must tell her that."

Sylvie turned to look at Nikos, standing in the middle of the kitchen with his arms folded across his chest, and his full mouth—*Rose's* mouth—drawn into a tight line.

"What are you saying?" she asked, fearful.

"That Rose deserves as much as you've given Rachel."

Sylvie felt something inside her snap. "Easy for you to say! Rachel isn't *your* daughter."

"She's not yours, either." In the moment of shocked stillness that greeted his words, Nikos stepped forward to seize her gently by the shoulders. "I'm not saying this to hurt you, Sylvie. But because I love you. I see how much pain all this has caused you—as much, in some ways, as it has Rose. How can Rachel's peace of mind be worth so much misery?"

"It's not just Rachel," she argued, a tear slipping down her cheek. "It's Iris, too. Are you willing to risk what might happen if she were to find out? That I'm no better than the mother who abandoned *her?*" She swiped angrily at her leaking eyes. "*Yes,* I want to shout from the mountaintops that Rose is our daughter! But don't you see? I can't. I can't take that chance."

How could she make Nikos understand? A secret, if kept too long, can become as frozen as a rusted padlock—one that won't open no matter how hard you hammer at it. Dear Lord, did he think that she hadn't *wanted* to claim Rose openly as their daughter? That she hadn't yearned all these years for things to be different?

Sylvie leaned weakly against the counter . . . and at once the hard lines in Nikos' face relaxed into an expression of concern. Faintly, as if from a great distance, she heard him sigh, "You're tired. Come, let me put you to bed. We can talk in the morning."

"I *am* tired," she admitted.

Sylvie allowed him to lead her out of the kitchen and through the darkened dining room, then up the marble staircase to the bed that all at once seemed the only place in the world where she would ever feel safe.

She wouldn't think about the party in just three weeks. And how, when it was her turn to toast to the happy couple, she'd have yet another lie to tell—one that, this time, might prove to be the end of any hope she'd had of winning Rose's forgiveness.

August

You are cordially invited to
celebrate the engagement of
our daughter, Iris,
to
Andrew Griffin
on Saturday, August 10th
at 6:30 p.m.
for
cocktails and buffet
at
12 Gramercy Park South
Apartment 5
New York, NY

❧

R.S.V.P. Mr. and Mrs. Brian McClanahan
889-9078

Chapter 4

Rachel took one look at the pigtailed schoolgirl on the examining table, then motioned to Kay Krempel, codirector of the East Side Women's Health Center. As they stepped out into the corridor, she asked in a low voice, "How far along?"

"Roughly? Around four months," Kay guessed. "We'll know more after Althea's examined her."

Kay was in her usual take-no-prisoners mode, Rachel could see. All five feet two inches of her drawn up as if to cast a shadow as tall as her reputation around here. Hands on hips, her chin thrust out as if in preparation to do battle. Her frizzy hair had gone almost completely gray, but the fire in Kay's hazel eyes burned as brightly as when they were roommates back in the seventies—when ideals had been more than warmed-over slogans in Nike commercials, when "just do it" had meant burning flags and marching in peace rallies.

Wasn't it Kay, all those years ago, who'd inspired her to abandon a promising internship at Good Shepherd in favor of a missionary hospital in a war zone at the other end of the world? Vietnam hadn't been what either of them bargained for, but Rachel had no regrets. For one thing, she wouldn't have met Brian. Nor would she have learned the true definition of a friend. *If I were ever shipwrecked, I'd want Kay in my lifeboat,* she thought, smiling to herself.

"Is it my imagination, or are they getting younger every year?" Rachel sighed as she handed the girl's chart back to Kay.

"We had one in yesterday, a thirteen-year-old expecting twins."

Rachel shook her head, more in weariness than disbelief. Fact was, these girls could easily be the *daughters* of women she and Kay had treated back when the clinic first opened—a storefront operation cobbled together out of donated supplies and a meager HEW grant, serving coffee and doughnuts to win over a neighborhood suspicious of well-meaning newcomers.

The East Side Center now occupied the entire building—a brownstone on the corner of Fourteenth and Third—but how much had they achieved, really? Teen moms bearing unwanted babies was as much of an epidemic now as it had been back then.

"Holy Angels?" Rachel asked.

To many parents, she knew, the all-girl Holy Angels and its male counterpart, St. Sebastian's, seemed the perfect answer to the Lower East Side's overcrowded, violence-plagued public schools. Though from what Rachel had seen here at the East Side Center, Holy Angels was as much a problem as it was a solution. Reading, writing, and arithmetic were being taught, all right, but its students had yet to learn the meaning of birth control—a subject best left to those who hadn't yet learned to exercise self-control, one nun had frostily informed them. Or, as Kay had put it, "They teach their girls to cross their legs as well as their 'T's."

Right now, Kay was nodding grimly, her mouth drawn into a tight line. "Seventh grade," she affirmed. "Maybe it's something in the holy water. I wonder what that old bat Sister Alice would say if we told her that praying is giving those girls of hers more than just sore kneecaps."

"She'd accuse you of being a heathen, no doubt."

"That's the least of it," Kay snorted. "Guess what came in this morning's mail? A copy of a petition that was sent to the mayor's office. Looks as if Our Lady of the Gadfly isn't satisfied with keeping her girls ignorant in the classroom: she and her minions want a ban on *us* giving out any information about the birds and bees."

Rachel shrugged. "City Hall won't give her the time of day. Not with all the AIDS activists finally getting people to vote with their heads instead of their hang-ups." She tried to sound unconcerned, but Kay clearly wasn't buying it.

"That's not all," she reported in an ominously lowered voice, and whisked an envelope from a pocket of the baggy vest that hung to the knees of her cotton trousers. "Get a load of *this*."

Rachel, with a sinking heart, scanned the sheet of paper Kay had thrust at her.

It was a copy of a letter addressed to Sister Alice, in response to her petition, from Philip Scanlon, executive director of the Community Health Fund. Scanlon had written that he, too, was deeply concerned about the morality of today's youth, and would do what he could to help Sister Alice in her efforts to address this unfortunate decline. Platitudes that would have been nothing more than words on paper, except for one thing: Community Health was the East Side Center's principal financial backer.

"It's never been any secret what we do here." Rachel crumpled the letter, wishing it were as easy to make the problem itself go away. Making reference to the fact that, like many independent clinics, they referred their patients to private physicians for all surgeries, including abortion, she added, with more than her usual dose of irony, "Anyway, we're the good guys, remember?"

"Just remember, nice guys finish last," Kay—their resident one-woman Greek chorus—was quick to remind her. "Our CHF grant comes up for renewal in September. If Sister Alice has her way, we'll be out of a job. Because, without that money, this place wouldn't survive a month."

Rachel clutched her head in mock despair. At the same time, she found herself thinking, *God, what if Kay's right?* She groaned. "I can't think about this right now. Not with sixteen calls to return, and a meeting uptown in less than an hour. Monsieur Henri arranged for a tasting, and I promised the man I wouldn't be late. Lord, what is it with these caterers? You'd think a buffet supper for forty was a NASA launch."

Kay shook her head, smiling. "The party's in four days. You're *supposed* to be running around like a chicken with your head cut off."

"I never said I was Martha Stewart."

"I'm sure your daughter would agree."

"So would my husband."

"Maybe. But at least you still have one." Kay cast her a bitter half-smile—a reminder that even the most solid-seeming marriages weren't iron-clad. Sixteen years ago, when Kay, after a string of disastrous relationships, married steadfast-seeming Simon Lieberman, a stockbroker with a large firm of his own, no one had cheered harder than Rachel. But shortly after their tenth anniversary, Simon had divorced her for a much younger woman . . . leaving Kay to joke acidly that her husband was better at long-term investments than personal commitments. Only Rachel knew how bitterly she'd grieved.

She sighed, thinking of Brian. The meals they used to prepare, bumping elbows and laughing as they sipped wine amid the flour and cucumber peels. When was the last time they'd so much as sat down to dinner together?

Maybe she could steal a moment to call home, just a quick hello to let him know she was thinking of him. . . .

Glancing at her watch, Rachel saw that she had just enough time for the calls that couldn't wait. Mason Gold, for one. A harried district attorney, sure, but he would always spare a minute for an old friend in need of a favor. She'd ask him to do a little fishing down at City Hall to see what, if any, reaction there had been to Sister Alice's petition. Next, Philip Scanlon at Community Health Fund—as if that two-faced old buzzard would part with a single grain of inside information.

That meant waiting until after lunch to get in touch with Brian. She sighed again—this time in frustration—before heading down the corridor in the direction of her office.

Striding past the L-shaped reception area, which was already packed at eleven-thirty in the morning, Rachel was acutely aware of the activity that hummed around her like an electrical current: phones ringing, the front door buzzing, voices chattering in Spanish, babies crying, doctors and nurses bustling in and out of examining rooms. Sounds and voices that normally filled her with a sense of accomplishment, the feeling that, yes, despite the headaches and gad-flies, they *were* making a difference.

Yet here she was, so tightly wound she felt on the verge of snapping—a pent-up frustration that had nothing to do with fanatical nuns, or spineless board presidents, or even her own hectic schedule. Because, damnit, this was *not* what she wanted. She was a *doctor*, not an administrator. How had she ended up in an Anne Klein suit instead of scrubs? Juggling a budget forever stretched too thin, writing grant proposals, lobbying for funds, not to mention constantly recruiting the best and the brightest—doctors and nurses willing to work for little or nothing.

What had happened to doing what she loved best, taking care of pregnant women and delivering babies? How long since she'd seen tears of gratitude in the eyes of an exhausted patient who'd just given birth, or cradled a newborn infant still slippery with its natal fluids?

She missed even the frustrations. Struggling to convey in her limited Spanish that, no, it wasn't a *woman's* orgasm that caused her to become pregnant. Refereeing the fights that occasionally broke out in the waiting room—usually between a teenaged girl about to become a mom and a boyfriend reluctant to be a father. Even the occasional emergency—a placenta previa spontaneously hemorrhaging, or a C-section that couldn't wait for an ambulance to arrive—had given her a heady sense of her own power—the greatest of all, the power to heal.

You're tired and overworked, she told herself. *What you really need is a vacation . . . a couple of weeks on a beach somewhere, doing absolutely nothing.* When her head had cleared, she would once again see how much more valuable a contribution she was making this way. How many more people she was helping.

But that still wouldn't change how she felt. How deeply she missed the hands-on doctoring she'd loved since she was an intern. Even in a field hospital in the middle of a jungle, with men dying in her arms, and nothing but coffee and adrenaline to keep her going, she'd felt more connected. More *alive.*

And what about Brian, what this was doing to *them?* It was as if all she could see right now was the surface glare, and underneath swam a whole ocean she wasn't prepared to confront. Unspoken resentments, and unfulfilled desires that would need more than a month in the sun to remedy. She didn't dare think about the possibility that, if things didn't change, one day it might be too late. Even the most patient husband had his limits, she knew. And even the strongest of passions, left untended, could wither and die.

Who would know better than she? Years ago, as newlyweds, they'd nearly been torn apart by a series of misunderstandings and mistaken assumptions. Yet Rachel couldn't bring herself to believe Brian would ever leave her. It wasn't possible. Any more than life without him would be.

Even so, she felt her chest constrict.

There was Iris, too. Her daughter, she knew, was *not* getting better—in some ways she was worse—and Rachel continued to worry about whether she was doing the right thing. Going along with this misbegotten engagement, throwing this party—wasn't it, she acknowledged deep down, a little like rearranging the deck chairs on a sinking *Titanic?*

Stop it. You're being melodramatic. Didn't Dr. Eisenger say she was okay now? He'd been experimenting with the dosages of her medication, he had explained, which could easily have caused her to react as she had at Brian's party. It made sense, yes. Rachel herself knew how tricky it was prescribing antidepressants. And Iris *did* seem better. So maybe marrying Drew, whom they *all* loved, would be a good thing after all. . . .

In the partitioned office she shared with Kay, Rachel sank into the swivel chair behind her piled desk. Just for an instant, she allowed herself the incredible luxury of simply closing her eyes. In the swimmy darkness, where fragments of light danced like fireflies, the biblical quote popped into her head: *Physician, heal thyself.*

Nice idea, she thought. But what do you do when you're caught on a treadmill and there's no way to stop? When you've put your husband on hold so many times he no longer bothers to call?

The party, she thought suddenly. Wasn't it an opportunity of sorts? A chance to demonstrate that her family *did* come first? She would make it wonderful, the best ever. She'd make the apartment glow, see that every detail was perfect. Candles everywhere. And music, the lovely mellow jazz she and Brian used to listen to on nights out at the Blue Note and Village Vanguard. The food would be carefully chosen with Henri; the champagne crisp; the floral arrangements from Gramercy Flowers, dazzling and fragrant.

It would be only a small start, not even equal to a romantic weekend in the Hamptons, but maybe it would show Brian how good things could be once again. How, with a little luck, and a lot of patience, even a marriage that had been blown off course could be brought safely to shore.

R Late Saturday afternoon, with her guests due to arrive in less than an hour, Rachel, who'd been doing exactly what Kay had envisioned—running around like a damn chicken with its head cut off—finally stopped long enough to take stock of all she'd accomplished. Standing in the living room, by the row of windows that overlooked Gramercy Park, she gazed about in wonder. Even with rain coming down outside in sheets, this apartment, which had stood listless for so long, seemed to glow as if sunlit. Gone were the drooping potted plants her well-meaning housekeeper was forever overwatering, and the piles of newspapers and magazines awaiting the proverbial free time when she could read them. The freshly waxed oak floor shimmered, and the marble fireplace had been polished until it shone almost as brightly as the mirror above it. Even the faded colors in the antique paisley shawl folded over the sofa back, just back from the dry cleaner's, seemed brighter and richer somehow.

Not even on Hanukkah, she thought, with the menorah lit in the window, had this room looked so beautiful. Now, for the first time in months, she could truly appreciate its vaulted windows and high ceiling; its lovely mirrored panels at either end of the fireplace, which on sunny days painted pale, fledgling rainbows on the cream-colored walls and balding Turkish carpets.

Today was not one of those days. The rain that had been pouring down all afternoon had left the sky the color of soggy cardboard, and turned the streets to soup. From where she stood, Rachel could see cars and taxis flying along Lexington Avenue on wings of muddy water. Pedestrians clutching the collars of their raincoats battled through the driving torrent, umbrellas held in front of them like shields. Only the postman, in his plastic-covered hat and poncho, darting out from under a dripping eave, looked more miserable.

But just listen to Iris in the next room: singing her heart out! As if she hadn't a care in the world. Her pure, sweet soprano made Rachel think of a canary they'd once had. One summer day, Iris had accidentally left the cage door open, and it flew out a window. She'd been inconsolable, Rachel remembered. Blaming herself, refusing even to *think* of getting another bird. Until Drew had brought over a parakeet, a bright-blue fellow with green-tipped wings Iris had named Sky. And then it was as if the tragedy had never happened. . . .

Drew and Iris. They were already looking for an apartment large enough for the two of them, and had talked about getting married next summer. In the meantime, Iris seemed to prefer Drew's studio, cramped as it was, to her old room here. Rachel didn't take it personally, nor did she object to their sleeping together. She'd have to have been blind, after all, not to know they were intimate.

The truth was, Rachel would have sacrificed almost anything to see her daughter looking so radiant—eyes shining, cheeks aglow, laughing at the smallest of jokes. Iris had even begun painting again, the floor around her easel awash in half-finished watercolors, the oversized shirts she wore speckled with every color in her paintbox. There was a lovely landscape of the park pinned to the corkboard wall in the dressing room off her bedroom that she used as a studio, and several more tucked away in her portfolio. Not even this weather had dampened her sunny mood. As Rachel listened, Iris' voice

seemed to float, light as the air itself, in a song from an old Anne
Murray album she'd come across while sorting through the CDs.

God, don't let her ever stop singing. . . .

"Dear, would you like this on the dining-room table, or over by
the sofa?" Mama's voice—light, brisk, yet somehow intrusive—
caused Rachel to whirl around.

She found her mother poised in the doorway to the dining room,
cradling a vase of artfully arranged flowers from her garden—asters,
hollyhocks, dahlias, mustard-yellow yarrow.

Mama seemed more drawn than usual . . . or was it just the watery light on her thin face making her look like a Goya portrait? She
was wearing a simple crepe dress the pale lavender of the sachets
Mama tucked into drawers at home, her only jewelry a strand of
opera pearls. Rachel felt a tug of yearning—for the kind of closeness
she'd always wanted with her mother, but forever seemed to fall short
of. The kind Mama and Iris shared. At the same time, she couldn't
help feeling a tiny bit irritated. Why had Mama insisted on bringing
flowers—as lovely as they were—when Rachel had specifically *told*
her she was having a florist deliver the arrangements she'd so carefully
chosen?

"Over there is fine," Rachel told her, distractedly waving a hand
in the direction of the refectory table behind the sofa. Not wanting
to seem ungrateful—her mother *had* meant well—she added with a
smile, "Henri's cordoned off the kitchen and dining room. No tres-
passing . . . not even for a cup of tea. He was very insistent."

Sylvie smiled knowingly, clearly no stranger to demanding caterers who viewed clients' kitchens as their own personal fiefdoms.
Rachel could hear Henri faintly in the kitchen, beyond the dining
room, clanging pots and rattling plates, barking orders in rapid-fire
French. He hadn't come cheap, to be sure, but, judging from what
she'd sampled so far, every bite would be worth the fortune they were
spending.

Rachel watched her mother set the vase down on a smaller table
by the bookcase—*not* where she'd asked—and felt her irritation flare.

Never mind that the flowers were perfect where Mama had placed them, spotlit by an overhead track light. Mother knew best. Hadn't it been that way as far back as Rachel could remember? Mama buying her pretty dresses that hung in her closet, price tags dangling from the sleeves, until she'd outgrown them. On birthdays and Hanukkah, presenting her with fat coffee-table books of Renoir, Sargent, van Gogh, which she leafed through once, then never looked at again. Serving family meals on her good Limoges china, even though Rachel constantly knocked over her glass and chipped the delicate gold rims of those plates.

"A cup of tea *would* be nice," Mama said wistfully. "In the summer, it never seems the thing, but on a day like this . . ." She sighed, arching her spine, her hand pressed to the small of her back. "Dear me, I do hope this rain lets up in time for the party. Some of your guests might think twice."

"I know of at least one who'd jump at any excuse not to come," Rachel muttered darkly.

"Oh? Who?" Sylvie was instantly alert, the stiffness in her back apparently forgotten. She settled on the sofa, her posture perfectly erect, looking as out of place against the green sailcloth slipcovers as an Easter lily in a field of clover.

Rachel hesitated, then thought, *Oh, hell . . . why not?* "Rose," she confided. "When she called to say she was coming, you'd have thought it was a public hanging we'd invited her to."

Rachel knew how fond her mother was of Rose, and it didn't seem fair painting her as a spoilsport. Who wouldn't have doubts? Rose was merely looking out for her son, as any mother would. On the other hand, no one had put a gun to Drew's head.

The problem wasn't Drew, she reasoned. It was Rose herself.

Let's face it, Rose lost a husband . . . and now she's afraid she'll lose a son. Since his father's death, Drew had been especially protective toward his mother. Stopping by to see her at least once a week, often staying for dinner. He was spending more time with his little brother, too. But once Drew and Iris were living together, Rachel suspected all that would change. Between his studies and Iris, there wouldn't be much left over for Rose or Jason.

If only Rose were involved with someone herself! A love affair, Rachel thought, would take her mind off Drew. She *had* heard from Brian that Rose was dating—Eric Sandstrom, of all people—but Rose hadn't mentioned anything to her. Either she was keeping it under wraps for the time being, or there wasn't much to tell.

In any event, Rachel couldn't imagine Rose becoming serious about Eric—a somewhat younger man who'd never been married, and had no kids of his own. Rachel liked him well enough, and Brian seemed to think he was about the only honest voice left in broadcasting. Even so, Rachel found herself wondering if she'd done the right thing inviting Eric to this party. What if it only succeeded in making Rose more uptight? *The last thing she needs is another excuse to be mad at me.*

"I know. Rose spoke to me about it. She was quite upset." Sylvie turned her gaze on Rachel, who noted with alarm, and some bewilderment, that there were tears in her mother's eyes. "Rachel, I've been wondering—you know I'm not one to mix in—but do you think perhaps she's justified?"

Again, that sharp prick of irritation. Why was Mama sticking up for Rose? Rachel felt an urge to say something mean, but in the end, she merely sighed and said, "I would have been happier if they'd waited, sure. But on the other hand no one can say this engagement was sudden or unexpected. Drew and Iris have been joined at the hip since they were kids."

"Perhaps they've been a little *too* close," Sylvie suggested with her usual polite conviction. "Some time apart wouldn't hurt."

"They were at separate colleges for *four years,*" Rachel argued.

"I don't mean just distance. Maybe they should see other people."

Rachel stared at her, absorbing the full meaning of her words. Mama wasn't just willing to accept the risk that Iris' world might crumble—she was actually *recommending* it.

"You and Rose seem to be in agreement," she replied coolly.

Mama shook her head. "This isn't about Rose."

Rachel's annoyance tipped over into anger, and she found herself snapping, "Of course it is! I wouldn't mind so much if her only concern was for Drew. If she wasn't doing this to hang on to him. I can't believe you don't see it, Mama. Just whose side are you on, anyway?"

Sylvie winced, and seemed to wrestle with herself before going on. "I'm merely suggesting you look at it from Rose's point of view. She loves her son as much as you love Iris."

"Loyalty to one's own family *should* come first."

Rachel's sarcasm wasn't lost on her mother. Mama's eyes went dark, like something slipping below the surface of cool green water. "I haven't forgotten my priorities." She rose, and walked slowly and with the utmost dignity over to where Rachel stood.

The rain was still pouring down in sheets, the wind hurling it against the leaded panes in furious smacks. It reminded Rachel of the jungles of Tien Sung, the relentless tropical monsoons, the ankle-deep mud—a Chicken Little world whose sky really *had* fallen.

"I'm sorry, Mama." Rachel rubbed one temple, where a pulse throbbed. "I've been working so hard I can hardly see straight. And, yes, you're right—this could all be a gigantic mistake. But what choice do we have? Brian and I have given her everything—unconditional love, and all *this*." She threw out an arm in a gesture that encompassed not just their home but Iris' entire upbringing—the best private schools, family vacations and sleepaway camp every summer, even the finest psychiatrists when nothing else seemed to work. "But somehow it's never enough. Maybe Drew can give her what she needs. Maybe all we can do is hope for the best."

Mama shook her head, placing a hand on Rachel's arm. "That's what I thought when I married your father. Please, don't misunderstand me—I loved him with all my heart. But, oh, my dear, *no one* can give you what is missing in yourself."

"Even if I said something, Iris wouldn't listen to me," Rachel argued. Mama's hand against her bare skin felt as worn and soft as old damask, unsettling in some deep way she couldn't quite figure out. "When Brian tried talking to her, she just got upset, and that only made it worse. She cried for hours."

"There are worse things than tears," Mama said.

"We want her to be happy. Is that so terrible?" Rachel, stung nearly to tears herself, drew away and stepped back.

Mama's cool green gaze rested on Rachel in a way that caused the back of her neck to prickle. "A good marriage takes work," she said. "And two people to share the burden equally."

Rachel found herself remembering once again that first rocky year with Brian, how uncertain she'd felt about him—especially his feelings for Rose. There was no doubt in her mind that, had he not been drafted, Brian would have married his childhood sweetheart. But he *had* gone to Nam, and over there . . . well, things were different. Even so, Rachel was often reminded of how unlike they were, not just their backgrounds, but the way they approached life. Their cataclysmic meeting, her literally bringing him back from the brink of death, the madness of Nam itself—all of it had drawn them together as nothing else could have. But even their shared experience—a history that had bound them tightly while excluding all others—might not be enough, in the end, to survive an enemy even more insidious than the one they'd faced over there: their own inability to close the gap that had sprung up between them.

When Iris moved out for good, what would happen to them? *Will we be able to find our way back to where we started?*

"Where *is* Iris, by the way?" Mama wanted to know. "I promised I'd help fix her hair." She gave a little laugh and said, "Heaven knows why, but she seems to think I'm not too old to know what's fashionable."

Rachel cocked her head, listening. But Iris had stopped singing; the only sound was the clattering of Henri in the kitchen. She was probably in her room getting dressed. Rachel looked back at her mother and smiled. "Oh, Mama." Suddenly struck by the realization that her mother *was* old, and that one day she wouldn't be around to make a fuss, Rachel felt her irritation dissolve. "She trusts you. It's as simple as that."

She wished that she had the same faith—not just in Mama, but in her husband and daughter as well—that she could simply trust that everything would work out somehow.

And what about Rose? There was more at stake here than their children's happiness. If Rose refused to make peace with this, Rachel could lose more than a daughter—she could also lose a friend.

The thought weighed on her as she watched her mother make her way slowly into the next room, with the elaborate care of an elderly woman too dignified to let on just how frail she'd become.

At half past six, the guests began to arrive. Mason Gold, accompanied by his wife and two grown daughters . . . tailed by a crew of Iris' and Drew's friends spilling boisterously from the elevator. Then several writers from the workshop Brian was giving this summer. And Kay—dear, dependable Kay—with two of the OBs from the clinic, Althea Turnbill and Ruth Jacobs. Others soon followed, appearing at the door in clusters, breathless with delight at finding themselves in a dry place, their umbrellas dripping wet circles onto the mat Rachel had laid in the foyer.

Within half an hour, every window was misted over, and at the bar that had been set up near the entrance to the dining room, the ice bucket was already in need of a refill. But if it was a bit warm with the press of so many damp bodies, no one seemed to mind. They all seemed to be having a good time.

Except Rose. She'd been among the first to show up, but seemed in no hurry to mingle. Rachel kept sneaking glances her way, hoping to catch her eye. But Rose was ignoring her. At the moment, she stood with her two sisters, who looked as if they, too, would rather be anywhere but here. Marie, with her skinny frame and sharp features, who made Rachel think of a twitchy cat poised to pounce. And

Clare, in her knee-length nun's habit, who seemed to cower like a plump little wren afraid of being gobbled up.

Rose looked nothing like either of them. Taller, darker, with her bold features and air of I-want-it-done-yesterday, she shared only the faintest family resemblance with her sisters—most of it in her expression and gestures. Yet it was obvious the three were united about one thing: Drew's engagement was no cause for celebration.

Rachel suddenly felt like marching over, confronting them. *Why the hell did you even bother to come? If that's how you feel, you should have stayed home.*

Almost in desperation, she turned to her journalist friend, Sue Garcia, queenly in a voluminous caftan and squash-blossom necklace. Several years ago, Sue had written a piece on the East Side Center for *Ms.*, describing Rachel, among other things, as "a brave pioneer in the frontier of inner-city women's health." Though somewhat embarrassed by all the praise, Rachel had called to thank her. They'd ended up having lunch, and had been buddies ever since. Okay, Sue was outspoken and opinionated, but at least she wasn't thumbing her nose at Iris' engagement.

"I'd marry that young man myself, if he'd have an old lady like me." Sue flipped her thick gray braid over one shoulder and laughed. "Screw all that feminist crap about single women needing to celebrate their independence. It's hell climbing into a cold bed at night."

Rachel's mind formed a picture of Brian and her, the two of them sleeping spooned against one another. She felt a light chill trickle down her spine. There was so much that she took for granted. . . .

A few minutes later, chatting with the Golds, she found herself thinking, *What if I'd married Mason instead?* Looking at him now, with his receding hairline and beginnings of a potbelly, it was hard to believe they'd ever been lovers—even if it had only been for one night. Mason, whom she'd known since elementary school, was more like a brother. And, luckily, he, too, seemed to have forgotten that misbegotten fumble at the Pierre, the evening of his twenty-first birthday celebration. Seeing how content he was, standing with an arm around his wife, Shannon, Rachel even felt a tiny bit envious of their happiness, and wondered if maybe Mason knew something she didn't.

"I checked with my friend in the mayor's office," he informed Rachel. "Nobody remembers a petition, but they *do* know Sister Alice. Seems she's been a thorn in everyone's side, not just yours."

"Should I be worried?" Rachel asked.

Mason frowned. She noticed that his lawyerly tortoiseshell glasses were slightly crooked. "Worried? That might be too strong. I'd be on my guard, though, if I were you. Troublemakers like her, they never give up."

"You ought to know." His wife poked him affectionately with her elbow before turning to give Rachel a knowing smile. "He's been consorting with criminals too long." Shannon, blonde, pert, and perfectly turned out in Yves St. Laurent, was like a different person from the long-haired hippie bride who for a brief time had called herself Cheyenne.

Rachel remembered those days a little wistfully. Mason, working for pennies at Legal Aid, refusing help from his parents. Shannon, teaching Montessori, with her own two girls in tow.

In her mind, Rachel was seeing the snapshot Mason had taken all those years ago of the girl he'd teasingly nicknamed Young Doctor Rosenthal, with her duffel bag and long hair parted down the middle, boarding the flight to Nam. Yet it was as if that fire in her, all those righteous beliefs, had gone up in smoke. She still had her clinic, sure, but what had once seemed a glorious undertaking now seemed a lot more like grueling work.

Maybe it would all seem more worthwhile if she could somehow manage to hold her family together. She looked over at her daughter, standing by the piano with a group of her friends from Bryn Mawr, every last one dressed in what clearly was the latest fashion statement—gothic black dresses and clunky black shoes. Among them, Iris appeared to float, butterflylike, in a perfectly fitted turquoise *chong sam* with braided silk frog clasps. Watching her proudly show off the simple sapphire ring she and Drew had picked out, Rachel felt a surge of pride. Whatever her problems, Iris had a good heart.

Rachel watched her flit off to join Drew, who stepped away from his own friends to slip an arm around her waist. In his pressed black slacks and a white dress shirt rolled up at the sleeves, he brought to mind a fifties teen idol—dark-eyed and heavy-lidded, with his curly hair falling over his forehead, and killer smile. The two exchanged a look that shot an arrow of pure, sweet nostalgia though Rachel's heart—it was exactly the way Brian used to look at her.

"Don't look now, but I think we've been infiltrated by the enemy."

Rachel turned to find Kay squinting up at her, dressed in what appeared to be striped silk pajamas, and holding aloft a glass of white wine. Kay jerked her frizzy gray head in the direction of the younger of Rose's two sisters, standing alone now, and looking a bit stranded. But even in her nun's habit, Clare, hardly seemed a threat.

"Drew's aunt," Rachel identified. "And don't worry, she doesn't bite."

Truthfully, she'd never much liked Clare, who was scared of her own shadow, and whose every conversation was sprinkled with "Mother Superior says . . ." and "Father Donahue thinks . . ." She wasn't anything like Rose, or her scrappy older sister, Marie, who, when life knocked her down, not only got up but hit back.

Kay peered at Clare, who ·was nervously toying with the silver cross around her neck, her round blue eyes blinking too rapidly in her scrunchy little pillow of a face. "Have I met her before? She looks sort of familiar."

"I doubt it," Rachel said. "Rose and her sister aren't very close. Clare's at some convent up near Albany." She nudged Kay. "Why don't you introduce yourself? She looks as if she could use the company."

"Good idea. If nothing else, I might learn some insider tips we can use with Sister Alice. . . ." Kay, nose in the air like a bloodhound on a scent, went plowing through the crowd toward Clare.

Speaking of Rose, where *was* she?

Scanning the room, she spotted Rose over by the fireplace, chatting with Brian. Her younger son, Jason, stood a few feet away, looking awkward and out of place, his hands shoved deep in the pockets of his slacks. If it hadn't been for Mandy, his redheaded half-sister, leaning over to whisper in his ear just then—something that brought a grudging smile to his lips—Jason would have been the picture of sullen dejection.

Poor Jay. Rachel knew how tough it was, losing a dad and having a mother so distracted by her own sadness that she could barely focus on her son's.

But now Rachel took a second look at the glamorous woman across the room, her head thrown back in laughter, her dark eyes aglow. In her bright yellow dress, gold hoop earrings swaying, Rose didn't appear the least bit mournful. Suddenly Rachel found herself regretting her own ivory linen shift; she felt plain and colorless next to Rose.

What the hell were she and Brian laughing about anyway? Some story about the old days, no doubt. They never got tired of reminiscing about when they were kids, growing up in the same building on Avenue K. Whatever, Brian hadn't looked this relaxed or happy in months. And, God, the way he was looking at her . . . Rachel felt the bite of old envy newly sharpened by her husband's recent coolness toward her.

She was distracted by the sight of Mandy reaching out, quick as a cardsharp, to snag a flute of champagne from a passing tray. Rachel winced inwardly. How much champagne had she downed already? How long before she drifted to sleep in some corner? Well, at least she wouldn't make a scene, Rachel reassured herself—that wasn't Mandy's style—though it might be better if she *did*. Maybe then her family would notice what appeared to be a growing problem.

Watching Rose go off to talk to Eric Sandstrom, who'd just arrived, Rachel felt certain she'd only imagined the spark between her and Brian. At the same time, she couldn't help feeling hurt that Rose was so clearly ignoring *her*. As if they were still the rivals for Brian's heart they'd once been. As if, all those years ago, Rose hadn't accepted Rachel's offer of friendship—a friendship that had grown through the years, until now Rose was practically one of the family.

And who could forget that it had been Rose who'd brought Iris into their lives? Back then, had Rose not acted so quickly, pulling strings, forging through the wilderness of forms and procedures, where would they be now? *I owe her, damnit. And she knows it.*

Suddenly eager to put an end to such thoughts, Rachel sailed over to greet Mrs. Isley—her daughter's fourth-grade teacher from Brearley, with whom Iris had stayed in touch ever since. The poor woman had been widowed last year, too, but, unlike Rose, she, with her bony figure, wasn't drawing looks from almost every man in the room.

Rachel was nodding in agreement to something Mrs. Isley was rambling on about—not hearing a single word—when Henri signaled that supper was ready to be served. Glancing around her, at her friends and family laughing and chatting animatedly with one another—and now helping themselves to the sumptuous buffet laid out on the dining-room table—Rachel felt oddly relieved. Maybe others besides Rose disapproved of the reason for this party, but if so they were keeping it to themselves.

Everyone feasted on the cold lobster-and-dill fettuccine, poached salmon, red pepper confit, and wild rice salad. Wine was poured. Second helpings were scooped up. Every available seat was filled, the younger guests sitting cross-legged on the floor. When they were finally finished eating, and the platters had been cleared away, Sean, the youngest of Brian's five brothers, rose to make a toast.

"I never thought I'd live to see the day my big brother would give his only daughter away in marriage," he began effusively, a little tipsy himself. A big, ruddy-cheeked, auburn-bearded man who resembled Brian only around the eyes, Sean added with a wink, "But may the happy couple be as blessed as Rachel and Brian—who can now take that second honeymoon they've been talking about since Carter was in office."

Rachel felt her face grow warm as she glanced over at Brian. Their eyes met, and she sensed, or perhaps only imagined, a distinct distance; it sent a chill through her.

Then Sylvie was lifting her glass and, in an oddly formal voice, saying, "My darling granddaughter, and you, dear Drew . . . I couldn't possibly wish you more than the happiness I've witnessed tonight. May you continue to be so blessed."

Rose, across the room, seemed to grow flushed, her eyes glittering with some suppressed emotion, but it wasn't until Rachel was heading into the kitchen to see about dessert that Rose finally approached her.

"Do you have a minute?" she asked. "We need to talk."

Rachel shrugged, and led the way down the hall to the privacy of Brian's study. Her chest felt tight. She was remembering another party—a long-ago summer night in London, when she and Brian were first married. By some freakish coincidence—or could it have been fate?—they had run into Rose, whom Brian hadn't seen since before Nam. It had been awkward and embarrassing for all of them, for there was no hiding how devastated Rose had been by the news of their marriage. But not even Rachel had been prepared for the intensity of Rose's reaction. . . .

In her mind's eye, she could see it as clearly as if it had only just happened: the bloody gash on Rose's palm where she'd squeezed her champagne glass hard enough to shatter it. And the fathomless black of her eyes, making Rachel almost glad for the task of cleaning and dressing her wound—anything to avoid looking into that heated, anguished face.

Yes, Rose had mellowed some with the years, but she was essentially unchanged—a woman capable of passion so great it could draw blood.

Shutting the study door behind them, Rachel didn't miss the

pinched whiteness around Rose's mouth, or the color now stamped on her broad, high cheekbones. Even her springy black hair seemed to radiate indignation.

"I wasn't going to come tonight," Rose informed her in a low, controlled voice. "I almost backed out . . . but Drew insisted. It was a mistake."

Rachel felt her chest grow even tighter. Wasn't that just like Rose, choosing to confront her *now*, with a roomful of guests just down the hall?

"Maybe you *should* have stayed home then," she suggested coolly.

"No doubt." Rose's gaze was flat and remote. But the outburst, when it came, was clearly overdue, as far as *she* was concerned. "Rachel, for God's sake, this is crazy! Iris needs *help*, not a party with everyone standing around pretending they don't remember what almost happened at the last one. You know this is wrong. Deep down, you *must* know."

Rachel, taken aback, sank into the Morris chair next to Brian's desk. Numbly, she looked about her, at the books crowding every wall, the stacks of rubber-band-bound manuscripts—various drafts of Brian's novels—his old electric typewriter under its shroud, which he'd stopped using years ago but kept as a sort of shrine. Rose stood in front of the window, staring pensively out at the darkness. On the wall behind her hung the framed header from the cardboard display for *Stolen Thunder*, showing a silhouetted figure emerging from the heart of a raging inferno.

"What would you have suggested I do instead—have her committed?" Rachel challenged.

Rose shook her head. "I'm not saying Iris is crazy. Or even that there's anything we can *do*." She paused, pushing a hand through her hair. "Look, I haven't had a chance to sit down with Brian and really hash this out. I wanted to speak with you first. Don't you see? By throwing this party you're giving your stamp of approval to something that is just plain wrong." Then, backing off a bit, perhaps realizing she'd come on too strong, "Drew needs to see things more clearly . . . without all the fanfare," she reasoned. "He doesn't know what he's getting into here."

"And you do." Rachel felt suddenly certain that Rose had set out purposely to wreck her evening, along with any chance Rachel might have had to shine for her husband and daughter. A slow anger seeped through her, like something hot spilled down her dress. "You have it all figured out, soup to nuts. Did it ever occur to you, Rose, that you might not have all the answers?"

Rose took a deep breath. "I'm not saying I always know what's right. But I *do* know a disaster in the making when I see one. And you're not helping any by hiding your head in the sand. A month ago, Iris nearly killed herself. What makes you think she won't try it again?"

Rachel flinched as if she'd been slapped. Then she realized: this wasn't just about Iris. Something deeper, more insidious, was at work here. In Rose's eyes, Rachel thought she saw the sparks of an old resentment, smoldering like one of those underground fires that can burn for years, decades even. Did it have something to do with Brian? Now that she'd lost Max, had some of Rose's feelings for her old flame returned? Certainly, she and Brian seemed chummy enough tonight.

"Are you doing this just to hurt me? Is *that* it?" Rachel confronted her. "Because, honestly, I can't think of any other reason for reminding me how close I came to losing my daughter."

Rose frowned. "Why would I want to hurt you?"

"I don't know. I'm asking you." She paused, then forced herself to say, "A little while ago, I saw you talking to Brian. Did you sound off at *him?* Or did you two just have a cozy little chat?"

"Rachel," Rose sighed. "I'm not trying to paint you as the bad guy. And, whatever you might think, there's nothing going on behind your back." She made the fatal error of dropping her gaze . . . and that's when Rachel knew. For Rose had the thin skin of the truly passionate: she couldn't hide it when she was lying.

Something is going on behind my back. I don't know what it is, but, damnit, I'm going to find out.

"Oh no?" she pressed. "Is that why my husband apparently spent more time tonight with *you* than with me, his own wife?" Rachel, in some deep part of her, knew she was overreacting, taking out her frustration at Brian on Rose. She and Brian had talked about their daughter's engagement, sure, but had they *really* shared with each other everything they felt?

"Look, if you and Brian are having problems . . ." Rose put a hand out, letting the suggestion trail off dismissively.

Rachel felt something snap apart inside her; some thin wire that had been keeping intact her crumbling hope that her marriage would somehow sort itself out on its own. *Oh, God, does she know? Did Brian tell her about us, too?*

"How dare you," she breathed. "You waltz in here making all sorts of assumptions. Not just about my daughter . . . but my marriage, too. *What gives you the right?*"

Rose met her gaze without apology. And there it was again, that look—like a flash of heat lightning in the black depths of her eyes. Ancient and dark and fierce. "You don't know the half of it," she said in a low, tight voice, almost under her breath. Then, as if to stop herself from elaborating, she rolled her full lips back against her teeth in a thin, hard line.

Brian. She must mean Brian. Being widowed had clearly raked up old memories for Rose. And maybe Brian was partly responsible, too, encouraging her in some way. Rachel felt the fear that had been swelling in her rise and crest like a wave. But to have spoken it aloud would only have made it more real, more scary somehow.

This isn't about Iris," she said. "Or even your son. It's about *you.* Some sick need you have to hang on to him. You lost Max . . . and now you feel as if you're losing Drew. Get over it, Rose. Your husband is dead, and nothing is going to bring him back."

Rachel regretted her outburst at once. A moment ago she'd felt strong and purposeful, but now she felt weak as a newborn; her legs trembled as if she were on the verge of collapse. *Oh God, what have I done?*

Something awful, that much was clear. Rose, her eyes iced over with unshed tears, was roughly pushing away Rachel's outstretched arm. But if Rachel's words had been sticks, the ones Rose hurled at her in return were stones, the sharp kind that leave nasty bruises and break bones.

In a trembling voice, she hissed, "I hope you never find out what it's like to lose a man you love. I *have*. Twice. Max is dead, true . . . but I lost Brian because you *stole* him from me."

Chapter 5

❧ Rose, storming out of Brian's office, was about to slam the door behind her when a prim voice in her head reminded her that you didn't go around slamming doors in other people's homes. Especially that of a friend . . . a friend who would soon be your son's mother-in-law. And certainly not with forty people in the next room, many of whom might wonder what the hell was going on.

She slammed the door anyway, as hard as she could.

To hell with Rachel, and her damn party. Rachel had everything a woman could want: loving husband, nice home, fulfilling career. Even a mother who would do anything to make her happy. And now she wanted Drew, too?

Kiss my ass, Rose swore inwardly, fury burning through her. Rachel was right about one thing: Max was dead. But *she* wasn't. And, damnit, she would make sure Rachel remembered that.

Rose collided with someone, and the red mist swirling inside her head cleared suddenly. Brian. His hand on her shoulder, steadying her. In the half-light of the hallway, his familiar face swam into focus.

"Whoa . . . what's your hurry?" In his free hand, he was holding what was left of a Scotch and soda. She stared at it for an instant, transfixed by the sweating glass, the lozenges of melting ice swimming in the inch or so of pale amber.

Then she tore her gaze away, and looked up at Brian, at the face she'd carried inside her head, all the time he was in Vietnam and for a long while after, like a snapshot of someone beloved who'd died. In a way he *had* died over there, just as she'd feared he would. Because the Brian who returned home didn't belong to her anymore. He was Rachel's.

Now all she saw was a man growing older in the best possible way—his angular features more defined somehow, each line and gray hair like a footnote that clarified him in some way. He wore a loose-fitting blazer with a pale-blue shirt open at the collar, and she noticed that the braided-leather belt looped about the waist of his pressed chinos was one she'd given him. He'd kept it all these years. Why hadn't she ever noticed it before?

"I have to go," she told him.

"So soon?" His eyes rested on her with the steadiness of someone who'd known her a very long time—and wouldn't be easily fooled.

"I have things to take care of at home," she lied. Rose looked down at the toes of her black patent-leather slingbacks, gleaming sullenly in the dim light. She felt like such a hypocrite. For getting all dressed up like this, for going along with the pretense like everyone else. And hadn't she been enjoying herself, too? Flirting with Eric. Basking in his attention like . . . like it could really lead to something.

"Where's Rachel? I thought I saw you two go off together." Brian looked past her, eyeing the closed door to his office as if he already knew something terrible had happened. "Rose, what's going on?"

Of course, she thought. *Brian always could read me like a book. Even when we were kids . . .*

"We talked," Rose told him, striking a cautious tone. "Look, Bri, I'm sorry. The only reason I didn't stay home tonight was because I didn't want to hurt Drew. But it seems I did more harm in coming."

Brian looked troubled, but not surprised. "I can't say I blame you." With a sigh, he stepped around her to set his glass down on the narrow hall table, his back to the office door. "Listen, can we talk about this some more—somewhere quiet, just you and me?"

A wedge of light appeared on the Dhurrie runner behind him. Rose could see Rachel's silhouette in the doorway.

"I'd like that." Rose said, just loudly enough for Rachel to hear. She was still smarting from Rachel's accusations, and, yes, her confrontation with Sylvie too, which, though weeks old, had chafed at old scars, causing them to itch and burn. Maybe it *was* childish, taking advantage of Brian's offer mainly to strike back at Rachel . . . but, oh, what the hell.

"Why don't I take you home?" Brian suggested. "We can talk on the way."

She stared at him. "Now?"

Brian shrugged. "Rachel can manage without me, I'm sure. She usually does." There was no resentment in his voice, only a kind of weary acceptance.

"I'll ask Mandy to keep an eye on Jay, see that he gets home okay," Rose said. Jason wouldn't be too thrilled, she knew. All his friends were allowed out at night unchaperoned, he was always arguing. It wasn't fair, she was treating him like a baby. *But life isn't fair!* she'd wanted to fling back at him. *Was what happened to your dad fair?*

"I'll phone for a car. Ten minutes, meet you at the door." Brian held up both hands, fingers extended. He didn't look at all sorry to be leaving. Anyway, the party would be winding down soon, Rose told herself.

A few feet down the hall, the office door clicked quietly shut.

Rose experienced a tiny stab of guilt, immediately swallowed by a wave of righteous resentment. After those awful things Rachel had said, why should she care if Rachel felt hurt? Anyway, Rose was sick and tired of tiptoeing around her precious feelings. . . .

From the little he'd said already, Brian, she suspected, would see it her way. And she could use an ally. More than that, she could use a friend.

From nowhere, the thought of Eric flashed across her mind.

They'd gone out a couple of times since she'd done his show. No big deal, she told herself. But one time in particular stood out. An evening last week, when she'd been nearly comatose from hours of poring over the fine print in a stack of depositions, and Eric had spirited her off to his favorite Italian restaurant—a funky Village hideaway. They'd sat tucked in a back booth, twirling their forks in plates of linguine, and listening to a group of old Italian men playing bocci ball in the alley outside.

"Do you believe people have the power to reinvent themselves?" Eric had asked. "I don't mean just correcting a bad habit . . . but a real sea-change." Locking his hands together, he'd leaned forward to elaborate. "The other day, a listener phoned in—the husband of that battered wife who did our show. He was on the verge of tears. Said he hadn't realized until he heard his wife on the air what total bullshit all his apologies had been. Now he's in counseling. He knows he can't control his behavior, and he's trying to find out why. But he swore he wouldn't go near her until he knew for sure he wouldn't hit her again."

"And you believed him?" she'd asked, incredulous.

He'd grinned. "I guess that answers my question."

"I don't mean to sound so cynical." Rose shrugged and sat back. Over the sound system, an old Righteous Brothers tune was playing softly—one that made her feel oddly nostalgic. "I guess I've been burned a few times."

All at once, there had been the warmth of Eric's hand stealing across the table to close over hers. And his blue eyes that seemed to cast a soft glow in the darkness, resting on her as if he understood exactly why she would find it hard to believe in miracles. She'd told him little enough about Max, and nothing at all about her mother, but nevertheless, he seemed to know intuitively everything that was most essential about her.

They'd talked on the phone, too—nearly every night, in fact. Eric was a good listener; she could bounce things off him—stuff about Jay and Drew, problems she was having at the office—and he didn't give advice unless asked. Rose would lie in bed with her eyes closed and the lights off, the sound of Eric's voice soothing as a touch.

In some ways, it was better than having him beside her. She found his real, physical presence too disturbing—exciting in a way that inflamed her to the point of irritation. This way, she wasn't risking anything. And she could walk away at any time, no hard feelings. However much a friend he was turning out to be, she mustn't let herself forget, not for one second, that Eric was no substitute for Max. She mustn't confuse loneliness and need—and, yes, desire—with the kind of love she and her husband had shared.

Even so, in her present state—raw, every nerve exposed—Rose found herself wishing for a dose of Eric's good sense and galvanizing sympathy. As she headed back into the living room, she found herself automatically scanning the crowd. . . .

She spotted him at once, perched on an arm of the sofa, a coffee cup balanced on one knee. He was chatting with Marie, who appeared genuinely disarmed for a change. In her rayon pantsuit that had to be at least five years out of date, her shoe-black hair tucked behind her ears, Rose's sister was almost glowing.

Rose felt her temperature rise as she began making her way toward him, and a pulse in her belly start to throb. It didn't matter what she told herself, or how often she said it, the fact remained she couldn't be anywhere *near* Eric without feeling like a teenager in heat.

I'll just say goodbye. . . .

Rose was halfway across the room when her attention was diverted by the sight of Mandy, seated alone in a corner by the bookcase. She, too, held a coffee cup, but the careful way she was lifting it to her mouth made Rose wonder if it was coffee Mandy was sipping, or something stronger.

Now, watching her stepdaughter's arm float up to brush something clumsily from the front of her kelly-green dress, Rose thought: *She's drunk.*

God, not again. When had she *ever* seen Mandy leave a party without being at least tipsy? Once or twice she'd even mentioned it to Max, but he'd always dismissed her concern. None of the junior partners billed more hours than Mandy, he'd point out. In the ten years she'd been with the firm, she'd taken no more than a handful of sick days. If Mandy had a problem, wouldn't it have shown up at work?

Rose thought about how lately Mandy was almost never in her office. She'd chalked it up to a killer schedule, but now she wasn't so sure. *Did* her stepdaughter have a problem?

Suddenly Rose wasn't at all sure she wanted to know. One more thing on her already heaping plate was more than she could handle right now . . .

"It stopped raining."

Eric's voice. Rose turned, finding he'd slipped through the crowd to meet her halfway. Her heart began to beat even faster. Damn. There ought to be a law against guys like him, she thought. Men who could set you on fire with a glance. He was looking at her that way now—as frankly sexual as if he were gazing up at her from a pillow, sandy hair rumpled, his blue eyes nearly making her forget there were other people in the room.

He wants me, too. She'd known for some time—how could she not?—but there was difference between simply knowing something and actually *feeling* it. Rose shivered, feeling damp between her breasts . . . and her thighs.

She was thankful for the excuse to look away, toward the windows; it had indeed stopped raining. "I won't be needing my umbrella, then," she said.

"You're leaving already?" He sounded disappointed.

"As soon as I can arrange a ride home for Jay." Lowering her voice, she added, "I was going to ask my stepdaughter, but I don't think she's in any shape."

She watched Eric glance over at Mandy, slumped in her chair wearing a blank, stupid look. He nodded in understanding.

"I take it this isn't the first time," he observed mildly.

"No. I'm afraid not."

"I'll see that she gets home safely." Eric made the offer casually, as if he were merely helping her on with her coat.

Rose was pierced by a gratitude that was disproportionate, she knew. But, oh, how good, just this once, to have someone pick up the slack.

"I'd hate for you to go out of your way," she protested, even so.

"It's no trouble."

"Well, then . . . thank you."

"No need. It wasn't so long ago that *I* was the one being poured into taxis," he told her. "I don't like being reminded of those days . . . but I don't want to forget them, either. It's what keeps me honest." His faint, enigmatic smile held a trace of something hard, like a precious mineral mined at great expense. "She'll be in good hands, don't worry."

"I know," she said.

Rose kissed his cheek lightly, catching his scent, which for some reason she associated not with objects or other smells, but with memories that had nothing to do with him: sleeping in on Sunday, and nibbling buttered toast; hot summer days at the beach, and skinny-dipping. She stepped back, feeling foolish and vulnerable, a locker-room joke: the lonely widow desperately seeking a man to fill the gap.

Excusing herself before she could give in to the tears pressing hotly behind her eyes, Rose quickly made her rounds. In the end, she decided she was being silly about Jason, and gave him money for a taxi. Jay was right—he wasn't a baby anymore.

She was slipping her raincoat on in the foyer when Sylvie, whom she'd been avoiding, caught up with her at last. In her lavender dress that floated about her slender calves, she seemed almost as ethereal as the Japanese lanterns she used to string across her patio on summer nights. Rose, stirred by mixed feelings that bumped against one another like rude passengers on an elevator, reluctantly took the hand Sylvie held out—a hand as cool and weightless as a ghost's.

"I couldn't let you go without at least saying goodbye." Sylvie's voice was warm, assured . . . making Rose wonder for an instant if she'd only imagined that awful afternoon just last month. Until Sylvie asked hopefully, "Perhaps we could get together for lunch, or tea, sometime next week?"

Rose ducked her head, becoming suddenly absorbed in knotting the belt on her raincoat. "Oh, I don't know," she muttered. "I'm pretty busy."

"What about the week after?"

Rose looked up at Sylvie and saw that she was struggling to maintain her composure: blinking rapidly to keep the tears in her eyes from spilling over, her bright smile tugging down at the corners. Despite herself, Rose felt a lump of sympathy form in her throat. *I can't take this,* she thought. *Not another minute.*

"Frankly, I don't see the point." Rose spoke more coldly than she'd intended, as if to freeze the emotions bubbling inside her.

Aching inside, she pushed past Sylvie.

Brian, thank God, was waiting at the door—with Rachel nowhere in sight.

Good, she thought, stepping ahead of him into the outer foyer. Maybe it was time for the shoe to be on the other foot, for Rachel to know what it felt like to be the one left behind.

🌺 Climbing into the hired car beside Brian, Rose realized how exhausted she was. All she wanted to do when she got home was crawl into bed and pull up the covers. But first, she and Brian needed to talk.

On the ride home, they talked about everything *but* Drew and Iris. Brian told her about the novel he was working on, and about his last book tour—ten cities—which had nearly done him in. Rose, in turn, told him about her big case going to trial next month, and how Mrs. Esposito's lawyers had squawked at the evidentiary hearing last week. Rose had introduced the receipts for a new TV and stereo their client had bought the same day she was supposedly bedridden, too sick to be deposed.

By the time they pulled up in front of the brownstone on Perry, Rose realized they hadn't once mentioned the real reason Brian had wanted to come along. Was he saving the big speech for when they were inside?

Brian paused on the sidewalk outside the street-level entrance to her duplex, giving her a thoughtful look. "Hey, I was just wondering," he asked. "You keep in touch with anyone from the old neighborhood?"

She smiled at him. "Just you."

He smiled back. "Remember that fort we built up on the roof? It's a miracle it didn't fall in on us—all that scrap lumber held together with rusty nails and baling wire."

"Instead, what fell apart was *us*." She laughed softly, looking at him poised in the hallway just inside the door . . . and, yes, remembering that fort, which had been more than just a playhouse. It had become a kind of sanctuary really, where Brian had first kissed her, and she'd discovered the most powerful force on earth: love. "Life really *is* strange. Now, all these years later, it's our kids who can't live without each other."

Brian climbed the stairs to the second-floor living room, and dropped heavily onto the sofa. She watched him kick off his loafers. He still wore Docksiders, she noticed. How could it be that so much had changed, and yet the little things remained the same?

"Strange, yeah." He sighed, and forked a hand through his hair.

A watery light slanted in through the tall front windows, whose multitude of panes drove her housekeeper insane. On the marble mantel, silver-framed photos gleamed—one of Max with his arms draped around their sons' shoulders; another, more recent one of Drew in cap and gown at his graduation. They made her sad for some reason, as if those cherished memories were no more substantial than the pale reflections of raindrops on the wall above.

Quietly, she said, "I'll make some coffee."

When she returned with a steaming pot and two mugs, she was surprised to find Brian screwing a new bulb into the brass sconce over the piano. She was grateful, and a little surprised, too—he'd remembered where she kept things like bulbs and picture hangers and loose string. She'd been meaning to replace that bulb herself—for months. That, and a million other small chores. Except usually by the time she got home she was either too tired or too loaded down with paperwork.

"You're hired." She laughed, handing him a mug. "When you're finished with that, I have a leaky faucet in the bathroom that needs a new washer."

Brian grinned. "Seriously, I wouldn't mind. It's nice to be appreciated for a change."

She ignored his remark, not wanting to tread any further on what might prove to be thin ice. Already, she was beginning to regret her petty impulse to get back at Rachel through Brian. If he and Rachel were having problems, well, that was for them to work out. Anyway, her main concern right now was for Drew.

"Bri," she began hesitantly, settling with her mug into the easy chair across from the sofa, "this engagement—please tell me you think it's as bad an idea as I do. I don't think I could bear it if *you* were against me, too."

He looked at her, his expression flat and unsmiling. "No, Rose. I'm not against you," he said. "That doesn't mean I have no opinions of my own, though." In his stockinged feet, he padded back over to the sofa and sat down. Leaning forward, elbows resting on his splayed knees, he fixed her with a keen gaze. "Look, I know how you must feel. If it were up to me . . ." He glanced away, reaching for the mug he'd placed on the coffee table. "It's *not,* though. Rose, you know as well as I do we can't prevent our kids from making the same mistakes we made. Hell, would *we* have listened to reason?"

Rose shook her head, not wanting to hear what he was saying. "I don't care about what's *reasonable.*" Her voice rose. "Bri, I'm scared. Mostly for Drew, sure. But, believe it or not, I care about Iris, too."

"I know that." He lifted his fine gray eyes to her. "Rose, if I spent the rest of my life trying, I could never begin to repay you. Don't think I've forgotten it was you who brought us Iris."

Rose shifted, suddenly uncomfortable. Brian didn't know the *whole* truth, she thought. Only that Iris' real mother had died of an overdose not long after they learned her identity—when she was picked up on drug charges. Rose had told no one about the night she'd been called down to the station. What would have been the point of repeating those disjointed ravings about Iris? Clearly, the woman had been out of her mind.

"You don't owe me anything," she told him, adding firmly, "Whatever you do, do it for Iris."

Brian dropped his head into his hands, and spoke in a voice that was muted and hollow. "Do you think we haven't tried everything already? She's fine now, sure, but any minute . . . Christ, it's like there's this bomb ticking, and I can't get to it . . . and I know if I don't it'll all just . . . blow up." He raised his eyes, and she saw the anguish in them—anguish, she guessed, from what Rachel had hinted at, which had to do with more than just Iris. "Rose, I don't know what else to do."

She stared at him, the past and present coming together in a jarring rush, as if she were seeing two Brians—the young man she'd once loved, and would have died for . . . and the anguished father before her, who would do anything to save his child.

"I don't know, either," she replied softly. "But we can't just sit back and do *nothing*."

"Hell, it took a fucking war to come between *us*." The smile he gave her was thin and mirthless.

"Rachel accused me of trying to hang on to Drew, because— because I can't accept that Max is dead." Rose, a hard stone of anger lodged in her chest, addressed the Chagall print between the two windows. "Maybe she's right. Maybe there *is* some part of me that's holding on."

"At least you had something worth holding on to." Brian's voice was uncharacteristically bitter.

"You have to *fight* for what you love. With Max I didn't have that chance." She turned to him, furious all of a sudden, wanting to shake him, or startle him at least; make him see at least a fraction of the world of grief of which she'd been afforded a full view.

The expression on his face just then made her stop instantly, the anger draining from her. It was so bleak, so unlike the Brian who'd looked out for her when they were kids. He was always the one with a long fuse, and yet at the same time fearless with his fists when he needed to be. Nor would she ever forget what Brian had said to her when he was drafted to fight in Vietnam: *If I don't go, somebody else's number will be picked. I couldn't live with knowing another guy might have died in my place.*

Where had that young man gone? Was it Iris who had carved those lines around his eyes and mouth—constantly being faced with a battle that couldn't be won? Or was it simply that they were getting older? Discovering that life was less a promise than a series of compromises?

Wordlessly, she sank onto the sofa beside him, and they held each other. She recalled a time when she'd believed she wouldn't live through the pain of his leaving her. And now it was Brian's despair reminding her that life *did* go on, that hearts mended.

Rose buried her face against his chest. Dimly, she was aware of Brian stroking her hair, murmuring softly. Responding to her, as he always had. With kindness. When he kissed her lightly on the lips, it seemed only natural that she kiss him back.

Tentatively at first . . . then with a desperation that seemed to rise from an aching hollow deep inside. She grabbed hold of Brian's shirt, clung to him as if to keep from drowning.

"Please," she whispered, not knowing what it was she was begging for. "Oh, please."

A memory rose in her, at once both exquisite and painful: pennies scattered over the floor of Brian's college room, hundreds of pennies from a jar she'd shattered in a moment of fury when he told her he'd been drafted to go to Vietnam. Winking up at her like crazed stars as she sank to her knees, sobbing. She and Brian had made love one last time, on the carpet—silently, furiously, with the kind of passion that can only come from knowing it will all too soon be spent. Their faces wet with tears, all those pennies—such small things, worth next to nothing on their own, unless collected over time, like memories—pressing cool circles into her hot naked flesh.

Now Brian brought a hand to her throat, caressing it with his thumb. With his fingertips, he stroked the tiny hairs on the back of her neck, and brushed his lips over her temples. His breath came in small, warm bursts. His need was evident in the faint trembling of his fingers. When at last he drew back, it seemed to require a tremendous effort from him.

"Rose," he murmured thickly. "Rose, I'm so sorry."

"Don't be. . . . We haven't done anything. And we won't."

"No, not about this. About *us*. All these years, I've wanted you to know. It wasn't that I'd stopped loving you."

She touched a finger to his mouth, the urgent passion of a moment ago spent like a struck match. There are some things, she thought, that can never be recaptured. Part of her wanted to sink back into the comforting burrow of the past . . . but mostly she knew it was just an illusion. At the time, she'd have done anything to hold on to Brian. Through the years, however, she'd learned that some relationships are made to last, and others are to be tucked away, precious reminders of the elusive joy that lies at the sweet heart of life.

"That was another time. We aren't even the same people anymore. You have Rachel. And I have . . . I *had* Max," she finished in a small, choked voice.

"I didn't mean . . ." He dropped his head, looking pained.

"I know you didn't," she said. "We're tired, is all. And wrung out. I miss my husband. I miss being *married*."

"I know what that's like," he replied bitterly.

"It's not too late for you," she urged, wishing she could express how utterly final it is when someone you love dies; how every harsh word, every unspoken endearment, becomes magnified in your mind. "You've just lost your way. Whatever's wrong, there's still time to fix it."

Rose thought of Max, of how long it had been—*years* after losing

Brian—before she'd felt able to relinquish her whole heart. Never again would she allow herself to be trampled, she'd vowed. And now here she was, a survivor once more, learning that there was more than one way to lose a loved one, or for a heart to break.

An image of Eric rose in her mind, and suddenly she felt afraid. She didn't want to go through it again, all that grief. She didn't want to fall in love, only to have it snatched away.

"Do you think our kids will have any better luck?" Brian asked.

"God, I hope so."

A long, uncomfortable silence passed, in which the only sound was the lonesome yowling of a cat somewhere out back—one of the colony of strays that had decided her garden was the next best thing to kitty litter. She hadn't the heart to report them to the Humane Society. It didn't seem fair somehow, having them put to sleep, just for doing what came naturally.

He pulled away from her, reluctantly unfolding to his feet one length at a time. As tall as ever, but with a slight stoop to his shoulders that hadn't been there when they were young, when the illustrations of princes in her books of fairy tales all seemed to look like Brian.

"I'd better go," he said.

Watching him head for the door, Rose thought wearily: *Yes, go home to your wife. And be glad you still have one.*

As he was leaving, Brian turned and said, as if he wished it could be more, "I'm glad we talked."

"Me, too," she said, meaning it.

Downstairs, Rose heard the faint click of the lock as he let himself out.

Alone, listening to the rain dripping from the eaves, a sound like the uneven ticking of a clock, she thought again of Eric.

What if it had been Eric kissing her? Eric, who wasn't married . . . who'd have been free to stay the night. And with whom she shared no complicated past. Would she have been so quick to see him leave? So able to resist the powerful longing to know again the feel of a man's naked body in her bed. A man who clearly wanted her, too.

One night, that's all she'd ask. All she'd dare risk.

🌹 Brian strode along the sidewalk, ignoring the cabs streaking like minnows down the rain-slicked stretch of Seventh Avenue where it intersected with Perry. He'd decided to walk back, needing the air, needing to think before he returned home. To Rachel. And to the scene that no doubt awaited him. He wondered what it would be like just to keep on walking, like in those songs about wandering cowpokes—just to keep putting one foot in front of the other until you couldn't go any farther.

Isn't that what you've been doing? What got you here in the first place?

Each day, telling himself it would get better; that the Rachel he'd fallen in love with all those years ago, and married instead of Rose—that tender-tough girl brimming with a passion to save the world, but passionate about him, too—would return to him.

Now he wasn't so sure.

Like ripples in a pond, something had changed for him with Max's death. It had brought home to him how easily it could all be snatched away. Now, tonight, with Rose, he'd been reminded of something else as well: how wondrous it had been with her. His first love. The memory of their time together unspoiled and undiminished, like some delicious fruit he could bite into again and again.

He'd believed it back then, when she told him she would have died for him.

He believed her capable of such depth of emotion even now. The Rose who'd clung to him their last night together before Nam, naked and weeping, hadn't changed. Though tempered by the years, and by loss, she had a streak of midnight in her that reminded him of the one and only time he'd attempted sky-diving, that first lurching moment of finding himself free-falling in midair—exciting, and at the same time mind-numbingly terrifying. Yet he'd never felt so alive.

What most people didn't get was how rare it was, he thought. And how fleeting. The irony was that even those lucky enough to experience that kind of love seldom appreciated it until it was too late. They left it to wither. Or allowed it to be snatched away.

He found himself thinking about his second novel, which, after the sensation of *Double Eagle,* had been a bit of a disappointment to some. *Kings Highway* was a quieter book in many ways, the autobiographical story of a kid growing up in Midwood, the son of a large Irish Catholic family, who befriends the lonely girl next door. A misfit who grows into a beauty . . . and whom he ends up nearly destroying through circumstances beyond his control.

Rachel, when she read it, had said very little. She had to have known who his model for Rowena had been, but whatever jealousy she might have felt, she'd kept it to herself. He'd admired her for that. She was smart enough to know a wedding ring didn't buy you all the shares of your partner's thoughts and feelings.

Now he wondered if Rachel's silence had been merely a sign that she ran slightly cooler at her core than he'd come to expect. Rose, under those same circumstances, would have yelled and cried . . . and then made fierce love to him. The things left unspoken in a marriage, he realized, didn't just melt away. They accumulated, like ice on a roof, until tiny leaks began to appear . . . and then, finally, the whole ceiling caved in.

Tonight, his daughter's engagement party, had reminded him of more than he wanted to remember. A time when, like Drew, he'd been too young to appreciate fully the gift he'd been given—a gift that comes only once in a lifetime.

Brian walked on. The huge marquees on either side of the avenue grayed into those of smaller storefronts as he turned east, toward Park, navigating his way around the small lakes left by clogged sewer drains. He passed the Barnes & Noble where he'd had the publication party for his last book. Two hundred people had shown up that night. Incredible. The memory warmed him . . . but only for an instant. Then the tide of emptiness came surging back in.

Turning onto Gramercy Park, he found himself thinking about his friend Eric Sandstrom . . . and felt more than a twinge of envy. Eric and Rose were dating, he'd heard. For some reason, the news had affected him more than Rose's being married to Max all those years. For one thing, Max had been older. Eric, though roughly his own age, made Brian feel over the hill—the father of a grown daughter, soon to be a father-in-law. His shot at the joys of youth long past.

But was that true? His life with Rachel was frustrating, not because he was past caring, but because he loved her, and wanted more. He'd believed his patience would eventually pay off. Now he wanted it all—everything that had been stored up for a rainy day.

Face it, man. You wouldn't be feeling this way if you had a wife who'd miss you half as much as Rose misses Max. Rachel, if he died, would mourn, he knew. But in the end, would his absence leave the kind of yawning gap Rose was experiencing? No, probably not.

It was close to eleven-thirty by the time Brian let himself into their apartment. He was surprised to find Rachel waiting up for him, curled on the sofa in her bathrobe.

She looked drawn, her eyes red, as if she'd been crying.

"I won't ask what took you so long. I won't stoop to that." Her voice came at him, hard and low, a bullet that caught him unawares.

"I walked home." Not an apology, merely an explanation. He tugged off his Docksiders at the door, realizing as he did so that they were soaked all the way through to his socks.

He could see the struggle in Rachel's face as she rose to greet him with crossed arms. "You might have called at least. Or better yet, given me some warning before you walked off and left me with a houseful of guests. What was I supposed to tell them? That you cared more about seeing your dear friend Rose home than about your own wife and daughter?"

"I'm surprised you even noticed." He walked over to the bar that was still set up, waiting for the caterer to take it down in the morning. A nearly empty fifth of Scotch was about all that was left; he helped himself from it—just enough to thaw the lump of ice forming in his belly.

"Damn you," she swore. "I will not let you make this about *me*."

"Who said anything about you?" He turned slowly to face her, too tired to argue. "Rachel, believe it or not, I wasn't doing this to punish you. Or take sides. As incredible as it might seem, I had a good time tonight."

"I don't doubt that." She stalked over to where he stood, her reflection flashing in the mirrored panels on either side of the fireplace. "God, Brian. Do you think I'm stupid? Do you think I don't know what this is all about?"

"You tell me."

"Rose. The lonely widow. Reaching out. *Needing* someone to fill the void. It's like every tear-jerker movie I've ever seen." She paused before flinging at him, "I can't believe you fell for it."

She was hurt, he could see. It was one of the things he found most maddening about her . . . and, at the same time, oddly endearing. The more vulnerable she felt, the tougher she tried to appear.

It's her toughness that saved your life, asshole. The memory jumped out at him. Waking up to find himself on an iron army cot in a whitewashed room, with the most vivid pair of blue eyes gazing down at him. The eyes of an angel, he'd thought in that first drugged moment . . . until he learned from one of the nurses how Dr. Rosenthal had fought like hell to keep him from being triaged onto the sidelines and into a body bag. Corralling everyone in sight to assist her in repairing his ruptured gut. Besides, angels didn't wear mud-clotted huaraches, and have fingernails that were bitten to the quick.

But this wasn't Nam. And he wasn't dying. Even if it felt like it sometimes.

Brian shrugged and turned away, knowing his coolness would only hurt her more. He *wanted* to hurt her, damnit.

"I'd almost forgotten what it felt like," he said. "To be needed."

Rachel fixed him with an unflinching stare, as if she could see right through him and knew what had almost happened tonight. *Would* have happened, if he hadn't stopped himself. And the worst part was, he felt no shame about it. Only regret.

Taking a step backwards, Rachel demanded anxiously, "What are you saying? What happened that you're not telling me?"

Brian didn't answer at first. It was a moment before he could muster the energy to shake his head. "Nothing," he answered truthfully. "Nothing happened. We talked. That's all."

Her gaze remained on him a moment or two longer, searching his face. She sighed. "I'm sorry. I didn't mean to accuse you." She pushed her hands through her hair. "It's been a long night. I'm upset, but I know you wouldn't . . . well . . . with Rose."

She couldn't even say the words. Suddenly he wanted her to say them. *Make love. Fuck.* Whatever you want to call it. Anything that might show she still wanted him in the same way—enough to get angry at the thought of another woman, Rose, *especially* Rose.

Something in him snapped, and he strode over, grabbed Rachel by the shoulders, his fingers sinking into the soft terry of her robe as if into sand that might slip between his fingers.

"Nothing happened," he repeated.

What came next surprised the hell out of him. Rachel burst into tears, clutching at him with an abruptness that nearly knocked him off balance. "Brian, what's happening to us?"

Despite himself, Brian's arms were lifting to soothe her—a gesture that comforted him, too, by virtue of its familiarity, if nothing else. He stroked her hair, pushing his hand up underneath, and running it along her scalp the way she liked.

When she tipped her head back to be kissed, he found himself responding with a need that was like some tremendous force of gravity. He couldn't remember the last time he'd felt this way about his wife. And that was because it wasn't his wife he was thinking of right now. *Rose.* He was on fire with Rose. Remembering her mouth, her heat. Not just tonight, but from years ago. Her touch on the back of his neck. The taut smoothness of her legs wrapped around his. The way she'd looked, naked in the half-light, all dark hair and dark eyes with those long golden limbs like melted butter. Looking wondrously pagan, like some sort of wicked sacrilege, in her white Catholic underpants with the tiny gold crucifix he'd given her gleaming in the hollow of her throat.

Filled with Rose, he drew his wife to him, roughly. He heard her whimper in pain, and tasted blood. It dawned on him, in some hazy recess of his brain, that he must have bitten her lip.

Brian didn't care. He was beyond caring. Beyond merely wanting. He *needed* this. Christ. More than anything in his whole life.

He tugged at the sash on her robe, but Rachel gently pushed him away. "Iris," she whispered. "She might hear us." She took his hand, and led him down the hall.

In the bedroom where they'd spent so many companionable nights, spooned back to front, he took her. With an urgency that was fierce and hard . . . and unlike anything he and Rachel had ever experienced. Even on their wedding night, in that hole-in-the-wall hotel with its drunken wooden shutters overlooking the Saigon River, he hadn't touched her this way. Pushing up between her legs with his hand. Sucking hard on her breast, as she arched up against him. She moaned, whether in pain or pleasure he couldn't tell, but it didn't matter. Because she was excited, too.

Wet. Not just down there. But moist all over with sweat. Christ, she was burning up.

On the candlewick spread that had been his Irish grandmother's, he drove into her. And felt her quicken almost against her will, every muscle contracted, as if part of her was resisting . . . but, at the same time, she desperately wanted it, too.

Images skated through his mind like scenes half glimpsed from a speeding train: Rose, at seventeen, going down on him for the first time. A little shocked by it all, but so willing . . . wanting to please him . . .

And a memory of Rachel, too. When they were first married, in

Vermont, hiking up a ski slope laid barren by summer. At the top, where the deserted lift stood like some giant abandoned toy, they'd made love. The sun beating down on his bare back. Rachel's moist skin sticking to his. Her eyes blazing up at him like the sky reflected in the still surface of a mountain lake.

He came hard, as if something was being torn from him. A searing rush in which the trembling of Rachel's climax was all but lost.

Then it was over, and he lay panting beside her. Several minutes passed before Brian realized she was crying. Softly, almost soundlessly, into the pillow she held to her face.

Brian felt jolted. *She knows.*

How could she not? Never, in all the years they'd been married, had he made love to her like that.

"Don't." She flinched when he tried to put his arm around her.

He wanted to say, *It's not what you're thinking.* But that would have been a lie.

She closed here eyes so she wouldn't have to look at him, tears squeezing out from under her clenched eyelids.

He felt an odd mixture of emotion—four parts shame, one part bitterness. He'd never cheated on Rachel, not in twenty-odd years, but what had just happened came about as close to that as you could get. The thought made him a little sick.

He willed Rachel to look at him, to give him one good reason to stay in this marriage. To keep from wanting to take Rose . . . and next time, not just in his fantasies.

But she remained balled up, her eyes squeezed shut, her body like a great fist closed against him.

The worst of it was, he couldn't stop seeing Rose in his mind. How he would have felt had Rose been lying beside him now. The thought of her sleeping with Eric sent a low pain ratcheting through his gut. *Had* she slept with him?

Not yet, maybe, but she would. Soon. If Brian wanted her—if she would even have him—he would have to act quickly.

He rolled onto his back, shocked by the enormity of what he was contemplating. Not just an affair. No, he wouldn't do that to Rose or Rachel.

Divorce?

The thought struck him like a sandbag hurled at his chest, but for the first time he wasn't pushing it away. Instead, he lay perfectly still, measuring its weight, testing his reaction. He found that he wasn't paralyzed by the thought, as he had been on previous forays into that wilderness. That he could actually bear to imagine such a thing, however terrifying and awful.

At the same time, he yearned to snatch Rachel up, shake her until it sank in: *she* was what he wanted. Not the pale version of a marriage they had now. But the way it had been in the beginning. Just the two of them.

He'd have gone to the ends of the earth for Rachel. Just like in Nam, when he'd risked his life to go back into the jungle—to the occupied hospital where Rachel was being held prisoner.

Brian would never forget how Rachel had looked when he walked through the door, the lightning play of emotions on a face stretched nearly transparent with exhaustion. Shock, recognition, disbelief . . . then absolute, incredulous joy.

Christ, what he wouldn't give to see that look on her face again.

There was only one thing he *wouldn't* do: settle for less than either of them deserved.

Quite simply, he wanted all. Or nothing.

Chapter 6

❧ "Sorry . . . so sorry . . . Don't be mad. . . ."

Mandy was muttering to herself as Eric helped her from the cab. Her head was down, her coppery hair obscuring most of her face. The corner on which they stood was just east of Battery Park City, where she lived. As far as Mandy was concerned, though, it might as well have been miles away.

Looking around him, Eric was struck by a sense of having narrowly averted a possible disaster. The street was pretty much deserted this far west. If Mandy had gone home alone, anything could have happened. . . .

A buried memory flickered through his consciousness, disjointed images of nights like this—stumbling from pillar to lamppost, negotiating each curb as if it were a precipice, fighting to maintain his balance on pavement that rocked like a suspension bridge. How he'd managed each time to get where he was headed, to *survive*, had to be some kind of miracle in itself.

His AA sponsor had put it best. Carl Jagger, a burly black trucker from Tennessee—with whom Eric had had only one thing in common, but whom he'd grown to love like an uncle—had listened intently as Eric haltingly told his tale about the car wreck that had taken his co-anchor Ginny's life, but which had spared his own. Then, bowing his huge head, whose tightly coiled hair had always made Eric think of a buffalo's, Carl had replied almost reverently, "Man, you got some powerful mojo workin' on you."

Mojo. Miracle. Call it what you like. It was out there, if not exactly available ready-made in your size. You had to fashion your own,

Eric had learned. From whatever scraps you were left with, and whatever tools you were given.

This lady here, he thought, hooking an arm about Mandy's waist as she wilted against him, could use some of that mojo herself.

As he steered her along the walk that led to her building, Eric felt connected to Mandy in a way that went deeper than with most people he'd only just met. A connection that had nothing to do with knowing Mandy . . . and everything to do with what they shared. They were alcoholics. Recovering or otherwise, one thing never changed: once a drunk, always a drunk. And God help him, Eric thought, if he ever forgot it.

"My keys . . . I can't find them. . . ." Mandy had stopped, and was fumbling in her purse, its contents spilling onto the pavement—lipstick tube, compact, fountain pen, eyeglass case, a small canister of Mace.

They stood under the granite awning that shielded the entrance to the sleek black-glass tower in which Mandy lived—one in a complex of residential high-rises, all of which looked eerily alike to Eric. Mercury-vapor lamps illuminated the walk on either side, as well as the strip of grass edged in boxwood that passed as landscaping.

He stooped, retrieving her leather-tabbed key ring from under a scraggly bush. "Here," he said. "You hold on to these while I get the rest." He dropped it into her outstretched palm, and gently folded her fingers around it.

Mandy just stood there, gazing at him stupidly, her head nodding like a sleepy child's. As he guided her through the revolving door and into the elevator, she leaned heavily against him. *Probably slipped in a few before the party,* he guessed. Oh yeah, he knew *that* terrain.

Letting them into her apartment on the twenty-second floor, Eric wasn't surprised to see an empty wine bottle on the pass-through counter of the kitchen that opened onto the small, austere living room. He didn't have to look inside the refrigerator to know it was well stocked. Not with much in the way of groceries, he imagined, but he'd bet cash money there was vodka in the freezer, and several bottles of wine chilling on the fridge's bottom rack.

Something burned in his gut, a not-so-old wound that hadn't quite healed.

He turned to find Mandy sagging onto the sofa, and grabbed her before she became dead weight. She muttered in protest, wriggling in his grasp, and pushing at him with fists made of rubber. Eric didn't resist, only tightened his hold about her. When he spoke, there was no judgment in his voice, no hint of blame. How many times had he walked this particular walk? How many helping hands had he pushed away?

"Come on, let's get you to bed."

With one arm looped about her, supporting her, he walked her down the hallway to her bedroom. Thumbing the light switch, he found only more of the same sterile hotel decor. Queen-sized bed covered in a paisley quilted spread, maple headboard with matching maple dresser and nightstands. Nice, expensive, but with about as much personality as a department store's model room. Nothing that bore even the slightest trace of its occupant.

It was a disguise, he knew. Mandy was hiding behind all this smooth banality as she would behind a mask—one that had fooled everyone, including Mandy herself. But that mask had begun to slip. . . .

Rose, he thought, would be good for her. Tough, uncompromising. Just the kick in the ass her stepdaughter needed . . .

Rose. Was he merely fooling himself about her? If she knew even a fraction of the complicated feelings she'd stirred in him, would she be scared into bolting for high ground? Probably. Hell, it scared *him.*

"So sorry . . . All my fault . . ." Mandy was seated on a corner of the bed like a Raggedy Ann doll about to topple over. She was crying, her jaw slack and her mouth drooping open. Tears sooty with mascara rolled down her cheeks.

Eric crouched down so they were at eye level.

"You have nothing to apologize for," he told her. "Not to me."

"Oh God . . . I'm such a mess." She was holding the knuckles of a clenched fist to her mouth, her eyes like twin smudges of carbon on white paper. "I need a drink," she said with sudden forcefulness.

She tried to stand up, but Eric seized her by the shoulders, holding her steady. "First, you need to sleep."

She blinked at him, screwing her eyes up as if trying to bring him into focus. "Who are you? Do I know you?"

"Not yet. But you will, I hope." *I'll be the guy sitting next to you at your first AA meeting, if you make it that far.*

Mandy nodded blankly, and closed her eyes. He felt the tension in her arms and shoulders abruptly ease. This time, gently, he eased her down onto the bed.

When Eric returned from the bathroom with a wet washcloth to wipe her face, she was out cold.

🙊 Fifteen minutes later, Eric stood alone on the windswept esplanade looking out over New York Harbor. Except for the scattered couples strolling along its curving pathways, Battery Park City—landfill he'd always thought of as phony real estate stuck onto the southernmost tip of Manhattan like some vast concrete prosthesis—was deserted this time of night. The hot-doggers on Rollerblades had all gone home, and the kid-friendly play area resembled an abandoned construction site. The only evidence that this phony city was inhabited was the row upon row of lighted windows in the cluster of residential towers behind him.

Eric leaned against the metal railing, gazing out at the skyline reflected on water the color of stale coffee. The Statue of Liberty, illuminated in the distance, her arm upthrust in victory—or was it merely in welcome?—reminding him for some reason of when he was a kid, when life had seemed much more clear-cut: a game that had come with a set of instructions. Win or lose, you always knew where you stood. And when you screwed up, you could always start over from scratch.

He smiled bitterly to himself. As he'd gotten older, he'd discovered that life was more of a test than a game—a test of endurance, the lesson of which was, for the most part, obscured. Each day like pushing a boulder up a hill that kept rolling back to flatten you.

Staying sober had become easier with time, yes. Otherwise, how would anyone manage it? But he hadn't forgotten how tough it'd been in the beginning. How seemingly impossible to make it through even one day.

Mandy? She hadn't even started the journey. Tomorrow, he knew, she'd dimly remember getting drunk at the party, and his taking her home. She might even feel humiliated enough to white-knuckle it for a day or two. But until she loosened her grip, and realized the impossibility of doing it alone, she didn't stand a chance.

Eric knew the territory well. Christ, yes—and then some. He was the Kurtz of that particular heart of darkness. Ten years of roadside bars, lost weekends, late nights in unfamiliar locales . . . plus another five of the seriously hardcore lock-the-door, unplug-the-phone drinking you do when it's become your only reason for living. Not until he'd woken up, at age thirty-nine, in the drunk tank of a Memphis jail, had he discovered just how far he'd wandered from any path he would have chosen for himself.

When they told him it was Ginny who'd been driving their rented car as it smashed through the guardrail, he supposed he should have felt relieved that it wasn't *him*. But even in his hungover state, with a square of gauze over one badly swollen eye, Eric had known exactly whose fault it was. Ginny, as timid behind the wheel of a car as she was gutsy in front of a camera, had hated driving at night, especially in strange cities. If he'd kept his promise to her and stayed sober during their stint in Memphis, Ginny Gregson would be alive today.

Eric Sandstrom, fair-haired boy of the top-rated *Morning Show*, on the other hand, had risen from the wreckage like a modern-day Lazarus. Even with network executives demanding he sober up "or else," and friends no longer returning his calls, he'd literally gotten away with murder.

His only punishment was to go on living.

Drinking helped deaden the pain. Sandstrom's Quart-a-Day Maintenance Plan, a friend had called it—Bill Stimson, who'd seen the humor in it as only a fellow drunk paying rent on a stool down at Duffy's Tavern could. *No down payment necessary, easy installments, just sign on the dotted line, if you will, sir.*

Bill died a few years ago, he'd heard. Liver failure.

These days Eric traveled the back roads of those memories only as often as he needed to in order to keep from reliving them. Blessedly, those months were largely a blur in his mind, marked by a few clear patches. Like the morning he'd woken with no feeling in his arm from the elbow down, and a voice deep in his fogged brain quite calmly pointing out that, if he didn't quit drinking, his next gig would be the county morgue. He'd shut that voice up with a bender that had lasted three days before washing him ashore on a strange lawn, where he was found baying at the moon at half past who-the-fuck-cares-what-time-it-is in the morning—a stunt that earned him a bed in the detox ward at Santa Monica Hospital.

For Eric, the experience was defined by a single watershed moment: looking around him, at all those winos in wrinkled hospital gowns reeking of Thunderbird, and thinking, *Christ, what am I doing in this place? I'm nothing like these guys. I don't belong here.*

The voice in his head had spoken up again—louder this time, in order to be heard above the jackhammer threatening to pulverize his skull. *You're wrong, my friend, this is EXACTLY where you belong. The only difference between you and these other guys is that they know what they are.*

At the time, he'd seen it as just one more reason to go on slowly killing himself . . . but what it had been, in fact, was the wake-up call that had jarred him hard enough to accept the offer of a kindly older man named Phil, who'd visited him the next day and invited Eric to attend an AA meeting. It had been the beginning of a whole new life. The first day in a series of days, weeks, months, in which he would be guided by a single objective: staying sober by living the program, by adhering to the twelve steps laid out by Bill W.

Now, five years and a hundred million miles of hard road behind him, it seemed to Eric that he hadn't come as far as he'd hoped to. There were still times when the collective memory of all those wasted years washed over him like sewage. When he felt less than whole—as if the ragged ends of his past and present lives didn't quite meet.

At this particular moment, however, it was enough simply to be standing here on his own two feet, gazing with clear eyes at the monument to a city that punished its huddled masses as much as it forgave them.

He would do what he could for Mandy . . . but he wasn't in the business of saving people. Only by continuing to save himself did he stand a chance of helping someone else.

Eric shivered in the cool breeze that rattled through the shrubs planted in neat columns alongside the esplanade. During his years of exile in Des Moines, and later in L.A., he'd dreamed of one day coming back to New York. There was a kind of majesty to this city that rubbed off on even its lowliest subjects. A hard beauty, as well as a gruff acceptance of its prodigal sons. Watching a tugboat churn its way upriver, he smiled to think how different this was from the triumphant return he'd imagined.

He'd pictured himself at this age with a wife, two kids, and a prime-time network slot—at a fat salary with the perks to match.

Instead, here he was, still single, about to head home to his comfortable—but far from fashionable—third-floor walk-up in Murray Hill. A few people still remembered him from the *Morning Show*. But with radio, he knew, unless your name was Howard Stern or Rush Limbaugh, you were nobody.

Yet Eric had no regrets. The radio gave him a freedom that would have been unthinkable—if not illegal—on television. He could explore at length issues that actually mattered. It was the hardest he'd ever worked, no contest—five days a week of three hours on-air, plus half a day's prep—but also the most rewarding. At times, it was even fun.

He didn't regret not having married, either. Women, Christ, there'd been *women*. One to whom he'd almost proposed. Susanne Whittaker had been his producer at the *Morning Show*. Smart, sexy, a solid ten . . . and he'd loved her, yeah. But in the end, he supposed, he hadn't loved her enough. Susanne wasn't the one he'd been searching for, the woman in his mind's eye.

As far back as he could remember, Eric had known she was out there, that woman. Somewhere. He hadn't known when or where they would meet, but he'd had a hazy idea of what she would look like: dark and long-limbed, with strong features and a streak of wildness. The details weren't important. It was her *essence* he carried in his head like a keepsake worn with handling. The only thing he'd known for sure was that when he saw her he would recognize her instantly.

And he had. The night of Brian McClanahan's party. A perfect stranger, yet someone he'd known all his life. From the moment she sat down next to him—tall and dark and lovely, with her shoulders braced for an evening she clearly wasn't looking forward to, and her cheeks flushed with that story about being caught in traffic—which he suspected had been exaggerated—Eric had been certain: this was the woman he was destined to marry.

Rose just didn't know it yet.

She wasn't *ready* to know.

Soon, he thought. With luck, and a little of God's grace.

Eric had never belonged to any church, and the notion of some heavenly father guiding his every move evoked an unpleasant image of himself as a puck in the magnetic hockey game he'd owned as a kid. His God was more meat and potatoes—work hard, do the best job you can, and the boss just might reward you.

Now, gazing up at the moon wrapped in haze like a milky blind eye, Eric, for the first time in years, found himself praying.

Just this one thing, God, that's all I ask.

A moment later, he was striding along the esplanade toward West Street—where finding a taxi this time of night, he thought, might prove difficult enough to make him regret playing the Good Samaritan—quickening his step as it occurred to him that Rose might still be up, that it wasn't too late to call when he got home. . . .

❧   Eric's taxi was turning off the West Side Highway onto Twenty-third when he remembered: Rose would be anxious about Mandy. Instead of calling, why not just stop by?

He glanced at his watch. It seemed hours since he'd left the party, but Eric saw that it was only a little past eleven. Not the time of night for a social call, but this wasn't exactly social. Besides, at the party, they'd had almost no time together; quite frankly, he missed her.

He'd been to her place once—last Friday, when she'd invited him in for a drink before dinner. Now, climbing out of the cab in front of her brownstone, Eric was relieved to see a light on upstairs—in the living room, where they'd sat sipping sodas, while Mozart played on the stereo.

Talking about nothing in particular, while Eric had thought about nothing but making love to her.

Now he wondered if she'd resent the intrusion. See it as some ploy to get her into bed. As if that were all he wanted from her . . .

Before Eric could change his mind, a curtain drew back . . . and a second later, the porch light switched on. Four stone steps led to the front door, which stood wide open, with Rose silhouetted against the light, nothing but a thin cotton robe between her and the warm breeze ruffling its hem.

"I saw the taxi pull up," she said. "I thought it might be Jay. He called to let me know he and Drew were going out after the party. But he should be home by now."

"I suppose I should have called, too," Eric apologized.

"As you can see, I was just getting ready for bed." Her tone was almost comically prim; it was that smile of hers, like something warm to drink on a snowy day, that gave her away. She added, "But come in anyway. I could use the company."

Upstairs, the living room was dim, the only light streaming from the kitchen beyond. He remembered it as cozy, but now her place seemed forlorn somehow. Filled with mementos that brought to mind a shrine. This time, Eric noticed the masculine touches—the leather club chair, the nineteenth-century mariner prints, the brass ship's compass on the wall by the bookcase. And the photos, of course—everywhere, framed photos of her family, featuring a stocky older man with a keen gaze that in every shot was fixed lovingly on Rose.

There was music playing low—something lyrical and sad. Schumann? He didn't stop long enough to ask. Rose was already motioning him into the kitchen, making room for him at the round oak table by scooping a stack of books and papers from one of the pressback chairs.

"I'm toasting a bagel," she told him. "Want to share it with me?"

She looked so delicious herself—face scrubbed of makeup, her hair standing up in wild dark scribbles—that it was all Eric could do not to show her, then and there, just what, exactly, he was hungry for.

"Got any cream cheese?" he asked.

Rose made a trip to the refrigerator, and set out butter, jam, a tub of Philly. Handing him a plate with half a bagel that looked more burned than toasted, she sat down across from him and asked, "How did it go with Mandy?"

"She'll live."

"That's not what I meant." He caught a note of impatience in her voice.

Eric shrugged. "There isn't much more to tell."

"What kind of shape was she in when you left her?"

"Out cold." He spread a thick layer of cream cheese over his bagel, enough to mask the burned edges.

Rose grimaced. "God, just what I was afraid of. Eric, how bad off do you think she is?"

"Bad enough to have her stepmother, and probably half the people at that party, wondering what's next," he said.

She looked down and sighed, her hands pressed flat against the table on either side of her plate. "Look, I know this is going to sound horribly selfish. I love Mandy, as if she were my own . . . but right now, I don't think I can handle this."

"Good. Because that's exactly what she needs—for you *not* to help."

"That sounds so harsh," she said, somewhat taken aback.

"No, just honest. What's she been like at work?"

"I hardly see her these days. We're both so busy."

"Maybe she's avoiding you."

"The thought *had* occurred to me," she admitted, frowning.

Eric looked at her, seated across from him in her bathrobe, so beautiful, so troubled, and found himself imagining a life of this— late nights with Rose, the two of them ironing out some knot, exchanging views, soliciting each other's opinion. God, it could be so good. If only she'd see what *he* saw . . .

Something hard inside his chest cracked open—a seed of hope he hadn't dared plant until now.

He brushed the back of her hand, lightly, his fingers curled like a question mark. "Speaking of trouble, you want to tell me about what happened at the party?"

"God, was it that obvious?" She cast him a stricken look.

"I don't think anyone else noticed," he reassured her. "I just happened to catch Rachel as I was leaving. She looked as if she'd been crying."

Rose drew back, reaching for her butter knife. "Well if she was, she brought it on herself," she said with an uncharacteristic lack of sympathy. "Rachel doesn't want to know how *I* feel. The only one in that family I can talk to is Brian."

"Is that why he took you home?"

Eric was unprepared for the violent flush that stained Rose's cheeks, and the suddenness with which she twisted out of her chair. He heard the soft slap of her bare feet against the tile floor as she padded over to the stove. "Want some tea? I have three kinds of herbal." She put the kettle on to boil. With a casualness that didn't fool him, not for one second, she replied, "Brian saw how upset I was. He was only being nice."

Eric knew that Brian and Rose had once been lovers—Rose had admitted as much—but it hadn't even *occurred* to him she might still be carrying a torch. Christ. Was *that* what this was all about?

He was seized by a jealousy so fierce it seemed to rise from some deep, primal place. When had he ever felt this way toward a woman? *Any* woman?

"I can't say I didn't see it coming. With Rachel, I mean." His voice was the controlled, even one he used when speaking into a mike.

"She accused me of being selfish—a lonely widow clinging to her eldest son. God, how pathetic is *that*." Rose's indignation seemed to be acting as some sort of tonic, strengthening her.

Eric didn't trust himself to speak. Finally, he dared to ask, "Is there some truth in it?"

She stared at him, and he could almost see the blood rising in her, swelling her veins.

"What exactly are you saying?" Her eyes narrowed.

He stared back at her, holding his ground. But when he spoke, it was softly, and not without compassion. "There's more than one way to mourn," he said. "Some of us get through it by drinking ourselves into a stupor. Others just hold on, as if letting go of their grief would mean they hadn't cared enough to begin with."

Silence rushed in like a tide, nearly swallowing them. Eric could hear the brush of wet leaves against a windowpane, and the soft whistling of the teakettle beginning to boil. Finally, Rose spoke.

"How I mourn my husband is nobody's business," she informed him coldly. She was standing so straight he could have dropped a plumb line from her squared-off shoulders. "Not yours, or Rachel's, or . . . or the man in the moon's."

He felt a flash of anger. *The man in the moon isn't going to warm your bed at night,* he itched to reply. Instead, biting down on his frustration, Eric said only, "Sounds like I hit a nerve."

She stared at him for a moment before replying coolly, "Look, I don't mean to be rude, but I didn't ask you in so you could psychoanalyze me."

"You could always ask me to leave," he calmly pointed out.

She snorted. "Oh sure. You'd love that, wouldn't you? It would just prove your point—that I'm a hopeless neurotic who can't stand hearing the truth."

"If the shoe fits . . ." He smiled, reminding her that he hadn't been born yesterday; he knew perfectly well what all this bluster was about: Brian. Something had happened here tonight with Brian. Something she apparently felt guilty about. But, why? Because of Rachel? Or, as she was implying now, because of Max? Either way, where the hell did that leave *him*?

"I still miss my husband, yes. Is that what you want to hear? Rose's expression grew fierce. "I miss him so much sometimes I can hardly stand it. Haven't you ever felt that way? Haven't you ever loved someone so much it hurt just to *breathe* when you weren't with her?"

"Once." *Are you blind, Rose? Don't you see it?*

She pulled back, regarding him with new curiosity. Finally, she asked, "What went wrong?"

Eric felt the kernel inside him send up a small green shoot. *Nothing. Yet.* Because damnit, he wasn't giving up—and he wouldn't let Rose give up, either, not if he had anything to say about it.

"It's a long story," he said. "I'll tell you about it sometime."

She leaned against the counter at her back, the barest glimmer of a smile touching her lips. "You haven't eaten your bagel. Shall I wrap it up to go?" She seemed to have forgotten all about their tea, and was oblivious even to the hissing of the kettle.

"Is that a hint?"

"It's late," she said. "I should get to bed."

"I won't keep you, then."

Eric pulled himself to his feet, the sound of his chair scraping over the floor tiles causing her bird, asleep under the cloth covering its cage, to stir. He wanted badly to take her into his arms—almost enough to risk what he knew would be the world's worst timing.

Instead, he walked over to the stove and switched off the burner under the kettle.

When he looked over at Rose, her head was tilted to one side, and she was eyeing him in an odd way—as if daring him. "Go ahead," she urged sarcastically, "you might as well just say it."

"Say what?"

"Aren't you going to remind me that life goes on? That I'm still young, and should think about getting married again? I've already heard it from practically everyone else." She folded her arms over her chest, her robe falling open a bit. She was breathing heavily, and he could see a line of moisture glistening faintly between her heavy breasts.

It was driving him crazy; if he didn't get out of here, this very minute, he *would* kiss her. And more.

"What I'm offering here isn't advice," he told her.

He let his words hang between them, measuring their effect in the hot depths of her eyes. She was the first to look away, and it pierced him somehow, pierced him to the core.

"What I said before, about Mandy?" she replied softly. "I meant it, Eric. I can't handle one more thing right now."

There was no mistaking her meaning . . . and nothing left to say. For now, for tonight, he'd just have to walk away.

Eric found himself remembering a trip to Paris some years back. Wandering through a church cemetery, where he'd stumbled across an ancient, lichen-encrusted headstone. Simple, unadorned—just a woman's name, and the dates of her birth and death, with a brief inscription above it, so worn it was almost indecipherable: *Tout Mon Amour, Toujours.*

All My Love, Always.

He'd been inexplicably moved, unable to imagine the depth of feeling behind that simple expression of a husband's grief. Now he understood. Deep down, it must have been what he, too, after years of giving only pieces of himself to women who'd deserved better, had wanted. To love someone that much—a woman in whose eyes he would see the reflection of everything he felt. A love that would endure, even after death.

Chapter 7

Rose was sweating under her white rayon blouse. Jury selection? More like torture, she thought. The endless drip, drip, drip of the same questions asked over and over. One answer bleeding into the next, as interminable as the last day of school before summer. Even the windowless room in which she sat, down the hall from the main jury pool, reminded Rose of her days at Sacred Heart—the austere counsel table opposite rows of wooden seats bolted to the floor, the atmosphere of cowed intimidation.

From her seat at the table she watched the opposing counsel, Mark Cannizzaro, pace the scuffed strip of floor separating them from the first row of prospective jurors, and thought, *Yeah, it fits.*

Esposito v. *St. Bartholomew's Hospital* as the Gospel According to St. Mark.

The way he was carrying on, like Clarence Darrow making his closing statement in the Scopes trial, except Mark reminded her more of Lieutenant Columbo—short and dark, with lousy posture. Everything about him rumpled, from his coarse black hair to the tan socks he wore with his navy Capezios.

Lord, she thought. If he got this worked up over voir dire, imagine what he'd be like once the actual trial was under way. Rose imagined herself smacking the back of his hand with a ruler, like the nuns used to do.

The very hand that right now was gesturing theatrically in accompaniment to questions any child would have known to ask, while Mark zeroed in like a hawk on the would-be juror seated before him—a retired schoolteacher from Central Casting, complete with regulation gray bun and half-moon glasses clipped to a chain around her wattled neck.

"Mrs. Merriman, this next question is *very* important, so, please, take your time, and give it some thought." Mark's voice husky with false portent, his heavy eyebrows raised so high they were nearly touching his dense hairline. "Honestly, now, would you have a difficult time finding *against* a seventy-six-year-old woman left partially paralyzed after routine surgery—even if the evidence and testimony should *fail* to prove my client's stroke was a result of the hospital's negligence?"

Translation: *We all know the doctors screwed up, and I'm going to prove it, but in the meantime, are you willing to play along?*

Rose squirmed in her seat. Really, this was too much. He'd been like this all morning; even the prospective jurors, judging from their expressions—which ranged from bored to outright disgusted—were fed up with Mark's crude attempt to twist things around, and make it look as if being favorably disposed toward St. Bartholomew's would somehow imply that they felt no sympathy for poor old Mrs. Esposito.

Except Mrs. Merriman, it seemed. To Rose's dismay, it appeared that Mark's cleverness in mentioning the age of his client was having an effect on her. The schoolteacher's face grew even more pinched, and her eyes narrowed. Rose guessed she was in her mid-seventies—a member in good standing of the AARP, no doubt. The type who'd spit on anyone low enough to bamboozle, much less cripple, a fellow Gray Panther.

Rose felt a worm of uneasiness burrow into her belly. True, Mark Cannizzaro was nine-tenths hot air and macho bluster. Based on what he'd presented in discovery, he had no solid evidence against her client. But with medical-malpractice cases, she knew, you couldn't discount the sympathy quotient. What juror *wouldn't* feel sorry for an elderly Hispanic woman scraping by on Social Security, who spoke only broken English—and now was confined to a wheelchair?

Never mind that Carmen Esposito was about as helpless as a fox in a henhouse, and that both her English and her stroke-induced aphasia faded in and out depending on who she was talking to. And in anticipation of the fat judgment she was confident she'd be awarded, the sly old lady had already charged up a storm on her daughter's credit card—new TV, new sofa, new everything.

What Rose also knew was that any attempt to paint Mrs. Esposito as a greedy opportunist would have to be handled very, very carefully. Too heavy-handed an approach could backfire; she'd seen it happen, time and again. And that would be a mistake she couldn't afford.

She *needed* to win this case; the stakes were too high. In a low-income neighborhood stalked by ambulance-chasers like Mark, forever on the prowl for telltale signs of blood, a sizable "sympathy" judgment would leave St. Bart's wide open to a slew of other, similar suits.

No, she couldn't afford a juror like Mrs. Merriman. . . .

She took several deep breaths, steeling herself. When Mark was finally finished with his grandstanding, Rose stood up. She strolled slowly, purposefully around the table, hoping her confident expression would fool at least some of the people looking blankly back at her. Underneath her perfectly-ironed expression, though, she felt as jittery as six cups of coffee on an empty stomach.

She perched on a corner of the counsel table, smoothing her skirt over her knees, and smiling at the retired schoolteacher as if she were an old student paying homage. In a low, conversational voice, she asked, "Mrs. Merriman, do you smoke?"

The old woman flashed Rose a startled look that immediately escalated to indignation. Drawing herself up even straighter, she replied crisply, "I should say not!"

"You mean, if you'd caught one of your students smoking, you wouldn't have approved?"

"It happened . . . on more than one occasion," Mrs. Merriman recalled tartly. "I never punished them, but I always gave them the facts—that cigarettes were habit-forming, and caused cancer . . . among other things." Now she was peering suspiciously up at Rose. "Why? Does it have something to do with this case?"

Mark, too, was glowering at Rose, his naturally ruddy complexion deepening alarmingly. She was straddling the line, she knew. One step in the wrong direction, and he'd insist—rightfully—that the whole bunch be dismissed on grounds that their impartiality had been tampered with.

Ignoring him, Rose plowed on. "Let me put it this way: if you were to learn that Mr. Cannizzaro's client, prior to her surgery, had been a longtime smoker, would it prejudice you against her?"

For the first time, the old biddy appeared flustered. Fiddling with her eyeglass chain, she stammered, "Why, I suppose . . . I can't imagine . . . Well, goodness, I don't know."

"Thank you, Mrs. Merriman. That'll be all." Rose excused her with all the somber regret she could muster—as if her working in that Mrs. Esposito had been a smoker were an innocent slip, nothing more. As if she hadn't purposely set out to eliminate this particular juror.

Rose ignored Mark, now madly scribbling on his legal pad. She wanted to savor her small triumph, but it was too soon. She hadn't won the war; she'd only succeeded in blocking a single juror. Without using up one of her precious pre-emptory challenges—this one, surely, Mark would pass on first. Max, she thought wistfully, would have been proud.

But all *she* felt was empty.

Suddenly it seemed as if the lifeline Rose had been clinging to—the long hours and endless round of court dates that kept her from dwelling on her loneliness—was slipping from her grasp. The water she'd been treading surged up in a wave that threatened to drown her. She'd been like this since the night before last, when she'd had her talk with Brian. But it wasn't Brian making her gasp for air, she knew. It was . . .

Eric.

She'd imagined that keeping Eric at arm's length would make her stronger, more able to resist him, but in the end, it had only left her more vulnerable. God, she'd wanted him. So badly that, after his brief visit, she'd lain awake in bed for hours, aching and hot as if with a fever. If he'd kissed her, as Brian had—and as she'd known Eric wanted to—there would have been no stopping. And where would that have led?

One glorious night in bed, she reminded herself, even one that blossomed into a glorious affair, was too high a price to pay for the upheaval it would cause, now and later on. She was half in love with Eric already. Dear God, if she were to *sleep* with him . . .

She'd be lost altogether.

Rose gave herself a little mental shake, and sat down to await the next prospective juror. She thought: *This is what I'm good at. What I have some control over.* Yes, that was it. Control. She needed to stay focused. Not just on her work—this case—but on her children. Drew and Jay, and, yes, Mandy, too.

Max? He was part of the picture as well. She had so little left of him, just memories . . . and the time she spent alone, reliving them. Allowing Eric inside would cause those memories to fade.

She'd loved only two men in her life. And twice she'd had to pick up the pieces of a shattered heart.

Rose wasn't stupid enough to believe she could spend the rest of her life playing the Italian widow. She missed hearing a man's voice calling to her from the shower, and the sound of newspaper rustling across the breakfast table. Sex, too—God, yes—she missed the sex. But was that enough to justify disrupting the whole, carefully balanced egg crate of her life?

No, she thought.

It all boiled down to one thing: you had to hold something of yourself back. Isn't that what she needed to somehow get across to Drew? But before she could teach her sons, she'd have to learn that lesson for herself. . . .

❧ "Mom? I'm going over to Drew's—okay?"

Rose looked up from the pot she was stirring on the stove. Jason hovered in the kitchen doorway, a teenaged scarecrow in baggy shorts and a T-shirt that was miles too big. His eyes were downcast; his thick brown hair, with its paler highlights, fell over his forehead.

She sighed, shutting off the burner under the marinara sauce— enough for an army. After getting through this morning's ordeal down at the courthouse, then spending most of the afternoon in a chilly conference room uptown taking depositions for a case involving sex discrimination, she'd been looking forward to a companionable evening at home with her sons. She'd even left the office early so that she would have enough time to fix a nice supper from scratch.

"What about dinner? I thought Drew was coming *here.*" Rose felt something sting her calf below the hem of her skirt and looked down; a drop of sauce had dribbled off the spoon she held frozen in midair.

"Oh yeah. I forgot. He said to tell you he can't make it." Jay glanced up, then down again—so quickly only a mother would have caught the furtive gleam in his eyes.

"You're telling me *now?* What does it look like I'm doing here— getting ready to open a soup kitchen? The least your brother could have done was let me know ahead of time." Her voice rose, and she winced at the Brooklynese inflections that had crept in—something that only happened when she was angry or overtired, or, as in this case, both.

Jay was chewing on his lower lip, a bad sign. Addressing the toes of his grubby sneakers, he muttered, "Something must've come up. He said he'd call later on and explain."

Rose fixed him with a steady gaze, willing him to look at her. Taking a deep breath, she asked, "Jay, what's *really* going on here? Why do I have the feeling you guys are keeping something from me?"

"Mom, it's no big deal. Would you just chill?" When Jay finally did look up at her, she flinched from the hot anger in his eyes. "If I had anything to hide, believe me, you wouldn't have a *clue.*"

Rose swallowed hard, and turned her gaze to the table around which they all used to gather at mealtime—the boys reaching over each other's plates, knobby elbows forever on the verge of knocking something over, while she and Max rolled their eyes and exchanged looks of fond exasperation. Oh God, she would give anything to have it all back. . . .

Now, whenever the three of them got together, they were like loose pieces from an old board game—bright-colored plastic markers with nowhere to go.

Looking back at her son, Rose saw that the jeans she'd bought him only a few months ago were already too short. He needed new sneakers, too. And a haircut. Why hadn't she noticed before? When had she last looked at his homework, or paid attention to what he was eating?

Poor Jay.

"Dinner can keep, I guess," she told him, her heart aching with all she wanted to say, but couldn't.

She watched Jay retrieve his backpack from the spindle-backed deacon's bench that stood against one wall like a ladder resting on its side. The bag's canvas pockets bulged suspiciously.

Jay saw her looking at it, and said defensively, "I was going to ask you. Drew said I could spend the night if I wanted."

Rose stepped away from the stove and walked over to him. Her legs, she realized with dismay, were trembling. She leaned close, close enough so that he'd have to look at her, and said, "Listen, buster, this isn't a hotel where you can just come and go as you please. You *live* here. We're a family, remember?"

He glared at her. She could feel her son's pain and anger radiating off him. Jay was nothing like his older brother, who wasn't ashamed to cry. Even as a very little boy, Jay would hold himself clenched like a fist, his face screwed up tight to keep from bawling. The way he was doing now, elbows tucked in against his rib cage, the muscles in his jaw working furiously. If Drew was like his father—for whom the proverbial glass hadn't been just half full but brimming over—Jay was like her: quick to imagine the worst, and slow to reveal his hurt.

Rose longed to go to him, take him in her arms. The last time she'd hugged her younger son had been at Max's funeral. Since then, he hadn't let her within summons-serving distance.

"Drew *is* my family," he replied coldly.

Rose ducked her head and rubbed the bridge of her nose, where pressure was building. "The big Tupperware container on top of the fridge, would you get it for me?" she asked, careful to maintain an even tone. "There's enough sauce here for a basketball team. I want you to take some to Drew."

"It's okay. We'll go out for pizza or something."

"Jay. I'm not asking. I'm *telling* you." She saw him take a step back, and realized she was practically shouting. This had nothing to do with making sure the boys ate a decent meal, she realized. It was to remind them that, whether they liked it or not, they still had a mother.

A mother who cared.

But Jay wasn't interested. In his hot, furious face, she read the whole story: he'd lost his father . . . and, in a way, his mother, too. Only Rose hadn't died—she'd abandoned him. Just when he'd needed her the most.

"Don't you get it?" he exploded. "We don't *want* your fucking spaghetti sauce. You only made it so we'd have to sit here and listen to everything that's the matter with us." His voice wobbled up an octave, then broke, reminding her of when he'd been thirteen and in the first awkward throes of puberty. "What about *you*, Mom? When was the last time you cooked dinner just because you felt like it? How come you never talk to us anymore unless something's wrong?"

His words were like tiny flung pebbles, their sharp edges pricking her. She watched Jay heave his overstuffed backpack onto his shoulder and shoot her a look of such scorn, it sliced her to the bone.

Then he was gone, vanishing from sight like a shadow slipping along a wall.

Rose wanted to go after him, but her feet wouldn't budge. She felt as hopelessly stuck as in the days right after Max's death. The things Jay had accused her of, they were all true. Except for tonight, when *was* the last time she'd cooked a real dinner? These days, their freezer resembled the frozen-food section in D'Agostino's—the casseroles and covered dishes from well-meaning friends and relatives had long since been eaten, or thrown out, and in their place were boxes of Stouffer's lasagne, Lean Cuisine, Hot Pockets, Sara Lee.

Rose sank into the nearest chair. The pressure in her sinuses had become a throbbing headache, but she was too tired even for the trip down the hall to the bathroom for an aspirin.

In the corner, Mr. Chips began to squawk, fluttering his wings and scattering pinfeathers over the table's polished oak surface like so many ashes. Time for the vet to clip his wings again, she thought. Not that there was much danger of her cockatiel's flying off. Poor thing, he'd been in that cage so long he actually seemed to prefer it to life outside.

She dropped her head into the crook of her arm, the tabletop cool against her cheek. It smelled of buttered toast and Pledge. How many glasses of spilled milk had she mopped up over the years? How many chins had she wiped? Did all of it count for nothing?

In her head, she heard Max's voice, faintly impatient this time: *It's not like money in the bank, Rosie. You have to keep spending it in order to earn it back.*

With a cry of frustration, she jumped to her feet and raced over to the stove. Blindly, without thinking, she seized the pot of spaghetti sauce and heaved it into the sink. Watching it swirl down the drain—blood-red that faded to watery pink when she turned on the tap—Rose was filled with fury. Not at Jay. Or Drew. But at herself. All that wasted time and energy, fantasizing about how she could have saved Max, when all along her children had been right here . . . and she'd done nothing, absolutely nothing, to save *them*.

She had to stop feeling sorry for herself. Stop wanting back what was lost forever. Max might be dead, but *she* was still alive. And it was high time she started acting like it.

Rose marched over to the bulletin board by the phone, which had become a junkyard of mostly forgotten reminders stuck up with bright pushpins—pink message slips, old shopping lists, a wrinkled dry-cleaning ticket, an invitation to some long-past charity event she'd neglected to respond to—and tugged free the slip of paper on which Eric's number was scribbled.

Before she could talk herself out of it, she was punching in the numbers, wondering if there was still a chance, however slim, that Eric was free for dinner tonight.

❧ "You subscribe to this? I'm impressed."

Rose, rummaging for her keys on the cluttered bachelor's chest by the entrance to the staircase, turned to look at Eric. He was seated on the sofa, thumbing through an old issue of *Harvard Business Review* he'd picked up off the coffee table. His blue eyes regarded her with bemused admiration, as if nothing she did or said would have surprised him.

"It's my husband's," she told him. "I haven't gotten around to canceling it." She would, though—first thing tomorrow.

Just thinking about it made her feel lighter somehow, as if a weight she hadn't even realized she was carrying had been lifted from her shoulders.

She wished she could feel as easy about Eric. Over the phone, he'd seemed hesitant at first—could she blame him, after the way she'd acted last time?—but when he arrived a few minutes ago, he'd greeted her as if nothing were wrong. Even so, she'd detected a certain reserve.

Was Eric having second thoughts? After the way she'd acted the other night, had he concluded that she was more trouble than she might be worth?

Or maybe, she thought, he'd merely come to his senses and realized what he'd be getting into with her. Not just Mandy, but the whole combination plate: Max, the boys, her law practice.

She wasn't getting any younger, either.

A stitch of anxiety formed in her stomach.

Relax. It's not the Last Supper, soothed a voice in her head. Just dinner with a friend at her favorite bistro, down the block. As soon as she could find those damn keys . . .

That reminded her: Mandy had stopped by this afternoon to ask—somewhat sheepishly—if Rose had an extra set of keys to the office. Her own, she said, had been missing since the night of the party. Rose had made a mental note to check with Eric but guessed that Mandy, as drunk as she'd been, had misplaced them somewhere in her apartment. And hadn't she been sloshed at last Tuesday's partners' meeting, too? Yes, Rose was sure of it.

Her thoughts were interrupted by Eric's recalling with wry affection, "My dad belonged to this book club, and after he died, the books kept right on coming. Mom just lets them pile up. Once, when I asked why she pays for books she doesn't read, she said she likes having them arrive in the mail each month—the same as if Dad were still around."

"I'm sorry about your father. Was it recent?" Rose realized that, as much as she'd told him about herself, she knew very little about Eric. He was too good a listener.

"Six years ago. Cancer." He smiled sadly, as if remembering something too personal to be shared. Then said, "You know what gets me the most? That he never saw me sober."

Rose felt her throat tighten at the thought of all the events yet to come that Max would never witness: graduations, weddings, births. "You obviously weren't raised Catholic," she observed, somewhat dryly.

"Close enough. Episcopal." He cocked his head, giving her a puzzled look.

"Well, then, I don't have to tell you. The Great Scoreboard in the

Sky—it lights up every time you make a home run. Your dad is probably cheering from the bleachers even as we speak."

He smiled. "Sounds like the Yankees versus the Dodgers."

"A hundred to nothing. World Series, 1956," she supplied.

They both laughed.

"What about your mom?" Rose inquired.

"Alive and well in Minneapolis." He leaned forward to rap his knuckles lightly against the coffee table. "At seventy-one, would you believe it, she's discovered the Internet. She e-mails me every other day. Usually about some exotic trip she's planning."

"If she's anything like you, it doesn't surprise me." Rose thought of Sylvie and felt a flicker of old sadness.

He shook his head. "If you could have seen her just after my dad died . . . Hell, all she did was watch TV and knit afghans. It's as if she's been transformed into this whole other person. She's actually starting to read some of those books that come in the mail. She's even *dating*." Eric grinned. "My brother can't forgive her for that."

"I didn't know you had a brother."

"Kenny. He's an orthopedist. Wife, three kids, lives in St. Paul. We talk on the phone every so often, but we're not close."

"No sisters?"

"Nope." Eric tossed the magazine down, linked his hands behind his head, and tilted back to look up at her. "*Your* sisters, on the other hand . . ." He hesitated, then asked, "Can I be honest?"

"Might as well."

"They're nothing like you. Not one bit. It's like you came from different families."

Rose froze. Eric wasn't the first to have said it, but for some reason, coming from him, it struck a nerve. Maybe because it would have been so easy to confide in him, as she had about so much else. She thought, *What would that accomplish? Except give him one more reason to feel sorry for me.*

In an attempt to cover her uneasiness, she joked, "Maybe I was left on the doorstep by gypsies."

"Now, *that* would make sense." He laughed heartily, and she felt a current of electricity shoot straight down through her belly.

It was his eyes, she thought. They were fixed on her in a way she found faintly unsettling. He seemed to be waiting for something . . . some signal.

He's looking at me the way Max used to.

Rose had to turn away, so he wouldn't see how much she wanted him, too. Tears filled her eyes, dissolving Eric's reflection, in the mirror over the mantel, to a watery shimmer. Only his shirt stood out, plain white against the sofa's dark upholstery, like a crisp envelope with an invitation to some delicious event tucked inside.

Rose longed suddenly for him to take her, right now, right here. On the sofa, on the carpet, it didn't matter where. No words, no coy flirtation, no dipping in one toe at a time.

She realized she was trembling. She felt feverish—icy cold one minute, burning up the next. And, oh God, this wicked heat between her legs. What on earth was *happening* to her?

Rose swung around to face him, bracing herself against the shock of his unguarded gaze as she might have thrown up a hand to shield herself from a too-bright light.

"Eric? Something you mentioned the other night—I know it's none of my business, but I can't help wondering. That woman you spoke of—why didn't you marry her?"

"I didn't ask." He spoke quietly, those scrubbed blue eyes never leaving her face.

"Why not? If you loved her that much."

"There are some things you don't ask unless you know the answer."

He's still in love with her, she thought, surprised to realize she was jealous.

But that was crazy, she told herself. Why should she care?

"I don't mean to pry," she apologized. "It's just that . . ."

"Anything you want to know about me, just ask," he told her. "I have nothing to hide."

"Okay." She swallowed hard, and met his gaze. "Why did you agree to have dinner with me tonight?"

"I wanted to see you."

"But *why?*" she pressed, beyond caring how pathetic she must seem—a woman who barely knew her own mind, asking questions she wasn't at all certain she was prepared to have answered.

"I love you."

It was his eyes that held her pinned against the mantel while he rose and slowly walked toward her. His expression tender, and at the same time uncompromising. She couldn't tear her gaze from him— the wry curve of his mouth, the tiny hooked scar over his right eye, his schoolboy's hair falling over the forehead of a man who'd been through hell and still believed in second chances.

When he took her in his arms and kissed her, his mouth on hers was like a slow dance, the last of the evening, when the chairs are stacked on the tables and everyone else has gone home. Rose swayed against him. *Oh God, it's been so long. . . .*

It was as if she were waking up from a long sleep, senses that had been dormant sparking to life, one by one. The tip of his tongue setting off tiny shock waves as it traveled down her throat. His hand on the back of her neck almost scorching her.

He was tender, so tender. As if not wanting to frighten her. At the same time, there was nothing tentative about his desire. His whole body felt charged with it. Wordlessly, he unbuttoned her blouse, pushing it off her shoulders. But they couldn't seem to stop kissing long enough for her to wriggle out of her skirt. She had never known a man with more levels to his kissing than Eric, each one more dizzying than the last. Oh, sweet Jesus, how had she survived without this for so long?

Rose would have followed him anywhere. To Zanzibar—to the moon, even. It wasn't until Eric seized her by the wrist and they were heading for the bedroom down the hall that the spell broke. A cold wave of panic swept over her.

No . . . I can't. Not in the same bed where she and Max had . . .

But it was too late. Turning back was impossible. Rose felt crazed with wanting, so crazed that when she lay down with Eric on the bed—the bed on which she and her husband had made love more times than she could count—it felt no more strange than a river following its natural course.

And now here was this delicious man with skin like something sweet poured over a rich weave of muscle and bone. Touching her in places she'd nearly forgotten were capable of sensation. Cradling her breasts as if they'd been as firm and lovely as a virgin's. Lovingly exploring her belly with his tongue as he moved down between her legs . . .

And, oh, God, he was . . . It felt so good. . . .

Max had been a skilled and patient lover. But nothing like this. *Stop. Don't think about Max.*

Putting Max out of her mind was easier than it should have been, her thoughts scuttling away like leaves caught in a current. There was only Eric's naked body, his hot mouth, the mounting heat between her legs. . . .

It happened with the force of a collision—the orgasm she'd never believed possible, not for her, not *this* way. Slamming through her, wave after wave of the purest pleasure. Bending her up like an arched bow, her limbs quivering. *Jesus, Mary, and Joseph . . .*

A narcotic haze descended over her. It was as if she were dreaming, and in dreams there were no rules. She could scream, thrash, sweat rivers. As Eric mounted her, she wrapped her legs tightly about his, drawing him tight against her. Beads of sweat from his forehead dropped onto her face like tiny warm kisses. He moved inside her, deep thrusts followed by slow gliding strokes, until she was once again on the verge of coming. She hovered deliciously. It seemed they could go on like this forever. She felt the muscles in his back go taut, but he was holding back, waiting until she'd had her fill.

"Your turn," she urged.

"Not yet," he whispered.

Rose moaned softly as he quickened, then slowed. Then she *was* coming. Again. Straining against him while he kissed her, catching her lower lip lightly between his teeth, filling her mouth with the taste of her own womanhood, like some forbidden fruit.

Not until she was spent, and lay gasping in his arms, did Eric allow himself to come, too: a single, almost savage thrust that tore a harsh cry from his throat.

It was several minutes before either of them could speak.

"Rose?" His voice was a low rustle in the darkness.

"What?"

"I meant what I said before."

She rolled onto her side so that she was facing him. In the dim light from the hallway, Eric's eyes gleamed. She felt an ache now where there had been only sweet release.

"I can't promise you anything," she told him.

"I'm not asking you to."

"What if this whole thing turns out to be a mistake?"

He tensed. "It won't. Whatever happens."

She shivered. "That's the part that worries me. Not knowing."

He was quiet for so long she began to feel panicky. Had she revealed too much? And, God, what if he *had* really meant it? How could she love him back? There was no place in her twice-mended heart strong enough for love to grow.

Then came that smoky voice again, rising out of the darkness—the voice of someone who'd learned the hard way not to pack more than he could carry.

"One day at a time, okay?" Smiling a little, he touched her cheek.

Past his shoulder, Rose could see into the bathroom, where a patch of blue terrycloth—the robe that hung on the back of the door—was reflected in the medicine-cabinet mirror. Max's robe. It brought memories of the day, shortly after the funeral, when Mandy had helped her empty Max's closets. The two of them briskly packing up sweaters, shirts, slacks, suits. Labeling boxes, putting everything in order for the Housing Authority Thrift Shop. Even managing to wring a small laugh out of a pair of never-worn reindeer-printed boxer shirts—a joke Christmas gift from a client.

The robe had somehow escaped the purge. Rose didn't notice it until after Mandy had left. Since then, it had become her secret vice—like Mandy's drinking. She hoarded it, sneaking into the bathroom every so often just to bury her head in its nappy folds, inhale her husband's scent. She knew it was holding her back in some way, but couldn't seem to stop.

Tomorrow would be exactly one year since Max's death.

She looked back at Eric, his profile outlined in the soft light, as clearly as a horizon. Oddly, she felt a pang of loss, not for Max, but for what she'd be throwing away if she turned her back on this chance.

One day at a time, that's all he was asking.

Could she give him that much?

You've made it through three hundred and sixty-four, urged the voice in her head. *What's one more?*

Chapter 8

🌺 Mandy Griffin stole a glance at her wristwatch, and thought, *Fifteen minutes, tops. Then I'm home free.* From where she sat, alongside her client at the polished beech conference table, across from Robert Greene and *his* client, she could see through the floor-to-ceiling glass wall into the reception area just beyond—a cool island of pale woods and brushed nickel, with double doors leading out to the elevators . . . and to salvation.

Luigi's wasn't far, just two blocks from the office—a low-key Italian restaurant with a bar tucked away in back, where the lights were low, the TV always on, and, most important, the drinks never stopped coming. She saw herself perched on a leather-padded stool, hefting a Jack Daniel's double on the rocks, the glass heavy in her hand, its icy cold numbing her fingertips . . . and was swept by a longing so intense it was all she could do not to bolt for the door.

Mandy gripped the arms of her chair. Her temples throbbed; each pulsebeat like a tidal surge squeezing through a narrow rocky inlet. Her mouth tasted of cotton balls dipped in rubbing alcohol, dry and faintly astringent.

Stay cool, she commanded herself. *You can't let them see.*

She directed her gaze at Robert, whose dark head was bent over the sheet of figures she'd just handed him—her proposed distributive award for the soon-to-be-ex–Mrs. Rifkin. Robert, she noted approvingly, wasn't allowing the rudeness of his client—bald, portly Mr. Rifkin, shifting in his chair like an overgrown first-grader—to distract him. In his slate-gray suit and Dunhill tie, a platinum watch thin as caviar toast showing below one starched cuff, Robert was every inch the white-shoe gentleman.

As polite and well mannered now as he'd been last night, when she'd declined his invitation to stay over—for the third time in less than three weeks. He'd said that he understood, and that, yes, if it got out, the Rifkins *might* take it the wrong way. He'd even kissed her lightly on the mouth as she was getting out of the cab.

But appearances, Mandy knew all too well, could be deceiving. Now she wondered, did he guess? The Rifkins, she thought with a stab of guilt, had been the furthest thing from her mind last night. The truth was that, as much as she enjoyed Robert's company—*desired* him, even—nothing was more alluring than the privacy of her own home, where she could drink freely, as much as she wanted.

You're imagining things, she told herself. If Robert had even the slightest idea, wouldn't his disgust show? When she'd suggested they get together this weekend instead, wouldn't he have made an excuse of his own?

Robert, as if sensing Mandy's anxious scrutiny, glanced up at her. He was rubbing his chin—a habit she found both endearing and somewhat irritating. "Off the top of my head, Mandy, I've got to say, eighty thousand for the contents of the Boca Raton residence seems pretty steep." He flashed her a smile that said, *Let's stop kidding around and get down to business.* "I know it's insured for that much, but—come on—realistically, what's the resale value here?"

"The yacht's included in that," piped Flora Rifkin, a gimlet-eyed blonde of a certain age, interchangeable with a thousand other wives of Jewish manufacturing barons who'd migrated to the East Sixties by way of the Grand Concourse. All of them, like Flora, with lacquered hair and nails, wearing chunky gold earrings and toting quilted Chanel handbags.

Tightly wrapped, Mandy thought. That's how Dad would have described Flora. The kind of package you opened carefully, lest it contain something other than new bank checks, or the latest offering from Fruit-of-the-Month Club.

"Yacht? You call that toy boat a *yacht?*" roared Leo, her estranged husband. "What, I'm Ari Onassis all of a sudden? A Sunday outing with the Freedmans is high-seas adventure?"

"Call it what you like. It's yours, Leo. *You* wanted Boca, so you could loll around all day watching Miss Sports Illustrated show off those boobs you bought her." Flora made a scornful gesture with a clawlike hand cured by the Florida sun into pemmican. "Me? I'll take the money. You want this divorce, buster, you got it . . . but, like I said, it's gonna cost you. Big. A lot bigger than what that *shiksele* of yours has stuffed in her bra."

"You leave Tamara out of it!" Leo's beefy face flushed an alarming red. Head wagging, he turned to Robert with an aggrieved look. "You see? You *see* what I've had to put up with?"

Robert, looking faintly embarrassed, cleared his throat and said, "Look, there's no reason we can't all be civilized about—"

"Civilized? Is that what you call shtupping a girl young enough to be your granddaughter?" Fury had twisted Flora Rifkin's heavily made-up face into a Kabuki mask. "Forty years, and this is what I have to show for it? An *alter kocker* for a husband, who doesn't have the decency to pay what he owes!"

Leo hauled himself to his feet. His pale-blue eyes bulged from the puffy flesh surrounding them, making him appear, in that moment, almost comical—Ralph Kramden bellowing, *One of these days, Alice, I swear . . .*

He jabbed a stubby finger at his wife. "I don't have to listen to this! You think I need another ulcer on top of the one you already gave me? Next time I see you, lady, will be in court."

Mandy's head was pounding like a St. Patrick's Day parade, and she had a sinking feeling that her escape wasn't so imminent. Sweet Jesus. How much longer—ten, fifteen minutes? Could she hang on that long? *Yes, of course you can,* a brisk voice assured her . . . a voice that made her think of her mother, when Mandy was little, declaring impatiently that she couldn't have to go *that* bad, surely she could hold it in until they found a restroom.

Bartender . . . make that two *doubles.*

Mandy, stepping outside herself for an instant, felt appalled. My God, had it gotten as bad as all that? It used to be she'd merely looked forward with pleasant anticipation to the bourbon and soda that awaited her at the end of the day. Now, swallowing hard against the dryness of her throat, she felt nearly sick with need. She could almost *taste* it—the chilled kiss of the glass against her bottom lip, that first tingling rush. It it were in front of her now, she wouldn't be able to resist. . . .

But drinking on the job, everyone knew, was strictly *verboten.* Even at lunch, Mandy seldom indulged in more than a glass of wine. Weeknights, too, she kept it to a minimum, unable to afford a major hangover. In ten years, she'd called in sick, oh, maybe five, six times. If anything, the other partners complained she was *too* compulsive about her work—it made them look bad, they joked.

But lately it was as if the internal brakes that used to respond to her slightest touch had grown glassy and sluggish. Each time, she had to pump a little harder . . . and even so she often felt herself skidding off the road. Her only defense was to remind herself, over and over, that if she had a problem it was nothing like that associate, Stan Mays, who'd worked here briefly, a few years back . . . before he was packed off to rehab in disgrace. Or how would she have been able to bill so many hours each month?

If everyone else slaved as hard as I do, they'd need a drink after work, too, she reasoned. Anyway, what was she talking about here? A couple of bourbons in the evening, just to unwind. If not for that, she'd never leave here; she'd work herself right into the ground.

It's not as if I'm an alcoholic.

Feeling stronger, Mandy spoke up confidently. "Mr. Rifkin, do you have any idea what taking this to court would cost you?" She leaned on her elbows, fixing him with her bulletproof gaze—perfected through years of handling difficult divorces. "Try two years of your life, and that's just for starters. By the time you walk out of that courtroom, you'll be at least a million out of pocket on legal fees alone. And as far as the distributive award goes, what judge wouldn't feel sympathetic toward a wife of forty years you abandoned for a younger woman?"

Leo opened his mouth and shut it again, like a fat goldfish. He dropped back into his chair so heavily that a little *chuff* of air was forced from its cushion—a sound that made Mandy think of the polite euphemism used by her mother—living in Florida now, God bless her 401(k)—for breaking wind: "poot."

Yes, she thought, that about summed it up. Leo Rifkin was nothing more than a silly, overblown poot.

Mandy had to clamp her lips tightly shut to keep from snickering. She was on the verge of really losing it, she knew. Her craving for a drink, like a long drought, had left her so parched, she was actually cracking apart inside. Even her stomach was burning now, making her think of the Alka Selzer she always kept on hand in the credenza behind her desk. That, and a fifth of Jack Daniel's—her first-aid kit, to be cracked open only in the event of a true emergency. Just knowing it was there brought a measure of comfort, its unbroken seal assuring her she wasn't anything like *them*—the bums she passed every day on her way to work, huddled in doorways with their wrinkled paper bags, reeking of cheap liquor.

Across the table, Mandy caught Robert's eye. He was frowning slightly, as if puzzled about something. God. Why was he *looking* at her like that? Had he guessed that, on the inside, she wasn't anything like the plastic Mandy doll she dressed each morning with such elaborate care? Powdering her nose to cover the tiny broken veins, making up her eyes to hide their puffiness.

Or, worse, did he suspect that the bottle of merlot they'd killed with dinner was merely a warm-up for what she'd put away after she got home?

Mandy was flooded with shame. Then something even more disturbing occurred to her. *He probably thinks it's something* he *did.*

She winced at the thought, wishing there was some way of reassuring him. It wasn't his fault. Robert didn't deserve this. Besides, she adored him. Honestly. He was kind, considerate, sexy, and intelligent. Handsome, too. That rare man her single girlfriends believed extinct.

Robert had only one major flaw: he didn't drink. Not to speak of. An occasional cocktail, wine with dinner, that kind of thing. She couldn't imagine him snatching back from a too-eager waitress a glass with a thimbleful of wine still left in it. And surely he'd have been hurt to know that the whole time they'd been holding hands at dinner—even during her bitchy imitation of Judge Forrester, which nearly gave him a hernia from laughing—she'd been eyeing the bottle on the table between them, gauging how soon she could pour herself a refill, and how much she could get away with before he started to notice she'd drunk much more than he.

Now, in the sleek conference room that always made her feel a bit queasy, as if she were in a glass elevator, Mandy saw that Robert's put-out expression was softening into one of admiration and affection. She relaxed, feeling some of her tension drain away. Incredible. He actually *believed* that what he saw was what he got.

God, let me out of here before I blow it.

Leo Rifkin was looking at her with respect as well—the kind you got for playing hardball with the big boys. She thought of her father, how strong he'd been, strong in ways the Leo Rifkins of the world couldn't begin to imagine. Wise, too. *It's simple, Monkey,* he'd say, ruffling her hair and smiling down at her as if no one else in the world was more important. *The secret to success is in truly believing you're as smart as the next person.*

Monkey. His nickname for her since she was a baby. But now she seemed to have a monkey of her own, sitting squarely on her back, and she didn't feel very smart. If she were, wouldn't she have been able to figure out a way to quit drinking? To put a lid on things before she *did* become an alcoholic.

Oh God, Daddy. Tears pressed behind her eyes. She had to look down quickly, pretending to scribble a note on her legal pad.

"What's everyone so excited about?" Leo boomed with ersatz

good cheer. "I blow off a little steam, and suddenly we're in court? Listen, I'm a reasonable man, but I can only be pushed so far."

Flora was dabbing at her eyes with a corner of her handkerchief rolled up so it wouldn't smudge her mascara. "I'm sorry." She sniffed. "I'm still not used to it. Season tickets to Carnegie Hall, how do you divide a thing like that? Tell me, Leo, how?"

"You alternate," Mandy suggested, not unkindly. She didn't add that some people—her stepmother, for instance—didn't even have that option. The first season at the Met after Daddy died, the nights Rose couldn't give away the extra ticket, she'd stayed home rather than face the empty seat next to hers.

Robert, flicking her a grateful look, quickly took up the rear, proposing, "As far as the Boca contents go, the reasonable thing, in my opinion, would be to have it independently appraised."

After a moment's reflection, Leo nodded.

Flora nodded, too, prompting Mandy to counter with, "*Two* appraisals. We go with the highest." She looked sternly at Leo. "We're not talking about profits from a garage sale here. Should my client wish to purchase a vacation home of her own, she'll need to furnish it. And buying new, as we all know, isn't cheap."

"Remember that first apartment of ours, Flo? Grand Street and Avenue A," Leo recalled with a low chuckle, shaking his head. "No hot water after nine P.M., except on Sundays." Mandy could have sworn there were tears in his eyes.

"Five flights, and we had to lug everything up." Flora's mouth flickered in a smile, and Mandy saw that her coral lipstick had bled into tiny pleats around her lips. "And the landlord's nine kids, the noise. *We* should have been so lucky. If we'd been blessed with children . . ." She dabbed at her eyes again, then, with a huge sigh, drew herself up straight. "Enough. When you remember what it counted for, Leo, all those years, have your lawyer call mine. Meanwhile, have a nice life." She rose abruptly, snatching her Chanel bag from the table, its chain strap making a hissing sound against the polished wood.

Mandy glanced at Robert, who shrugged and looked over at his client.

Leo, palms flat against the table, made a show of pushing himself to his feet. Mopping his glistening pate with the handkerchief he fished from the pocket of his tailored fat-man trousers, he heaved a massive sigh, as if to establish who the *real* injured party was here.

Robert began gathering up papers, shoveling them into his briefcase.

Mandy nearly wept with relief.

At the door, Leo Rifkin extended his hand. She hesitated before taking it, praying he wouldn't notice how clammy hers was. Not until she'd ushered the Rifkins out, and had returned for a few words in private with Robert, did she feel the invisible wing nut between her shoulders loosen a half-turn.

"Nice work," he praised. "Looks like you may have saved us a couple more years of those two." Privately, they'd dubbed the Rifkins the Dynamic Duo.

She cocked her head in a wry smile. "Since when do you object to billing in the six figures?"

"Since this divorce started cutting into my time with you," he replied in a low, intimate voice. He brushed an invisible speck of lint from the lapel of her pink linen jacket, no doubt cognizant of their being on display to the secretaries, associates, paralegals scurrying down the corridor on the other side of the glass partition—all those in a hurry to catch a train, or get home for dinner . . . or a drink.

Looking up into his hazel eyes—eyes that shifted from green to amber, depending on the light, with lashes thick enough to inspire envy in a fashion model—Mandy felt wrenched. *Why isn't he enough?* Most women would have killed for a man like Robert. And here she was throwing away everything those amazing eyes seemed to promise.

"I miss you, too." Only she kept her voice light, teasing almost.

"You could have fooled me. Last night, you acted like you couldn't wait to get rid of me." He was smiling, but she could see the question in his face.

She stiffened, and it took all her training to keep smiling. "You're right . . . but it was in a good cause," she hedged.

"And what might that be, counselor?"

"The proposal for Mrs. Rifkin—I wanted to go over it one more time before I hit the sack. Good thing, too, or this meeting would've dragged on even longer. I don't know about you, but I've had enough of the Rifkins to last *three* lifetimes." She made a show of rolling her eyes.

Robert laughed knowingly, and the moment of tension evaporated. Mandy seized the opportunity to glance at her watch. "Listen, Robert, I've got to run. I'm meeting a client downtown."

"I'll drop you off," he said. "I have a car waiting outside."

Guessing he was on his way back to his office, at Madison and Forty-fifth, she took a gamble, and said, "Thanks, but it's on the West Side. I'll catch a cab."

He grabbed his briefcase and fell into step with her as she headed out the door. "We still on for Thursday?"

Thursday? Had they made a date? Mandy struggled to remember.

Robert must have seen the confusion in her face, because he sounded a little surprised at having to remind her. "The reception at the Carlyle, for Cynthia. Remember?"

"Of course," she lied, feeling herself start to sweat. Cynthia Robbins, one of her oldest friends, had just made partner at Cravath, Swaine. How could she have forgotten?

You must have been drunk.

Mandy suddenly felt weighed down by the burden of her secret self. There was so *much* Robert didn't know, and that she couldn't explain. There was absolutely no logic to it, unless you understood that everything in her life flowed from a single, working premise: drinking came first.

God knew she *wanted* what Robert was offering. Everything her father and Rose had had—love, passion, marriage. A partnership of two professionals supporting one another emotionally as well as financially. Kids, too. She'd be thirty-four her next birthday.

If she could get a handle on this thing, maybe, just maybe, the life she'd imagined would come true. If she could find a way to not always *need* that next drink . . .

It was so close now, she could almost taste it. The sweet burn of the bourbon going down, melting into her veins, and loosening her joints. In her mind, she could hear the rattle of ice cubes, and felt warmed by the liquor's amber glow.

Mandy had to clutch her briefcase to her chest in order to keep from flying past Robert, flying right out into the street. Luigi's, two blocks away, beckoned like the Emerald City at the end of a Yellow Brick Road that wasn't on any map.

On the crowded sidewalk, as he was heading for the curb where his chauffeured car was idling, Robert turned to Mandy, his handsome face open—and utterly clueless. "I'll call you later. Will you be home?"

"Where else?" She rolled her eyes, hefting her briefcase to show how much work she had. A lie that wasn't really a lie. Robert didn't have to know she had other plans for this evening as well. Plans that didn't include him, or anyone.

"You never quit, do you?"

For a panicked moment, she imagined his remark had to do with her drinking. Then reason kicked in. Work. Of course. He was always kidding her about working too hard. And right now, it was just the opening she needed.

"Leave a message if I don't pick up. I'll probably have my machine on," she told him, feeling sick inside, and hating herself more than ever.

But even as she kissed Robert goodbye, Mandy was already miles away, wondering which of the three liquor stores among which she alternated she should stop at tonight, after Luigi's, on her way home.

➷➷ The following morning, at seven-thirty, Mandy was at her desk with a large paper cup of Starbucks coffee growing cold at her elbow.

Her secretary wouldn't be in for at least another hour, but in addition to preparing a list of phone calls for Rhonda to make, she'd red-penciled a separation agreement for retyping, and dictated two letters.

She liked this time of the day best. *Carpe diem* . . . before the day seized *her*. Before the cacophony of phones and beeping intercoms, and the endless round of meetings began. Mostly, she liked the buffer zone it provided—time in which to try her hangover on for size.

Today's hangover, she'd rate, oh, about 7.8 on her own private Richter scale. From the very first moment, when she'd opened her eyes and found herself on the sofa, still in her clothes from yesterday, she'd known it was going to be bad. She just hadn't known *how* bad. A cold shower and half a gallon of coffee had made only a tiny dent in the concrete block encasing her head.

Vaguely, she recalled Luigi's, a safe cocoon smelling of stale cigarettes and Chianti, where she was lulled by the clink of glasses and the warmth of the bourbon spreading through her. An hour or so later, on her way home, she'd stopped at Westside Discount Liquors. After that, things got a little fuzzy. . . .

"Mandy, hi, glad I caught you. Got a minute?"

Startled, she glanced up at her stepmother, poised in the doorway. Rose looked striking, as always, in a turquoise shantung suit and jewel-patterned scarf. Her curly black hair with its ribbon of white was swept up on top of her head, and dangling from her ears were her signature ruby earrings. Yet something was different about her, Mandy observed. Her face—it was more alive somehow. Rose's eyes sparkled, and her high cheekbones seemed to glow.

Mandy thought: *She's getting laid.*

Something inside her buckled, like soft metal giving way. She felt a jolt of bruised anger. Daddy had only been gone a year, and Rose was jumping into bed with the first guy to come along. How much could she have loved Daddy? What could she be *thinking*?

Mandy immediately felt ashamed. Who was she to judge? It was about time Rose climbed down off the funeral pyre, she told herself. And this guy she was seeing seemed nice enough. Mandy remembered Eric Sandstrom from last Saturday's party . . . vaguely. She'd been pretty out of it toward the end, but had a hazy recollection of Eric helping her downstairs, then hailing her a cab. Had she thanked him? Probably not. It was a miracle she'd managed to make it the rest of the way home on her own.

Never again, Mandy resolved, her head throbbing in protest as she drew herself upright in her chair. She was going to cut back from now on. This time she meant it.

"I'm just finishing up," she greeted Rose, beckoning her inside. "I always come in early to clear my desk before I get gobbled up by the day. What are *you* doing here this time of the morning?"

"I wanted to speak with you. Alone." Rose wasn't smiling, and when she stepped inside, she was careful to close the door behind her.

She knows, Mandy thought, a red light flashing on in her head. Twice last week, Rose had called her at home, no particular reason, just to say hello. And yesterday, at the partners' meeting, Rose had seemed to watch Mandy out of the corner of her eye.

Now the other shoe was about to drop.

Please, God, don't let her say anything. I can't take it right now. Not with this head.

Mandy, in a sudden fit of agitation, began scooping up papers, stuffing them into file folders. Even so, she could feel Rose's dark eyes on her, and wriggled inside like a bug on a pin. Heat spread up her neck, into her cheeks.

"I have a conference call in fifteen minutes," she lied smoothly. "But until then, I'm all yours. What's up?"

Mandy watched her stepmother ease into the leather sling-chair opposite her desk and cast a quick glance around the office—like a detective scanning it for clues. An open wine bottle, a corkscrew, a dirty glass. Mandy nearly laughed out loud. *Do you really think I'm that stupid?*

Her office, in fact, was almost excruciatingly tidy. The smallest of the partners', it was also the most private, tucked away at the end of the corridor. Every night before she went home, and before the janitor arrived, she spent ten minutes or so straightening it herself. She couldn't afford a cluttered desk, overflowing shelves, files in disarray. People might talk.

Even the decor was simple, minimalist. Plain walnut desk, beige sofa, a pair of Jasper Johns prints on the wall. No family photos, except a snapshot of her dad tucked in a corner of her desk blotter—Daddy at the beach in Cape May, a few weeks before he died.

"I won't keep you," Rose said, her tone softening. As if she, too, were remembering that weekend, the five of them—Drew and Jay had come, too—bicycling around town, stopping here and there to sample Cape May's famous fudge, or simply to take in the ocean view. At an antique store, Daddy had insisted on buying Rose a weathervane she'd admired, a brass rooster gone green. She'd scoffed at the idea—where on earth would she put it? But he'd laughed, earning a sock on the arm by joking, *When I die, put it over my gravestone—that way you'll always know which direction I'm headed.*

Mandy shuddered, remembering.

"If it's about those résumés," she jumped in quickly, "I set aside the ones I think are worth interviewing. I've got them right here. . . ." She thumbed through the manila files in her organizer and pulled one out, sliding it across the desk so Rose wouldn't notice her hand was trembling. One of their paralegals, Nancy Chen, was due to give birth in less than a week—but what difference would it make who they hired to replace Nancy if her *own* career was at stake? "My first choice is the guy from Cornell," she told Rose, forcing herself to breathe slowly. "He seems the most ambitious. Also the brightest. That's his résumé on top."

Rose quickly glanced through the other résumés. "What about the Haverford girl? Summa cum laude, top ten percent of her class."

Mandy shook her head. "I counted two typos. Anyone who doesn't bother to proofread a cover letter can't be trusted with a contract, right?"

"We'll know more after we interview them." Rose tucked the résumés back into their folder and looked up, her expression turning grave. "Anyway, I'm not here to discuss business." She hesitated, as if uncertain of her footing.

Mandy imagined herself wrapped in a giant blood-pressure cuff, its rubber bulb squeezing. Each heartbeat causing her whole body to swell, and her head to pound.

Yet, when she spoke, her voice sounded perfectly normal. Amazing.

"Let me guess. You're worried about Drew." Mandy was concerned about her brother, too, but right now all she could think of was covering her own ass. "Honestly, Rose, if you want my opinion, this will just have to play itself out. If we're lucky, he'll wise up before the wedding."

It worked. Rose sighed, momentarily distracted. "I wish I could at least talk to him. He's been avoiding me lately. I can't even get him on the phone."

"Why not ask him over for dinner?" Mandy suggested. "Make it Friday and I'll come, too. For moral support."

Rose seemed to brighten at the idea, but then her face fell, and she replied gloomily, "I already tried that. He canceled at the last minute. I think he was hurt because I didn't include Iris."

"So invite her, too. That way, Drew won't suspect a setup."

"A setup?" Rose snorted. "As if I'd do that to my own son."

Rose was right, she thought. Subterfuge wasn't her style. When she confronted you about something, it was more like a Mack truck. In fact, Mandy could feel it coming at her now, bearing down. Rose was going to say that there'd been talk around the office. People were starting to notice. . . .

A bolt of alarm shot through her. What would she do without her clients, without this office to come to every morning? What else *was* there?

Then she was struck by an even deeper fear, one that ran below the surface like a fault line: *What if it means I can't drink anymore?*

Her hands, tightly knotted in her lap, were slick with sweat, and she was trembling all over. She laughed her patented Mandy-doll laugh, which sounded high-pitched and mechanical even to her own ears. "You're a mom, right? Everyone under the age of thirty thinks their mom is out to get them."

She ought to know. Her own mother was a black belt in that sport. Moving to Palm Beach hadn't slowed Bernice down one bit. Mandy wondered sometimes if the real reason she drank was her mother; if she was merely blotting out all those painful memories of growing up, Mom criticizing her every move, making her feel dirty and ashamed. Even when she got her *period,* for Christ's sake.

Mandy remembered vividly the first time she'd gotten high—at a cousin's wedding, shortly after her parents had split up. She'd been twelve, and everybody had thought it was cute, watching her flit from table to table, finishing off the dregs in champagne glasses. By the time the bouquet was thrown, she'd been so smashed she'd felt as if *she* were flying. It was as if she'd been stumbling around in the dark her whole life . . . and suddenly here was the key to a magic kingdom, dazzling in its brightness, where the brightest light of all was Mandy herself.

"Drew isn't the only one I'm worried about," Rose said, her dark eyes fixed on Mandy. "I don't know quite how to put this, but I guess there's no polite way. Your drinking—it's gotten out of control."

Mandy felt the world tip sideways. She clutched the arms of her chair to keep from being pitched to the floor. Yet her first instinct was to fight back, to cry out against the unfairness of it.

"Three hundred thousand in billings last year, you call *that* out of control?" she shot back. "If people are talking, Rose, maybe it's because they need to look more closely at their own records."

"Mandy, this isn't an indictment. I only want to help." Her stepmother's eyes seemed to plead with Mandy.

Never mind that I lost Daddy, too.

"Do I look like I need help? Do I act like I'm out of control?" Mandy made a sweeping gesture that took in her entire office, where every slip of paper was accounted for, every file labeled and color-coded, where even the volumes in the bookcase behind her desk were alphabetized. She added frostily, "Rose, I'm sure you mean well, but whoever is spreading lies about me has it all backwards. If I relax with a few drinks now and then, it's *because* of all I do around here."

"I know what you're capable of, that isn't the point," Rose persisted. "You're a good lawyer, Mandy. And a wonderful stepdaughter. Your father wasn't the only one cheering when you joined the firm."

"Are you saying I'm letting my father down?" Mandy was quick to assume the worst.

"Thank God your father can't see you like this." The sympathy in Rose's voice was like salt sprinkled on an open wound. As if Mandy were just one more nut case, like Iris. "You think it doesn't show? I can *smell* it on you. At last Tuesday's meeting, you were so hung over you were practically falling out of your chair. Even old Gib noticed, and he's practically blind."

Mandy sat back, feeling as embarrassed and frightened as a child caught in a lie. But she couldn't admit the truth—that would have been like giving away the combination to the safe guarding her most precious possession. What she needed more than anything else right now was a shot of bourbon, straight up. Just one. Otherwise, how would she ever manage to get through this?

"I see," she replied coldly. "*You* can go off the deep end, but if once in a while I have too much to drink, I'm some kind of deadbeat? I loved my father, too, you know. Did you ever stop to think you're not the only one who misses him?"

"What I *think* is that you need help," Rose told her. "Mandy, listen. I'm not the enemy, I'm on *your* side."

"What are you getting at, exactly?"

"I know someone you might want to talk to. Eric. I'll ask him to dinner on Friday. That way, you two can get to know one another." She stood up, her expression stern, uncompromising. "I'm counting on you to be there."

Mandy stared at her for a long moment before crying out, "You wouldn't treat me this way if Daddy were alive! He wouldn't have *let* you."

Rose shook her head, looking pained. "You're wrong. Your father loved you, Mandy. It would have hurt him deeply to see you this way."

She closed the door soundlessly behind her. Alone, Mandy slumped forward, dropping her head onto her folded arms. Her outrage had dissolved, leaving her as boneless as a protozoan under a microscope. Down the hall, she could hear a phone ringing . . . but the noise seemed to be coming from inside her head. An urgent bleating that wouldn't stop, that she had no way of answering.

With an effort, Mandy pulled herself to her feet. Her face was wet, which surprised her. She hadn't realized she was crying. Help? She knew of only one thing that could help her now. . . .

As she drew the bottle out from its hiding place in the credenza, she noted with pride that the paper seal was still intact. See? That proved it. She wasn't out of control, no fucking way. Otherwise, wouldn't she have helped herself to a nip before this?

Hadn't she been extra careful while Daddy was alive? Never more than a glass or two of wine at family dinners. Rose was right about that much—he *would* have been hurt and disappointed to see his little girl like this.

Even around her mother, who was always making snide remarks about Daddy and Rose, Mandy was careful to maintain her two-drink limit. Finding out from his ex-wife that their daughter had a drinking problem would have been worse for Daddy than discovering it himself.

But now Daddy was gone . . . and things had gotten a little slippery. From now on, she'd just have to make more of an effort. And she could. She *would*.

Starting tomorrow.

What she needed right now—more than Rose's approval, or even her own self-respect—was *this*.

The sealed cap, as she twisted it, made a delicious crinkling sound. She brought the bottle to her lips, sweeter than any lover's kiss, and was dimly aware of a line being irretrievably crossed. There was no turning back. She could no longer fool herself into believing she wasn't as bad off as those who drank during the day, *at work.*

But all that lay far ahead in the future—as unreal as the distant threat of being audited by the IRS would be to someone choking to death *right now.* If she didn't have this—*just one sip, I promise*—she wouldn't survive the next hour, much less the rest of the day.

With a low moan that might have been a plea for mercy, Mandy tipped the bottle back and drank.

❧ By Friday evening, she was sober as a parson. Arriving at Rose's promptly at eight, she thumbed the front-door buzzer. Mandy felt weak—unsteady, even—but she nonetheless wanted to shout it to every passerby, to anyone who would listen: *I haven't touched a drink in two whole days!* Not so much as a sip of sherry. And yesterday, on her way to the subway, hadn't she walked a block out of her way to keep from passing Luigi's?

Yet, oddly, she was in no mood to celebrate.

She felt jittery. Faintly queasy, too. In fact, she'd almost called to cancel . . . but in the end had decided she'd be damned if she'd slink off with her tail between her legs. What she had to do was put on a show, fake it for all she was worth. Her whole future depended on it—her standing with the firm and in the legal community, her friendship with Rose, her license, once she got this little problem under control, to continue . . . well, *everything.*

The door swung open.

"On time, as usual. And I'm running late." Rose, looking flushed and wiping her hands on a dark green butcher's apron, greeted Mandy with a light kiss on the cheek. "Go on up, make yourself comfortable while I check on the roast. The gang's all here, except Eric."

Climbing the stairs, Mandy felt confused. Rose was acting as if nothing had happened, as if this evening weren't some sort of a test.

The other day, in her office, had her stepmother's warning been just that—a mere notice, no more than a minor traffic violation, that she needed to watch her step?

It should have been a relief . . . but Mandy felt as if the sky were falling and she was the only one who could see it. The only one running for cover. Chicken Little with a monkey on her back. The image caused a mildly hysterical giggle to surface, which she disguised as a cough.

Entering the living room, with its jumble of books and family photos and nautical prints, she felt a familiar tightening in her throat. Everything about this place reminded her of her father—of how Daddy had *believed* in her. Making her feel special, always, even after the boys were born. Rose, too, she acknowledged grudgingly, had gone out of her way to be nice. *I didn't make it easy on her, either.* A gawky teenager with braces on her teeth and a chip on her shoulder. It was a wonder she'd found anyone at all to love her.

Jay loped over to envelop Mandy in a rib-crushing hug. She yelped, but was grateful for the show of affection, which she badly needed. Though she never would have admitted it, Jay was her favorite. She couldn't help it—there was something so achingly vulnerable behind those carefully guarded defenses of his. He reminded her of herself at that age, only better-looking.

"Hey, bro, what's up?" She ruffled his hair, making it stand up in spiky clumps. "New girlfriend—or did last week's make the final cut?"

He gave an embarrassed laugh and ducked his head. Unlike every other sixteen-year-old male she knew, Jay wasn't constantly on the make. But could he help it that girls seemed to find him irresistible? That cute redhead he'd dated his sophomore year still phoned regularly. And last summer's romance with Annalise, the *au pair* for the family upstairs, had resulted in a steady stream of letters and postcards from Denmark.

"Your love life must be pretty boring if you're so interested in mine," Jay shot back, treating her to a rare grin.

Mandy thought of Robert . . . and a shadow fell over her heart. Yesterday evening, after the champagne reception for Cynthia—a white-knuckle test worse than any hangover—she'd risked a late supper at their favorite French restaurant on Madison. But the whole time, she'd been on edge. No appetite, either. Her stomach, like the rest of her, one large contracted muscle.

She'd excused herself early, saying she had a headache, which wasn't far from the truth. But Robert was no fool, she knew. In the cab on the way home, he'd hardly said a word. No kiss, either. By now, he *had* to have guessed she was hiding something.

Or was she just being paranoid?

Maybe I'm *the one who should be seeing a shrink,* Mandy thought as Iris McClanahan rose from the sofa to greet her.

Not that you'd ever guess Iris was anything but normal. In a red halter dress that showed off her tanned shoulders, with her butterscotch hair falling loosely down her back, Iris looked as healthy and sunny as the brightest of summer days. Yet what always impressed Mandy most was how *nice* she was. As if it had never occurred to her that another woman might be jealous of her. Or that Rose had invited her simply as a way of twisting Drew's arm.

"Isn't this great? All of us together." Iris looked so delighted, Mandy half-expected to see her clap her hands like a child being given a special treat. Her face was literally glowing. "I barely got a chance to talk to you at our party. All those people! You look wonderful, by the way."

"Thanks," Mandy murmured, knowing it wasn't true. She looked like shit. Pale, with dark circles under her eyes. At the office, she'd told everyone she was coming down with the flu—as if anyone would buy that, with all the rumors that had to be flying. Now, looking into Iris' amber eyes which, up close, weren't quite so cloudless, she realized that in some ways their predicaments were similar. Iris, too, was treading on thin ice with Rose. Tentatively, she asked, "By the way, when's the wedding? Have you two set a date yet?"

Iris cast an uncertain glance at Drew, who was over by the liquor cabinet, pouring himself a glass of wine—something Mandy dearly wished she could do. He appeared tense, uncomfortable. Rose's plan had worked, sure, but he looked none too happy about being here. He had to know how worried his mother was, and was probably worried himself that Iris would notice.

Poor Drew. Was he having cold feet as well?

"Next summer, I hope," Iris said a bit too brightly. "Drew doesn't want to set a date until we find an apartment. He's superstitious." She crossed the room and slipped an arm about Drew, who smiled and kissed the top of her head.

If Drew doesn't watch out, he'll be eaten alive. Over the years, Mandy had witnessed enough of Iris' moods to know that her brother wouldn't have an easy time of it.

"You sure you know what you're getting into?" Mandy asked, masking her concern by pretending it was for Iris. "Knowing my brother, before long you'll be knee deep in lab rats he couldn't bear to euthanize."

"If you're trying to scare her off, you'll have to do better than that." Drew laughed, looking so like their father just then, Mandy felt her throat catch.

Except her brother's blue eyes, unlike Daddy's, were utterly vulnerable—a window standing open to anything that might fly in.

They were interrupted by the buzzing of the doorbell downstairs. Minutes later, Rose was ushering in the man responsible for that giddy look on her face. Eric Sandstrom, in faded jeans and pressed navy blazer, his deceptively laid-back gaze seeming to size up the situation with a glance.

"Hey, sorry I'm late. I was subbing for one of the other hosts." Friendly without appearing too eager, greeting everyone with a warm handshake.

Yes, Mandy could see it. Eric, though not conventionally handsome, was more interesting in some ways than Robert even. He bore the irresistible stamp of a man who . . . well, who'd *lived.* It wasn't just the lines around his eyes and mouth. His expression embodied something both wise and sad. It puzzled her, because at the same time he appeared happy—joyous, even.

Meeting his almost uncomfortably direct gaze, Mandy had the strangest feeling she knew him from somewhere other than Drew and Iris' party. A vague memory drifted lazily just below her consciousness. Lying on her back, looking up at Eric, his face like a bright sun at the mouth of a dark cave.

But that was crazy. At the party, they'd only exchanged a few words. And afterwards, when he'd helped her downstairs and into a taxi, she'd been in no shape for conversation.

Yet Rose had been so eager for Mandy to get to know him. Why? The memory surfaced again, more clearly this time. Eric hovering over her, with those sad and knowing eyes—*A dream? Yes, it must have been*—and goosebumps scuttled up the backs of her arms.

Suddenly Mandy couldn't wait to get away. Whatever Eric's story, she didn't want to hear it. Not now. Not ever.

Warily, she watched him greet Drew, then Jay, who hung back a bit, reminding her of a jealous boyfriend checking out the competition. Iris was the only one who greeted Eric warmly, as if he were an old friend of her family. Which he was, Mandy remembered.

"You're invited, too," Iris told him. Then, noting his puzzled expression, she began to giggle. "To the wedding. That's what we were talking about before you got here."

Rose's face turned to stone. She tried to hide it, but there was no disguising her dismay. Drew must have seen it, too. He frowned, shoving his fists deep into the pockets of his chinos. Meanwhile, Jay—who, like any sixteen-year-old, would sooner walk over hot coals than see a family problem aired in public—did his usual fadeout, melting into the background without actually leaving the room.

Even Mandy was embarrassed. Though, at the same time, she couldn't help feeling relieved that the focus was on someone other than her.

Rose was quick to shift gears. As deftly as a poker player disguising a losing hand, she smiled and said, "Why don't you all come to the table? The food is just about ready."

Dinner was more relaxed—the exhalation of a pent-up breath. Drew talked about his summer job at Computer World, how crazy it was now, with everyone flocking to buy laptops for their school-age kids. And Eric amused them with stories about the celebrities he'd interviewed while cohosting the *Morning Show*—the blind jazz pianist who'd remained seated while his wife, out in the audience, took a bow; the macho movie star who'd squealed in fright when one of the other guests—a zookeeper—thoughtlessly allowed a marmoset to scramble up onto his lap.

Even Jay laughed at that.

When Eric stood up to help Rose clear the table, Mandy was surprised at how quickly the time had gone. Somehow, she'd managed to get through an entire meal without obsessing about not drinking— a feat she would have believed impossible. Nor had she been the center of attention.

Nobody is out to get me, she realized.

Eric was too busy concentrating on Rose. Any fool could see he was in love with her. And yet Rose seemed skittish, as if not quite wanting to believe it. As if that kind of happiness might be a thing of the past. *She's not over Daddy,* Mandy thought, feeling suddenly sad for her stepmother.

Mandy got up, too, and began stacking plates, carrying them into the kitchen. Anything to keep her hands busy, to keep from thinking about the lonely weekend ahead, when she'd be climbing the walls to keep from walking to the liquor store ... while at the same time wishing she could be with Robert.

"You don't remember, do you?"

Startled, Mandy looked over to find Eric at the kitchen sink, rinsing off a plate. In the next room, she could hear Rose taking orders for coffee, and Drew arguing good-naturedly with his brother about something. She glanced nervously over her shoulder.

For the moment, at least, she and Eric were alone.

"Remember what?" Mandy asked innocently, though she had the distinct feeling she didn't want to know.

"I took you home after the party." He bent to load the plate into the dishwasher, then straightened to smile at her.

Mandy tensed, searching his face for the judgment she was used to seeing in other people's. There was none. Eric met her gaze with the cool look of someone living in a glass house of his own, who knew better than to throw stones.

She relaxed slightly and admitted, "I was kind of out of it."

"No shit." He chuckled, as if amused by her understatement.

Mandy remembered again why she was here, and felt her face grow tight. "I should have thanked you. I'm sorry." She added caustically, "I guess it's a good thing I have Rose to remind me of my manners."

He shrugged, refusing the bait. "You don't owe me anything. But if you ever need someone to talk to, I'm around." He fished in the pocket of his blazer, and handed her his business card. "Call me anytime."

Mandy just stood there, holding the card between her thumb and forefinger as gingerly as a lighted match. What was he? Some kind of preacher? That must be what his radio show was about—telling people how to fix their lives.

"That's why you came tonight, isn't it? To lecture me," she snapped. Taking a deep breath, she fought to bring herself under control. "Look, I don't mean to sound rude. But I hardly know you. Why should I listen to anything you have to say?"

"I know what you're going through, that's why."

"How could you?"

"I'm an alcoholic." His tone was matter-of-fact.

Mandy stared at him, feeling slightly dizzy. Of course. How stupid of her. She should have known. Eric wasn't just being the Good Samaritan—*He thinks I'm an alcoholic, too.* Instinctively, she found herself backing away, wanting to put as much distance between them as possible.

"You can't think . . ." She licked her lips, which suddenly felt as dry as old, bleached bones. Words of denial bubbled to the surface. "I sometimes drink too much, sure, but I'm not . . . I can stop anytime."

He smiled. "I used to think that, too."

"But you did. Stop, I mean."

"I'm sober, yes. There's a difference. I learned that in AA."

"I'm not like you," she insisted. "I don't need AA."

"None of us think we do. In the beginning, at least."

She eyed him, curious in spite of herself. "What changed your mind?"

He surprised her with a hollow laugh, rubbing his eyelids as if tired. When he opened them again, his eyes were bloodshot, their bright, unsettling blue like a bolt of lightning in an overcast sky.

"I began losing things," he told her. "My friends, my job, my house. Toward the end, even my sanity."

"I haven't lost anything," she declared, defiantly almost.

Eric eyed her thoughtfully before reaching once more into his pocket. When she saw what he was holding, Mandy gasped. Her missing keys. She'd been looking everywhere. How had Eric gotten them?

"I would have returned them sooner," he apologized, "but I didn't realize I'd pocketed them until Rose mentioned something the other night. I went looking in my closet, and found them."

Mandy's cheeks burned as she reached for them.

It seemed suddenly vital that he understand. "I haven't had a drink in two days," she blurted.

Eric merely shrugged as if to say, *So what? What's two days stacked up against all your years of drinking?* "Like I said, you can call me anytime. We'll go to a meeting together." In the weary curve of his mouth, she saw something that struck more than just a nerve . . . something that jarred her to the bone.

"I can't," she whispered. "It . . . It would mean . . ."

She stopped. God, what had she been about to say?

She saw from his expression that Eric *did* understand—more than she'd bargained for. He was looking at her with compassion, as if he knew precisely how she felt.

". . . not being able to drink anymore," he finished for her. "Yeah, I know. It's a bitch, all right. But it gets better, believe me. Or I wouldn't be here. You'll see."

But Mandy didn't want to see. Or know. She wanted only to escape. Abruptly turning her back on Eric, she darted from the kitchen. Her head was pounding, her scalp on fire. She wanted to be home, where she could . . .

No. No booze. I can't. That would prove he's right.

She had to be good. Even if it killed her.

Chapter 9

✒ "Your mother hates me," Iris declared mournfully.

She was lagging behind, and Drew had to slow his steps in order to keep pace. The taxi had let them off at the corner of Gansevoort, a block from his place—a fifth-floor walk-up the ad in the *Times* had billed as a "quaint studio in historic bldg, ideally located in Village." In other words, a dump. But it was *his* dump . . . and the more he thought about giving it up for something roomier that he and Iris could share, the less he liked it. Particularly at times like this, when Iris was stewing about something.

It'll get better, he told himself. *It has to.*

He took a deep breath. The humidity that all week had gripped the city like a sweaty fist was beginning to ease. He thought he could feel the first hint of fall in the air—or was it just his imagination? Tomorrow was his last day at the computer store where he'd spent the summer peddling laptops to college-bound kids who made him feel as if his own undergrad days had taken place long enough ago for him to smile with wistful nostalgia. *An engaged man,* he thought. *I'm engaged to be married.* However many times he said it, he couldn't quite see himself that way. It was as if he'd turned a corner onto an unfamiliar street . . . and if what he was seeing now was any indication of what lay ahead, Drew wasn't at all sure he was headed in the right direction.

Once school starts, I'll be too busy to notice, he told himself.

In a just few weeks, he'd be submerged in lectures and labs, where his only concern would be keeping his head above water. And Iris at Parson's, all her tiny worries—worries that tended to grow, like mushrooms in damp rotting soil, into *big* worries—lost in a storm of drawing paper, charcoal stubs, gesso, and paint. Soon, he thought, this summer would seem like one of those dreams from which you awake sweating and short of breath, only to forget, a minute later, what it was all about.

"She doesn't *hate* you." Drew squeezed her hand. "She's worried, that's all."

"Because she thinks I'm some kind of psycho, right?" There was no resentment in Iris' voice, only a kind of bruised despair.

"Jesus, Iris." Drew sighed. When she got like this, he never knew quite what to say, how to console her. "Nobody thinks you're a psycho. Look at it from my mom's point of view—Dad's only been gone a year, and now her oldest son is engaged to be married. Plus, you have to admit, it hasn't always been hearts and roses with us."

He grinned crookedly, casting like a fly fisherman on a still lake for even the tiniest glimmer of a smile. But Iris wasn't biting. She regarded him gravely, her eyes in the hard glare of the street lamp deeply pocketed with shadow.

"More like Dungeons and Dragons," she groaned without so much as a hint of irony. Drew couldn't remember the last time he'd seen her look so unhappy. Not since . . .

The memory, still fresh, resurfaced. Iris perched on the terrace ledge, the wedge of bare back exposed by her dress glowing in the darkness like a lighted windowpane between a pair of parted curtains. A window he could look into, but never get past.

Fear edged its way up his throat.

No, he wouldn't think about that night. Or that other time . . . in high school. Things would never again get that bad, he told himself. Iris was in therapy, and took her medication twice a day, just as prescribed. Drew had kept an eye on her, to make sure. He hated having to check up on her like that, but what choice did he have? He couldn't risk another of those episodes; the last one had scared the shit out of him.

Even so, her moods tended to strike without warning. She seemed to have no control over them. When she got like this, and worse, she wasn't even *Iris,* for Chrissakes. Not the Iris who'd been so comforting and supportive when Dad died, and who'd taken charge that time an elderly woman had slipped on the subway steps in front of them—heading off rubberneckers, then snagging a cell phone from a startled passerby to dial 911. When Iris got upset, *really* upset, something happened to her. Sort of like a car going into a skid on an icy road.

Drew felt a sudden urgent need to seize control of the situation, to find traction before it was too late.

Nice and easy, he told himself. A favorite expression of his dad's—one he'd found himself using more and more often lately.

"It's been a weird summer," he agreed, careful not to sound patronizing—she was way too smart to fall for that. "I guess it's not helping, either, that our mothers aren't speaking to one another." They passed a packing plant, shuttered for the night. It reminded him of what he liked least about the Meat District—at night, this neighborhood was a frigging ghost town.

Iris forced a shaky laugh. "No kidding. After our party, when Dad got back from taking your mother home? Even with the door to my room closed, I could hear Mom light into him. She's jealous, I think."

"That's stupid." Drew laughed, not because the idea was so impossibly far-fetched—after all, his mother and Brian *had* been in love at one time, even if it was practically a lifetime ago—but because he sensed Iris needed reassuring. "Between you and me, I doubt your mom has anything to worry about."

Iris stopped, and swung around, her face seeming to leap out at him, frighteningly, like headlights appearing suddenly on a dark road. "Don't you see? *We're* the reason they're at each other's throats. Your mom thinks our engagement is a huge mistake . . . and *my* mom sees it as the answer to her prayers."

"You know what? They're both wrong." Drew cupped her anxious face in his hands, as if he could somehow anchor her. "This is for *us,* nobody else. Because we love each other."

"*Do* you love me? Oh, Drew, I need to hear that you do." She tipped her head up, as if to keep the tears in her eyes from spilling over.

"Of course, I do, baby." He wrapped his arms about her, pulling her close. He could feel her heart beating, and thought of a tiny bird he'd once scooped off the ground—it had weighed nothing, nothing at all, but its quivering terror had seemed almost more than he could contain. Iris was trembling like that now—so hard he thought at first she was crying. But she made no sound, only a small cry in the back of her throat as she buried her face against his shoulder.

As they stood with their arms wrapped around each other, Drew felt suddenly, acutely aware that the sidewalk was nearly deserted. If they didn't get moving they'd be sitting ducks for—

Muggers?

He shook off the thought. But the vague sense of danger wouldn't let go. He looked around at the corrugated security gates gleaming mutely along both sides of the dimly lit street. Even the cars bumping over the cobblestones, headed for the West Side Highway, were few and far between.

A cool, reasoning voice spoke up inside his head. *Man, don't you get it? It's not what's OUT THERE.* This was like one of those horror flicks where the victim runs around locking doors and windows only to discover that, all along, the monster was INSIDE.

Only one thing stood clear: he loved her. There had never been anyone but Iris. Not really. As little kids, they'd slept side by side in their respective sleeping bags on the rug in front of the fireplace at his parents' rented Lake George cabin. He had a clear picture in his mind of seven-year-old Iris in her footie pajamas, her hair trailing across her pillow and tickling his cheek. He'd even known something about her that *she* wasn't aware of: ladylike Iris—who picked the crusts off her sandwiches and was squeamish about wading barefoot in the lake—snored like a longshoreman.

Drew remembered their first time, when he was fifteen. They'd been watching TV in her parents' bedroom one evening when Brian and Rachel were both working late. They started tickling each other, and before he knew it Drew was on top of her, his breathing coming in ragged gusts, the zipper on his jeans about to pop. He'd felt embarrassed, disgusting; then there was Iris looking up at him with her Mona Lisa smile, calm and knowing—*womanly* somehow—her soft hair spread over the rumpled bedspread like a blanket over springy grass. Inviting him to lie with her. He'd kissed her, not like the few tentative pecks they'd exchanged on other occasions, but deeply, unashamedly. And she'd kissed him back, opening her mouth, folding her own tongue about his and pressing a hand to the nape of his neck. Offering herself to him with a trust that was both innocent and, yeah, a bit frightening.

He'd been so blown away by it all, so excited, he'd come before he was even inside her. But Iris hadn't seemed upset, or disappointed. She merely stroked him until he was ready again. Then, clinging to him so tightly he seemed to bear the imprint of her body for days afterwards, she'd come, too.

If Iris was unpredictable, it was part of what made her so different from other girls, so impossible to pin down. Like static electricity, or a color too vivid to be captured on canvas. She was light, energy, motion, all at once.

At Bryn Mawr, at the art department's end-of-year show, even her paintings had stood out—delicate washes that evoked a mood, an expression, a time of day with the merest suggestion of a line or stroke. Yet she seemed almost unaware of how talented she was. It was as if, for her, painting was no more a stretch than humming along with the music, or recounting a dream aloud.

Did she have any idea how truly exceptional she was? And how beautiful? Like in those paperback romances Iris made fun of but secretly liked to read, it made his heart ache just to look at her.

Holding her tightly, Drew vowed to keep Iris safe. To protect her as best he could. Whatever it took.

"I love you so much," Iris murmured. He heard the words catch in her throat as her lips moved against his neck. "If you ever left me . . ."

"I'm not leaving." Drew squeezed her, then stepped back. "Hey, I have an idea. Why don't we go away Labor Day weekend? It's our last one before school, and we'll have three days. We could drive up to Vermont."

He recognized the fleeting smile she gave him even before she answered, "I'd like that . . . except I was sort of hoping we could look at apartments. It'd be a good time, with everyone out of town. If we see something we like, there won't be a dozen other people in line ahead of us."

Drew felt unreasonably disappointed. No, more than that—shot down. But that was dumb. It wasn't like they'd made any plans. Even so, he hesitated a moment before saying, "We could do that."

Iris instantly withdrew, hunching her shoulders and folding her arms tightly across her stomach. "You don't sound too excited." She kept her head low as they continued along the sidewalk. "Really, Drew, if you'd rather not, it's no big deal."

"Can't it wait?" he asked.

"I suppose. . . ."

"I mean, it's not like my lease is up tomorrow or anything."

At the entrance to his building, as Drew fumbled for his keys, he could see Iris out of the corner of his eye, her shadow knifing up against the graffiti-scrawled brick façade. She looked tense and angry. "I thought the whole idea was for us to have a place of our own," she said in a low, hurt voice. "But I wouldn't dream of *forcing* you to move. If you'd rather live here, be my guest."

Drew sighed, struggling to control his impatience. "Iris, if I didn't want to *be* with you, why in God's name would I have asked you to marry me?"

"Honestly? Sometimes I don't know."

"Oh Christ, here we go again," Drew swore. He rammed his key into the lock and elbowed the door open with such force that Iris flinched. This time, he didn't stop to reassure her, or even to wait for her to catch up as he bounded up the stairs.

Four flights that, in his fed-up state, felt as steep as a mountainside, leaving him sweaty and winded by the time he reached his own floor. Letting himself into the apartment, Drew had a sudden, shocking impulse to slam the door, lock Iris out. When was the last time he'd been able to *breathe* without her jumping down his throat?

He caught himself, shaken by this unexpected fury. Leaning against the doorjamb, he forced himself to take slow breaths as he waited for her to round the last flight of stairs.

He watched Iris sweep past and throw herself onto his futon. The bed had been comfortable when it was just him sleeping on it, but now, with Iris staying over most nights, it felt cramped. The place was filthy, too, Drew noted, looking around him with disgust. Dirty plates were piled on the kitchen counter, newspapers and magazines strewn everywhere else. Wire hangers jammed the doorknobs—Iris' clothes mostly—and he caught a distinct odor of rotting garbage. Why hadn't he noticed before? Come to think of it, Iris spent more time here than at home—why hadn't *she*?

"I'm sorry," she said, seeming to wilt. "I guess I overreacted. I get scared sometimes, that's all." She picked at her thumbnail, looking childlike beneath the poster on the wall behind her—Pearl Jam at the Knitting Factory. Only three years since that concert, he recalled. Christ. What wouldn't he give just to cut loose the way he had that night—yell, dance, throw himself into the wild meshing of limbs? An old man—that's what he was becoming. Old and stuck. As if echoing his thoughts, Iris added plaintively, "I wouldn't want you ever to feel . . . responsible for me."

"Yeah? Well, even if that was the case, who elected *me* savior of the world?" He realized he was shouting. It wasn't just Iris. Since Dad's death he'd felt responsible for Mom, too. Not to mention his brother.

"Oh, Drew. I know it hasn't been easy." She sounded more like her sane, sensible self now—the Iris he loved best.

Drew felt the tension go out of him, and this time he spoke gently. "That doesn't mean I see you as some kind of burden." He walked over to the kitchen area, no bigger than a closet, with its two cupboards and a counter the size of a breadboard. He cranked on the tap, splashed water over his face.

"I just . . . I really *don't* know what I'd do if you ever left me." Her voice hovered just above the rushing water, so that mostly what he was aware of was its tone—high and anxious.

"Iris, I'm not going anywhere."

"You left me once before."

"Great—this is just *great.*" Drew spun around and slammed his fist down. Droplets of water sprayed out to form a damp radius on the chipped Formica. "You want to keep on until we *do* break up? Is that what you're after?"

Iris' head whipped up, her face screwed into something that made him think of an ancient baby, all sucking need and bright, shocked outrage. She sat there a moment, staring at him with those huge, injured eyes, as if he'd hit her. Then, without a word, she stood up and walked into the bathroom. The door clicked shut behind her.

A minute went by, then two. Drew listened for the flush of the toilet, or the sound of a running tap. Nothing. He waited a while longer before knocking.

"Iris? Are you okay?" He rapped gently on the heavy old door. Silence.

He knocked again, harder this time. "Listen, Iris, I know you're upset. Maybe dinner at my mom's wasn't such a good idea. You're right, she *was* pretty uptight." When she didn't answer, he began to feel truly worried. It was a struggle to maintain an even tone. "You don't have to come out—just let me know you're okay. Iris? *Iris?*"

He pressed an ear to the door, but couldn't hear a thing. Not even the click of the medicine cabinet. Jesus. What the hell was she *doing* in there? He found himself running down the mental list of what was in his medicine cabinet. Toothbrush. Right Guard. Shaving cream. Aspirin. An old prescription of Seldane for his hay fever. A packet of Gillette cartridges—

He stopped. *No, she wouldn't. Not that. Not again.*

Drew felt his worry slip over into panic.

"Iris!" he shouted. "Open up!"

The only sound was the faint creaking of footsteps overhead—the old lady in 6-F. Mrs. Casey, who'd recently confided to him that, last year, after she'd fallen and broken her hip, it had been a whole day—twenty-four hours and then some—before she was found and taken to the hospital.

A picture formed in Drew's mind: Iris lying on the bathroom floor in a puddle of blood. Fear swelled in him, breaking in an icy wave that nearly brought him to his knees.

He hammered on the door. Hard enough to bruise his knuckles and send jabs of pain down through his wrists.

"Iris! If you don't open up, I swear to God I'm going to kick this door in!"

He waited a moment, scowling down at the porcelain knob, willing it to turn. But it only seemed to taunt him with its fixed, sightless stare. Either she hadn't heard him, or she didn't care.

Drew stepped back, and with a low grunt drove the heel of his Timberland boot into the door's raised center panel—an effort that succeeded only in jarring him to the bone and sending a flurry of paint chips spraying like misbegotten confetti.

Breathing hard, his leg throbbing, he jerked an arm across his forehead, from which greasy beads of sweat had begun to drip. What now?

Drew leaned into the door frame, squeezing his eyes shut. "Iris . . . for God's sake," he panted.

Her silence seemed to mock him. Damn her. Was she doing this to punish him?

His gaze fell on the iron barbell sticking out from under the futon—a relic from the days when he'd had the time to work out. Dragging it out, he hoisted the fifty-pound weight to his shoulder. *"Iris!"* The cry tore from his lungs with a violence that left his throat burning.

No response. There was only the rushing of blood in his ears, and the distant sound of a horn blaring in the street below.

Drew, his sweaty hands gripping the cold iron bar, its weight digging into his shoulder, once again charged the door. This time he felt something give, then heard a loud cracking sound. He stared at the split center panel—a foot-long gash of bare wood showing through the countless layers of ossified paint.

With a savage growl, he charged again, driving the barbell into the crack he'd made. Then, suddenly, the door was flying open, banging against the inner wall hard enough to send the toothbrush glass spinning off the edge of the sink onto the tiles below with a tinkling crash.

He found Iris on the floor, wedged in the corner between the sink and toilet, her legs tucked in tightly against her chest, her arms wrapped about them, her head resting on her knees. No blood. Oh, thank God.

Feeling suddenly weak, his heart pounding, sweat pouring off him, Drew picked his way around the broken shards glinting against the old Pepto-Bismol–pink tiles, and knelt to touch her arm.

"Iris?"

The hand he took hold of was limp and clammy. He squeezed it hard. No response at first: then he felt the quick, faint pressure of her fingers. At last, she dragged her head up with an effort that caused it to wobble on her slender neck.

Drew had to suck in his breath to keep from revealing his shock. She looked awful. Her eyes sunken and bruised in a face pale as chalk. Her hair a tangled mess. The sharp smell of urine stung his nose, and when Drew looked down, he saw with dismay that she'd wet herself.

Jesus. What had happened? Had he pushed her too hard? Or was this merely a sign of something worse to come?

Gently, he pulled her into his arms. His shoulder ached, but he hardly noticed, not with the relief that was sluicing through him like cool water. She was all right. It wasn't anything . . . well, *irreversible*. The only casualty was a broken door, and a landlord who would raise bloody hell.

"Baby, are you okay? Please tell me you're okay," he choked, pressing a wet cheek into her springy hair. In spite of everything, it still smelled of her apple-scented shampoo. "Oh God, Iris, I was so scared."

An endless, almost unendurable silence ensued. Finally, when he felt on the verge of losing it himself, Drew felt her stir in his arms.

"Don't tell," she breathed in a breathy little voice that sounded eerily childlike. "Promise me you won't."

"*Who* don't you want me to tell? Who is it you're scared of?" Drew felt an almost frantic need to know; somehow, to pry open the sealed tomb of Iris' past.

But she only shook her head violently, her eyes squeezed tightly shut, and whimpered, "Matches. She has matches. Something sharp, too—it's poking her." Her hold on Drew tightened until he could hardly breathe. She began to sob, a deep, wracking anguish that seemed to threaten to tear her from his arms, like a loose shingle in a strong wind.

"*Who?*" Drew, in his distress, almost shouted it this time.

"My mother," she said. Not in her little-girl voice this time—and *not,* he sensed at once, referring to Rachel.

Whatever she was struggling to remember, Drew realized, it went much farther back than anything he knew about her . . . and was clearly more than Iris herself could express. The expression of dawning horror she wore was that of someone uncovering a scrap of memory, like a shard of bone in freshly dug soil, one that might have been better off left buried.

September

"Goodbye," said the fox. "And now here is my secret, a very simple secret: It is only with the heart that one can see rightly; what is essential is invisible to the eye."

Antoine de Saint-Exupéry, The Little Prince

exore x

Chapter 10

Rachel gazed in astonishment at the diminutive nun seated before her at a massive oak desk that, by contrast with her almost childlike form, seemed absurdly outsized. Not the fire-breathing monster she'd been expecting—more like a character out of a comic strip. Little Lulu meets Mr. Magoo. She fought an urge to peek underneath the desk to see if Sister Alice's feet were touching the floor.

Instead she kept her eyes riveted on Holy Angels' elderly principal. A starched white band framed a round face like bread dough rising in a bowl, in which her small pink mouth, pursed in disapproval, formed a deep dimple. Harmless enough . . . except for her eyes. A pale, wintry blue, they regarded Rachel with an unblinking calm that was downright creepy. Was it possible Sister Alice didn't *know?*

She must, Rachel thought. *Or she wouldn't have agreed to see me.* With the fall term starting, Sister Alice had to be busy. Under ordinary circumstances, nothing short of the near-death of one of her students would have prompted the old bat into allowing Rachel— her sworn enemy—into the inner sanctum.

"Have a seat, Dr. Rosenthal," she offered mildly, gesturing toward a pair of sturdy oak chairs facing her desk. "I have a few minutes before the final bell; then I have to be in chapel to lead the afternoon prayer."

"I won't keep you."

Rachel herself had a mountain of work back at the clinic, which she'd put on hold in order to come here, in the hope that—what? Sister Alice would come around to her point of view? That would happen when the Pope declared himself in favor of birth control, she thought. But in light of the desperate call Rachel had received last night—the mother of one of her young patients, a Holy Angels student—was it too much to ask that Sister Alice show at least *some* sense of responsibility for what had happened? That she agree to stop circulating her petition, at least, even if she *didn't* sanction sex education?

Rachel lowered herself stiffly into the nearest chair, glancing around the gloomy office. It was unadorned except for the carved wooden crucifix on the wall, and a second-rate oil depicting what appeared to be the Resurrection. The walnut bookcase was neatly lined with age-darkened buckram spines—a certain cure for even the most hopeless insomniac, no doubt. And on the desk stood only a clear pitcher of water, which grudgingly reflected back what little sunlight trickled from a pair of high, reinforced windows.

Clearly, when God had said, *Let there be light,* He hadn't had this cheerless room in mind, she thought. No. Here, Sister Alice ran the show.

Rachel, seeing not even a chink of warmth she might have been able to ply with pleasantries, dove in with her usual headfirst bluntness. "I'm not here to discuss our differences," she began. "I doubt it would accomplish much, in any case. But this situation . . . well . . . it's serious."

Sister Alice nodded sagely. "What could be more serious than the Lord's business?" she agreed in a faintly wheezy voice that suggested asthma, or maybe the onset of emphysema. "We at Holy Angels are committed to instilling our girls with the divine teachings of the faith."

Rachel stiffened. "Religious education, as I see it, should be about teaching little girls how *not* to become mothers," she responded tartly.

Sister Alice gently shook her head. "Faith in God is what keeps our girls from straying. *Not,*" she added with emphasis, "filling their heads with a lot of ideas they wouldn't have had otherwise."

Suddenly, unbelievably, it was Rachel who was being scolded—

an errant schoolgirl hauled up before the principal. Outrage rose in her like a blast of hot dry air from a furnace.

"Tell that to Elvie Rodriguez. When she's out of Intensive Care, that is." Rachel was trembling with her effort to keep from shouting, *You sanctimonious old BITCH.*

She took hold of herself, shocked by how close she'd come to actually losing control. What was *wrong* with her? Sister Alice was a menace, sure . . . but . . .

It's not Sister Alice, it's YOU, a voice in her head piped up, maddeningly. She'd been on edge for weeks, not eating, hardly sleeping, ever since Brian . . .

No. She wouldn't think about that. It was too painful. Too frightening. Better to focus on an enemy she could see.

Rachel, taking a breath, raised her eyes to the resurrected Jesus on the wall, a bearded figure in sandals and flowing white robe, who appeared to be hovering several inches above the ground on which the rapturous throng around him stood huddled. But the picture she couldn't get out of her mind was of Elvie, the shy eighth-grader in pigtails who'd come to the East Side Center weeks ago hoping for some kind of miracle, only to be given the bad—but hardly unexpected—news that she was pregnant. She'd nodded in understanding, dutifully accepting an appointment card. And that was the last they'd seen of her. Until yesterday.

Rachel had been at her desk yesterday evening when the call came—Elvie's mother, jabbering hysterically in Spanish, something about her daughter being rushed to the hospital. Would the señora doctor please come?

Rachel had dropped everything to race over to St. Bart's. Something in Mrs. Rodriguez's voice—a panic that only another mother who'd come close to losing her child would recognize. A remembered fear that had followed Rachel up the elevator and into the ICU, where the petite, dark-haired fourteen-year-old lay half conscious amid a thicket of tubes and blinking monitors.

Rachel had taken the girl's hand, which felt as limp and flat as a paper doll's. "*Está bien*. It's going to be all right, Elvie. You lost a lot of blood . . . but you'll be fine." Mechanically, she'd repeated what she'd been told by the attending resident, hoping it was true.

But Elvie had merely shaken her head, tears slipping down her temples to darken the starched white pillow. "No. I did a bad thing. A mortal sin. I'll be punished in hell, just like my teacher said."

Rachel had fought to keep from crying herself. At the meanness of small minds. At the loss of innocence. In her mind, she couldn't help seeing Iris in the hospital at fourteen: pale from loss of blood, with great bruised-looking smudges under her eyes. The circumstances had been different, but weren't both girls victims of their own despair? Mere children who'd felt painted into a corner—one by her own private demons, the other by self-proclaimed spokespersons of God—and had seen no other way out.

Iris. Since the party, Rachel had scarcely seen her daughter, except in passing. Iris was almost always either at Drew's or off looking at apartments. And, truthfully, Rachel had been so preoccupied, she'd hardly noticed. All she'd been able to think about was Brian.

That night, making love to her when any fool could see the one he'd really wanted was Rose. God. It was worse than humiliating. It was . . .

Exciting. Admit it. You were turned on.

The memory brought a rush of heat to Rachel's cheeks, which even the funereal gloom of Sister Alice's office failed to dampen. Had she sunk that low? Was she so frightened of losing her husband? That she'd *enjoyed* it made her feel even more degraded. Not because there'd been anything wrong with what they'd done, but because she'd known, oh yes, from the very first, that it was Rose he was kissing, not her. Rose in his mind's eye as he'd taken her.

Rose, as a young woman.

How could Rachel possibly compete with a memory that was gilt-edged, like the pages of a storybook? With none of the everyday wear and tear of a marriage. No silly fights over whose turn it was to take out the garbage. No flashes of irritation over someone's forgetting to enter a check. No shared anxiety over a sick child.

Rachel felt sick herself. Furious, too. She wanted to throw something at the wall, do anything to rid herself of the awful suspicion that she'd compromised herself—not only with her husband, but professionally, too. Marching over here for a showdown with Sister Alice, instead of merely calling, when the person she *really* wanted to confront was Rose.

Rachel blinked hard, forcing herself to focus on Sister Alice, whose smooth white forehead, she saw, was pleated with concern. "Elvie, yes . . . poor child," the old nun clucked, her small plump fingers steepled under her chin. "Her mother called this morning to tell us what happened. One of our most devout, Mrs. Rodriguez—she was quite upset."

Because her daughter nearly died giving herself an abortion . . . or because your church considers it a sin? It was all Rachel could do to keep from slamming her fist down on the desk.

Instead, she fixed Sister Alice with an icy glare. "Mrs. Rodriguez had every right to be shook up. Elvie confided in her teacher and told her she was pregnant. That woman—*your* staff—called her a sinner, and said she had to confess to the priest or she would go to hell."

The elderly nun shook her head sadly, as if the effort of explaining God's ways to someone as unenlightened as Rachel would simply be too taxing. "Salvation lies in seeking God's forgiveness," she said, turning up her hands in a gesture of humility. "I'll ask Father to say a rosary for Elvie and her family at Sunday's mass."

Rachel's anger boiled over. "While you're at it, ask him to say one for the souls of narrow-minded hypocrites," she snapped.

Rachel watched Sister Alice's gaze narrow slightly, and thought of an expression Kay often used: *Always keep your eye out for the zipper in sheep's clothing.* The zipper in the sheep's clothing of this particular wolf had shown itself at last—in a glint of something cold and steely in the old nun's eyes.

"I have no doubt you and your clinic serve a useful function in

our community," she replied in a voice that was as frosty as it was labored. "But you overstep your bounds when you provide more than
is strictly necessary. It is *you,* Dr. Rosenthal, who are a threat to our
community's youth. By encouraging girls like Elvie to practice birth
control, you're implying that you *approve* of their immoral activities."

"In Elvie's case, the barn door was already open," Rachel informed
her. "She was almost twelve weeks pregnant when we examined her."

Sister Alice, for the first time, looked troubled. "I don't understand," she said, shaking her head. "She was such a good girl."

Rachel bristled at the past tense. As if Elvie Rodriguez were
dead—or might be better off that way. "Maybe it's something in
your holy water." She couldn't resist the dig.

Sister Alice's face betrayed no emotion. There was only the odd
whistling noise that accompanied each strained breath, and the har-
nessed fury in her voice. "Keep in mind, Dr. Rosenthal . . . that the
Church . . . has been in existence for thousands of years." She
brought a hand to her heaving chest. "Misguided crusades such as
yours . . . are merely ripples . . . on the ocean. Enough to rock the
boat . . . but not capsize it."

A bell jangled in the hallway outside. Sister Alice rose, and
stepped out from behind her desk. Her breathing seemed to have
calmed, as if saying her piece had loosened the tight girdle holding
her emotions in. But there would be no miracle, Rachel saw; if she'd
come here hoping for a change of heart, if not mind, what she'd gotten instead was a dose of dime-store piety. Even as she extended her
hand to Rachel, a faint ray of sunlight made Sister Alice's pale forehead gleam like that of a plastic Day-Glo saint.

"I'm afraid I must excuse myself." The regret in her voice was the
final blow—she sounded truly sorry to be missing this opportunity
to educate Rachel further. She was even gracious enough to add,
"Thank you for seeing to it that Elvie is in good hands at St.
Bartholomew's. Her mother is very grateful. We will include *you* in
our prayers as well, Dr. Rosenthal."

With a rustle of gray gabardine—a modified habit that fell to just above the ankles of the diminutive nun—Sister Alice ushered Rachel out into the corridor, tiled in toothpaste-green linoleum. Down this she glided as if on an invisible current, without so much as a backward glance.

Rachel, her head pounding with suppressed fury, stalked past the front office's poodle-haired secretary, and through the double doors to the street. As she paused on the steps outside, her gaze was drawn to the detached building on her left, which she assumed was the chapel. Young girls in dark-blue uniforms streamed across the concrete yard separating it from the school building, most of them dark-haired and amber-skinned, the daughters of working-class Hispanics.

Watching as they disappeared through the chapel's side entrance, Rachel was struck by how many of the younger ones—nine- and ten-year-olds in ponytails—had already begun developing. Before long, they'd be having sex. And next thing you knew . . .

. . . they'd be showing up at the East Side Center. Pregnant.

And what would prevent the next Elvie Rodriguez from panicking and doing something equally misguided?

Rachel felt helpless, just another administrator—not so different from Sister Alice—spouting opinions and doctrine in the absence of real aid. Where had she been when Elvie Rodriguez, alone and afraid, had aborted her baby with a crochet hook? That day at the clinic, if Rachel had sat down with her, taken the time to draw her out, hear her worries, maybe things would have turned out differently.

That was what she'd never been able to communicate fully to Brian. How critical it was—the situation of the girls and women who drifted through the doors of East Side when they had nowhere else to go. How tenuous their existence, and their trust. And how one missed opportunity could mean the difference between life or death.

Sometimes, all it took was an extra minute.

The trouble was, all those minutes added up.

Starting down Fourteenth Street—back toward the clinic, two long blocks to the east—Rachel walked with her head low, her shoulders hunched forward, more miserable and tense than before she'd set out to see Sister Alice.

By the time she reached the corner of Fourteenth and Second—where the four-story building housing the East Side Women's Health Center stood as solid and reassuring as a lighthouse amid the surrounding tenements—the pressure in her head had become a non-stop jackhammer. Oh, what wouldn't she give for five minutes to stretch out in one of the examining rooms! Instead, she'd have to settle for a couple of aspirins gulped down with lukewarm water from the tap. That, and maybe half a minute in her office to put her feet up.

As Rachel swept in through the plate-glass doors, skirting the waiting room with its usual crush of patients, the last thing she was prepared to deal with was her codirector, Kay, barreling toward her with a howling toddler in her arms.

"Mind holding him a sec? Mom's in with Mary Ann having an ultrasound, and everyone else is tied up. I can't seem to get him to stop crying." Kay thrust the red-faced child at her. "You're a mother. *You* know what to do."

"You've had more practice with babies than I have," Rachel protested, letting go with a weary laugh of any wild idea she might have had of snatching a moment to herself. She tried to balance the little boy on her hip, but he was wiggling so hard he kept slipping off. He couldn't have been more than two, with a mop of dark curls and swooping eyelashes that twenty years from now would be breaking women's hearts all over town. She sighed. "Hold my calls, Monique," she tossed over her shoulder to the receptionist—a young Haitian woman with an elaborate weave of beaded braids, who had her own hands full at the moment, manning the phone lines and smoothing the ruffled feathers of patients who'd been waiting for hours, some of them all morning.

As Rachel lugged the little boy down the hallway to her office, the two-year-old's howls downshifted into hiccoughing sniffles. Wide-eyed, he watched Carlene, one of their nurse-midwives, pushing a pregnant woman in a wheelchair who was obviously in labor. Thank goodness St. Bartholomew's was only a block away, Rachel thought. Here, they weren't equipped to deliver babies—but on at least half a dozen occasions in the past, the babies had had other ideas.

She felt a stab of longing. God, she missed it—the thrill of ushering a brand-new life into the world. The wondrous awe that accompanied each birth, in which her own role always seemed almost inconsequential. The wild whoop of joy all around when every toe and finger was accounted for.

She had to remind herself, again and again, of all that she and Kay had accomplished with this clinic—all the reasons she was more effective, in terms of scope at least, as an administrator than as a doctor. Since East Side had first opened its doors back in the early seventies, with a hand-lettered sign in the window, they'd made a real difference in this community. Infant mortality had dropped 15 percent. Abortion referrals were down as well. And the AIDS-awareness program they offered, along with free condoms, had been adopted by at least a dozen schools.

They'd weathered federal budget cuts, the let-them-eat-cake eighties, two major renovations, and the Christian Coalition. They would survive Sister Alice, too. Somehow.

In the office she shared with Kay, decorated in Early Salvation Army, Rachel plopped the sniffling toddler on the carpet along with the basket of toys she kept for just such emergencies. At once, he became absorbed in banging at the Playskool barn with a toy truck.

"See? I told you. It's some kind of magic known only to mothers." Kay parked herself on the shabby arm of an easy chair, donated years ago by a patient, which they'd never gotten around to replacing. It seemed there was always some other, more pressing expense—medical equipment in need of repair, computers to upgrade, a new fax or Xerox machine. Not to mention the cost of removing the graffiti that appeared outside the building as regularly as the garbage that littered the sidewalk.

"Magic? I wish I had a wand I could wave over Sister Alice that would stop her from circulating petitions, at least," Rachel muttered. "That, or a voodoo doll." She crouched down to help the little boy at her feet stack colored plastic rings on a post. "You should have seen her—it was unbelievable. I didn't accomplish a single thing by going over there. If anything, I made it worse."

Kay brushed absently at her baggy linen blazer, which was as hopelessly rumpled as the rest of her. "Good thing I wasn't there. I have strict rules about decking nuns."

"I came close to hitting her myself." She lowered her voice. "Do you know what she said? That *we're* responsible for what happened to Elvie."

In Kay's brown eyes, etched with wrinkles she made no attempt to camouflage with makeup, Rachel was dismayed to see a hint of hardened disillusionment where there had once been only fire. "It doesn't surprise me," Kay snorted. "The only thing I'd like to know is what the Sister Alices of this world expect us to *do* with all those unwanted babies."

"I guess she hopes couples like Brian and me will adopt them." She thought of her own home fires, dwindling to ash while she sat here, wringing her hands over the world's ills . . . and for the first time felt so discouraged she didn't know which way to turn. "Oh, Kay, I honestly don't know *what* to do."

Kay eyed her thoughtfully. "Are we still on the subject of Sister Alice?"

Rachel fell silent. Kay was her oldest friend; they'd roomed together in college. They'd toiled side by side in Vietnam. Who else was she going to confide in?

"Things aren't so great at home, either," she confessed.

"Why does that not surprise me?" Kay crossed her arms over her plump chest, taking advantage of her perch to peer down at Rachel. "Iris?"

"It's not just Iris." Rachel became suddenly absorbed in arranging alphabet blocks into words. She spelled out C-A-T and N-O-N-E.

"Brian, huh?"

Rachel nodded, keeping her head low so Kay wouldn't see the tears in her eyes. She hadn't told her friend the whole story, only the part she could bear to talk about—her fight with Rose, and Brian's leaving her in the lurch to take Rose home. "We've hardly spoken two words to one another since the party," she said. "Tomorrow, he leaves for Michigan. Some writers' conference. Every year they invite him, but this is the first time he's accepted. It doesn't take a genius to guess why."

Kay fixed her with a curiously unsympathetic gaze. "What did you expect? Given the choice between cold sheets and cold weather, I'd do the same."

"It's not as simple as that."

"What? You think I was born yesterday? *Nothing's* ever that simple. Especially with two people who've been married as long as you and Brian. But somebody has got to break the ice, and it might as well be you."

Rachel thought of her mother's garden, how every day Mama was out there, among her roses, weeding, clipping, trimming. A garden will tolerate anything but neglect, Mama liked to say. Turn your back, and it either dies or takes on a life of its own.

"I wouldn't know where to begin," she said.

"Bullshit." Kay leaped up, startling the little boy at her feet, whose face screwed up, as if he were about to start crying again. Rachel caught him just before he came unglued, and snatched him up onto her lap.

That didn't stop Kay. Pacing the narrow strip of carpeting that separated their two desks, she ranted, "Rachel, I swear, sometimes you can be so dense. The guy is crazy about you. He's over the moon, always has been. If you don't see it—this cold war, or whatever you want to call it—for what it is, then I give up. You don't deserve Brian."

Rachel stiffened. "Since you're such an expert, why don't you tell me what it is I should be doing differently?"

Kay threw her hands up, blowing out an exasperated breath. Her outburst deflated just as abruptly, and she sank back onto the chair. "Look, I don't have all the answers. The only thing I know is that nothing broken ever got fixed by sticking it up on a shelf. Why don't you start by asking yourself why a husband who loves you would choose to see an old friend home when he could just as easily have put her in a cab?"

Rachel flinched, and thought, *If you only knew . . .*

She hadn't planned on dumping all this on Kay. Yet when Kay and Simon split up, Rachel recalled, hadn't Kay cried on *her* shoulder more than a few times? Who was better equipped than her oldest friend to advise what to do if you think your husband might be cheating on you?

With a sigh, Rachel confessed, "Oh, God, it's so hard for me to say this . . . but I think . . . I'm scared something might be going on between Brian and Rose. Or, if nothing's happened yet, he *wants* it to."

Suddenly, Kay was all ears, leaning forward, her eyes full of concern. "Have you talked to Brian about it?"

She nodded. "He denies it, of course. But . . ." Rachel drew the line at confiding what had happened *after* they'd talked. She felt too ashamed; telling Kay would only make it more excruciating.

"But what? You think he's lying?" Kay pressed.

"If he is, then he's lying to himself," Rachel answered as fairly as she could. "I'm not sure he knows *what* he wants, at this point."

"Well, that's pretty obvious, isn't it?" Kay said. "He wants *you*. From what you've told me, none of this would be an issue if you two were spending more time together."

"Yeah, and if wishes were horses, beggars could ride." Rachel shook her head. "Honestly, I wish for the same thing. But every time I think I'm a few steps ahead of the game, I get swamped all over again."

"The question is, what are you going to do about it?"

"For someone who believes there's a solution to every problem, I feel pretty stupid admitting I don't have a clue." Rachel aimed for a weak chuckle that fell short of its mark. "Some days, Kay, I swear, I wish I could just walk right out that door. Leave this place to run itself, and let everybody just look after themselves."

"Why don't you?"

"Can't you just see it? I'd be climbing the walls within a week."

"What about a vacation?" Cagily, Kay added, "Unless you don't trust me to look after everything until you got back."

The thought glimmered in Rachel's mind, as tantalizing—and ultimately false—as a mirage. As much as she'd like to believe there was a quick, obvious cure to what ailed her marriage, she knew better. "I don't know if that's such a good idea right now," she said. "Plugging holes in a sinking marriage is one thing," she said. "But when the boat's about to tip over, you don't set out to sea in it."

"A quiet dinner, then." Kay was not giving up. "A restaurant where you can sit down like two civilized people. And talk."

"For someone who solved her own problems by getting a divorce, you sure seem to have all the answers," Rachel observed dryly.

"Yeah? Well, maybe it taught me something." Kay's expression turned wistful. As tough as she sometimes talked, and as many calluses as she'd built up around her heart, she had truly loved her husband. "Look, Simon and I—there was nothing much either of us could have done to make it work. But I happen to think what *you* have is worth fighting for."

"So do I." A reluctant smile forced its way to the surface, surprising Rachel. She eyed Kay with a mix of admiration and fond exasperation. "Have I ever told you that you remind me of my mother?"

"Practically every day since college. Except now I'm even starting to *look* like I could be." With a rueful laugh, she pushed a hand though her graying mop, which more and more these days reminded Rachel of an owl's ruffled feathers. "Maybe that's why I haven't gotten serious about anyone since Simon. Every guy I meet, I wind up nagging him to put the lid down and pick up his socks." Kay shook her head. "Speaking of your mother, how *is* she?"

"About the same," Rachel sighed. "She insists she's happy with Dr. Choudry. It's just that I'd feel better if she got a second opinion."

"What about *you?*" Kay suggested. "I know cardiology isn't exactly your specialty, but when was the last time you visited her and saw for yourself?"

Rachel felt a twinge of guilt. "It's been a few weeks." Part of her problem, she realized as she spoke, was not wanting to face the fact that her mother might *not* be doing as well as she insisted she was.

"Go see her. But first, see to your husband." Kay's brisk tone left no room for argument. She squatted down in front of the toddler, now growing droopy-eyed on Rachel's lap. "Hey, little man, you ready to go back to *your* mama? It sure smells that way." She wrinkled her nose as she scooped him into her arms.

Kay was halfway out the door when Rachel, still seated cross-legged on the floor, feeling a little foolish, and wondering if the snag she'd just noticed in her pantyhose was on the verge of becoming a full-fledged run, called softly, "Kay? Thanks."

Kay grinned over the toddler's dark curls. "I know you don't quite believe it yet, but things *will* get better. You won't regret taking my advice."

Watching her go, Rachel wondered if even dear, wise Kay could know how regretful she already was. It was killing her that she couldn't just pick up the phone and call Brian. Share with him everything that was troubling her, the way she used to.

But when the person you want most to comfort you is the one making you ache, what then? When the love you need isn't there because you allowed it to wither?

Something tipped over in her, and the blood drained from her head as if from an upended bucket. Feeling suddenly dizzy, Rachel—for the first time in more than twenty years as director of the East Side Women's Health Center—allowed herself to stretch out on the carpet and close her eyes.

❧ The restaurant was only a ten-minute stroll from their apartment, but as far as Rachel was concerned, it might as well have been a journey to the dark side of the moon. Along the way, she and Brian hardly exchanged two words. Ambling along at her side with his hands stuffed in the pockets of his oldest twill blazer, Brian seemed distracted, and not the least bit apologetic about the other night. Rachel, despite her every good intention, felt her outrage mount with each silent step.

Who was the injured party here, anyway? Who'd been left high and dry the night of Iris' party? How dare he act as if all this was somehow *her* fault.

At the Gotham, she waited until they were seated at her favorite table—on the raised area that skirted the main floor, where it was a little quieter than among the Deco-chromed banquettes below. As soon as their waiter, a young man with the slicked-back hair of an extra in a Fred Astaire movie, had taken their drink orders, Rachel leaned forward and with quiet emphasis said, "I can see this isn't going to be the romantic evening of either of our dreams. But I *was* hoping we could at least talk."

"I'm listening." Brian leaned into the soft glow of the candle, his gray eyes, which had always struck her as wonderfully pensive, now merely remote.

She wanted to stay mad, damnit. Mad kept her from having to face the truth: that a good portion of why she was so angry at her husband was because she knew she'd mostly brought it on herself. Yet she pleaded, "Don't do this, Brian. Don't make *me* out to be the bad guy here."

She caught a flicker on the lenses of his glasses, a spark of reflected candlelight that made her think of the thin rind of ice that forms on pavement when a rainstorm is followed by a sudden drop in temperature.

Then he reached across the table, and Rachel had to suppress a small shudder of delight at the familiar warmth of his hand. She gave it a light squeeze and withdrew—he mustn't think she was making too much of it.

"Do you *really* want to talk about it?" he asked. "Without pointing fingers?"

"Yes," she said. "But first, I need to know the truth. About you and Rose."

There it was again. His face closing against her, shutting her out. "I told you already."

"You haven't told me anything!"

"That's because there's nothing to tell."

Rachel felt her blood heating, swelling upward, making her scalp feel like a too-tight cap. She whispered furiously, "How can you say that? After . . . after the way you . . . that night. The way you made love to me."

Brian's eyes cut away; if he'd said something cruel, it couldn't have hurt more. Clearly, she'd struck a nerve in him. "Nothing happened," he insisted softly, still not meeting her gaze. "But I won't lie to you. I won't pretend that part of me didn't *want* to just turn back the clock."

Rachel clapped a hand over her mouth. Just like in a bad play, some distant corner of her brain observed dispassionately. Or that fairy tale about two princesses, one who spewed forth diamonds whenever she spoke, and the other toads. The image of a toad popping out suddenly made her want to giggle—a knee-jerk reaction to extreme circumstances that she'd struggled for years to curb. Apparently without success.

She dropped her head, both hands pressed to her mouth now, squeezing hard to keep from laughing hysterically. Tears rose in her eyes.

"Rachel, are you all right?" she heard Brian ask, his voice full of concern.

Her head jerked up, and now the words came with no trouble at all: "No. I'm not. How could I be?"

"It's not what you're thinking." His face softened, and once again, he reached for her hand. "Rachel, I . . ."

She jerked away. "Do you love her?" There. She'd spit it out: a toad, a great slimy warted thing with yellow pop-eyes and a long forked tongue.

Watching Brian sit back, Rachel felt unexpectedly bewildered, as if she'd been groping for a light switch in a dark room and been hit with the sudden realization that there was none; she was doomed to stumble about, sightless.

"That would make it easier for you, wouldn't it?" he said. "Having someone else to focus on. Someone to keep you from looking at the *real* problem."

"I see. It's all *my* fault, then. Everything."

"I didn't say that."

"You didn't have to."

When he spoke at last, her husband's voice was flat with defeat. "Look, it's my fault, too, okay? Nothing in a marriage, good or bad, happens in a vacuum. All I know is that, with Rose, she needed me. As a friend," he was quick to add. "It was nice to be needed for a change."

"*I* need you." Rachel dared not raise her voice above a whisper. Otherwise, she might burst into tears.

"No . . . you don't." Brian shook his head with regret. "You don't need anyone. It's the other way around—*you* trying to hold the world on your shoulders."

"Look, if you're referring to the clinic—"

"I don't want to *hear* about the clinic," he cut in, as sharply as a jab. Then his voice softened. "Max's death changed something for me, too," he said. "I look at Rose, and think, 'Damn, life really *is* short.' And I don't want to spend it alone. Yeah, I know—there's always some crisis you have to rush off to, usually at ninety miles an hour. What I want to know is, when does this particular train ever stop?"

"That isn't fair. It's not as if you're sitting still yourself."

"It's not the same," he told her. "And you know it."

She *did* know. Brian, unless he was on tour or racing to meet a deadline, had always been there—not just for her, but for their daughter. Yet, for some reason, that only made her more defensive. "You're right. It's *not* the same," she shot back. "The difference is that when *you* slow down your novel still gets written. And even if it didn't, no one would *die* as a result."

He offered her the crooked smile that had made her fall in love with him all those years ago. Only now it was more like a treasured keepsake she'd somehow lost . . . or given away. "Rachel, let's face it. If you were any less driven, I wouldn't *be* here. I'd have been shipped home from Nam in a body bag. But"—the angles of his face seemed to grow sharper—"the war is over. It's been over for a long time."

Rachel looked out at the tables below, each a candlelit island no doubt with its own quiet little drama. Husbands, wives, lovers, friends, business partners . . . all struggling in their own way to maintain what they believed were their inalienable rights.

Hadn't she, too, once believed her marriage was inviolate?

"Are you saying . . ." She stopped, unable to get the words out. Divorce. Did Brian want a divorce? She swallowed hard. "Look, I know there are things we need to work on."

She waited in stricken silence for Brian to answer.

"You have to be around in order to work on things," he reminded her gently.

She took hold of the wineglass their waiter had set in front of her, clutched it with both hands as if to steady herself. "It won't always be this way," she said. "I've already talked to Kay about taking some time off. In a month or so, when things settle down."

Brian smiled, and shook his head. "Do you know how many times I've heard that, Rachel? How many plane reservations we made that had to be canceled? It's *now* I'm talking about. Right now. I can't wait for an opening in your busy calendar. And neither can Iris."

"What's Iris got to do with this?"

"Maybe you haven't noticed, but she seems to have gone into hiding."

"That's ridiculous. She's at Drew's."

"Then why is it so hard to reach her? And when she *does* pick up the phone, it's like talking to a stranger. She can't get off fast enough. Drew, too. It's like anything other than the weather is suddenly classified information."

"I've noticed." Rachel sighed, relieved that this was a concern they could both share. "I figured she was just busy. You know, with starting school, finding an apartment. Oh, Brian, I guess I *have* been preoccupied. I didn't stop to think that maybe—" She broke off abruptly, too superstitious to say aloud what she was thinking, for fear it might come true: that Iris might be slipping back into that dark place, beyond their reach.

She looked across the table at the husband with whom she'd shared so much through the years—the agony of coming to terms with the fact that they would never have children of their own, coping with Brian's overnight celebrity, but, mostly, the crises with Iris that they'd weathered by holding tightly to each other's hands, like a pair of mountain climbers negotiating a sheer drop.

"There's one thing we tend to forget." Brian's richly textured voice, with its hint of Brooklyn, was like a tonic—healing and, at the same time, cruelly tantalizing her with the illusion of a quick fix that simply wasn't possible. "Iris is tougher than anyone thinks. She's survived this far, hasn't she?"

"True," Rachel acknowledged, though at times she wasn't so sure. "We're survivors, too, in a way."

He nodded thoughtfully. "That we are."

"You know," she said softly, "there's one thing I've always envied about you and Rose—the fact that you never grew old together. You never had to fight about who was spending more money. Or which one was doing most of the housework. You never had to take turns getting up in the night to take care of a sick child. When you look back, it all must seem so perfect and beautiful ... like a flower pressed between the pages of a book." She took a shaky breath. "That's what makes memories so precious. If they're not handled carefully, they fall apart."

"The only thing falling apart is us." Brian shook his head, and this time the glint in his eyes wasn't a reflection.

It was as if they'd found themselves, near the end of a long sea voyage, facing yet another tempest. Her first instinct was to reach for his hand. She held on, squeezing hard. She didn't know what else to do.

"Oh, Brian. What can I say?" she managed in a choked whisper.

"Nothing," he told her. Firm but kind. "We've talked enough. Things have to change, Rachel. That's all. Something has to give. And it won't be me. I've given my fair share already."

She couldn't argue with that. But what he hadn't told her was *how* to change. How was she to separate the strands of her life—strands that had somehow gotten tangled into one giant knot?

Rachel knew no other way than to tug hard, but that was only making it worse. There *had* to be a way to weave those strands into a tapestry that would encompass what she and Brian wanted, both for themselves and for each other; something that would prove both lovely and serviceable.

Out of nowhere came the thought of her mother. Why hadn't Mama married Nikos? Except for her usual glib response about being too set in her ways, she'd never offered any real explanation. Did she fear that it would compromise her? That marrying again would somehow trample the tender sprig of independence she'd nurtured over the years into a strong tree?

Tomorrow she would ask Mama's advice. See what words of wisdom, if any, Mama had to offer.

It was ironic, Rachel thought. She'd planned on visiting simply to make sure everything was all right. A concerned daughter looking in on her elderly mother. But now *she* was the one in need of solace, longing for her mother's cool hand against her brow, and for Mama's sensible voice telling her what to do.

Chapter 11

Sylvie, dozing in her bed, propped nearly upright by a mound of pillows, was aware of a faint humming noise. In her half-dreaming state, she imagined a honeybee trapped against a windowpane, deceived by the blue sky on the other side into believing it could fly straight through the glass. When she was little, she would always capture the poor things in a Mason jar, and set them free outdoors. Otherwise, they just kept at it until they perished. People weren't much smarter, she mused; they only imagined they were.

Bzzzttt.

Not an insect's droning, Sylvie realized. It seemed to be coming from the intercom.

Her eyes fluttered open, and she muttered thickly, "What?"

No answer. She lay alone in the four-poster bed, gazing up at the ceiling, which, with its rose-medallion centerpiece and curlicued brackets, had always made her think of an upside-down wedding cake. Not even the safe bulwark of Nikos' broad, sleeping back to comfort her. Good Lord. Had she slept away the entire morning?

It had to be nearly lunchtime, judging from the sunlight flung like a bright shawl across the eyelet duvet. So late! But these days, time had a funny habit of folding in on her. She'd be out on the patio, reading or enjoying her afternoon tea, and she'd close her eyes to rest them, just for a minute . . . only to start awake and discover that somehow a whole *hour* had gone by.

I'm old, she thought impatiently. *An old lady snoozing my life away.*

Not just old, but *weak*. Day by day, her strength leaked from her like water from a cracked pitcher. Lying down was the only way to keep from being drained altogether. By the same token, nothing ever seemed to replenish her. She could sleep all day, and wake up feeling no more rested than if she'd spent the night reading or watching TV. A trip upstairs left her as exhausted as if she'd climbed to the top of the Empire State. And however deeply she breathed, her lungs were always starved for air.

Dr. Choudry, at her last appointment, had clipped X-rays of her chest to a lightboard and pointed out the cloudy areas where fluid lay trapped. In his courtly, faintly accented English, which reminded her of Nikos when they'd first met, her cardiologist had warned about the risk of developing pneumonia. Antibiotics would only prolong the inevitable, he explained, his soft brown eyes fixing on her with a gravity that would have made her smile—how oddly formal he appeared, like a Victorian suitor gathering the nerve to ask her hand in marriage!—if she hadn't been on the verge of tears. It was time they discussed the possibility of a transplant, he said.

"No. Thank you." She'd cut him off, firmly but politely, as if it were an unwanted magazine subscription he was trying to interest her in. "Whatever time I have left, I don't intend to spend it on a waiting list, hoping for a healthy heart that ought to go to someone young, with his whole life still ahead of him."

Now, as the faint murmuring of voices drifted up the stairs, she wondered if Nikos had company. The past few weeks, he'd insisted on staying home to keep an eye on her. But that only meant his work now came to him. Anteros' chief foreman, Joe D'Angelo, had stopped by twice yesterday. The den was now littered with blueprints, punch lists, specs on various interiors, not to mention the endless coffee mugs and overflowing ashtrays that had their overworked housekeeper muttering under her breath.

Poor Nikos. This was hard on him, too. Occasionally, she'd catch him with his guard down, watching her with an expression of fierce apprehension, as if she were a precious vase teetering on the edge of a narrow shelf. Sylvie longed to put his fears to rest . . . but how could

she? There was no way she could reassure Nikos of what she only suspected was true: her time had not yet come. One day, perhaps
not too far away, she'd be stretched out in her coffin instead of on
this bed. But first, she had important business to attend to. Family
business.

And until it was taken care of, she could not, *would* not, go without a fight.

Something has to be done about Iris. The thought had been lodged
in Sylvie's mind like a splinter since yesterday afternoon, when her
granddaughter had unexpectedly stopped by.

The girl who'd sat at her kitchen table bore no resemblance to the
joyful young woman who'd celebrated her engagement only weeks
before. Iris had looked—well, mournful. She'd lost weight, too; her
jeans hung on her as if from a clothesline.

Sylvie, shocked to see her so despondent, had insisted on fixing
Iris a toasted cheese sandwich. But the girl had only picked at it,
crumbling the hard crust into tiny crumbs that lay sprinkled over her
plate like birdseed.

"Would you rather have soup instead?" Sylvie had offered. "I
could heat some up. It won't take a minute." She'd felt silly, useless—
only stupid, old women believed food was the cure for whatever
ailed. But what else could she do?

Iris shook her head. She looked small and lost, seated at the
sturdy pine table that had been a fixture of this kitchen since Sylvie
had come to the house as a timid young bride. It was the table at
which she'd first interviewed Nikos for the job of handyman, over
half a century ago, never dreaming they would end up spending their
lives together. And where Rachel, as a little girl, had stood on a chair
with an apron tied around her neck, rolling out scraps of piecrust.

Iris had loved to play underneath it with her dolls, pretending it
was her secret fort. As much as she loved her own home and parents,
this house had always been a refuge for her. Sylvie could see Iris in
her mind, a little girl racing up the front steps, her arms flung wide.

She knew every cupboard and closet, every corner in which to curl up and read. She loved the defunct bellpulls in the kitchen, artifacts from the days of many servants.

But her favorite place of all had been the attic. How often when Rachel or Brian arrived to pick Iris up, had they had to search high and low, calling from room to room? When at last they found her, it was usually by climbing the ladder to the attic. She'd be rummaging in one of the old trunks, or playing house with the baby furniture that once upon a time had been Rachel's. She'd especially loved the wicker bassinet, passed down from Sylvie's own grandmother; she'd spend hours arranging her dolls in it, and rocking them to sleep.

Like a cloud passing over the sun, a shadow scudded over the surface of this happy memory. Sylvie found herself remembering the time she'd come upon her seven-year-old granddaughter playing with matches in the attic. No, not *playing*. Iris had been holding a lit match to her baby doll, watching, as if in a trance, as the flame caused a portion of the doll's plastic arm to bubble, then begin to melt. Only when Sylvie cried out in alarm, startling her, had Iris snapped out of whatever spell she'd been under . . .

"I'm sorry, Grandma." Iris now pushed her plate aside with a sigh. "I guess I wasn't as hungry as I thought."

"Something to drink maybe?" Sylvie started to get up.

Iris' hand circled her wrist, stopping her. "Really, Grandma. I don't need anything. I'm only here to see you."

Sylvie sank back into her chair. Her granddaughter's fingers felt strangely weightless, as if her bones were hollow, like a bird's. More shaken than she dared let on, Sylvie replied warmly, "We'll just sit and visit, then. I was feeling a little low, and you're just the medicine I need." She lightly touched her granddaughter's cheek. "How's my *shainenke?*"

"Fine, just fine." Iris stared sightlessly out the window, where the morning glory that twisted up the drainpipe had begun to die back, its leaves riddled by insects and the onset of cold weather into something that resembled old, tattered lace. In a queer, disconnected voice, she said, "Drew and I have been looking at apartments. But the ones we can afford are either too small or too dark."

Sylvie hesitated only an instant, not wanting to seem too eager, before offering, "Do you need money, dear? I could lend you some, if you'd like. Pay me back whenever you can . . . or not at all. All I care about it is that you're happy."

Tears flooded Iris' eyes, making them appear huge and luminous. "Oh, Gran." Her voice trembled on a note so wistful it was almost heartbreaking. As if she wished desperately it could be that simple. "You've always been so generous. Too generous. But I don't want your money."

"Well, then . . . I'm sure you'll find something." Sylvie spoke firmly and brightly. "In the meantime, you must be busy with school. Are you enjoying your classes so far?"

"School?" Iris blinked, as if she'd just woken from a nap, and swung sluggishly around to meet Sylvie's gaze. In a dull voice, she finished, "Oh . . . well . . . The thing is, I dropped out. For now. I asked the dean if I could defer until next semester. To be honest, I'm not sure if I ever want to go back. I can paint on my own, can't I?" She shrugged, but a wary look had crept into her eyes. "You won't tell my parents, will you?"

"I'm sure they'd understand. If you explained it to them." Sylvie tried to keep the alarm from her voice. She didn't know which was worse, Iris dropping out of school, or the fact that she was keeping it from her parents. Ever since she could remember, Iris had wanted to be an artist. As far back as kindergarten, her drawings had been more colorful and imaginative than any of her classmates'.

But her change of heart wasn't the real problem, Sylvie suspected. It was just the handwriting on the wall.

"I will. Soon." Iris smiled, the corners of her mouth tucked downward in a faintly rueful expression that Sylvie found not the least bit reassuring. "You know how Mom is. She worries if I miss a doctor's appointment." She dropped her voice. "And, anyway, between you and me, things haven't been so great at home. That's another reason I've been staying away."

"Do you want to talk about it?" Sylvie asked, though not at all sure she wanted to hear.

Iris shifted in her chair and began twirling a hank of hair—a childhood habit she reverted to when she was anxious. "It's been going on for a while, I think," she confided. "All the stuff that happened over the summer with Drew and me just turned the flame up. Now Mom is furious with Rose. She thinks Dad and Rose might be having an affair."

Sylvie felt her heart catch, and she slumped back in her chair. "Oh dear."

Just like before, she thought. In the early years of Rachel's marriage, when she'd fretted over the fact that they couldn't have children, using Rose as her scapegoat. Imagining Brian still loved Rose . . . and wanted to go back to her.

Now, decades later, Sylvie found herself wondering if there had been more than a grain of truth in Rachel's jealous imaginings. If Brian really did still carry some sort of torch for Rose. Certainly, from what Sylvie had seen, Rachel had done nothing to discourage him from wandering.

"What do *you* think?" she asked her granddaughter.

Iris shrugged, but Sylvie could see she was troubled. "I don't think anything's happened. But Mom . . ." She let the sentence trail off. "I just wish sometimes she'd stop worrying about everyone else and worry more about *herself*."

Well said, Sylvie thought.

"I'm sure your parents will work it out." She spoke with more confidence than she felt. "What I'm worried about, frankly, is *you*. Iris, dear, pardon me for saying so, but you don't look well."

Iris shifted away from her, and sat chewing her bottom lip in silence. Finally, she said, "Drew thinks we should wait to move in together. Until things are more settled."

This is about more than finding the right apartment, Sylvie thought. The look on Iris' face told a story much deeper, and darker. "Tell me," she urged softly. "What is it? Why so sad?"

Iris shook her head, and a tear from one brimming eye spilled down her cheek. "Oh, Grandma . . . it's not Drew's fault. It's *me.* The way I get sometimes."

"What way is that?" Sylvie asked, dreading yet already knowing the answer.

"Drew is always telling me he loves me," Iris began, her head tucked low. "But I never believe him. After a while, I start thinking that maybe he's just saying it to make me feel better. And the next thing I know, I'm picking a fight. Accusing him of stuff. And . . . well . . . you can pretty much imagine the rest." She looked up, her lashes stuck together in dark wet spikes.

Sylvie felt tired, so tired she could have put her head down right then and there. But she had to say alert, find a way to help. Cautiously, she asked, "Have you spoken to anyone about this?"

"Just Dr. Eisenger. He says that when a negative thought creeps in, I should ask myself, 'Is this real, or am I just looking for an excuse to feel bad?' But it's hard to know sometimes." Elbows propped on the table, she rested her chin in her palms, her fingers cupped delicately about her face. "With Drew, I hold on so tight I end up choking him . . . but I can't seem to make myself stop." The tears were flowing freely now, but Iris wasn't wiping them away—as if she was so used to crying she hardly noticed. "Grandma, have you ever wanted something so bad you'd *die* to keep from losing it?"

Sylvie brought a hand to her chest. A cold heaviness sat squarely over her heart. Not painful exactly—more like a dull ache. She took slow, careful breaths, consciously relaxing her body as she'd been taught. But the anvil above her heart wouldn't budge.

Softly, she said: "I know what it's like to lose someone you love."

The thought of Rose gleamed like some ancient, unalloyed mineral below the heavy layers of her shame. All these years, believing time healed all wounds, she'd only been fooling herself. Rose would never forgive her. And why should she? Sylvie couldn't forgive herself.

Iris, she saw, was now eyeing *her* with concern. Pulling herself up straight, Sylvie added, "The important thing to remember is that you *are* loved. Not just by Drew. Your mother and father would do anything for you. And I hope I don't have to tell you how *I* feel."

Iris dropped her head into her hands. The muffled voice that emerged from between her fingers sent a chill through Sylvie; it was as hollow and desperate as that of a prisoner behind a locked door. "You're the only one I can talk to, Grandma, the only one who understands. Rose hates me. And Mom and Daddy . . . they act as if my getting engaged is the answer to their prayers. I *can't* disappoint them."

"Nonsense." Sylvie reached across with both hands and lifted her granddaughter's face as she would a drooping rosebush in need of staking. "The only thing that matters is whether or not *you're* happy. Now, let's begin at the beginning. Tell me everything. . . ."

Iris took a deep, uneven breath. "Once in a while, I have these . . . weird blackouts. Usually, it's when I forget to take my medication. But I can't always predict when it's going to happen." The color had drained from her face, and Sylvie saw she was trembling, her whole body, as if in the grip of a fever chill. "One night, I locked myself in Drew's bathroom, and . . . and I . . . just blanked out. All I remember is that it—it smelled like something was *burning*. But there was no fire. Drew told me—after he broke the door down—that I'd only imagined it. But I *didn't* see the razor. I didn't know it was there, on the bathroom floor, until Drew showed me. Oh, Grandma," she whispered, her teeth chattering as she hugged herself. "What's *wrong* with me?"

Sylvie felt her alarm slip over into panic. It was as if a puzzle she'd been struggling with—the puzzle that was Iris—had suddenly revealed itself to be more complicated than anything she, or anyone, could solve. They'd all been clinging to the belief that her therapist knew what he was doing. That, in time, and with proper medication,

Iris would be able to lead a normal life. Even that Drew's love could save her somehow. But, Sylvie knew now, that simply wasn't the case.

Her granddaughter's confession had shocked Sylvie deeply. What shocked her even more, however, was that all this time, while Iris had been gradually disintegrating, practically before their eyes, not one person in the family had done a thing to prevent it. Least of all herself.

I should have done what Rose asked, she thought in anguish, *I should have spoken up.*

By holding her tongue, she'd failed not only Iris, but both her daughters as well. Iris was *sick.* Clearly, the time had come for drastic measures. . . .

She would gather the whole family together for a summit meeting, Sylvie decided then and there. Drew and Rose, too. Together, they would decide what was best.

But by the time Iris had left, Sylvie was too exhausted even to pick up the phone. It was all she could do just to crawl into bed.

Now, after a whole night and half a day of sleep, Sylvie felt no less tired. Lord have mercy. How would she ever summon the energy to mobilize an entire family into action?

Hearing the muffled thud of footsteps on the stairs, she felt her spirits lift. Nikos. He would help. If only to soothe and encourage her. Long ago—in another lifetime, it seemed—she'd hesitated to lean on him, but now the thought of his strong shoulder brought real tears of relief to her aching eyes.

In response to his light knock, she called, "Come in, dear. I'm awake."

The door swung open . . . but it wasn't Nikos who stepped inside. Sylvie didn't immediately recognize the silhouetted figure emerging from the dark hallway into the bright room.

Then the figure moved out of the glare and into focus . . . materializing at once into a slender middle-aged woman with light-brown hair threaded with gray, wearing a stylish black coatdress with gold buttons that flashed in the sunlight.

Rachel.

Sylvie smiled, her spirits lifting. "Just who I wanted to see."

"Did I wake you?" Rachel approached the bed as any doctor might have, briskly and with a sense of authority, but her blue eyes were soft with concern.

"No, dear . . . but you should have called," Sylvie chided gently. "I'd have been up and dressed if I'd known you were coming. And here I am indulging myself as shamelessly as a lazy old cat." She patted the mattress beside her. "Come, sit with me. And stop looking at me like you're afraid I'll shatter if you breathe on me."

Rachel looked unconvinced by Sylvie's display of lightheartedness, but she didn't argue. Something else was troubling her, Sylvie could see. And, unfortunately—for in many ways Sylvie believed that ignorance truly was bliss—she had a pretty good idea what that might be.

Sylvie became aware of her heart laboring in a way that was truly frightening. She considered asking Rachel to fetch her the vial of Hytrin from her medicine chest, but decided to wait. *It's probably nothing,* she told herself, *and I wouldn't want her to worry.* Instead, she smoothed the covers over her lap, staring down at the bumps of her knees under the lace duvet, which made her think of tree roots buried under a blanket of snow.

Sylvie thought: *I can't protect her.* The realization—long overdue, she supposed—brought a bittersweet pang.

Rachel hiked herself onto the bed, which as a child she used to make believe was a wooden ship, its four carved posters the masts by which it sailed to far-off lands. Peering closely at Sylvie, she observed with her usual bluntness, "I don't like your color, Mama."

Who am I fooling? She's a doctor. She knows a sick person when she sees one.

"I haven't been able to spend as much time outdoors as I'd like," Sylvie confessed lightly. "But, heavens, you didn't come all this way to listen to me complain."

"When was your last appointment with Dr. Choudry?" Rachel folded her arms over her chest, refusing to be diverted.

"Tuesday of last week," Sylvie informed her. "So, you see, you have nothing to worry about. I've been examined from head to toe. Nothing new to report, except that he and I have become quite chummy. Did you know that in England, where he went to college, Tinoo Choudry was a nationally ranked polo champion? Personally, I find it fascinating. To think of someone so athletic choosing medicine instead. He told me—"

"Mother . . . you're changing the subject." Rachel was trying to look stern, but couldn't keep from smiling. "If you won't tell me, I'll have to put in a call to this famous Dr. Choudry myself."

Sylvie knew, without even having to ask, that Rachel had done so already. She also knew that Rachel couldn't have learned much. Dr. Choudry was a man of his word—Sylvie was too good a judge of character to be wrong about this—and would honor his promise not to reveal to her family how sick she was.

"I'm only trying to put you at ease," she soothed. "There's nothing wrong with me that a little rest won't cure."

"I'm not here to check up on you."

"You're a wonderful daughter," Sylvie shook her head, "but a terrible liar."

Rachel smiled back. "Okay. But that's not the *only* reason I came."

"Fair enough."

"Mama . . . there's something I need to talk to you about." Rachel looked pale and tired herself, Sylvie noted as she covered her daughter's hand with her own. "Brian and I have been having some problems. . . ."

"I know," Sylvie stopped her before she could go any further. "Iris stopped by yesterday. She told me."

Rachel's eyes widened in alarm. "Iris?"

"She seems to think it has something to do with Rose," Sylvie hedged delicately.

Rachel's face flushed an unattractive mottled pink that made Sylvie remember when she'd had the measles as a child. "I didn't mean for her to hear. Oh God. It's all so embarrassing."

Embarrassing? Sylvie found herself growing impatient. Rachel, since she was a little girl, had been this way—understating when she should have been shouting, always holding her cards close to her vest.

Sylvie lifted an eyebrow. "I would have thought suspecting your husband of having an affair would be more painful than embarrassing."

Seeing Rachel's face twist with a pain deeper than any she could have put words to, Sylvie immediately wished she'd kept her thoughts to herself. Rachel's visible struggle to hold her emotions in check was so huge, it exhausted Sylvie just watching her.

Finally, Rachel said, "I never would have believed something like this could happen. Not *now,* after all these years. That's the worst part. I feel so *stupid. . . .*"

The thought of Gerald flashed across Sylvie's mind, the stricken look on his face the day he'd surprised her coming up the steps from Nikos' basement room. "Don't," she advised, more sternly than she'd intended. "Whatever happened. Whatever you imagine—it's not something you could have prevented, believe me."

"That's not the way Brian sees it." Anger seemed to lend her a welcome refuge from her vast, formless dread, but the refuge proved temporary. Her shoulders sagging, Rachel gripped the bedpost. "Oh, Mama, I'm afraid he's going to ask me for a divorce."

In spite of herself, Sylvie gasped. "Whatever would possess him to do a thing like that?"

"He thinks I don't love him."

"Well, *do* you?"

"How can you ask that?" Holding on to the bedpost, Rachel hauled herself up and stood swaying slightly on her feet, like a sailor testing his land legs. "Mama, I don't know what I'd do if Brian ever left me."

Sylvie instinctively pulled back on the throttle; right now, her daughter needed a dose of good sense more than a mother's outrage.

"Well, for heaven's sake's, why wait until then? What's keeping you from doing something about it *now?*"

Rachel looked at her askance, as if not quite sure what to make of this new, sharp-tongued mother. "You sound angry, Mama. Are you all right?"

"I wish people would stop asking me that. You have no idea how tired I get having to reassure everyone all the time." Suddenly Sylvie *was* angry. *Good for me,* she thought. It proved she still had a few drops of gas left in her tank.

Rachel shook her head with a helplessness that was almost jarringly out of character. "I want to change things. I just don't know how. It's like I'm on this giant hamster wheel, and the more I try to get off, the faster it turns."

"Then you haven't tried hard enough."

It hurt Sylvie to be so harsh . . . but it was essential that she get the message across. Not only for Rachel's sake, and Brian's . . . but, indirectly, for Iris'. Rachel needed to focus on something even more pressing than her marriage. She had to find a way—just as Sylvie herself was attempting to do now—to help her child.

Sylvie, with great difficulty, drew in a deep breath. "There's something else you should know," she said. "Iris didn't stop by just to chat. She was terribly upset. And not just about you and Brian."

As if an alarm had sounded, Rachel gave a little jerk, becoming instantly alert. "Did she say why?"

"Sit down, darling," Sylvie urged gently. "I'll tell you everything I know. But first, you must understand what's involved. Iris is . . . well, she's beyond what a weekly appointment with her therapist can handle. Frankly, I'm not even certain this doctor knows what he's doing."

Sylvie's heart was thundering in her chest, and suddenly she felt dizzy.

"Mama . . . Mama . . ." She could hear Rachel calling her, but it seemed to be coming at her in a blizzard, muted by snow and howling wind.

Sylvie squeezed her eyes shut. Her chest felt tight and clogged, as if she were drowning, her lungs filling with water. She tried to breathe, but no air was getting through.

A sharp pain exploded just below her windpipe, spreading downward in a fiery arc. She clutched at the front of her nightgown, clawing at it, as if this thing that was burning its way through her could somehow be dislodged. Her mouth opened, then snapped closed. Rachel's face grew fuzzy . . . then loomed once again into view. The four-poster bed she'd shared with Nikos for more than twenty years—and her husband, Gerald, before that—canted sideways, becoming the imaginary ship of which Rachel had once been the captain . . . and which now was threatening to capsize.

The room turned gray, then black, as Sylvie felt herself dissolve into thousands of bright pinpoints, like stars in some distant galaxy, far beyond human reach.

🙊   Sylvie struggled mightily, swimming her way up through blackness toward the faintly glimmering surface just over her head. She heard voices, but they were distorted and droning, like an old-fashioned phonograph played at the wrong speed. Wavery shapes above her materialized slowly into faces. Rachel . . . then Nikos.

Rachel was pale as an egg. But she was also a doctor, Sylvie comprehended in some corner of her brain. Rachel would fix whatever was wrong. She would know what to do.

"Mama . . . can you tell me where it hurts?" A cool hand pressed against Sylvie's chest, where her nightgown had come unbuttoned. "I can help you, but you have to help, too. Can you talk?"

Sylvie turned her head toward Nikos, kneeling beside her, his weathered face, like old, rubbed leather, shining with tears. Slowly, almost reverently, he took her hand and lifted it to his mouth. The warm pressure of his lips against her knuckles caused the fiery pain in her chest to recede slightly.

"Sylvie . . . you are going to be all right," he murmured. "Do you hear me?"

Sylvie croaked a noise meant to be "yes" through a mouth that felt numb, like after she'd been to the dentist. Somewhere in the midst of the roaring pain, she was dimly aware of her heart weakly flopping. There was an odd tingling in her arms and legs . . . and the bed beneath her felt damp.

"Call an ambulance," she heard Rachel command.

It was like a bucket of icy water dashed over Sylvie. Out of nowhere, she found the strength to grab Rachel's sleeve. "Please . . . no."

"Don't be ridiculous." Rachel's voice rose. "Mama, if we don't get you to the hospital, you might . . ." She broke off, casting a sharp glance at Nikos.

But instead of rushing to the phone, he remained kneeling beside the bed, his broad shoulders bowed as if in prayer. It wasn't until Rachel started to get up that he rose to his full height, reaching out to grip her shoulders gently.

"No," he said in his deep rumble of a voice. "Let her be. It's what she wants." Tears had found their way into the deep crevices of his face.

"That's crazy." Rachel stared at him in disbelief. "She'll die!"

"I want to . . . die . . . ," Sylvie gasped, "in my own bed."

Rachel shook her head violently. Sylvie knew it went against everything she believed in. She also knew that, in the end, Rachel would do as her mother wished. For her daughter was brave as well as smart—brave enough to give what was asked of her, rather than insisting on what she felt was needed.

I raised her well. The thought rolled to a stop somewhere amid her surging agony, smooth and lovely as a perfect ocean shell washed onto a shore.

But what about her other daughter? What about Rose?

Abruptly, the shore turned sharp, full of broken, scattered shells.

I'll go to my grave leaving her nothing but a legacy of lies.

Suddenly it struck her that Iris wasn't the only reason she'd hung on until now. It was because of Rose, too. She couldn't leave this earth without letting go of the burden she'd carried in her heart all these years—the secret buried so deep she'd believed it impossible to unearth.

There was time. Just *thinking* about it was like struggling to turn an ancient faucet that had been rusted shut, but she knew that if she tried hard enough she could open it. She had to. This was her last chance. *Rose's* last chance.

You'd do that to Rachel? a voice cried out in protest.

Sylvie's resolve faltered. Then she reminded herself that there was *never* a good time for the revealing of long-kept secrets. And if she hesitated, it might be too late. Rachel was strong. She would survive. And Iris, Lord help her—her problem went much deeper than anything that was within Sylvie's power to alter, one way or the other.

It was Rose she had to think of now. Rose, from whom she'd withheld the final measure of her love . . .

Sylvie, through a swimming haze, looked up at Nikos. In his dear face, hewn, like something for the ages, with anguish, she found the strength to move forward, to do what was right. . . .

A kind of lightness overtook her, causing the pain to diminish just a little—enough for her to speak clearly.

"Rose," she whispered. "Please. Ask her to come. There's something I need to tell her. . . ."

Chapter 12

꒑ The stuffy, paneled anteroom appeared crowded. Four members of opposing counsel huddled at one end, like players in a high-school football team. Rose—accompanied by Christina Overby, house counsel for the insurance company—stood poised in readiness by a frosted-glass door, which opened onto one of the labyrinthine corridors that cross-sectioned the fourth floor of the New York County Courthouse at 60 Centre Street.

Somebody throw the frigging ball, Rose urged silently, literally tapping her foot with impatience.

The trial of *Esposito* v. *St. Bartholomew's* had been under way for exactly one week. The jury had heard medical testimony from a lineup of medical personnel—from the attending physician to the orderly assigned to OR-8 on the morning of Mrs. Esposito's surgery. They'd been taken step by step through the surgical procedure that had allegedly left the elderly woman partially paralyzed. They'd even heard expert witnesses testify as to the high rate of cerebral aneurysms among long-term smokers.

Rose had introduced foamcore-mounted exhibits of Mrs. Esposito's X-rays and CAT scans both before and after the surgery. As well as blowups of invoices tracing her spending habits, which had escalated sharply in the months she'd supposedly been bedridden and incapacitated. Rose had even found a witness—a former son-in-law of Mrs. Esposito—to refute the plaintiff's claim that she'd been in perfect health before her stroke.

The jury, which at the outset had seemed sympathetic to the elderly woman slumped in her wheelchair, was slowly bending Rose's way. She could feel it the way a sudden rise in temperature affected her sinuses. Nothing she could put her finger on—the odd wince here and there, the disapproving little head-shake, their refusal to make eye contact with the plaintiff.

For one thing, Mrs. Esposito, when she took the stand, had appeared anything but helpless—swatting at the bailiff when he attempted to push her wheelchair to the front of the courtroom, snapping defensively when Rose questioned her about certain inconsistencies between her testimony and her sworn deposition.

Not to mention a paucity of real evidence—which, during pretrial discovery, had prompted numerous fishing expeditions on Cannizzaro's part. And which now, in the second day of the plaintiff's attorneys' presentation, was becoming obvious to the jury as well.

Certainly, the huge compensatory award for Mrs. Esposito that had seemed in the bag was rapidly dwindling to Las Vegas odds. And now Mark Cannizzaro was ready to talk settlement.

Yet Rose knew it would be a mistake for her to get too cocky. After all, she'd been wrong before. Who could have predicted the jury's decision in *Maxwell* v. *CoreTech Industries?* The plaintiff had claimed severe damage from exposure to asbestos, but suffered from nothing other than what was described as "debilitating migraines." The jury had awarded him damages of eight million.

It's not over till it's over, she could hear Max say. She felt her armpits grow damp, and shifted her leather portfolio to one hip.

She watched Mark pull away from the pack, his forehead below his bushy hairline shiny with sweat. "A million two," he growled at Rose.

Was it her imagination, or had he shrunk in the past five days? Or maybe, she thought, he was simply reverting to his simian roots—a reverse of those diagrams charting the evolution of man from apes.

Rose steeled herself before setting foot on what might prove to be nothing more than quicksand. "Four fifty," she shot back. "Plus, you drop the suit against Diagnostics." Diagnostics, Inc., the largest shareholder of which happened to be her client, St. Bart's, was the independent laboratory that had run the plaintiff's tests—erroneously, according to the Esposito home team.

Mark shot her a stagey grimace. "That's highway robbery, and you know it. Nine fifty, that's as far we'll go. Consider it cheap at the price."

"Robbery? Mark, may I remind you that *my* client isn't the one holding a gun to anyone's head," Rose responded coolly.

Beside her, Rose felt her co-counsel, Christina, grow as tense as a terrier straining at its leash. Rose accidentally on purpose bumped her elbow to distract her before Christina could blurt something that would screw this deal. Christina, thirtyish, yet prematurely gray since her teens, was often mistaken for Rose's elder—a fact she didn't appreciate. And she was in no mood now to sit back and let Rose steal the show.

"Mr. Cannizzaro, I don't think you fully appreciate the negative impact of what—" Christina began, chin raised, chest up, vowels rounded—a white-glove Vassar girl to the hilt.

"Five hundred," Rose interrupted her.

She understood the Mark Cannizzaros of the world; she'd grown up with them on Avenue K, watched them playing games of pickup in their raggedy shorts and line-dried T-shirts. She'd learned to negotiate with them long before law school—helping them with their homework for the price of a homemade cannoli; haggling over baseball cards; getting them to pony up their lunch money in exchange for the mimeographed copies of the "shit" list Sister Perpetua kept in her office: the titles of all the books banned by the Church.

The rules of the game? You could rob them blind, you could even trick them. But you must never, ever make them look foolish.

Cannizzaro laughed—a hard, gritty sound, like shoes scuffing over gravel. "You drive a hard bargain, Griffin. Seven fifty, and we ditch Diagnostics. That's it. Final. I swear on my mama's grave, I can't go any lower than that."

Rose fixed him with a look that said, *We're paisanos, you can't pull that shit with me.* "Face it, the jury isn't buying. Six fifty, take it or leave it. This offer expires in exactly one minute."

Christina started to open her mouth again, while Cannizzaro's boys—all graduates of the Academy of Wannabe Yuppies—simply stared.

Mark Cannizzaro shifted from one navy Capezio loafer to the other before grunting, "Make it seven hundred and you've got a deal."

Rose shook her head, and folded her arms over her chest.

"Six fifty won't even cover my expenses!" Mark protested.

"That's your problem." He might not like it, but he would respect her for hanging tough.

"Ahhh, Griffin, come on. . . ."

"It's that, or nothing," she told him. "You won't be able to get a shoe shine with what *that* jury is going to award your client, trust me."

"We'll appeal."

"Be my guest. Do you know the percentage of overturned decisions in cases presided over by Judge Delehanty? Less than two—and that's in the past ten years."

After what seemed like an eternity, in which she could have sworn she actually felt steam rising from her armpits, Mark hunched his shoulders defensively and muttered, "I'll run it by my client."

Translation: *I'll make it happen, one way or another.*

Rose allowed herself a tiny smile of triumph. She wasn't quite there yet; Mark could change his mind, or his client could refuse to play ball. But Rose doubted either of those things would happen. In court, you took your chances, and you cut your losses. Everybody knew that.

Forty minutes later, Rose was sailing through the courthouse's Corinthian-columned portico, and down the wide marble steps, with a bona-fide accepted offer in hand. The jury had been thanked and dismissed. Though there were still a million details to be negotiated, the matter of *Esposito* v. *St. Bartholomew's* had, for all intents and purposes, been put to bed.

Which was where Rose wished she could be right now.

It was just past eleven, and already she felt as if she'd put in a full twelve-hour day. Tense, her mind racing. Neck and shoulders steely enough to set off a metal detector.

She grabbed a taxi on Worth Street, gave the driver her office cross streets, and sank into the back seat. She was meeting Eric at one, but she could get a few things cleared off her desk before then.

Rose closed her eyes, rubbing the bridge of her nose between thumb and forefinger. She knew she ought to feel triumphant. Instead, she felt merely restless—a restlessness she suspected had nothing to do with the trial.

Eric. She couldn't stop thinking about him: the things they'd talked about, the faint raspiness of his voice late at night over the phone, the light pressure of his hand against the small of her back when ushering her through a door or bending close to kiss her.

In bed, too. The tip of his tongue circling her navel, the practiced motions of his hand between her legs. And making love, dear God, his almost supernatural ability to hold back, minute after minute, until she'd had her fill.

But more than all that, the thing she'd longed for and, at the same time, dreaded had come true.

She was in love.

When had she discovered this to be true—without a shadow of doubt? Oddly enough, it wasn't in Eric's bed, or even in his arms. Her revelation had come on a day, two weeks ago, when she'd been at her wit's end with Jay. Her youngest son had been sulking over the fact that she was going out again—the third evening that week—and when Eric arrived to pick Rose up for the concert to which he'd scored free tickets, she'd feared his being there would only make things worse.

But after darting into the kitchen for some cold drinks, she'd returned to find Eric and Jay deeply absorbed in a conversation about blues artists. Turned out they were both big B. B. King and Muddy Waters fans. They were discussing the finer points of various recordings, their heads bent over a handful of CDs from Jay's collection. Instantly, Rose had been struck by the age-old picture they formed. In that unguarded moment, so at ease with one another that they might have been father and son.

She'd felt a hard lump of ice inside her start to dissolve, and it was further melted when Eric suggested that Jay join them. He'd snag an extra ticket at the door, he said; besides, he'd added with a wink, it might be time for Jay to expand his repertoire to include a little Beethoven and Brahms.

No fireworks. No bells. But with that one gesture, Rose had been shown the gateway to a path that, she sensed, could lead to something rich and wonderful.

Even so, she continued to hold back in some ways, careful to maintain certain limits. She had yet to spend a whole night with Eric, for instance.

The official excuse was Jay, but her teenaged son wasn't the only reason. Deep down, she feared it was too risky—like crimes that become federal once a state line is crossed. She wasn't prepared for that level of intimacy. It would feel too much like . . .

. . . *being married.*

And that would be cheating somehow. Because she was already married. To Max.

To hell with what the therapists counseled, and the books on coping with loss. Rose didn't care if she was hanging on to her grief long past the expiration date. All she knew was that, in those first moments of blinking awake in the morning, it was Max she reached for.

Her husband. Now and forever.

She couldn't let go of that, not for anyone. Even Eric.

In the farthest reaches of her mind, a small voice whispered: *Admit it, Rose Santini Griffin, you're scared. Not just of Max's being pushed aside. You're scared it might not last with Eric. That you might lose him, too. And that next time, you just might not survive it. . . .*

Eventually, this heat would cool a bit, wouldn't it? The intensity would wane. She wouldn't feel damp between her legs all the time, longing for Eric within minutes of kissing him goodbye.

She was a sensible, middle-aged woman. The mother of grown boys. Managing partner of her own firm. Certainly, she could manage a love affair without letting her heart run away with her.

Yet Rose, arriving at her destination, was still so preoccupied she had to count out the money for the taxi twice before she got it right.

Minutes later, accosted by her secretary as she was striding toward her office, Rose felt as if she'd been ambushed. She had to blink to bring her into focus. Mallory, wearing a jumper and black tights, her hair—which blew with the wind of every new fashion—a shade and style that could only be described as Madonna Platinum.

"Lockwood wants a word with you. He's in your office," she informed Rose, *sotto voce*. "I told him you might be a while, but he said he didn't mind waiting. He . . ." She bit her bottom lip. "He seemed pretty upset."

Hayden Lockwood? In her office? Upset? Rose felt her mind click back into the groove worn by years of dealing with one crisis after another, both here and at home. Hayden was the newest of their associates, and easily the brightest. If there was a problem, she'd better deal with it.

She found him seated in the easy chair by the window—a lanky black man with close-cropped hair who, no matter how he arranged his long, knobby limbs, always reminded her of a young father on Parent Day, seated at his child's desk.

"Sorry to sneak up on you like this," he apologized, standing up. "Do you have a moment?" He spoke in round-toned, Harvard-educated English that Rose suspected he accentuated on purpose, to let people know he was no scholarship kid. Both his parents were college professors, and his oldest sister was chief counsel for the Democratic National Committee.

Right now, Hayden looked troubled, his dark eyes thoughtful behind the lenses of his conservative tortoiseshell glasses. And Rose didn't need two guesses as to why. *Mandy,* she thought, her heart sinking.

Hayden had been assigned to Mandy's department. He'd be the first to know if she'd fallen off the wagon.

Just what I don't *need right now.*

Rose gestured for him to sit down, and sank into the chair across from him instead of the one at her desk.

"I've been hearing good things about you," she began, hoping to put him at ease. "Mandy tells me she's never seen anyone bill so many hours. Besides herself," she added with a tiny smile. "And that bit of detective work you did on the Anderson divorce was brilliant. Really."

He smiled shyly, and ducked his head. "Thanks. I appreciate your saying so, but it was mostly common sense, along with some digging. I had to go through about sixteen boxes of those financial statements we subpoenaed, but eventually I noticed a pattern. How many times do you have a restaurant or hotel receipt in the Cayman Islands unless it's connected somehow to hidden assets?"

"Well, it looks as if you may have saved our client some money, not to mention a fair amount of grief." Smiling, she added, "The threat of unleashing the IRS on her husband is going to give Mrs. Anderson quite a bit more leeway in her own bargaining."

"No doubt about it." Hayden nodded enthusiastically, but looked uncomfortable. He cleared his throat as if wanting to say something else, then fell silent.

Rose prodded gently, "Hayden, is something the matter?"

He looked down at his enormous hands, loosely linked in his lap. "Actually . . . there is. It's, uh, about Mandy." He stumbled a bit over his words.

Rose felt her stomach contract. "What about her?"

"I wish there was some other way to handle this," he said. "I didn't want to come to you. But it's not the kind of thing I could just let go, either." He lifted his expressive brown eyes, and she saw how conflicted he was. "The other day, Mandy was late showing up for an appointment—with Mrs. Anderson, it so happens—and then, when she finally *did* get here, she . . ." He cleared his throat again. "I think it would be fair to say she was under the influence. Or maybe it was just that she'd had a lot to drink the night before. Whatever, I could smell it on her. She wasn't very steady on her feet, either." Despite his obvious discomfort, Hayden kept his gaze level with hers. "I have a lot of respect for Mandy, she's a fine lawyer . . . but, see, I know a little something about this. I have an uncle who . . . well, let's just say Uncle Willie is always the last to leave a party. Usually, he has to be carried out."

Rose felt a headache coming on, a real McWhopper. How could things have gotten so out of hand so quickly? Mandy had been really good lately, not even a glass of wine with dinner. Now this. And not just one little slip, either. Good God, the whole office had to know.

"This isn't the first time. Is that what you're saying?" she asked as calmly as she could, though her head was pulsing like a yellow caution blinker.

"No," he said, so softly it was almost a mumble.

His gaze shifted to the window, with its view of the Helmsley arch and the gilded clock that resembled a giant Krugerrand. The strained expression on his earnest young face made her think of Drew.

She winced inwardly. Her older son had dropped by last night to pick up his brother; he had two tickets to a Knicks game. Rose had asked after Iris—pleasantly, she'd thought—and somehow she and Drew had wound up arguing. He'd accused her not only of trying to run his life, but of running it with a friggin' *backhoe*. Which had triggered the Flatbush Avenue in Rose into shouting back, "Great, just great. *You* dig the hole, then. Just don't expect me to be there to pull you out when it gets too deep!"

Now here she was, looking down into the hole that *Mandy* had dug for herself, and wondering what the hell she was going to do about it. How had things come to this? Since when had she, Rose Santini Griffin, been appointed to King Solomon's throne? At the moment, she'd have swapped this serious young man before her, who meant well and was only trying to do his job, for an extra-strength Tylenol and ten minutes on a treadmill.

Rose sucked in her breath. "You did the right thing in coming to me," she assured him. "I'm sorry you had to be placed in this position. I hope it won't affect your opinion of the firm as a whole. You're a tremendous asset to us, Hayden."

"Thank you," he said.

Hayden smiled in gratitude, but it was the look of someone who knew perfectly well he'd be snapped up by another firm in an instant. How many young men, white or black, could boast a Harvard degree, and a résumé that included two summers interning at the white-shoe firm of Milbank, Tweed?

"I'll take care of this," she promised in a voice that left no doubt as to her sincerity.

Hayden nodded gravely and rose to his feet. His awkward bobble, as if he hadn't quite grown into his height, made her smile in spite of herself.

He shook the hand she extended, meeting her gaze with an expression that hovered between relief and resolve. Making it clear that, however much he might like and respect Mandy, he had no intention of compromising his career for a drunk.

And that's what Mandy is, Rose thought darkly. *A drunk.* Thank God, Max had been spared this.

But it didn't have to be this way, she told herself. Look at Eric. *He* had somehow managed to get sober, and get his life back on track.

Rose's spirits lifted a fraction of an inch. Yes, that was it. She would ask Eric what to do. Maybe if he spoke to Mandy . . .

Who knew? Mandy might even listen. The night Rose had had them both over to dinner, they'd seemed to hit it off—though Mandy apparently had no memory of his taking her home from Iris and Drew's party.

Rose glanced at her watch. Past twelve-thirty already! She'd have to hustle to make it to the restaurant by one. She realized she hadn't so much as glanced at the mail on her desk, or the neat pile of pink phone slips . . . but suddenly none of that seemed important.

Eric. In exactly twenty-eight minutes she'd be seeing him. His well-traveled eyes, which lit up when she walked in, as if he'd never seen anything so lovely. His delicious mouth, which never ran out of surprises. His hands, which always made her blush, because she couldn't stop thinking of how they'd touched her in bed.

All the anxiety of a moment ago trickled out of her like sand from an upended shoe. Rose dashed for the door, her face flushed, her heart racing as it hadn't since she was sixteen, and in love for the first time.

I won't think about it, she told herself, *how quickly it evaporates, this kind of love.* What she and Max had built together was solid, capable of withstanding any kind of weather. What she'd felt with Brian, what had made it so sweet, though she hadn't realized it then, was that it hadn't been for keeps.

And soon this, too, would be gone—the guilty pleasure of her new love affair with Eric, like every other bright, shining thing in her life, would eventually vanish like the moon with the first light of dawn.

❦ They met at an Indian restaurant at Lexington and Twenty-sixth, which, according to Eric, was one of the city's best-kept secrets. If you have an asbestos palate, or don't mind dining with a fire extinguisher on hand, he'd added slyly.

What Rose found even more appealing than the prospect of a delicious meal was the unlikelihood of running into anyone she knew. She didn't want her colleagues to see how she behaved around Eric, blushing like a schoolgirl with a crush; neither of them able to go five minutes without reaching for the other's hand, or sneaking a quick kiss.

Getting out of the cab in front of a yellowish stucco façade, Rose had to peer closely at the discreet sign. Pongal, she read. And, yes, there was the blue elephant in the window, just as Eric had described.

Stepping inside, she was enveloped in a bouquet of exotic aromas. Rose felt suddenly ravenous. It wasn't that she'd skipped breakfast—in her rush to get to work, she often did. It was Eric. Somehow, the prospect of seeing him stimulated *all* her appetites, made her blood race and her juices flow.

She spotted him at once, seated at a table in back, but paused for a moment, savoring this opportunity to observe him unnoticed. He wore what she recognized as his favorite pair of jeans—washed so many times they were the whitish blue of old love letters penned on airmail stationery—and a navy blazer over a light-colored shirt. His hair was windblown, and he was leaning back in his chair, reading a folded-over section of the *Times*.

Abruptly, as if sensing her presence, he looked up. Eyes that would have been just as blue had they been directed elsewhere, but which seemed to blaze with an almost blinding intensity as he lifted them to her. He was smiling—a secret little smile meant just for her—as if remembering their last time together.

She flushed, feeling sure that it was stamped on her forehead like a brand, that everyone in the place could see her for what she was: a woman in love.

Suddenly, in her mind, Rose was seeing a much younger version of herself: huddled on the scuffed kneeler before the statue of the BVM that had dominated the altar at her church, saying penance for her "sins" committed with Brian. Sins of the flesh that, no matter how many Hail Marys and Our Fathers she said, she'd been helpless to keep from committing all over again.

Admit it, you never felt this way with Max. She'd loved her husband, desired him deeply, and the sex had become fuller and richer with each passing year . . . but she couldn't remember a time when she'd burned for Max, when just the scent of the sheets after they'd made love had sent her spinning into orbit all over again. Max had known exactly how to please her; he'd been patient and loving and creative. But never, even in the very beginning, had memories of what they'd done in bed the night before caused her to twist in her seat, unable to cross her legs without feeling almost excruciatingly stimulated.

As Eric stood up to greet her, Rose felt as furtive as an adulteress meeting her lover for a secret rendezvous. To her horror, that only made her want him more. As he leaned close to kiss her on the mouth, she turned her head, presenting her cheek to him instead. It didn't stop her from catching his scent—a scent she couldn't quite identify, but which somehow brought to mind all the smells she loved best: new books, line-dried sheets, leaves freshly polished with rain.

Feeling overheated and jittery, she made a great show of unbuttoning her coat and arranging it over the back of her chair. Eric just stood there, his hands in his pockets, regarding her with faint amusement, as if he knew perfectly well what was on her mind.

"What are you looking at?" she asked with a self-conscious laugh.

"Prom night. Circa 1964." He grinned, and sank back down into his chair. "Right now, you don't look a day over seventeen."

She arched a brow. "Gray hairs and all?"

"You're prettier now than I bet you were back then."

"I never went to a prom," she told him. "The closest I ever got was being confirmed. You could call it a date with Jesus." She gave a short laugh laced with irony. "My grandmother was a big believer in going to bed early Saturday night in order to be up at the crack of dawn for Sunday mass."

"I wish I'd known you then."

"No, you don't. I was a mess. If it hadn't been for Brian . . ." She let the sentence trail off, shaking her head as if to clear it. "But that's yesterday's news. You want today's headline? My case was settled. The other side was smart enough to realize a bird in the hand is worth more than two million in the bush."

"Hey, congratulations." He grinned, and lifted his water glass. "What brought them around?"

"Insufficient proof. Not even a *prima facie* case." She grinned. "In other words, they didn't do their homework."

"Either that, or you were more thorough. How did it go with Professor Highsmith, by the way?"

"Oh Eric, I can't thank you enough. We flew him in to testify. He was terrific. His clinical study on the effect of smoking on the cardiovascular system was incredibly persuasive." Highsmith, a professor at Stanford, had come to her courtesy of Eric's Rolodex—the subject of an interview he'd done last year.

"In that case, you can buy me lunch." As if remembering something, he added, "But, listen, about Brian . . . there's one thing I'm curious about."

Rose, thinking of the night she and Brian had kissed, felt herself grow warm. "What's that?"

"He and I met for lunch the other day. Just to catch up, but somehow the conversation kept coming around to you. Brian wanted to know if I was still seeing you, how serious it was—that kind of thing."

"What did you tell him?"

"I told him, yes, I was seeing you. That's about it. Brian's a great guy, and a friend . . . but I got the funny feeling he was doing more than just make conversation." Eric himself seemed almost too nonchalant, as if he, like Brian, were soft-pedaling his interest in all this.

"Brian's always been sort of a big brother. He . . . he's very protective of me." A lame excuse, she knew, but she was too flustered to come up with something better.

Eric wasn't buying it. "You really loved him, didn't you?"

"Yes. At one time I loved him very much." She was surprised at how easy it was to talk about. "He was . . . everything. I think I must have been in love with him from the time I first started wondering if a Near Occasion of Sin included kissing." She took a sip from her water glass. "By the time I graduated from Impure Thoughts to Mortal Sin, I was a goner."

Eric smiled. "What happened after that?"

"Vietnam." She shrugged and said, "You know the rest. He was badly wounded. Rachel saved his life. They got married."

Rose was relieved when their waiter arrived just then to take their order. All this was ancient history, sure, but even memories that had grown dull with time could still cut. Even now, so many years later, she couldn't remember it without bleeding just a little—those letters he'd sent that had never reached her, that Nonnie had spitefully hidden away. And when Brian didn't hear back from her, he was sure she'd forgotten him. Nothing could have been further from the truth; the only thing that had kept her *alive* was the hope of something in the mail. When she did finally get word—that he'd gotten married—she was devastated. The only thing worse would have been learning that he'd been killed.

In time, and with Max's love, she'd grown to understand . . . to see that even if she *had* kept on writing to him, the Brian to whom those letters were addressed wouldn't have been the same Brian reading them. Not the boy she'd grown up with, or even the young man who'd believed it noble to fight for his country, who'd promised tearfully to come back to her—the girl next door.

But back then, Rose had wanted only to die. To close her eyes and never wake up.

"It's funny," Eric observed thoughtfully. "When I turned the tables on Brian, and asked about you and *him*—he couldn't get off the subject fast enough."

"What would be the point of raking it up? It all worked out for the best in the end." Rose felt something in her gut twist even so. "If it hadn't been for Rachel, I wouldn't have married Max. It hurt, yeah—honestly, I didn't think I was going to survive—but with time, I came to see that it was meant to be."

She saw something flicker in Eric's eyes. "You believe in destiny?" he asked with a faintly ironic lift of his brow.

"Depends."

"On what?"

She smiled, wanting to keep the discussion light, fearing that if she didn't it might lead to questions she wasn't ready to answer.

"On whether or not it comes with a prize at the bottom of the box."

Eric laughed softly. He was leaning on his elbows, his sandy hair falling over his forehead in that endearing way of men and boys who spend as little time in front of mirrors as possible. Along the stucco wall behind him hung a row of halogen lights, like tiny conical hats, suspended from a long wire like Christmas-tree lights.

"I wasn't referring to Cracker Jacks," he said.

"Eric, what are you asking?"

He regarded her thoughtfully for a moment, then said, "I've heard how you felt about your husband. And Brian. What I'm not so sure of is how you feel about *us*."

Rose shifted back in her chair, as if she'd been cornered. "Us?"

"Don't look so panicked." He smiled, but this time there was no humor in it. "It doesn't have to be written in blood."

"Eric." She folded a hand over his. "Listen . . . can we talk about this some other time? I'm feeling kind of overwhelmed at the moment."

He held her gaze for longer than she could physically bear— longer than it would have taken to tell him she was sorry, she hadn't meant to sound so heartless, could they please just leave now and go to his apartment, where they would draw the blinds and make love in the light that trembled in paper-thin slices between the slats.

"Is this a polite way of saying you want to cool it for the time being?" Eric was as blunt as ever. It was one of the things she admired most about him.

"I just thought . . ."

"I'm not in this to make life more difficult for either of us," Eric cut her off sharply. His eyes fixed on her with a keenness she found uncomfortable. "I have only one favor to ask. If you *do* decide to end it, do it in a minute. I promise I'll be out of your life before you take another breath."

Rose sat back, stunned by his intensity.

"I didn't say we should stop seeing each other," she told him.

"What *do* you want, then?"

"I don't know. That's the point." She frowned, nervously toying with her pendant—a ruby-studded heart on a slender gold chain, Max's gift to her on their fifteenth anniversary. "Except for my husband, you're the first man I've slept with in over twenty years. To be honest, I don't know quite how to handle it. It *does* feel a little like when I was a teenager."

He drew his hand across her cheek, his fingertips lighting briefly on her mouth before curling back into his lap. His slightly off-center smile made her think of a crooked pictured frame in need of straightening. "Is that good or bad?"

"Both."

"I'll never hurt you."

"Oh, Eric." She sighed. "It's not *you* I'm afraid of. It's me. My family is falling apart, and I'm supposed to be at the center holding things together—only I'm not. I'm either at work, or running back and forth between your place and mine."

"It doesn't have to be that way." He regarded her coolly, but underneath she sensed a heat that might scorch her if she got too close.

Rose took a sip of water that tasted flat, coppery. Indian sitar music played softly in the background. She felt something stirring in her, she didn't know quite what—either the beginning of something she wasn't ready to face, or the end of something she wasn't quite ready to give up.

Who was she kidding? Well, the least she could give him was an honest answer. "I guess I'm just not ready for more than what we have right now."

"I don't mind taking it slow."

She gave him an upside-down smile of contrition. "It doesn't seem fair. All I've done is dump my troubles on you."

"I don't see it that way," he said. "But if it helps to talk, I don't mind listening."

"You've done more than listen. Especially with Mandy."

"What's going on with her?" he asked, his expression sharpening.

Rose filled him in on her conversation with Hayden Lockwood. "The thing is, it's not *like* her," she puzzled aloud. "Until now, she never let her drinking get in the way of her work. Mandy has incredible willpower. She's like her father that way."

"In AA we have a saying: 'snatching defeat from the jaws of victory,'" Eric told her. "Sometimes it takes losing the next-most-important thing in your life to give up the *most* important."

"What could be more important than her job? Than *us*—her family?"

Eric smiled at her—a knowing smile. "Booze," he said simply. "To a practicing alcoholic, *nothing* is more important."

Their waiter appeared once again with several steaming bowls, reminding her of how hungry she was. Later they would decide what to do about Mandy, she decided. Right now, she was simply going to enjoy what was in front of her.

The savory dishes arrived one after the other, and she devoured everything, including most of the warm breads Eric had ordered for the two of them. The red-hot spices made her eyes water and her mouth smart. The dense chewiness of the *chapati* soothed her. The entire spread was like some elaborate seduction of the senses she was helpless to resist.

When Eric suggested they head back to his place, a thousand excuses—all of them valid—rose up in her mind like a frenzied flock of geese. But she couldn't think of a single one more urgent than the delicious prospect of Eric's making love to her.

Half an hour later, she stood naked before him in the bedroom of his Murray Hill apartment, which made up in sunniness what it lacked in charm, watching him undress.

She wanted him so badly she could hardly bear it. For years, she'd heard men talk about such urges, and had always come away feeling slightly superior. Women weren't so base, she'd thought smugly. They knew how to proceed at a more civilized pace—mutual regard for one another that built toward mutual desire; knowing what was appropriate, and what wasn't.

To hell with it, she thought. *I need this.*

Soft jazz played on the stereo—tenor saxophone that curled like silk ribbons about her naked limbs as she stretched out on the bed, looking up at the sturdy pine shelves that marched up toward the ceiling like rungs on a ladder. They were crammed with books, CDs, framed photos of vintage airplanes, promotional coffee mugs sent to him at WQNA, along with a curious array of boyhood baseball gloves so stiff with age they resembled chunks of wood oiled and polished to a dull shine.

"Stan Getz," Eric informed her. "Would you rather I put on something different?"

"No . . . I like it. Just come here."

He did. As Eric wrapped his naked body about hers, it was like sinking into a warm pool. She felt his breath against her neck, patient and still. He understood how it was with her, she thought. Instinctively knowing to allow her a minute or two to adjust to the floating sensation brought on by their combined bodies. Until she felt ready to begin stroking her way toward the deep end.

Eric smoothed his palms down the length of her arms, leaving a slipstream of goosebumps. In the semidarkness, his eyes glinted from under lids gone heavy. "You're so beautiful," he murmured. "The most beautiful woman I've ever had the pleasure of seeing naked."

"Flattery will get you everywhere," she whispered into his hair with a throaty laugh, running her hand down his back.

On the rag rug beside the bed, her pale-blue silk half-slip and matching bra lay in a puddle like melted ice. Several weeks ago, she'd succumbed at long last to the Victoria's Secret catalogue that showed up in her mailbox each month as faithfully as her period. Instead of tossing it into the recycling bin as she usually did, she'd picked up the phone and dialed their 800 number, ordering two hundred dollars' worth of lingerie. Since Max's death, she'd worn nothing but plain white cotton underwear. Catholic birth control, Marie called it.

What difference did it make? she'd reasoned. Nobody was going to see her undressed. Now, suddenly, it mattered. At work even, under her tailored suits, the whisper of silk against her skin made her feel sexual, desirable, the kind of woman a man would want to be trapped in an elevator with.

She felt as if she were on an elevator now, ascending rapidly. Her stomach floated somewhere up around her sternum. She felt prickly with sweat, and unable to swallow. She stroked him where she knew he liked to be stroked, gratified when he shuddered and cupped her buttocks, drawing her closer.

"Mmm . . . you're good at this," he murmured.

A breeze blowing through the open window caused the blind to undulate, sending delicate fingers of light and shadow rippling over his face and bare torso. A patch of skin below his collarbone, roughly the size and shape of a palm print, glistened with perspiration.

She squeezed lightly, and heard a hissing intake of breath as his stomach muscles clenched, tightening until they quivered.

"You make it easy," she teased.

His hand began moving in slow circles down her belly, lower, lower, leaving her breathless. His fingertips explored the soft hair below, parting her like sections of ripe fruit. Without her even drawing him a map, he knew each tributary and blue road as if he'd traveled it a hundred times.

"Like this?" he asked softly, thrusting deeper.

Rose moaned, feeling drugged with pleasure, soaking up each delicious sensation—his touch, his scent, the mere sight of him, even.

Eric was muscular in the long, lean way of swimmers, with low-slung hips that tapered into legs roped with tendon. What saved him from being annoyingly perfect was an inch of spare tire around his waist. And thank God for it, Rose thought, or she'd have been far too embarrassed to let him see *her* naked.

She could feel the seams in the old quilt on which she lay pressing a row of plump little diamonds along her naked spine. Rose gasped as Eric plunged into her again . . . then just as abruptly withdrew.

"Preview of coming attractions," he whispered.

"I don't know if I can wait." The marvelous thing about being over forty, she thought, is that you didn't have to be coy.

But Eric, instead of answering her, was easing downward. She could feel his breath tickling her belly, causing the muscles in her abdomen to contract so sharply it was almost a cramp. Dimly, she was aware of her hips arching, rising to meet his mouth where he was kissing her now. . . .

She rocked against him, crying out softly, words that made no sense, even to her, as if she were listening to some strange woman talk in her sleep. But who the hell cared? This *was* a dream, she decided. The kind of erotic dream that left you damp and trembling, and almost sick to your stomach with yearning.

She pulled away from him, and scooted down on the bed. "Your turn," she whispered.

Rose took him in her mouth.

A minute later, he was on top of her again, and she was guiding him into her. This time he didn't withdraw. As she strained against him, he held on to her hips in a way that, for once, made her grateful for their generous curves. Their bodies, slick with sweat, made soft sucking sounds as they drew together, then apart. She couldn't remember when she'd felt so consumed, so utterly shameless, like an animal in heat.

When she came, it was like summer thunder. Endless rolling waves promising blessed relief from the heat. Then Eric was coming, too, arching against her with his eyes closed and his mouth parted in a silent cry. Deep inside her, she could feel him pulsing. Low and quick, like a panicked heartbeat.

Eric collapsed onto her.

"Christ," he gasped.

She let out a breath that felt like the last, drawn-out chord at the end of a symphony.

Eric twisted around, his profile silhouetted in the dim light. "You really think you can turn it on and off?" he asked in a voice soft with wonder. "A woman like you? Rose, if nothing else, believe this: you weren't made to sit on a shelf."

"Who said anything about sitting on a shelf?" She drew away slightly, feeling the tiny sweat-soaked hairs on her chest and stomach begin to prickle as they dried. "Just because—"

"Rose, I want to marry you," he cut her off, speaking as calmly as if they were driving down the street discussing the traffic up ahead. "I know all the arguments—that it's too soon, your life is too crazy right now. That's why I'm not asking. And I'm not going to until you're ready. All I want is for you to know where I'm coming from— and where I hope we're headed. Fair enough?"

Rose was too stunned to reply. Of course. She should have known. What all this had been leading to. At the same time, it was crazy; it made no sense at all.

"Eric, I . . ."

He laid a finger across her lips. "Wait. I have a story for you. About the woman I fell in love with before I met you." His arms wound around her, holding her close, as if he were afraid she might slip away otherwise. "She *was* you. I know this is going to sound either cracked or ridiculously New Age—I barely believe it myself— but there it is. I saw you in my mind's eye long before we ever met. I actually knew more or less what you would look like . . . except you're even more beautiful." He kissed the top of her head, where her snowy stripe radiated outward like a falling star. "The only thing I haven't nailed down is the ending."

"You couldn't possibly have—" She stopped, forcing herself to think carefully about how best to put into words the feelings trapped inside her, bumping furiously against one another. In a more measured voice, she finished, "Maybe you *did* have someone particular in mind . . . or maybe I just happened along at the right moment, when you'd gotten tired of looking."

Something flashed in his eyes. In a clipped, almost brusque voice, he answered, "If you really believe that, then you're selling yourself— and *me*—short."

"Eric, I . . ." She felt curiously numb, even as she lay shivering in the circle of his arms. "I can't marry you. Not ever."

"That's it, case closed?" Behind his light tone she sensed the pull of something far more weighty than anything he could put into words.

"What about children?" she argued. "You said you wanted a family."

"*We'd* be a family. You and me. Rose, I want you to be my wife."

"Eric . . . no. I can't. It wouldn't be fair." She tensed, and tried to turn away, but he wouldn't let her. His fingers gently closed about her upper arm, raising gooseflesh.

"Fair to whom?"

"To either of us. I was married for twenty-one years. I have grown children. That woman in your mind's eye? She wasn't me. You just mistook me for someone who hasn't yet come along." She felt a stab of sorrow as full comprehension of what she was saying kaleidoscoped into sudden, jarring focus: that the best years of her life were behind her.

"Just think about it, okay? That's all I ask."

Rose, a deep regret softening the hard muscle of her resolve, opened her mouth . . . but whatever she'd been about to say—she didn't quite know herself—was canceled by the jarring sound of the phone on the nightstand.

Eric snatched it up, impatiently, as he might have in his studio at work. "Eric here." He listened for a moment, his look of annoyance shifting to one of concern. He handed her the receiver, mouthing, "It's for you."

Startled, Rose reached for it.

"Mom?" Jay. His voice was shaking. "I tried you at the office . . . but Mallory said you were out. With Eric. I'm glad I found you." A sharp inhalation of breath. "Mom . . . it's Sylvie. She's in really bad shape. Rachel wants her to go to the hospital, but she won't . . . Mom, she's asking for you. . . ."

Sylvie? Asking for her? But no hospital—how serious could it be? Was it some kind of ruse to lure her over there?

Then reality kicked in. Sylvie, Rose knew, would never drag her over under false pretenses. If she wouldn't go to the hospital, it was because she saw no point in it. She . . .

She wants to die in her own bed.

Dear God.

Her hand flew up to cup her mouth.

Suddenly none of the thousand and one reasons for being angry at Sylvie seemed to matter. Maybe they'd never mattered. Maybe everything that was truly important was embodied, like the seed at a fruit's core, in the plainest of all facts: Sylvie was her mother.

Sylvie had acted selfishly, yes. But in demanding more than her mother was prepared to give, Rose herself had thrown away something valuable and rich. Was it too late? Would Sylvie be gone before Rose could get there—before she could give her mother the one thing *she* had withheld?

Forgiveness.

A sense of desperate urgency seized her and jerked her off the bed. Her bare feet slapped down on old floorboards that, though sanded and varnished, seemed to ripple in waves as she steadied herself, holding a hand pressed to her heart.

"Tell Rachel I'm on my way," she said to Jay before hanging up.

Chapter 13

So this is how it feels, Rachel thought.

In med school, during her psychiatry clerkship, she'd often tried to imagine what it would be like to experience a nervous breakdown. Whether you would comprehend what was happening, or merely think it was the people around you who were acting crazy.

Now she knew.

Because it couldn't possibly be real, what she was hearing. It was as if the mother she'd known all her life had been replaced by a perfect stranger—one of those talkative, harmlessly cracked women on buses and planes who always seemed to attach themselves to her. A woman with sunken cheeks and ashen lips, saying things that made no sense . . .

"I was afraid, so afraid. Overjoyed and terrified at the same time. Pregnant after all those years of trying, but—" Mama's green eyes flooded with tears. "I could only *pray* that it was Gerald's baby. . . ."

Propped against a mound of pillows and bolsters, Sylvie resembled an old doll in a museum, her porcelain face a web of tiny cracks. Yet the hand clutching Rachel's wrist was achingly familiar—the hand that had soothed Rachel to sleep as a child, and guided her across a thousand busy intersections.

"Mama, please, don't try to talk," Rachel pleaded, her throat tight from held-back tears.

Sylvie went on as if Rachel hadn't spoken. "I was young . . . too young. . . ." Her voice was a cracked, feathery whisper. "Married to a husband old enough to be my father. Oh, I loved him! Don't ever doubt that. Gerald *was* like a father to me in many ways. He sheltered me . . . kept me safe . . . gave me everything I asked for and more. But he couldn't . . . give me . . ." Her tear-filled eyes sparkled with a queer, glancing light, and she seemed to be straining, not only to breathe, but to find the right word. ". . . *passion,*" she forced out at last.

"I fell in love, you see," she continued, the effort showing in her face. "With Nikos." Sylvie blinked, as if struggling to bring Nikos—perched on the mattress beside her, across from Rachel—into focus. In her blurred gaze was a love so naked, so exquisite, Rachel had to turn from it as if from a too-bright light. "What could have been more *wrong?* He worked for us, you see. . . . But you already know that. What you *don't* know is that it was way back then that we first became lovers." Her bluish lips parted in a wisp of a smile. "I was in love, yes, but every night I cried myself to sleep . . . hating myself, that I could do such a thing to my husband." She closed her eyes a moment, allowing herself the luxury of an uninterrupted breath.

"Mama, you don't have to . . ." Rachel's words were cut off by her mother's fingers tightening about her wrist.

"Yes . . . I *do,*" Sylvie insisted. "Please . . . listen . . . before it's too late." She paused, her gaze drifting to the paneled door that stood open at the far end of her spacious bedroom, as if, any second, she expected Rose to appear, though it had been only fifteen minutes or so since Rachel had spoken to Rose's son.

Rose. Why *was* Mama so anxious to see her?

Sun poured in through the windows' old leaded panes like water into a pale-blue vase, bringing to life the room's surfaces—a bouquet of delicate tapestries, sprigged fabrics, buttery woods. The Aubusson rug by the bed was more threadbare than Rachel remembered, but still as lovely as ever. As was the four-poster bed, with its carved garlands and rosettes, where, as a child, she'd spent hours playing. The same bed where . . .

Had she? Here? In this room . . . with Nikos?

"I'm listening, Mama." Rachel, though she couldn't quite absorb it, was morbidly spellbound by her mother's tale.

But Sylvie only squeezed tighter, her thumb rubbing fretfully against the tender underside of Rachel's wrist, making it burn. "Rose is coming? She *did* say she was coming?"

"Yes, Mama. Jay said she's on her way over." Rachel maintained a low, soothing tone, but she felt like screaming, *What does Rose have to do with any of this?*

Sylvie seemed to relax, sinking deeper into her throne of pillows. She looked so frail, all crumpled in on herself, like a withered leaf. Rachel wanted to snatch her up, physically *carry* her to the nearest hospital. She was aware of a steady pulse of alarm throbbing in her, as unremitting as a flashing red bubble light. *Mama, please don't die!* she cried inwardly.

"And then, yes . . . pregnant. After all those years, I was pregnant." Sylvie closed her eyes, and her speech became slurred, as if she were drifting off to sleep. But her twisted tale continued to steal past her lips like wind whistling through a window someone had neglected to close all the way. "Gerald and I had been to every specialist, had every kind of test. They never found anything wrong . . . but even so, as much as I prayed I might be wrong, I knew in my heart the baby wasn't his. There was a slight chance, though . . . and that's what kept me going." She opened her eyes, and cast an apologetic glance at Nikos, who patted her shoulder comfortingly. "I'm sorry, my dear. But it's the truth. I was such a timid mouse—afraid of my own shadow. Imagine what Gerald would have done had he guessed the truth!"

Rachel was shocked to see that Nikos was crying. Tears trickled down his staunch, weathered face like snowmelt from a mountain ridge. He didn't bother to wipe them away. When had she ever seen him cry? Never, she realized, and was filled with a deep affection for this man who had been so much more than her mother's faithful companion; he'd been like a stepfather to her, and a grandfather to Iris. As steady as the axle about which the wheel of their family turned.

She watched him struggle mightily to gain control over the emotions threatening to wrench him apart, his great knot of an Adam's

apple working. Rachel forgot her own anguish for the moment, her
heart going out to Nikos as he bent over Sylvie, cupping her face in
his large, work-worn hands as gently as if it were an eggshell that
might crack. He kissed her tenderly, first on one cheek, then the
other.

"I don't blame you," he said, his voice a soothing rumble. "You
did what you believed you had to."

Sylvie gazed up at him in gratitude, and in that instant she appeared almost transparent, as if the sunlight slanting across her face
were radiating from a source deep inside her. "Darling Nikos," she
whispered. Then, slowly, she swiveled her head toward Rachel. "*You*
were the reason I kept silent, my *shainenke*. Remember the story
about the fire? The night you were born, the hospital burning down?
It happened just as I described it. What you didn't know, *couldn't*
know"—she swallowed hard—"was that the baby girl I rescued, carried in my arms down that fire escape—she was you, just as I said,
but you weren't *mine*."

Rachel seemed suddenly to be looking at her mother from a great
distance, as if the room had telescoped, leaving only Mama's face,
floating like a pale petal at the end of a long tunnel. The bed on
which Rachel sat seemed to sway, and she gripped hold of one of its
carved posts to keep from losing her balance.

"I . . . I don't understand." She was aware of her lips moving, but
the words seemed to have come from someone else.

Her mother's eyes fixed on her—huge and overbright. "My own
baby was dark, with black hair . . . like her father," Sylvie whispered.
"After the fire . . ." She winced, bringing a hand to her chest. "Your
mother, your *real* mother, she didn't get out in time. Everybody just
assumed you were mine. . . .

"I didn't want to go along, not at first. But then I began to wonder if the fire . . . and your mother's death . . . if it had happened for
a reason. I felt almost as if God were . . . guiding me somehow." A
single, perfect tear slipped from the corner of one eye and trickled

down her temple, disappearing into her hair. "Only now I know it wasn't God."

Rachel heard herself ask, "What about the other baby? *Your* baby?" She was dreaming this—or her mother was. It couldn't possibly be true. *Could it?*

Behind her, Rachel heard the faint creak of old flooring muffled by carpet. She turned slowly . . . and in her dreamlike state, which some functioning part of her brain recognized as profound shock, it felt as if the *room* were turning—slow, lazy revolutions, like a carousel. Lightheaded, almost tipsy, Rachel blinked. In the doorway stood a shadowy figure, a tall woman whose outline was strikingly familiar, but Rachel, momentarily unhooked from her moorings, couldn't place her.

The figure emerged into the room, and Rachel saw that it was Rose. Her wild black hair was strewn every which way, and her cheeks were flagged with color. Even her raincoat was askew; perhaps she'd been in too much of a hurry to notice it was buttoned wrong.

"Rose," Rachel breathed. And that was when she knew. Turning to face her mother, she asked with soft incredulity, "It was Rose, wasn't it? The baby you left behind. Your real daughter. Yours and Nikos'."

Sylvie went so still, Rachel felt an urge to lean close to see if she was still breathing. But Mama's eyes—oh God, nothing so tortured could be anything but alive. Huge, vivid, blisteringly of this earth, they held Rachel's gaze as if trying desperately to convey to her some truth that couldn't possibly be contained in mere words. Then, with a sigh that seemed to sever the last thread holding her together, she whispered: "Yes."

Rachel went instantly numb. Random chunks of memory rolled and clicked in her head like tossed dice. Memories that hadn't seemed connected to one another in any way, but which now formed an excruciatingly perfect whole. She saw herself, as a very little girl, crying to her mother that she didn't *fit in.* She hated the frilly dresses her mother bought for her, and had always felt out of place in this great old house with its delicate fabrics and teetery-legged antiques. And there was Papa, the quizzical way he sometimes looked at her, as if hunting for something—a resemblance?—that wasn't there.

And the way Mama had looked at her, too. Mournfully, almost, as if . . .

It wasn't ME she was seeing. This thought was accompanied by a blow so crushing she had to brace herself to keep from being flattened by it. *All that time Mama had been wondering about Rose . . . regretting her mistake. . . .*

Only Rose hadn't been given away. She'd been abandoned. To strangers. And she, Rachel, had been . . . well . . . *stolen.*

The enormity of it swooped upward in her head like a flock of crows bursting into flight. There was a rushing sound in her ears, like the whirring of hollow-boned wings, and the edges of her vision were feathered with black. In the midst of it all, she was aware of the sound, sane beating of a heart that refused to believe what her mind was shrieking.

Lies! Everything I was told, everything I believed in was a lie. My own family isn't even mine. My mother isn't really my mother.

Rachel, with a moan, buried her face in her hands. She couldn't bear it. Everyone she loved and trusted seemed to be slipping away from her, as inexorably as a retreating tide. Iris. Brian. Mama.

Her family, her whole *history*, had been nothing more than an elaborate deception. . . .

A low, muffled cry prompted Rachel to lift her face.

The day's dying light, streaming through the mullioned windows, illuminated Rose as if in a portrait. She had come to a standstill several feet from the bed, with its four gleaming posts lifted to the ceiling like arms raised in exultation. Her face was tilted upward, hands clasped together just below her breasts as if in prayer.

"I've waited so long to hear you say it aloud: that I'm your daughter. You have no idea." The words were muffled by a gusting sob that seemed to send Rose lurching forward; she staggered the few remaining feet separating her from Sylvie.

Sylvie raised her head from the pillows on which she lay. Her face, pale as parchment, crumpled with pain. No, not pain. *Relief,* Rachel saw. A relief so profound it was almost shattering. Nikos must have felt it, too. Trembling, he opened his arms, embracing the daughter he could at last claim, fully and without apology. Rachel, from where she sat on the opposite side of the bed, could see his throat working, and the grateful wonder with which he smoothed a huge, callused hand over his child's heaving back.

As if in a dream, Rachel watched Rose ease from her father's arms and sink onto the mattress beside Mama. She felt a cool rush of perfumed air as Rose bent close to kiss her mother, who lay between them like a slender volume of poetry between two mismatched bookends. Yet Rachel might have been invisible. It was as if only Sylvie and Rose existed, mother and child, joined at the cheek, a Renaissance sculpture.

With a soft intake of breath, Rose began to weep.

And like a knife twisting in her heart, Rachel heard the woman whom all her life she'd believed to be her mother murmur, "Rose . . . oh, my precious girl. Can you ever forgive me?"

Forgiveness was something Rose Santini Griffin had long ago checked at the door. By age six, she'd come to the conclusion that the God her grandmother prayed to in church, on Sunday and every First Friday, listened only to thin-lipped Italian ladies dressed in black. And also that the word "fair" was not only used to describe little girls with blue eyes and blond hair, but applied generally to how they were treated as well. The reason God had made her so dark, Rose had believed, was to punish her. Why? Maybe she'd been *born* bad, she'd thought, like with Original Sin, only a whole lot worse.

Her only hope for redemption had been to do well in school, and keep her mouth shut instead of complaining or even crying into her pillow when Nonnie punished her. Nonetheless, she'd fantasized about Mother Mary appearing to her as she had to Bernadette—a miracle that would wipe her soul clean with a single stroke.

Only the vision, when it appeared, wasn't at all what Rose had been hoping for. The beautiful blonde lady who showed up one day outside her school wasn't barefoot, dressed in a blue robe. She wore a fur coat, and a stylish hat with a veil that dipped down over one eye. And ruby earrings in the shape of teardrops—one of which, startlingly, she'd plucked from her earlobe and thrust at Rose. Though her eyes were sad like the Blessed Virgin's, she'd turned away without speaking, without giving a clue as to why she'd come.

Rose hadn't realized it then, but the strange lady was her own mother.

Now, more than forty years later, Rose reached up to finger the ruby earring she'd worn pirate-style until an accident of fate—or *was* it just fate?—had brought her back into Sylvie's orbit . . . and led her not only to the earring's missing twin, but to the truth about her mother.

Gazing down at the frail, elderly woman on the bed, Rose felt pierced by an emotion she couldn't quite place. This was her mother . . . the woman who'd given birth to her . . . her flesh and blood. In the end, it didn't matter what Sylvie had done, or what Rose had missed growing up. What mattered was that they were connected—a connection that no amount of guilt or resentment had been able to sever. Why? Because there *was* a God, Rose understood at last in some deep way she hadn't as a child, and He had listened. He had provided her with the love she'd yearned for. Just not in the way she'd been expecting.

Rose brought an unsteady hand to her mother's cheek, and was shocked by its coolness. But Sylvie's heart must still be beating, she knew, because it was still capable of feeling. The tears trickling down her face were proof of that.

"Mother." Rose, for the first time ever, addressed Sylvie as she had yearned to all her adult life, the name like a sweet balm spreading through her.

How easy that was, she thought.

Sylvie smiled faintly. Her face gleamed as pale and smooth as a seashore washed clean by the tide. "I . . . wish. . . ," she murmured, straining to draw each breath, "it could have been different. That . . . I could have told the truth sooner." She turned her bright gaze upon Rachel, who wore the fixed, disbelieving expression of someone startled in her own home by an intruder. "I was afraid. For *you,* Rachel, dear. Of what it would do to you. But now I see that the one I was most afraid of hurting was myself. I'd lost one daughter already. I couldn't bear the thought of losing another."

"You didn't lose me." Rose brushed roughly with the heel of her hand at her own tears. "I've been here all along."

Sylvie motioned her closer, murmuring thickly, "In my nightstand . . . a key." She waited until Rose had slid open the drawer of the delicate burled table. "Do you see it? On a silver chain, next to my heart medicine. It's to the locked drawer in my desk downstairs. There's something in it I want you to have."

"What. . . ?"

Sylvie smiled. "You'll know when you find it."

Rose stared at the tiny key in her hand. She couldn't imagine what might be in that locked drawer. A family heirloom? A piece of jewelry like the ruby earrings Sylvie had given her?

"Your sons . . . my *grandsons* . . ." Sylvie's breath came in short, whistling bursts. "Tell them . . . please. That I love them. As much as I do Iris. Remind them that they still have Nikos. He can't be a father to them, not like Max . . . but he's their grandfather. They need to know."

"I'll tell them." Rose felt something in her chest give way, like an eroded embankment crumbling.

"There's something else. . . ." Sylvie's voice was so low Rose had to lean close to hear. She didn't know how much more she could take; she felt as if she were being ripped apart inside—torn into tiny bits, as she had been after Max died. "I loved you," Sylvie whispered. "From the moment I first held you in my arms. Even though I was frightened of what might happen . . . of what Gerald would do. You were *mine*. If it hadn't been for that fire . . ." She shut her eyes briefly, her chest rising and falling in fitful little bursts. "I would have kept you. It wouldn't have been easy, but I would have found a way. I . . . I was wrong to have done what I did."

Beside her, Rose heard a sound halfway between a gasp and a sob. Rachel. Rose swung around to face her. For the first time in all the years since Rachel had become known to her—first, as Brian's bride; then, incredibly, as the daughter Sylvie had raised in *her* place—Rose felt truly sorry for her.

She touched Rachel's sleeve, but Rachel didn't respond. She just sat there, her head bowed, her chest heaving with inarticulate grief. And for once, Sylvie—gazing at Rachel with the helpless, agonized eyes of a mother who wished desperately she hadn't had to make such a choice—wasn't reaching to console her.

What was there for Rose to say either? *You had her all those years—please don't begrudge me these last few moments.* How could she expect Rachel to understand the preciousness of the gift Rose had been given?

Common compassion caused Rose to seize hold of Rachel's icy fingers. Their past differences—even their recent clash—paled in comparison to this. Rachel was suffering, that was all that mattered. Rachel wasn't to blame for the choices Sylvie had made.

You won't die, Rose reassured Rachel silently. *Some days it feels like you're going to . . . and if one more person says, 'Take it a day at a time,' you'll hit them, you really will, because you can't think that far ahead—you don't know how you're going to make it through to the next* minute. *But you will make it.*

"Come. . . ." Sylvie extended her arms shakily. "I must have a moment alone with Nikos . . . but first let me hold you. *Both* of you. My girls . . ."

No one had called them "girls" in at least a hundred years. But as Sylvie, her eyes afire in a face pale as ashes, gathered them to her, both Rose and Rachel felt exactly the way they had as little children—when the one thing each had desired most was the comfort of a mother's embrace. For Rose, it was a comfort made all the more sweet for having been denied; for Rachel, a sense of coming home so powerful she had to throw an arm about Sylvie to keep from drowning. As they lay with their heads pressed to her laboring breast—one fair, one dark—a cloud passed before the sun, plunging the room into shadow, and making the burst of light that followed all the more brilliant.

Caught in its glow, the three women clung to one another, and wept.

🌹 Randomly, a line from a poem memorized in childhood drifted into Sylvie's head as she lay against Nikos, her eyes closed.

I remember, I remember . . . the house where I was born. . . .

She'd grown up in a Bronx tenement, a railroad flat with a kitchen so cramped that the bathtub by the stove had doubled as a table when covered with a folding screen laid flat. There had been just the two of them, she and Mama, who each night before bed had regaled little Sylvie, in her thickly accented voice that seemed to lend drama to the most ordinary of anecdotes, with tales of the museum where she worked. Describing works of art that had survived centuries of war, massacre, floods, famine: Egyptian vases dug out of tombs, along with mummies wrapped in rotting cloth; precious carvings from the Orient imported by tea and silk merchants in wooden sailing ships; hundred-year-old portraits so lifelike you'd have sworn their subjects were breathing.

But even those stories couldn't warm Sylvie on winter nights when the landlord turned the heat down so low they had to huddle together under the covers to keep from freezing. Sylvie's asthma would flare up then, and Mama would sit her up in bed, rubbing her thin chest with Vicks VapoRub.

What Sylvie remembered most about those nights was how hard she'd struggled, not only to breathe, but to keep from panicking. Lying in bed, surrounded by pans of hot water emitting ghostly fingers of steam. The sharp eucalyptus odor of Vicks barely penetrating the thick fog clogging her lungs. And Mama, dear Mama—singing to her softly, Viennese lullabies that made Sylvie cry even as they soothed her fears.

She felt now as she had then, as if the only thing keeping her alive was the familiar torso against which she lay, the arms that circled her as securely as a gold band. Mama was gone, but she had Nikos. Sylvie opened her eyes and smiled up at him, a smile that felt like a thin line traced by a fingertip along a frosty windowpane. She was cold . . . so cold. Not even Nikos could warm her.

At the same time, she felt oddly weightless. The thorn that had been plucked from her heart had liberated her in some way. She was sorry for the years of pain her silence had cost Rose . . . and for the anguish and confusion Rachel would suffer in the months and years to come. She was sorry, too, about Iris. But none of it could take away from this wondrous lightness.

My children will survive, she thought.

Rose? If there had been time, Sylvie would have counseled her not to view her solitary widowhood as some sort of virtue; a sturdiness that doesn't know how to bend can become a weakness, she'd have said.

Rachel? She needed to understand that saving the world began with shoring up one's own ramparts.

Iris was the one who worried her most. The thought of her granddaughter tugged at Sylvie. She'd wanted to say goodbye, and to plead with Iris not to turn away from the family who loved her.

So little time . . . so much left unsaid!

Panic set in again. Sylvie, drowning, struggled to stay afloat. She had to fight this, she told herself. Hoard every moment that remained.

Then a voice, so real she could have sworn she felt its breath against her ear, whispered, *They'll miss you, but their lives will go on.* Mama's voice.

Yes, Sylvie thought, relaxing a little. Even her garden, she knew, would survive without her. Nurtured by other hands, and by God. Come winter, its branches would grow bare, and its roots curl in on themselves . . . but in spring, it would bloom again. . . .

I remember, I remember . . . the roses, red and white. . . .

Sylvie labored mightily to draw in a breath; it felt like a rope being pulled through the eye of a needle. She no longer had any sensation in her hands and feet—and that was a blessing. She hardly felt the cold that had ached in every corner of her being. It would be over soon, she knew. And she understood that to be a blessing, too.

But before she let go, there was one last loved one she needed to say goodbye to. . . .

Sylvie lifted her face to the man she had known nearly half her life . . . the man with whom she'd shared thirty years of sorrows and joys in every shape and size.

"I . . . will . . . miss you." She managed to speak the words, but only barely. "I . . . never asked. Do you . . . believe . . . in heaven?"

Nikos nodded. It was as if some invisible bolts holding his expression intact had loosened, causing the rough planes of his face to sag. "I believe in God," he said. "And if I am made in His image, then He is a builder like me. Heaven must look like New York City, I think . . . lots of skyscrapers."

"I'll save a room for you."

"Next to yours, I hope," he answered in an unfamiliar choked voice. "One with a view."

"A . . . garden, too."

"Of course."

Nikos cupped a hand about her face, tipping it so that her chin rested against his rib cage. He didn't want her to see him crying . . . and that was okay. In all these years with Nikos, Sylvie had been unsuccessful in only one respect: she'd been unable to convince him that to cry was to feel, and to feel was to be strong.

My spirit flew in feathers then, that is so heavy now. . . .

"Nikos?" she breathed. "Are you . . . sorry. That we never married?"

He was silent, his broad chest lifting and falling with a reassuring steadiness. When he spoke, it was with the same unwavering directness, like a skilled hand on a plow, cutting wide, straight furrows in the earth.

"You *are* my wife," he told her. "In every way that counts. I used to think it mattered what people would say. I believed, as my father did, that only when a woman wears his ring on her finger can a man feel she is truly his." Nikos sighed. "But I know now that to love someone . . . there is no piece of paper for that. And a ring . . . it is empty in the middle. The emptiness can be filled only by the person who wears it."

Sylvie laid a hand over his. "I love you," she whispered. The weight on her chest seemed to have eased for just an instant, enabling her to speak clearly the words he needed to hear. "You are my husband."

"I'll look after her . . . our Rose," he promised.

"Look after Rachel, too," she pleaded. "And Iris. See that she gets . . . the help she needs."

"I will."

I remember, I remember . . . the fir-trees dark and high; I used to think their slender tops were close against the sky. . . .

The room seemed to fade, like a picture exposed to sudden intense light. But she wasn't at all frightened. Even as her senses began to fade, too, she felt she was being lifted, borne on some invisible current of brightness.

Oh, how lovely! she opened her mouth to cry out. But no words came. There was only a rushing sound, like the wind stirring the tops of tall trees, like the silken murmuring of pine needles in a forest too vast for any map. She could feel that breeze against her skin, the warm lick of it sliding along her arms and legs as she was lifted toward the sky—like when she was a little girl, swinging in the playground, her bottom snug in the leather sling-seat, its creaking chains seeming to writhe against her palms, the little bits and pieces of sun that shone through the narrow leaves of the ailanthus trees falling against her face like warm kisses.

I remember, I remember where I used to swing, and thought the air must rush as fresh to swallows on the wing. . . .

The sun wasn't coming in bits and pieces anymore. It was shining down on her with all its might . . . with a brightness that seemed to beckon her toward its source. She felt as if she were floating . . . as if her childhood fear of swinging so high she would actually be plucked right up into the sky were coming true at last. Only it wasn't scary at all. . . . It felt perfectly natural, in fact.

Sylvie, in the end, found it quite easy to let go. *Dying isn't hard,* she would have said, had she been able to form the words. Dying was a rose without thorns—beautiful, with nothing to prick you. *It's life,* she thought in her last instant of consciousness, *that makes us bleed. . . .*

Chapter 14

✿ The funeral service was held at Temple Emanu-El. But those who came to mourn—the synagogue was filled to overflowing with relatives, friends, former employees—agreed that the real tribute to Sylvie came afterwards, when she was laid to rest on a green slope shaded by a Norway maple just beginning to lose its leaves, under the most brilliant fall sky in recent memory.

In accordance with her faith, the coffin was fashioned from plain pine, without adornment of any kind. No flowers—that, too, was forbidden. In exactly one year, there would be a ceremony to unveil the headstone yet to be carved, and small stones would mark the presence of those who'd come to pay their respects. But until then, Sylvie would be blanketed only in the green, growing things she'd loved—soft grass spangled with the bright coins of dandelions; fallen leaves offering themselves up like small curled hands.

Rachel watched as Nikos sank to his knees before the open grave. Any weeping he might have done, he'd done in private, and the face that stared vacantly into the gouged earth, except for his bloodshot eyes, made her think of an Easter Island statue—blocky, rough, pagan somehow. She saw his lips moving, as if in silent prayer, but if Nikos belonged to any church—or even believed in God—Rachel had never heard about it.

It occurred to her, as she stood with her head unbowed, and her hair blowing in the faint breeze, that there was a great deal she didn't know—and not just about the people in her mother's life. If Mama had been able to keep Rose a secret all these years, what else had she hidden? What secrets had she taken with her to wherever she'd gone?

Even more troubling was that Rachel, who should have been

frantic to explore every dark corner, every twisting path of her mother's life, felt nothing more than mild curiosity. The wrecking ball that had swung down out of the blue had leveled her whole existence, leaving her utterly empty. It was as if Mama's secret had robbed her of her ability to feel as well as her identity.

Rachel looked around her, at the grieving faces forming a ragged wreath about the grave. Aunts, uncles, cousins—all the people whose blood she was supposed to have shared.

Her gaze shifted to Rose, defiantly resplendent, not in black, but in a muted red suit. Or maybe she'd understood Mama better than anyone—Mama's impeccable taste, and her love of bright colors. Rose wore a pale, strained look, but she, like Nikos, remained dry-eyed.

Flanking Rose were her sons, Drew and Jay, sober in suits—though Jay seemed to have shot up an inch or two since he'd last worn his. They looked more dazed than sorrowful, but it was touching to see how solicitous they were of their mother. Drew, muscular and dark-haired like his father, with an arm around her shoulders, and Jay standing guard with all the macho seriousness of a rookie cop. They were a closed corporation, those three, Rachel thought. Even Eric, standing a few feet away, remained outside that circle.

Rachel had to search the crowd to find Iris. Throughout the funeral service, her daughter, who'd been devastated by the death of her beloved grandmother, had sat dutifully between Rachel and Brian, but since arriving at the cemetery, she'd more or less melted into the background. When Rachel finally spotted her, half hidden behind the mountainous bulk of Morris Beder, a childhood friend of her mother's from the Bronx, she felt a pang that brought the faint sting of tears to her eyes. So thin! How was it possible, in just a few weeks, to have lost what looked like at least ten pounds? In a long black cotton-piqué dress that hung forlornly about her ankles, Iris was like some spectral vision.

Rachel thought: *I need to talk to her, alone, find out what's the matter.* Whatever it was, Mama had been alarmed. If it hadn't been for . . .

Her sense of urgency dissolved suddenly as a sudden gust of wind shook a fistful of raindrops from the maple tree—a souvenir from last night's storm—onto the grass at Rachel's feet. It was a full-time job, Rachel thought dully, just looking after herself. Like a ventriloquist, she had to be conscious every minute of making sure her arms and legs moved in concert, that the words coming out of her mouth weren't gibberish.

Even Brian, standing beside her, seemed far away. They were like two people on opposite sides of a glass wall. She could see him—hear him, even—but if she'd tried to touch him, she felt sure her fingers would have met only with cool, slick glass. Brian must have felt it, too, for his eyes, she saw, weren't on her, or even the rabbi chanting the mourners' *kaddish,* but on Rose.

Rose caught his gaze and held it, the two of them seeming to share a private communication that needed no words. Rose, in her dark-crimson suit—the one flower adorning Mama's grave. Rose, who for years had kept silent out of respect for the mother that Rachel, in many ways, had taken for granted.

Had Brian known about Mama? Had Rose confided in him all those years ago? The thought, like some nasty hornet that wouldn't be brushed away, was almost enough to stir Rachel from her strange lethargy. Almost . . . but not quite.

Watching her husband reluctantly tear his gaze from the woman he would have married but for an act of God, Rachel gave herself a mental shake. *Do something! FEEL something, damnit!*

But all she felt was impotent. Like someone in a wheelchair willing her paralyzed limbs to move. How could she keep her husband, her child—her *life*—from slipping away, when she herself had come undone?

Rachel felt someone touch her elbow, and looked down into the concerned brown eyes of her friend Kay. "You dropped this," Kay murmured, handing Rachel a crumpled handkerchief. Dear Kay, who'd had the good sense to wear a purple so dark it was nearly black, even if it made her look like a plump eggplant.

"Thanks." Rachel tucked it into the pocket of her black coat-dress. In storybooks, she thought, it was the lovelorn gentleman who returned the handkerchief. She glanced again at Brian, for whom she might have been invisible, and was ambushed by the first real emotion in days: a sorrow that pierced through the cottony layers in which she felt swathed, all the way down to her heart.

Touch my hand, tell me we'll be all right . . . anything, she pleaded silently.

If only to let her know she was still here. Still important to him.

But when Brian did speak, as the rabbi's wailing chant reached its crescendo, it was only to murmur, "Peter wants us to meet at the house afterwards. To go over the will. Is that okay with you?" Peter Harbinson, Mama's lawyer and good friend.

Rachel nodded, unable to speak.

The will. Of course. Somehow, in all the shock and confusion, she'd forgotten there was a will to be read, a sizable estate to be distributed. As if Mama's things were a pie to be divided up into even slices. As if Sylvie's house, her garden with its lovingly tended roses could ever be anything but her own.

You believed you *were part of her, too, remember? But that was only an illusion.*

No more real than the hand she slipped into the crook of her husband's elbow. For, had she been flesh and blood, wouldn't she have felt something—some warmth, some answering pressure—from him? Instead, there was only cool gabardine, against which her fingers made barely a ripple.

When it was time to go, Rachel felt almost grateful for the soft wet mud that sucked at her shoes as they made their way slowly back to the car, reminding her that she was still alive, still firmly grounded on this earth.

Back home, at her mother's, the family gathered in the library, while the friends and relatives assembled upstairs—among them Mama's Filipina housekeeper, Milagros, who, for once, was a guest in the home she'd cared for so faithfully.

Peter Harbinson, scarecrow-thin, with his stiltlike limbs and narrow face, sat in the leather-upholstered swivel chair that had once supported the more substantial girth of Rachel's father—or, at least, the man she'd *believed* was her father. In his dark-brown suit, Harbinson reminded Rachel of a long Dunhill cigar, like the ones in the embossed-leather humidor that still occupied a corner of the massive Edwardian partners desk.

He cleared his throat and looked around him. Rachel was only vaguely aware of the others in the room—Brian and Iris, Rose and her sons, and Nikos, of course. But Harbinson's lugubrious gaze seemed to take them all in at once.

"First, I'd like you all to know how sorry I am for your loss," he began in his reedy voice. "Two years ago, when my wife was diagnosed with leukemia, it was Sylvie who found us the best oncologist in the city, and who visited Margaret in the hospital nearly every day. I echo my wife's sentiments in saying that Sylvie was that rare and special friend—the kind who is there for you in times of need. Her generosity will long be remembered. Which is what brings us here today." He cleared his throat again, glancing down at the thick document in front of him. "As you know, she . . . ahem . . . was a woman of some means. I think it's fair to say that everyone in this room has been amply provided for. . . ."

Adjusting the half-glasses on the end of his long, skinny nose, he began to read from Sylvie's last will and testament. Rachel sat stiffly upright in her chair, trying hard not to succumb to the tug of familial gravity exercised by Papa's favorite room. The dark, polished shelving lined with books, and bound librettos of the operas he had so loved. The framed hunting prints matted in dark green. The collection of antique letter-openers on the small table next to the leather sofa. It even smelled of him, like pipe tobacco and old sweaters.

But the man she'd called Papa—who had carried her up the stairs to bed every night until she grew too heavy for him to lift—had been *no one's* father. . . .

Lies. All of it lies . . .

When Rachel heard Harbinson list all her mother's assets, which included a sizable bank account, an investment portfolio worth close to six million, and several limited partnerships in office buildings, she wasn't surprised. Even when she learned that it had been bequeathed to her—with the exception of the trusts set aside for her grandchildren—it left barely a scratch on the glassy surface of her detachment. Only when Harbinson got to the disposition of the house itself did Rachel come suddenly, sharply to attention.

" '. . . I give, devise, and bequeath title to the property located on Riverside Drive to Rose Santini Griffin, with the understanding that my longtime companion, Nikos Alexandros, shall have full use and occupancy thereof for the remainder of his lifetime. . . .' "

Rose? This house? Rachel felt like a sleepwalker slapped awake. She swiveled around to face Rose, who looked equally shocked. Her olive complexion pale as old, bleached clay. Rose sat gripping the arms of her spool-backed chair, shaking her head slowly as if to deny what she was hearing.

Mama gave her this house, and she doesn't even want it.

The enormity of the betrayal sluiced down over Rachel. She felt as if she were tumbling over and over, with nothing to grab hold of. *Brian . . . please . . . help me.* But Brian, though seated next to her, seemed to be a distant figure on some far-off shore. He wasn't reaching out to her; he merely watched with a somewhat bewildered expression as she sat gasping for air, her mouth opening and closing.

It was Iris who broke the stunned silence. Iris, who had barely uttered two words the entire afternoon. Now, suddenly, like a flame from a seemingly dead ember, she was shooting up from the ottoman at Drew's feet. Crying, "No! You can't! I don't *care* what you were to Grandma. This house doesn't belong to you!"

Watching her daughter fly across the room, Rachel found the strength to rise up, to beat at this numbness that had settled over her like a bell jar. She started toward Iris—sluggishly, for her limbs were stiff with disuse—but it was too late. Iris was out the door, the rapid tapping of her high heels against the tiled hallway like an urgent message being telegraphed. A message Rachel desperately wished she could decipher, before it was too late.

≈ "How are the boys doing?" asked Rachel.

"Not too badly . . . considering." Rose shrugged.

They stood side by side on the flagstone patio, near the steps leading down into the garden, two women—one tall and dark, the other slight and fair—their elongated shadows like the hands of a mammoth clock that had wound down. The afternoon sun was low in the sky, its storybook light striking the far brick wall and cutting a glorious swath of green through the dark tumble of ivy, where a rogue purple blossom from a late-blooming climber clung in stubborn defiance.

It had been more than two weeks since the funeral. But for Rose, every day was like the day before: a bizarre, through-the-looking-glass world where nothing was quite what it seemed. Strangers to whom she was now officially related, calling or dropping by to offer condolences that were merely an excuse to pry. Mandy, at work, eyeing her strangely, as if wondering what had given Rose the right to comment on *her* life while harboring such a huge secret of her own. Nikos, at her dinner table, attempting to explain to Drew and Jay, both of them confused and more than a little hurt, why it had taken so long for them to learn the truth about their grandparents.

This house, too. Rose couldn't get used to it being hers. It made no sense! Sylvie's bequest would accomplish nothing, except to alienate her further from Rachel. Look at the trouble it had caused so far—like that awful scene with Iris during the reading of the will. Rose, who'd been just as stunned, had felt personally responsible somehow, as if she were robbing Rachel and her daughter of their legacy. Which was why—last week, when Rachel suggested they meet today to go through the papers in Sylvie's office—Rose had welcomed the chance to be alone with her, to confront the five-hundred-pound gorilla neither of them could bring herself to mention.

Yet now here they were, hours of clearing and organizing behind them, no more at ease with each other than at the outset.

In the awkward silence that had descended, Rose surveyed the garden that only a short time ago had been Sylvie's pride and joy, idly noting the bushes and bowers that were drooping, the yellow leaves scattered over grass withered by last night's cold spell. She thought, *We ought to get a gardener in here sometime in the next month or so, before it freezes.* To trim back where it had become overgrown, if nothing else.

At the same time, she rebelled at the very idea. A gardener? Sylvie was the keeper of this garden. Anyone else puttering among her rosebushes and flower beds would seem like a trespasser.

Your mother is dead, a voice reminded her.

Mother. The brief euphoria Rose had felt in the beginning—oh, to be able to speak that word at long last!—had passed. The deepest cut of her grief was healing. But her resentment at the unfairness of it all, like a weed broken off at the top instead of pulled out by its root, had begun to grow back. How could Sylvie have done this to her? Left the most important thing until the very last, when it was almost too late to be of much value?

She turned to her old friend—whom she now regarded warily, but not without affection. Rose had set aside any resentment she might have felt toward her friend. What she was having a hard time coping with was how cold Rachel had been acting—as if the secret Sylvie had revealed on her deathbed were somehow Rose's fault, as if Rose herself weren't suffering.

At the moment, Rachel stood gazing out at some distant horizon, lost in thought, her eyes as blue and empty as the sky overhead. A light breeze had kicked up, ruffling her hair and scouring her cheeks pink, making her look years younger. Girlish almost, in her white dungarees and oversized navy sweatshirt.

Rose felt a sudden rush of tenderness. She touched Rachel's shoulder, and felt her jump slightly. "Do you want to call it quits? We don't have to do it all at once. There's so much—it looks like she never threw anything out." The irony of this caused a hollow laugh to surface. The same woman who'd safeguarded her secrets with such care had also saved every sales slip and taxi receipt . . .

"Quit?" Rachel echoed, shaking her head as if to clear it. "Sure. Why not? What difference will another day make? Or another year, for that matter?" She swiveled around to face Rose, her expression no longer blandly vacant, but a mask of hard angles. "I just want it to go away . . . for everything to be the way it was. And I know that's not going to happen. It's funny, because that's about the *only* thing I can be sure of these days—that my life will never be the same. I'm not even the same person."

"You're wrong about that," Rose told her with the assurance of one who knew. "You're exactly who you've always been. It was your *place* in all this that didn't make sense."

Rachel went back to staring fixedly into the distance. Softly, she said, "I always thought it was me, that the reason I felt as if I didn't quite belong here was because there was something the matter with *me.*"

Rose's mouth stretched in a smile of shared bitterness. "I know. I felt the same way, only like I didn't belong in my own skin. But at least you had a mother who loved you."

She looked down at her feet as if that might stop the tears forcing their way up the bridge of her nose. With the toe of a scuffed brown loafer, she pushed at a fallen leaf.

A muffled sob escaped Rachel. "What kind of love was that? Keeping me in the dark all those years? Denying me my own *family?* I like your sisters well enough, don't get me wrong. Marie, especially. But they're *yours.* How am I supposed to wipe the slate clean and start over?"

"I didn't say that what Sylvie did was right. Only that she loved you."

"How do you *know* that?" Rachel turned angrily to face her.

"Because," Rose said slowly, lifting her face to the light that all at once appeared to be radiating from every sunstruck surface—the rosehips like tiny polished apples that dotted every rosebush, the silvery bangles of a wind chime tinkling below the latticed bower. "Because, if she'd loved me half as much, she'd have told the truth sooner."

She tried to keep the resentment from her voice, but failed. Rachel felt cheated? *How can she possibly not realize how much better off she is for having been lied to?* On Rose's wedding day, there had been no mother to beam at her from the front pew. At her sons' baptisms, no grandmother to cradle them in her arms as they were blessed with holy water. Even when Max died, Rose had been careful not to lean on Sylvie too much.

So what *had* Sylvie given her?

This house. In which Rose had been conceived, but not raised. Could Sylvie possibly have imagined it would make up for all those lost years? Had she believed, even remotely, she could somehow *buy* Rose's forgiveness?

To make things even more complicated, Nikos had insisted on moving out. He couldn't bear the idea of being here without Sylvie, he'd said. Hearing her voice behind every door, imagining each time he walked into a room that he'd find her waiting. Anyway, as far as he was concerned, the house belonged to Rose. Money wasn't an issue; Nikos was wealthy in his own right. A week after the funeral, he'd taken an apartment in one of his own newly constructed buildings.

Now the house, and its garden, stood empty.

As empty as Rose felt inside.

A part of her understood that Sylvie's intentions had been good. In her own way, Sylvie had wanted to balance the scales, to do what was fair. This place had to be worth several million at least. But what the hell was Rose going to do with a mansion? She certainly couldn't see herself living here. Yet how could she sell it? Whether she liked it or not, it was as much a part of her heritage as it was Rachel's.

"Look! Over there . . . the tree peony." Rachel pointed. "I remember when Mama planted it—just after Brian and I were married. In honor of us, actually, because of its name—'Bridal Gown'."

She blushed slightly. "I didn't know peonies bloomed this late in the season."

"They don't," Rose said.

Nevertheless, she caught a flash of something snow-white through the weeping branches of the Japanese maple: a single teacup-sized blossom, like some ghostly reminder of Sylvie. Rose glanced over at Rachel, who was smiling—a real smile that softened her whole face. Rose smiled, too. A peony, of all things. God *was* in the details, she supposed.

"Will you miss it . . . this place, I mean?" she asked cautiously.

"What I *miss* is my mother," Rachel replied firmly.

Rose shook her head. "If I'd known she was planning on leaving me the house, I'd have told her not to." She hugged herself, shivering. "What on earth am I supposed to do with it?"

"Sell it."

Rose darted a glance at Rachel to see if she was joking. But Rachel was perfectly serious. Her blue eyes, narrowed against the bright light, regarded Rose with the directness that had always been her trademark.

"You can't mean that," Rose protested.

"As a matter of fact, I *do*." Rachel's voice was coolly emphatic. Rose had long presumed that this house meant as much to Rachel as it clearly did to Iris. But, like so much about Rachel, there was more to her than met the eye. "You want to know something?" Rachel went on. "My whole life, I never felt at home here. Not really. I was always tiptoeing around, afraid of breaking something. I even used to wonder if Mama felt that way, too. If that's why she spent so much of her time out here, in her garden."

"I don't know." Rose shook her head. "Selling it would seem wrong somehow."

"It's yours now," Rachel reminded her. "You can do what you want with it." She drew in a breath that seemed to set her back on course, like a sailboat that had been on the verge of capsizing. With quiet bitterness, she said, "You've gotten what you always wanted—Brian. You might as well have the house, too."

A flicker of guilt caused Rose to drop her gaze. She felt as if she were crossing a dangerous intersection. *Proceed with caution,* every instinct shouted.

"There *was* a time when I'd have gone off with Brian, in a heartbeat—even if it meant his leaving you." Rose paused, knowing she had to weigh each word carefully. "I haven't forgotten how much I loved him . . . but that was a long time ago. We're not even the same people anymore."

"Maybe Brian sees it differently."

Rose looked at her, more bewildered now than anything else. "Rachel, what are you saying?"

"You tell me."

Rose felt herself growing warm, despite the cool shadows that had slipped out from under the old house's copper-lined eaves. "You're asking the wrong person," she said.

Color rose in Rachel's cheeks, and her eyes glittered. In a hard, flat voice, she said, "I know. Nothing happened the night he took you home. Brian already told me that. But you and I know the truth has more than one face."

She was referring to Sylvie, Rose knew. But it seemed as if Rachel's grief and confusion over her mother's death had gotten tangled up with her fears about her husband.

"If you know that," Rose said, "then you must also know that what was true yesterday isn't necessarily what's true today." Gently, but not too gently, she added, "A word of advice: don't go looking for skeletons in empty closets."

"What are you saying? That I'm imagining things . . . that I don't know what's going on?" Rachel crossed her arms over her chest.

"Neither. All I'm saying is that you won't find out how much Brian loves you by asking *me.*"

You're a fine one to preach about love, a voice in her head chided.

What had she done about her feelings for Eric except try to squash them? She'd seen little enough of him since the funeral ... but not, as she'd told Eric, because she was so busy. The truth was, she was avoiding him. She'd told him she couldn't marry him, yes. But until she could look him in the eye, and say with absolute honesty that it was because she didn't love him enough, how could she face him? It would never happen—she *couldn't* stop loving him— and she would only risk stirring up feelings that were better left dormant.

Rachel's shoulders sagged, and she cupped her hands over her face. "Oh God, I miss Mama so much! She'd have known what to do. She would have made it better."

"The way she did with us?" Rose challenged.

Rachel shot her a stricken look over her steepled fingers. "I wish it had been different for you growing up ... but that would have meant *my* not having had her as a mother."

"It wasn't up to either of us," Rose reminded her. "We weren't given a choice."

"I still can't quite get used to the idea. Not just of Mama's being gone, but of our being ..." Rachel took an unsteady backward step and leaned against the low stone wall, using the back of her arm to wipe her eyes, the way Rose imagined she had as a little girl. "What *are* we? Not sisters ... but it *feels* that way, doesn't it?"

"We're ..." Rose had started to say, *We're friends*. But that wasn't quite true, either. Not at the moment. "... survivors of the same storm, you could say," she finished.

"What now? Where do we go from here?"

"We'll do what we've always done. Just keep putting one foot in front of the other."

Rachel fell silent, seeming to ponder this—a minute that stretched into several. Finally, glancing at her watch, she said, "It's late. I should get going."

"Go ahead," Rose urged. "I'll lock up."

She was in no hurry. The truth was, she needed some time to herself. A moment alone in Sylvie's house—*her* house now—simply to think.

About where she was headed. And what, if anything, could be salvaged out of the muddle Sylvie had left behind. She felt so lost. And confused, too. Wasn't this what she'd wanted—for the world to know she was Sylvie's daughter? Why, then, did it feel so hollow?

Some instinct made Rose grope in her coat pocket—the same coat she'd been wearing the day Sylvie had died. Her fingers closed over something small and metallic—the key Sylvie had given her. In all the confusion, she'd forgotten it. Now it lay gleaming in the curve of her palm. Sylvie had mentioned a desk drawer, she recalled. With something in it she'd wanted Rose to have.

You'll know when you see it. Sylvie's words echoed in her head.

In the small office that had been a butler's pantry when the house was originally built back in the 1850s, Rose found what she was looking for. A locked drawer in the beautiful old Chippendale desk—where Sylvie had written to her many friends, paid bills, kept her meticulous accounts. She fitted the key into the brass keyhole shaped like a tiny grass harp.

The drawer slid easily, as if it had been opened often.

But instead of finding more of what she'd seen so far—ledgers lined with neat columns, boxed receipts, canceled checks in bundles bound with rubber bands—Rose was confronted by something entirely unexpected: a bundle of letters.

Dozens of letters that had never been sent. Loosely tied together with a faded red ribbon. All of them handwritten, on various types of stationery—some yellowed with age, but all bearing the identical salutation: *"My dearest daughter."*

Tears filled Rose's eyes and spilled down her cheeks, unnoticed, unchecked. She scanned the letters, one after another—*decades'* worth. Letters rich with all the feelings and observations Sylvie, for one reason or another, had been unable to share with her.

August 12, 1977. . . . *Today you became a mother. When I learned you'd given birth—a boy!—I was overcome. So many feelings. Mostly joy, but some sadness, too. If only I could be a grandmother to little Drew . . .*

And ten years later . . .

November 22, 1986 . . . *When I saw you on television, the way you handled yourself with all those reporters and cameras crowding in, I felt such pride! You were so poised . . . so regal . . . standing there on the courthouse steps. My daughter the lawyer . . .*

Rose sat without moving, her trembling hand the only part of her that seemed able to function. Page after page, some brittle with age, slipped from her lap onto the carpet, like so many autumn leaves. It was almost too much to contemplate—the extent of what Sylvie had kept inside. Even after they'd been reunited, Sylvie had gone on writing these letters, sharing her innermost thoughts with a daughter who might never read them.

It was the most recent letter, written only a few months earlier, that affected Rose the most. Sylvie's revelation that she was dying, and her appeal to Rose—a sort of last wish—for understanding, if not forgiveness, of Sylvie's inability to acknowledge her true daughter openly.

Yet she *had* acknowledged Rose at the end. The courageousness of that act, as well as the unalloyed love evident in every line of these letters, touched a far corner of Rose's heart she'd believed was sealed off to her mother for all time.

In the deep, cold well of her sadness something tremulous was taking hold. A feeling that was too new, and maybe too alien, to have a name, but which brought an odd flicker of comfort nonetheless. Slumped in Sylvie's chair, her lap full of her mother's letters, Rose did something she hadn't done in ages.

She bowed her head, and prayed.

For Sylvie. For Drew and Iris. For Mandy. And Jay—the youngest of them all, who in some ways was having more difficulty coping with his father's death than her other children.

She prayed for Eric, asking God to be gentle, and not let it cause too much hurt when the time came for her to let him go—free him to look for that woman in his mind's eye, who Rose could never be.

But mostly, she prayed for herself.

🌹 Eric punched the blinking line button, and the caller's voice came squawking through his earphones. "You want to know what it's like? It feels like you been kicked in the stomach." An older woman, who sounded as if she'd been crying. "People nowadays, they got no respect. They treat you like you was dirt."

"We've got Gloria from Hoboken on the line." Eric leaned into the mike, finding a place on the wood-grain Formica desktop—strewn with tape reels, scripts for ads, loose pages from press kits—to prop his elbows. "Gloria, what was going through your mind when you got fired after thirty years on the job? You must have been pretty upset. What reason did your boss give?"

"He said I couldn't keep up no more . . . that the other ladies on my shift were complaining. But that's a lie, he never had *nothing* on me." A note of outrage rose in the bitter voice at the other end.

"What do you *think* was his reason?"

"I don't *think*. I know. It's 'cause of that health plan BS y'all are talking about. He'd've had to pay extra, on account of my bad back. Way he figured it, why should he have to shell out for an old lady who's retiring in a few years anyway?"

"Gloria, what do you do for a living?"

"You mean what I *used* to do? I worked in a commercial laundry plant. You know, sheets and towels, that kind of thing, for hotels and stuff. I was real good at it. I was manager of my shift."

"In thirty years, you must have seen your fair share of work-related illnesses, then. Did your job require any heavy lifting?"

"Well, sure . . . we had them big presses. Some you really had to wrestle with."

"Gloria, does your bad back have something to do with the heavy lifting you did at work?"

"Yeah, sure. Everyone in that place bitchin' 'bout something or other."

"Sounds as if you might have grounds for more than just a discrimination suit here. Have you spoken to a lawyer?"

"Humph." She sniffed. "What am I s'posed to pay a lawyer with? Food stamps?"

"Stay on the line, Gloria. My producer will take your address and send you the names of attorneys who handle cases like yours on a contingency basis. . . ."

"Con—*what?*"

"You won't owe a cent, Gloria. Only a piece of the pie if you win. Good luck with everything . . ." He punched the hold button; the call would be picked up by his producer, Greg, now giving him the thumbs-up from behind the soundproof Plexiglas of the engineer's booth. "For those of you who just tuned in, I'm Eric Sandstrom, and some of the folks we're hearing from today are wondering if their HMO is actually doing them more harm than good. . . ."

The rest of the show passed in a blur. Eric felt as if he were on automatic pilot, punching line buttons, responding to callers—most of them wanting to gripe on air. He wasn't without compassion for those who'd been genuinely screwed over. It was just that the meter measuring his sympathy appeared to be temporarily out of service. He was functioning okay, he could even think of intelligent things to say, but it was as if his feelings were baffled in carpet and foam, just like this studio.

When the signal came—Greg holding up a hand with his index and middle fingers extended to show they had only two minutes left—Eric wrapped up the hour with a taped commercial for a group medical practice in New Rochelle, which may or may not have been an intentional bit of irony. At that moment, he wondered if maybe everyone would be better off placing their trust in Native American medicine men. In his opinion, what people needed as much as doctoring was a dose of magic, a sprinkle of stardust, a pinch of faith. Some things, he thought, were better off left unexplained.

Wasn't that where he'd gone wrong with Rose? Not only pushing her too hard too soon, but attempting to make sense of the irrational, get her to see something that existed only in his mind's eye. What the hell had he expected? To Rose, it must have sounded crazy. The wild imaginings of someone whose brain was pickled from booze. And yet . . .

When was falling in love ever logical? When was there ever a right time? He understood why she was scared. Twice, she'd had the kind of love he was offering snatched away from her. And there was no guarantee it wouldn't happen again. Either of them could get sick or die. All he could promise was that he'd never willingly leave her. But for Rose, damnit, that wasn't enough.

These past weeks, they might as well have been in different time zones. He'd hardly seen her since the funeral. And their phone conversations were usually so brief and strained, he found himself half-listening for the hiss of long-distance static, the minute whirrs and clicks of trunk lines spanning the imagined miles between them.

I should have waited. She wasn't ready.

He'd been too impatient. And now—despite his grand vision and bursting heart—he could do nothing but sit back and wait . . . and hope.

It was slowly killing him.

To a recovering alcoholic, he reflected grimly, patience wasn't a virtue—it was a discipline. Something you strapped on every morning when you got out of bed. An alarm calibrated to react to the slightest tremor, arming you against your own impulses. Each day, each new challenge, was a catwalk suspended high off the ground, requiring the balance and nerve of an acrobat.

Eric, in a surge of defiance, thought, *You don't want what I'm offering? It doesn't come with a guarantee? Well, fuck you, lady. . . .*

Just as quickly, his anger faded. This cramped studio was getting
to him. He'd been holed up for hours. He needed to get out, stretch
his legs. Otherwise, he'd go nuts.

Twenty minutes later, having gone over tomorrow's schedule
with Greg—back-to-back interviews with a right-wing Republican
senator and a former Hollywood stuntman—Eric was walking
briskly up West Broadway. After a few blocks, his head began to
clear. He was once again seeing the point of it all, the light at the end
of the tunnel, so to speak. Rose. He was seeing Rose. . . .

On an impulse, he stopped at a phone kiosk. From memory, he
quickly punched in the number for Rose's office . . . only to be informed by her secretary that Rose had taken the day off. But he'd
already pegged Mallory as a die-hard romantic—the kind who reli-
giously watched *Melrose Place*, and devoured paperback romances. It
didn't take much coaxing to get her to tell him that Rose was at
Sylvie's, helping Rachel sort through their mother's papers.

Eric punched in the number Mallory had given him for Sylvie's
house, but an automated voice informed him it was no longer in service. Damn.

He glanced at his watch. Four-forty-five. Mallory had said that
Rose would be at Sylvie's until around five. It was a long shot, but if
he took the subway he might still catch her. Besides, he was curious.
He had yet to lay eyes on this mausoleum Rose had inherited.

Like everyone else, including Rose's own family, it appeared, Eric
had been stunned to learn of the connection between Rose and
Sylvie. Yet now he saw that it made sense in a way. Not that he could
ever imagine a set of circumstances in which he would abandon his
own child . . . then force her to live in some shadowy realm of lies
and half-truths. But he *did* understand the nature of concealing a
powerful secret—hadn't he managed to keep his drinking under
wraps for years?—and he knew how such secrets can ultimately reveal
much about their guardians. Though his initial knee-jerk reaction
was one born of hurt pride—why hadn't Rose felt she could confide

in *him?*—Eric had come to see a deeper message in Rose's silence: her commitment to a promise made had truly known no bounds.

And maybe that was the message, too, in her refusing to marry him. The same capacity for love and loyalty evidenced in her relationship with her mother had been the guiding force in Rose's marriage . . . and in the tenacity with which she clung to her husband's memory.

If only there were a way for *him* to harness that surfeit of love, Eric thought, full of anguished longing.

He had to see her, speak to her. Now.

But if she *was* at Sylvie's house, what would he say?

He'd already said everything there was to say. The only thing left was for her to have faith—Rose had to *believe* what her heart was telling her.

And if in the end she refused him?

He'd survive. Somehow.

But surviving, he knew, better than most, was a far cry from truly living.

At the Broadway and Lafayette subway station, fueled by a surge of adrenaline more intoxicating than any high since he'd quit drinking, Eric raced down the grimy steps in hopes of catching the train he could hear rumbling in its depths.

🌸 Rose was getting ready to leave when she heard the door buzz downstairs.

Rachel? Back for something she'd forgotten? But Rachel had her own key, Rose remembered.

Wearily, she thought, *Whoever you are . . . please just go away.* Probably one of Sylvie's friends or neighbors, someone well meaning who would offer to help, but now Rose would have to spend time chatting with the person—precious time when she could be home.

Rose made her way down the curving staircase, gripping the polished walnut banister for support. On the ground floor, against one wall of the tiled vestibule, stood a Biedermeier hall table, over which was hung a gilt-framed oval mirror. She caught a glimpse of her reflection, and in that instant was struck by a resemblance to Sylvie that she'd never noticed before. Something in the way she carried herself, with the determined air of a woman bearing up under a heavy load.

At the front door, she reached distractedly for the knob, not thinking to bother with the intercom. But the visitor, as it turned out, wasn't a neighbor, or family friend, she could quickly and politely dismiss. A tall, fair-haired man stood on the stoop, his shoulders bunched in nervous anticipation, his blue eyes squinting slightly, as if the sun's dying light was too bright.

Her heart flew up into her throat.

"Eric! What are *you* doing here?"

The stone portico under which he stood was twined on either side with clematis, now past its peak, its leaves as limp and forlorn as crepe streamers long after the party has ended. But what struck her most was the naked longing in Eric's eyes—the longing of a man for whom the *real* party had yet to begin.

Damn, she thought. *Damn, damn, damn.*

"I was in the neighborhood," he greeted, his voice light and teasing—disconcertingly so, in contrast to the intense emotion playing across his face. "Feel like some company?"

"Sure," she said, deciding to play along. It was easier than any of the thousand and one things she longed to say to him. "Only I can't even offer you a cup of coffee. The kitchen cupboards are pretty bare. Milagros comes just once a week now, to dust and vacuum."

She stepped back to usher him inside, suddenly aware of how she must look, in her oldest Levis and an old shirt of Max's knotted at the waist. After hours of lifting boxes and pawing through files, she was a wreck.

"You look wonderful," he said.

Rose felt pleased, in spite of herself. "You lie like a rug," she told him, laughing, "but thanks anyway."

He kissed her cheek. With the brush of his lips, she felt all her hidden parts that Eric had explored so lovingly inch into the red zone. Catching the familiar scent of his hair, she tried not to breathe in too deeply, for fear of remembering too much.

"I'd settle for a quick tour, if you have the time." Eric looked around, his lips pursing in a silent whistle of appreciation. "This is quite a place. I feel like I should be leaving my calling card on a silver tray. No offense, but it's hard to imagine someone actually *living* here."

"Sylvie once told me she had the same reaction the first time she walked in," Rose confided. "But it had been in her husband's family for years, so there was no question of their moving. Then I think it just grew on her. Amazing, what a person can get used to, isn't it? Come on, I'll show you around."

She gave him the standard dollar-fifty tour of the ground floor. The rose-hued sitting room, with its plump chintz loveseats and needlepoint firescreen, where Sylvie used to serve tea on a silver tray with her best Limoges china. The walnut-paneled library that had been Gerald Rosenthal's study. The formal dining room furnished in Chippendale, and the old-fashioned kitchen with its walk-in pantry. And, last but not least, the sunny little morning room in back, over-looking the garden, where Rose could almost see Sylvie in her fa-vorite wicker rocker, tucked under the pale-pink mohair afghan with her cozy English novels and gardening magazines.

Reciting the provenance of various antiques and paintings, Rose was amazed, not only by how much she'd retained from Sylvie's sto-ries over the years, but how calm she sounded. No one would have guessed her heart was pounding, and her throat thick and dry, forc-ing her to stop several times in mid-sentence to take a breath.

Eric, on the other hand, said next to nothing until they'd come to a stop by the French doors that opened onto the patio. Unlike most first-time visitors, who oohed and aahed until Rose wanted to throw up, he didn't seem overly impressed by the lavish decor. But maybe that was because, the whole time she'd been showing him around, he'd hardly taken his eyes off her. *Oh, Eric, you're not making this easy on me,* she thought, a lump forming just south of her collarbone.

"Not bad . . . if you like living in the past," he commented dryly. "Somehow, I can't see you here."

"Who said I was moving in?"

"You *didn't* say. We haven't talked much lately, if you'll recall." A note of regret in his voice—or was it accusation?—caused her to look away in discomfort.

He moved closer to the window to get a better look of the garden, shrouded in shadows cast by the setting sun, but in his easy movements she sensed a current that was anything but mild.

Rose tightened her grip on her emotions, which threatened to spill out like the endless papers from Sylvie's neatly organized files. "To answer your question," she began, "the answer is, no, I don't plan on moving in. I don't belong here. This house would only remind me of things I'd rather forget." Her legs felt suddenly wobbly, and she sank down onto the ottoman on which Sylvie's pink afghan lay folded.

Eric cocked his head, a faint smile touching his lips. "Where *do* you see yourself from now on?"

Rose didn't need to get hit over the head to know he wasn't referring to her address.

She was abruptly swept by a longing so fierce and primal that, before she could wrestle it to the ground, it had her by the throat. Eric, standing there, looking so *right* in this house that was somehow all wrong—what if she were to grab hold of his hand, and, like in chase movies where the hero and heroine escape their pursuers with seconds to spare, simply run off into the night? If she were to leave in the dust all her perfectly valid rationalizations and understandable caution? Oh, how magical! Rose could almost *feel* it—the real, physical thrill of hitting the open road with the top down, and the wind in her hair.

But this wasn't a movie, she told herself. In real life, good people didn't just run away. And Rose's first responsibility—before her practice, or even her family—was to *herself*. She needed to keep a steady hand on the wheel, and her eye on the white line . . . or she would veer off the road. Because the next time, Rose felt sure, she wouldn't survive the crash.

What guarantee did Eric have to offer that some act of God wouldn't cast them apart? None. Oh, she'd believed him when he'd promised never to leave her. But who knew better than she the various twists and turns in life that weren't on any map? The sudden storms that can strike without warning?

Her mother's death had affected her deeply, on more than one level. Night after night, she awoke with a start—drenched in sweat, her heart pounding—from some vivid nightmare in which she was chasing after an ambulance, or trying to find her way through a maze of hospital corridors . . . needing to get to Max before it was too late. But, of course, it was already too late. Max was gone. The only thing left for her to do, the only thing she had the slightest bit of control over, was the power to remove herself from the threat of its happening again. . . .

Still . . . her heart wouldn't let her turn away quite so easily. The urge to seize what was good and fulfilling *now*—an urge as instinctive as that of a baby's reaching in wonderment for some bright shining thing—was so strong, Rose nearly gave in to it.

"Eric . . ." She swallowed hard. "It must seem as if I've been avoiding you, I know. Honestly? It's not just because I've been so busy. The truth is . . . I'm a little afraid of you."

Eric started, clearly taken aback. "Me?"

"Yes, *you*." She forged ahead. "When I told you I couldn't marry you, I left out the most important part: I love you. I know it must not seem that way to you. But I *do* . . . and that's what scares me."

Rose looked down at the carpet, at its garland of leaves twining out from under the ottoman on which she sat.

"Rose, look at me. *Look* at me." Eric spoke sternly, waiting until she'd dragged her gaze up to meet his. "Nothing's changed for me. I want you. In my bed. In my life. For all the days to come. But I'm no fool. I knew what I was getting into. I'm prepared to wait, as long as you need me to. Until you're good and ready. The one thing I *won't* do is pretend we're heading somewhere if there's no chance we'll ever get off the ground. Say you love me enough to take a shot at this. Give me that much."

Rose could feel the lump in her throat expanding. Tears stung her eyes. "You want the truth?" she asked in a low, choked voice. "I can't sleep nights, thinking of you. I go around wanting you all the time. Reliving over and over in my mind the things we've said to one another. The things we've done." Using the flat of her palms, she propelled herself to her feet. "But I'm not ready to commit myself . . . to anyone. Not even you. And I can't promise I ever *will* be."

Eric strode over to grab her by the shoulders, his fingers biting into her, hurting her in a way she perversely welcomed. "Rose, I understand—it's a huge risk, coming at a time when you must feel like another loss would wipe you out. But when did you ever let being afraid of something stop you?"

A bitter, teary laugh bubbled to the surface. "Never. But it looks like you can teach an old dog new tricks after all."

"It doesn't have to be this way."

"I know. That's the whole point. My whole life, I've depended on other people to make me happy. And mostly, except for Max, I've been let down. Now, for the very first time, it's entirely up to *me*. Don't you see? I *have* to find out if I can stand on my own two feet."

He studied her hard, as if trying to understand. "I can't imagine why that would ever be a question. It certainly isn't how *I* see you."

Rose shook her head, and her eye fell on an eight-by-ten photo in a sterling frame propped on the low table by the sofa. A black-and-white image of a much younger Sylvie posing with a little girl who had to be Rachel. A stray thought popped into her head: *It should have been ME on her lap in that photo.* But she couldn't rewrite her history, any more than she could alter the fact that Eric had come along too soon after Max's death.

"What I need right now is . . . time," she told him gently. "Time to sort things out for myself. *By* myself." She took his face in her hands, savoring for the last time the smoothness of his fine-pored jaw beneath its nearly invisible beard.

With a sudden, convulsive gesture, Eric tugged her into his arms. He held her to him, an arm about her waist, the other against her back with his hand cupping the nape of her neck—tenderly, but firmly, the way Rose had cradled each of her babies. She felt him tremble with the effort it took not to demand more of her than what she'd already given; not to show her with his body what she'd be missing if she walked away from him now. Rose, no longer caring if she cried, or what weakness it might display, tipped her head back to look up at him.

A tear slid like a warm caress down one cheek as she closed her eyes, and offered her mouth up to Eric. And in that instant, there was no past or present, no pain—remembered, or imagined—no wishful thinking, even. There was only this: Eric's lips against hers, his gentle breath, his scent filling her like the ocean's on a summer day at the beach. His kiss lifted her, and carried her, for the span of several heartbeats, to a place where memory had no meaning, and even angels dared to rush in.

Then Eric was pulling back, giving her a look that was a mixture of longing and sadness. Outside, pigeons muttered in the eaves, and in the garden, the rising moon had made a black-and-white photo of the stone birdbath and ivy-shrouded walls. His voice soft with regret, he said, "You're everything I imagined you'd be. Strong. Beautiful. Passionate. Except one thing: that woman in my mind's eye, she was willing to meet me halfway. Rose, I love you more than you can even begin to imagine . . . but I'd be a fool to settle for less."

Watching him head for the door, Rose felt as if she were being torn in two: wanting to run after him, and fearing it would be a mistake, that if she could just hang on a few minutes longer she'd be okay. Even after hearing the distant click of the front door, she had to fight the urge to race outside, see if she might still catch him. Instead, she stood as rigid as if bolted into place. She couldn't move. She could hardly breathe. The only part of her that didn't feel dead was her heart—her poor, glued-together Humpty Dumpty heart, which, despite all her precautions, was somehow breaking all over again.

October

My home was hiding a secret in the depths of its heart. . . .

The Little Prince

Chapter 15

❧   Mandy felt as if she were hanging on by her fingernails, as if the slightest movement, even a shift in the wind, would send her sailing over the edge.

It was the first Monday in October—a month since her showdown with Rose over what Mandy had come to think of as "The Anderson Incident"—a lapse of judgment, sure, but one that had been blown out of proportion by holier-than-thou Hayden Lockwood, no doubt angling for a promotion. She was nonetheless acutely aware of the razor-thin margin between her plush corner office at her father's firm, and being out on the street. As she sat facing the bench in Room 452 of the courthouse on Centre Street, struggling to keep her mind on this morning's proceedings—the third and final day (please, God) in the seemingly endless divorce hearing of *Epstein* v. *Epstein*— her nervous system buzzed like an overloaded circuit about to blow.

It had been weeks since her last "slip." Six hundred and sixty-eight hours, to be precise. And she needed a drink. Badly. She'd been a good girl, staying on top of this case, poring over bank statements and actuarial tables until late last night in preparation for today's session. Didn't she deserve a reward? Just one little drink? A glass of wine to take the edge off? How could it hurt?

But what if it doesn't stop at one glass? A small, quiet voice asserted itself. *What then?* In her mind, she was seeing the firm resolve in Rose's face, hearing her warn that another incident like the one with the Andersons and Mandy would be out the door, no ifs, ands, or buts.

Now, like wavery images glimpsed through the bottom of a glass, the ugly episode that had sparked it all swam into view. Her clearest

memory was of negotiating the corridor to her office, doorknob by
doorknob, pausing to steady herself when the yawing floor threatened to throw her off balance. Head throbbing, mouth dry, the sweat
that had gathered in her armpits reeking of the bourbon she'd put
away the night before. Incredibly, it seemed she'd forgotten her
eleven o'clock with Rob and Gillian Anderson. By the time she'd remembered, it must have been close to that, but even with her quick
shower, and race to the office, she'd arrived almost an hour late.

Then, blessedly, the door with her name engraved in shiny brass.
But something was wrong. Hayden, darting out of the tiny office
next to hers, seemed distressed, not his usual cool, collected self. He'd
tried to stop her, but Mandy had shoved past him. Angry. Shouting.
What the fuck is going on? Then there had been Gillian Anderson,
gaping at her, horrified. Gillian's Philadelphia Main Line face a
shocked white circle against cool gray wallpaper chosen for its soothing effect. And, standing by the window, arms crossed, fleshy face
furrowed with outrage, Gillian's estranged husband—accompanied
by his attorney, Al Gottlieb, whose ferrety eyes had glittered with delight at this unexpected coup.

Mandy had struggled gamely to regain the ground that had been
lost—apologizing profusely, even tossing off a little joke about having tied one on at a party the night before—but it was no use. From
the disgusted expressions of the crew gathered in her office, Mandy
had comprehended—yes, even in the bleary midst of her eighty-
proof hangover—that her cover had been blown. No one believed,
not for an instant, that there had been a party last night. Unless it
was a party for one.

Oh, the humiliation! As soon as the Andersons had left—taking
about a thousand billable hours with them—Mandy had fled for the
elevator. Home. The image blinked on in her head like a green traffic
light, spurring her on, blotting out every other thought. She had to
get home, where she'd be safe. Where she could fix what was wrong.

That time, a fifth hadn't been enough. She'd needed a whole
quart of bourbon to dull her panic.

Sylvie's passing, as sad as it had been, had bought Mandy some time. But a few days after the funeral, Rose had called Mandy into her office and really given it to her. Another stunt like that and she'd be out the door, Rose had threatened. No second chance this time.

Since Rose's ultimatum, she'd been dry as a chalkboard. No more benders. She'd made up her mind. She'd have to be *really* good this time. But, oh, what she wouldn't give for just a hair—a single hair—of the dog that *hadn't* bitten her.

Are you willing to take that risk?

No . . . better keep a low profile for now. Then, when enough time had gone by, when everyone at the office had stopped acting as if she were some freak science project gone haywire, when she'd proved she was every bit as much in control as they, she'd be able to treat herself to an occasional glass of wine—and no one would even notice.

Mandy, pushing the Anderson debacle to the back of her mind, forced herself to tune back in to the nasal squawking of Mr. Epstein's attorney. Janet Braithwaite—thirtyish, brunette, reasonably attractive, though at least forty pounds overweight, had a voice like fingernails on a chalkboard, and, as usual, didn't know what the fuck she was talking about. After a minute, Mandy rose from her chair.

"Your Honor, may I remind the court that my client, Mrs. Epstein, was an active participant in her husband's business *before* they were married," she interjected. "Therefore, we believe she's entitled to a share of the premarital profits, as outlined."

Out of the corner of her eye, she could see her client sniffling into a balled-up handkerchief. Missy Epstein was using her allergies to advantage, subtly reminding everyone in the courtroom who the victim was here. *Nice going,* Mandy thought. Missy—with her thin lips and close-set eyes that looked squinty and shrewish even when she was sincere—needed all the help she could get.

Janet jumped to her feet. "She was his *secretary,* Your Honor!"

Janet was wearing a fitted burgundy suit, but no matter how expensive the cut, she always appeared to be spilling out of her clothes.

"Your point, Ms. Braithwaite?" Judge Kornfeld, trim and white-haired, whose strong, beaked profile made Mandy think of the eagle on a silver dollar, peered down from the bench.

Janet frowned, and abruptly dropped back into her chair, tapping her pencil against the notepad in front of her in a way that reminded Mandy of a bird pecking for insects. Clearing her throat, she began in a voice amplified by false bravado, "My point? My point is that, as a salaried employee, she was . . . Mrs. Epstein was adequately, um, compensated at the time. In any event, whatever she may have contributed, it doesn't appear to have had a lasting impact. Your Honor, as you can see from the figures in front of you, Mr. Epstein's hardware chain has shown a steady loss over the last eight years."

"Is that so?" Kornfeld pursed his mouth as he examined the document he was holding up to his nose, on which a pair of spindly half-glasses were propped. "Well, for some reason I'm not *seeing* those figures, Ms. Braithwaite. They seem to be missing from this proposal of yours."

Janet raked a hand through her hair, inadvertently rearranging its sculpted waves into a welter of crazed squiggles. "There should be a separate report . . . from the accountant. I'm absolutely *certain* I included it. Perhaps it was misplaced . . ." Her eyes darted about the gallery, as if half-expecting the bailiff, or one of the handful of witnesses, to produce the missing addendum. When it became clear that no one was coming to her rescue, she requested meekly, "Your Honor, may I approach the bench?"

Watching Janet jiggle her way to the front of the courtroom, Mandy felt mildly triumphant. For a change, *she* wasn't the one in the hot seat, being whispered about behind cupped hands. Nobody was eyeing her with contempt for having failed her client in some ghastly way.

It made it almost worthwhile—her abstinence, which felt as endless and punishing as a trek across the Sahara. Days of scarcely being able to answer the phone without screaming into it, wanting to slap clients silly when they bitched about having to divide up their Fiestaware collection, or their time-share in the Poconos. Evenings at home, so jittery she could hardly sit still, but not daring to go for a walk even, for fear of where it might take her. Nights of lying awake in bed, dry-mouthed with panic, wondering if it would *ever* end. Would she ever feel normal again? Would there ever be a time she could honestly say, when offered a drink, "No thanks, I don't feel like it?"

But she'd kept her word. That *proved* she wasn't an alcoholic. Borderline maybe, but not full-blown. Or she wouldn't have been able to quit just like that. This was the longest she'd ever gone.

The week of her last binge was more or less a blur. Her memory was of a boozy twilight that seemed to wrap endlessly around itself, as if she were on a transcontinental flight where each time zone melted into the next. Though, judging by the looks she'd been getting around the office, she must have been more out of it than she'd imagined. Why else would Hayden have gone behind Mandy's back to give Rose the lowdown on her?

And look at Robert. He'd cooled off, too. Not because of anything embarrassing she'd done, thank heaven. But how many times can you blow off a guy like Robert? After the string of excuses she'd given him, he'd stopped asking when they could get together, and now even his friendly calls "just to see how she was doing" had tapered off, too.

Mandy pulled a crumpled tissue from the pocket of her blazer and dabbed furtively at her sweaty brow. She felt like a rusty bucket leaking in a dozen places—never knowing when she might burst into tears, either. It seemed as if everything had begun to go south with Sylvie's dying—which was odd, because she hadn't been all that close to the woman. It was partly the shock of discovering Sylvie had been Rose's biological mother. Which Rose had known, and kept secret, for years. But mostly it was Rose herself. Her stepmother—to whom Mandy had always felt close, and who, as a child, she had practically *worshipped*—was like a different person. Harder. As if the experience had toughened her resolve in some way. Mandy had no doubt Rose *would* follow through on her threat to bring the hammer down if she caught Mandy drinking again.

So Mandy had *had* to be good. She simply had no other choice. And now here she was, not only sober . . . but vindicated, in her own eyes at least. As shitty as she felt, it was good to know she was capable of exercising such control. And maybe, in time, it would get easier. Maybe one day she'd be able to get through a whole day without even *thinking* about taking a drink.

Meanwhile, knock on wood, she still had her job, and business was good. Divorce, Mandy thought, was always a bull market.

Judge Kornfeld jolted her from her reverie by growling sternly, "Ms. Braithwaite, we don't have all day. Can you produce this missing—or is it *mythical*—report or not?"

A flurry of titters caused the color to rise in Janet's cheeks. "I—I don't know how it could have happened," she stammered as she thumbed frantically through the papers she'd retrieved from the bench. "It must have slipped out somehow." She lifted a stricken face to the judge. "I'll have it delivered to your chambers no later than this afternoon."

Mandy was relieved when the morning's proceedings thumped to a close with a rap from Kornfeld's gavel—he was granting a continuance until tomorrow. She politely refused Missy Epstein's offer to buy her lunch, electing instead to pick up a sandwich at a nearby deli on her way back to the office. Restaurants weren't safe these days, she'd found; the temptation to order a drink was simply too great. Besides, she was meeting Drew at his place around six, and would have to work straight through in order to have her desk cleared by then. Last night, when he'd called, her brother had sounded really stressed out. He'd said he needed to talk to her—it was important. She didn't want to keep him waiting.

Mandy was nibbling at her chicken-salad sandwich, while jotting her notes on the third draft of a separation agreement, when the intercom beeped. Her secretary announced she had Mrs. Griffin on line two, Mrs. *Bernice* Griffin. And judging from Lori's tone, it was clear that Mandy's mother—in less than a minute, and from the relatively safe distance of Boca Raton, had already managed to offend her in some way. *God, I do not need this right now.* Mandy lifted the receiver carefully, as if it were a snake that might strike.

"Mandy, is that you? My goodness, that girl of yours had me on hold so long I thought she'd forgotten me." Bernice gave a brittle laugh in which was buried a note of accusation, as if Lori's thoughtlessness were somehow Mandy's fault.

Mandy could feel a familiar kink forming in her neck, in the certain spot it seemed to favor, like a cowlick. "Sorry, Mom. I've been in court all morning. I just walked in." Why was she apologizing? Her whole life, it seemed, she'd been atoning for sins against her mother she had no knowledge of having committed. Sins that in Bernice Griffin's book were nonetheless scrupulously recorded and tallied. "What's up? You don't usually call me at work. Everything okay?"

Her mother released a sigh that seemed to go on forever, like air being let out of a tire. Then she said, "I was about to ask the same of you. When you didn't call on Sunday, I thought maybe you were ill . . . or had been in an accident. I was worried sick."

"Why on earth would you think that?" Mandy's mind raced frantically. What had been special about Sunday? Mother's birthday? No. That was in April . . . and Mandy had remembered to send flowers. Roses, for which her mother had thanked her, while at the same time remarking offhandedly that her back yard in Boca was so overrun with flowers, her gardener had had to deadhead every bush.

"If it wasn't important enough for you to remember, there's no point in my telling you," her mother replied with the long-suffering air of a woman accustomed to having her needs ignored.

The kink in Mandy's neck tightened, digging in like barbed wire. "Mom, don't do this. Of *course* I want to know. It's just that I've been so busy here at the office. Whatever it was, it must have slipped my mind."

"I'm perfectly aware of how busy you are. Do you think I called to complain? I was *concerned*, that's all." Mandy heard the click of her lighter, followed by a hard little *huff* of expelled breath. "How *is* the divorce business these days? Booming as usual?"

"It pays the rent." Mandy squeezed her eyes shut. "Listen, Mom, if there's something on your mind, I wish you'd tell me. Or did you call just to make me feel guilty?"

"Well, if that's the attitude you're going to take, I'm sorry I bothered," her mother snapped. "Pardon me if I'm taking up too much of your precious time."

Mandy could just see her mother, once a natural redhead, her hair now dyed a vivid henna, and so heavily sprayed it resembled an overturned clay pot. She would be out by the pool in her back yard, the remote phone in one hand, a Virginia Slim in the other. In Hacienda Harbor, the retirement community to which she'd moved six years ago (described in the brochure Mom had sent her as "ideally suited to the mature, active adult"), she was among the youngest of the residents—a fact that incited frequent mention of the interest paid her by the men of the community.

"I'm sorry, Mom, I didn't mean it that way." Mandy sighed. "I've been really stressed out lately."

Her mother exhaled forcibly, which came out sounding like a snort of derision. Mandy imagined her with her eyes narrowed against smoke that was drifting upward in lazy currents. She thought she could hear the faint hiss of a sprinkler in the background, and could almost smell the shorn wet Bermuda grass that, against bare soles, always felt spiky and inhospitable somehow.

"I'm not surprised," Bernice said.

Mandy was immediately on the defensive. "What do you mean?"

"Do I have to spell it out? Any fool can see. That woman, your stepmother—she's been working you to the bone. Ever since your father passed away, God rest his soul, you haven't been yourself."

"Mom . . . this has nothing to do with Rose." In a way, it *did.* But Mandy would rather walk naked down a crowded sidewalk than try to explain to her mother about her drinking.

"What about that young man you're seeing? You haven't mentioned him lately." There was a sudden sizzle of static, and her mother's voice grew faint. Mandy could picture her padding around to the other side of the pool, where the phone's signal was weakest. No doubt she was plucking at a dead blossom on one of the hibiscus shrubs that drove Bernice absolutely crazy with their lush disregard of the seasons.

"You mean Robert? We see each other when we can. We're both so busy." Many unthinkingly crossed her fingers behind her back, like she had as a little girl when telling a fib. "Don't worry. If I ever *do* decide to get married, I'll warn you far enough in advance so you can shop for a dress."

"No need to be flip. I was just asking." A rustling sound, like a branch being yanked at. "But since you brought it up, may I remind you that you're not getting any younger. By the time *I* was your age, I had a husband *and* a daughter."

"Yes, Mom, I know." *A husband and a daughter you drove crazy with your constant nagging.*

"Don't think I'm not aware of what the problem is."

"Who said I had a problem?" The barbed wire in Mandy's neck gave a vicious twist. Sweat broke out on her forehead and prickled under her arms. She felt as if she were in a steambath.

Her mother barreled on as if she hadn't heard. "I read books. I watch TV. I'm not stupid."

"Mom, what on *earth* are you talking about?"

"Divorce, that's what. You were twelve when your father left us—don't tell me that didn't leave scars."

"I don't see—"

"Of course you don't. You were too young to understand. It was that woman. She had her eye on him. I should have seen it. I was so blind! There he was, going to the office every day, not suspecting a thing—until she moved in for the kill."

"It's been twenty-two years." Mandy fought to hold back the scream mounting inside her. She'd been hearing the same story for years, and knew every bitter accusation and reinvented scrap of history by heart. "What's the point of going over and over it? Daddy's dead. And Rose isn't here to defend herself."

"You always stuck up for her. From day one." More thrashing of leaves, an effort that caused her mother's words to emerge in staccato bursts. "That must be why you forgot whose anniversary it was last Sunday. Daddy and I would have been married forty-two years. But who's counting?"

Mandy winced. The barbed wire was wrapped about her whole neck now. She didn't dare move, not even an inch, or it would rip her apart.

Damn . . . I should have remembered.

But what was the point? Every year, when she'd called or sent a card, she'd only loathed herself for giving in, for feeding her mother's delusions. Maybe that's why it had slipped her mind, Mandy thought. On top of the teetering pile that threatened to swamp her, it was simply one lie too many.

"Happy anniversary," Mandy congratulated in a voice as empty as the hole that had opened up in her stomach. "I'll send you a card."

"Don't bother. It's too late, anyway. . . . Oops, there's the door." Mandy could hear the faint chiming of the doorbell, followed by the slapping of rubber thongs against patio tiles. "It's the pool man— something to do with the filter. He promised he'd stop by. It's been two *weeks,* do you believe it? When I called again to remind him, he acted like he was doing *me* a favor. As if I don't pay him enough every month."

"I'll call you sometime this weekend," Mandy promised, silently blessing the pool man.

Hanging up, she was overwhelmed with thoughts of her father. Daddy. God, how she missed him. His booming laugh, and his habit of dropping by her office at odd times during the day just to ask how she was getting along, or to give her a quick hug. She missed his irrepressible sense of humor, the dumb jokes he told with such gusto you had to laugh anyway. And how, when they were alone, he'd call her by her childhood nickname. "Monkey," he'd tease, mussing her hair like when she was little. "You were such a little monkey, up a tree faster than I could say boo."

Right now, Mandy wanted nothing more than to put her head down on her desk and bawl like a baby.

Because the thing she *really* wanted she couldn't have.

Her mother had been right about one thing: she wasn't getting any younger. What *about* Robert? Mandy tried to remember when he'd last phoned. Yesterday, or was it the day before? No ... last week. She'd been watching TV, and his call had interrupted a Budweiser commercial.

He'd said he had tickets to Carnegie Hall for this Saturday, and would she like to go? Mandy had had to bite her lip to keep from blurting the truth—that she'd love to, but was terrified of his seeing her this way. Instead, she'd told Robert she was having dinner with her brother, which was only partly true. Jay had said that either night, Friday or Saturday, was fine.

Okay, so Robert hasn't called since. What did you expect? He's smart, he can take a hint. If you still want him, why the hell haven't YOU called?

Before she could talk herself out of it, Mandy snatched up the phone and punched in Robert's office number.

"Mandy Griffin for Mr. Greene," she announced briskly to his secretary, hoping it wouldn't be so obvious that her voice was trembling.

The woman hesitated before answering pleasantly, "I'll see if Mr. Greene is in his office."

Mandy waited what seemed an eternity before she came back on the line. "I'm sorry, Ms. Griffin, he's in a meeting. May I take a message?"

Something in her voice told Mandy she was lying. What was the secretary's name, anyway? She couldn't remember. But, then, so *much* seemed to have slipped her mind just lately. Only one thing was clear—a terrible certainty that throbbed in Mandy's head like an infected tooth—the tables had turned. Now it was Robert who was avoiding *her.*

"No . . . thanks. I'll call back later," she muttered.

She hung up, and for several minutes sat staring at the papers on her desk, trying to muster some interest in domestic crises other than her own . . . but it was hopeless. She couldn't stop thinking about the last time she and Robert had made love, his hurt look when she gently nudged him into leaving. It must have seemed like a rejection, her mumbled excuse about having to get up early the next morning to be in court. What he hadn't known was that she'd wanted him to stay. And that she'd hated herself for needing to be alone. Alone to drink . . .

Now it no longer mattered.

Not to Robert.

This time, Mandy couldn't hold in her despair, any more than she could have stopped a severed artery from bleeding; she could only muffle with her hands the cry that tore through her.

🌺   As lousy as Mandy felt, Drew looked even worse. Pale, unshaven, the flesh under his eyes bruised with anxiety. In the tiny studio apartment she'd teased him about when he moved in—saying it was perfect, if you happened to be very short and collected nothing larger than stamps—her brother sat dejectedly on the futon sofa, hunched forward with his elbows propped against his knees.

The last time Mandy had seen him was at Sylvie's funeral. Then he'd seemed sad, but not shaken. Now it was obvious something was dreadfully wrong. She glanced around at the normally tidy room, noting the dirty dishes in the sink and the laundry piled haphazardly in one corner.

The apartment wasn't just messy, she thought; it looked downright neglected. And that was *so* unlike Drew. As a kid, he'd existed in a cheerful jumble of hamster cages, terrariums, fish tanks, but there had been a certain *order* to it all. This was . . . well, it was *gross.*

"Drew, what is it? Are you sick?" Mandy, feeling a surge of genuine concern, forgot her own misery for the moment.

Her brother shook his head and lifted his handsome, haunted face—which always gave her a little jolt, it was so like Daddy's. "It's not me. It's Iris. I don't know where she is. Last night, she called from a phone booth to say she was on her way over. But she never showed up. None of the friends I've called have heard from her. She's not at her parents', either."

"Jesus. Did you two have a fight?"

The smile he gave her was so bleak, Mandy had to look away. It was like driving past a car wreck—a flash of something twisted and ghastly that makes you think, *there but for the grace of God* . . .

"We don't fight—not like normal couples." His voice was hoarse with weariness. "Some of the shit that's gone on, you wouldn't believe it if I told you."

"Try me."

He thought for a moment, spreading his hands in a helpless gesture, as if it would be useless to try and explain. "It's like . . . we'll be getting along just fine," he began haltingly, "and all of a sudden she'll just . . . she'll go off about something that . . . well, that doesn't make sense. It's like she has all these little rooms inside her head, and you never know what's going to pop out from behind the doors."

Drew's dark-brown hair stood up in a brushy rooster comb, reminding her of how, when he was a kid, no amount of hair goop would ever make it lie flat. It used to drive him crazy, but right now he hardly seemed to notice. She watched as he absently ran a hand over the top of his head. His fingernails, she saw, were bitten to the quick.

"Those rooms—what are they like?" Mandy felt as if she were in one of the Nancy Drew mysteries she used to devour as a kid, like she was creeping up a dark staircase armed with only a flashlight. And she wasn't at all sure she wanted to know what lay ahead.

Drew gave her a long, searching look. "Promise you won't tell? Not anyone. She made me swear."

Mandy shivered, wanting to turn back. She had her own staircase to climb, as steep as it was treacherous. She was the last person Drew should be turning to for help. But Drew was family. In some ways, the more than ten-year gap in their ages made her feel closer to him than if they'd grown up together—more like a mother than a sister. She'd been thirteen by the time he came along. She remembered exactly how he'd looked as a newborn, swaddled in his receiving blanket like a shrimp in its shell. How his miniature clown-face would go all scrunchy when he yawned. Holding him in her arms, she used to pretend he was *her* baby, better than any doll or pet.

How could she refuse to help him now?

"I promise," she said.

Drew took a deep breath, as if to fortify himself. "A couple of months ago, Iris really wigged out. I mean, big-time. I probably should have told someone then, but she made me promise not to. She swore she'd talk it over with her shrink, do whatever *he* thought best."

"How bad was it?"

Drew waved a hand in the direction of the bathroom . . . and that's when Mandy noticed that the door hung slightly askew on its hinges, and the splintered jamb was crudely patched with wood putty. Drew's hollow voice was like an echo rising from some deep chasm. "I kept begging her to open up . . . or *say* something, at least. If I hadn't busted the door in . . ."

His expression grew taut, and once again it was their father's face she was seeing—Daddy's look of confident decisiveness in an emergency. Except Drew didn't look heroic; he looked young, too young to have to deal with such terrible things. In a low voice hoarse with exhaustion, he confided, "She had the razor out. It was on the floor next to her. She would have cut herself if I hadn't gotten to her when I did." He started to cry—great gasping sobs that left Mandy torn between a fierce urge to wrap her arms around him, and a desire to tiptoe away so as not to intrude on something so excruciatingly private.

Suicide. Christ. Mandy couldn't imagine feeling that hopeless. Even with her drinking, as low as she'd gotten, not once had she ever considered putting a gun to her head. There was *always* another way out—even if at times the escape hatch seemed impossibly narrow.

Mandy, more disturbed than she dared let on, shook her head. "No wonder she looked so awful at the funeral—like she was sick or something." She seized her brother's hands, which felt clammy and inert. "Drew, she *is* sick. None of this is your fault. You've *got* to believe that."

Drew straightened, his mouth trembling. "It doesn't matter how *I* feel. Don't you see? She could die. Whatever's wrong, she could fucking *die* while we're all sitting around trying to figure it out. Listen, I'm no doctor, not yet, but I know enough to be scared."

"Why haven't you told her parents, then?"

"I don't know." He shrugged, and took a fierce swipe at his nose with knuckles clenched hard enough to hit someone. "I guess I wanted to believe it as much as they did—the whole myth about me making a difference. Sir Galahad to the rescue." He gave a grunt of grim laughter. "The thing is, I *do* love her. None of this changes anything." The look on her brother's face brought tears to her own eyes. "Mandy, I need your help. Please. Help me find her."

Mandy drew in a deep breath. She felt as if she were drowning—every ounce of energy drained by the immense effort it took just to keep her head above water—and now she'd been asked to save someone else. It was too much.

Yet, looking into her brother's ravaged eyes, she couldn't bring herself to say no, either. What if something terrible happened because she turned away? She'd never forgive herself. And didn't she have enough shame to live with as it was?

Against every instinct, every selfish bone in her body crying out for her to help herself before she extended a hand to her brother, Mandy said, "I'll try."

Dear God, get ALL of us through this in one piece.

Minutes later, Mandy was dashing downstairs on her way to the corner deli. Drew confessed he hadn't eaten since yesterday—and after a quick check of his nearly empty refrigerator, she didn't doubt it. She'd insisted they both grab something before heading off on what might be a wild-goose chase.

But at the hole-in-the-wall Pakistani deli, when she opened the refrigerator case, it wasn't the cartons of milk and orange juice that immediately caught her eye. What jumped out was the rack of wine coolers, rows of tall bottles misted with condensation. She thought of how one of those bottles would feel in her hand, its wonderfully familiar heft, its sweet chill wetting her palm. Even the brand, Aker's Orchard—it sounded so quaint and harmless. How could it hurt, just one? They weren't much stronger than soda; hardly enough alcohol to give you a buzz.

Mandy began to tremble. She swallowed, hearing a clicking sound at the back of her parched throat. She couldn't remember ever wanting anything so badly.

Squeezing her eyes shut, she tried to will away the almost palpable image of herself lifting one of those bottles to her mouth, head tilted back, lips parted. But it was no good. She couldn't shake it. And now the craving was even *worse.*

She felt herself start to reach into the case. Her hand, as if magnetized, drawn inevitably toward its pole.

Just one. I promise. . . .

But who was she kidding? It wouldn't stop at one. It never did.

With her last shred of willpower, Mandy jerked her arm back and, in that instant, experienced an almost physical sensation of something tearing—as if the narrow gap separating her from what she craved were a hank of hair being ripped from her scalp. Leaning up against the cool glass of the case, she mopped her sweating forehead with her sleeve, feeling not the least bit virtuous, merely deprived.

Grabbing one of the plastic baskets stacked just inside the door, she began throwing things into it. Bread. Cheese. Sliced turkey. A jar each of mustard and mayonnaise. It wasn't until she'd plunked the basket down on the counter that she remembered the milk. Should she go back? Risk the temptation?

As if in a trance, Mandy walked back over to the refrigerator case. The gleaming row of bottles, with their bright labels like children's crayon drawings, seemed to wink at her. She almost laughed out loud at her fears. How could anything so cheery—so *benign,* really—be cause for concern?

Before her conscience could get the better of her, Mandy reached for a bottle . . . and grabbed two instead. One for her health . . . and, oh hell, one for good measure.

At the register, as the bored-looking owner was ringing up her purchase, she rummaged in her shoulder bag for her wallet and pulled it out. Something fluttered to the floor. She bent to pick it up—a dog-eared business card. Frowning, she examined it. *Eric Sandstrom, WQNA Talk Radio.* His home number was scribbled on the back.

It all descended on her like a wheelbarrow tipping over in her mind—the night she'd had dinner at Rose's, Eric cornering her in the kitchen. This man she hardly knew—a stranger, really—looking at her as if he understood her in a way even her own family never could. *Call me anytime,* he'd said. They'd go to an AA meeting together.

The guy had some nerve, Mandy thought. Just because he'd escorted her home one night, did that give him the right to lecture her?

She felt a slippery brush against her calf that caused her to jump, her heart lurching into her throat. But it was only the store cat, a fat yellow tabby that scooted away as if she'd stepped on its tail. The Sikh store owner, too, was giving her a strange look. Mandy froze, staring at the plastic bag of groceries on the counter, while her mind screeched, *What are you waiting for? Just pay for the stuff, and get out of here.* But when she glanced toward the door, in anticipation of a fast getaway, she saw something that she hadn't noticed on her way in: a pay phone on the dingy wall above a rack of newspapers.

Call Eric now. This instant. A voice she didn't recognize, it had been so long since she'd heard it. Daddy's voice.

She felt a stinging rush behind her eyes.

At the same time, she balked. How silly, she told herself. What was the big deal? Anyway, she couldn't just walk off and leave these groceries. This guy was already eyeing her as if she were some kind of nut. And Drew was sure to start wondering what was keeping her.

And let's not forget the frosty wine coolers with your name on them.

Mandy fumbled with the clasp on her wallet. If she had no quarters, that would be a sign, wouldn't it? A sign that she wasn't meant to call Eric. But if, on the other hand . . .

She unzipped the change compartment . . . where a single quarter stared boldly up at her from a pile of dimes, nickels, pennies. With trembling fingers, she dug it out.

Damn.

Mandy formed a fist, squeezing so hard she could feel the coin digging into her palm like a dull blade. She was only dimly aware of the rise and fall of nasal singing from a radio tuned to some Indian station. And the store owner waiting impatiently with the register open.

Ignoring him, she let out a sigh of defeat that, oddly enough, seemed to lift her, making it almost easy to put one foot in front of the other as she walked over to the pay phone and dropped the quarter into its slot.

Chapter 16

❧ "Did you remember to pack the liner for your raincoat? It'll be cold in Cincinnati." Rachel watched her husband carry his luggage over to the door and set it down—the old green duffel that must have at least a hundred thousand miles on it, and the scuffed leather photographer's case he used as a carry-on.

"I'll be fine. I packed an extra sweater." Brian glanced at his watch—it was just past five, rush hour—then, just as cursorily, at her.

The prospect of his leaving worried her in a way she couldn't quite put her finger on. But it was only a business trip, she told herself. Two nights and a day to shmooze with a major wholesaler. Just like a hundred other publicity jaunts. Except for one thing: his cool, businesslike attitude toward *her,* as if she were just another item on his itinerary.

And why were they talking about the weather in Cincinnati, for God's sake, when the temperature in this very room felt close to freezing? Sure, couples got angry, yelled, fought—but this was worse. *We're like strangers,* she thought. Like seatmates on an airplane, acknowledging one another with polite nods but secretly terrified they might be forced into a conversation. Careful, oh so careful, even while dozing, to keep their elbows from brushing, their faces turned away.

If Brian should leave her for good, was this how it would be? No fuss, no muss. God, how awful. Rachel felt her low-grade anxiety start to rise, like mercury in a thermometer, and remembered a breezy term Mandy used to describe a particularly easy case: "low-impact divorce." At the time, Rachel had smiled, amused. Now she wondered if there really was such a thing. What might look like two adults handling a situation in a mature way—wasn't that just the product of emotions piled so high they had to tiptoe around, and talk in whispers, to keep it all from tumbling down?

"Did you leave a copy of your itinerary for me?" she asked.

"On your desk, in the den." Distractedly, he waved a hand in that direction while riffling through the packet containing his airline tickets and hotel vouchers. In his khakis and navy windbreaker, with his glasses slipping down his nose, he made her think of an archeologist heading off to a dig in some remote part of the world.

"I won't call unless it's an emergency," Rachel told him. "I know how busy you'll be."

Brian looked up sharply. This wasn't like her, they both knew. In the old days, she'd have expected him to phone as soon as he'd checked into his hotel. And then, later, she'd have called to wish him good night. On a few memorable occasions, for no particular reason, they'd talked for several hours.

Now she waited, hoping against hope, for Brian to break through the ice. To laugh, as if she'd only been joking, and say something cute like, *Hey, baby, you up for some phone sex later on?* Oh, he'd been wonderfully understanding about her mother. Tender and solicitous in the days following the funeral, taking on most of the household chores while Rachel had wandered about in a daze. Nikos, in accordance with Mama's wishes, had quietly informed Sylvie's family about Rose, so, along with everything else, there had been aunts, uncles, cousins, asking nosy questions Rachel wasn't in any shape to deal with. Brian had headed them off at the pass, explaining just enough to satisfy them, while at the same time keeping them at bay.

But as for any true intimacy between husband and wife, there had been only the briefest of hugs, the most generic of kisses. That's what hurt the most—Rachel felt her husband slipping away, but sensed she was powerless to stop it. Each day, the wall of ice separating them grew thicker.

It wasn't even about Rose. Not really. Whatever had happened between Brian and Rose, whatever he'd *wished* would happen, Rose was just the point of disembarkation after the long and tumultuous voyage of these past few years. But whatever storms Rachel and Brian had faced, none had been worse than this . . . this . . .

Becalmed, she thought. *That's what we are—becalmed.* The thing that sailors in the old days dreaded even more than high seas. Food and water in limited supply, and no land in sight.

"You'll be plenty busy yourself, I'm sure." Brian was trying to sound lighthearted, but it came out sounding like an accusation. More gently, he added, "I'll phone you when I get there, just to make sure you're okay."

When had the tables turned? Once, it had been Rachel worrying. Now it was Brian voicing an awareness of the potential danger lurking around every corner. Only he wasn't talking about plane crashes or car wrecks. He, too, must have sensed it—the chasm opening at their feet.

"I'm heading over to the clinic to catch up on a few things. I may be late getting home," she told him, feeling the sudden need to withdraw, protect herself. "I'm so behind. You know, with everything that's happened . . ." She let the sentence trail off.

"I'm sure." Brian's tone was clipped, impatient.

There was a grim set to his jaw, a remoteness in his eyes, that hadn't been evident even a few months ago. This evening, watching him pack—socks, shirts, ties, his favorite pen for signing autographs—she'd been struck by his efficiency. His . . . self-containment. As if he'd have been just as comfortable living elsewhere; as if it made no difference how long he'd be away. A day, a week, a month—maybe it was all the same to a man with nothing much to come home to.

But was it all *her* fault? If their roles had been reversed, with Brian running his own firm, say, wouldn't she have been more understanding? Why was it that all the successful women she knew felt continually torn—and their husbands almost never did?

Rachel felt a flare of resentment that just as quickly died.

Marriage, she thought, was more than a feminist issue. Like God, it was in the details—the small courtesies, the loving touch in passing, the thoughtful remembrances. She remembered the days when whoever had to get up earliest would leave a little love note for the other by the coffee machine. When she'd bring Brian supper on a tray if he was racing to meet a deadline; or, if it was the other way around and she'd had to work late, he'd show up at the clinic with a picnic basket. And winter nights, when she'd climb into bed, her feet blocks of ice, Brian would let her warm them against his with only a good-natured grunt of protest.

The night of the engagement party was the last time they'd made love—if you could call it that. Since then, they'd slept with their backs to each other. Even so, the thought of losing Brian brought a depth charge of panic exploding to the surface. What would she do without him? How would she survive? Oh God, dear God, *who would love her?*

Except for Iris, she had no family. No *real* family, not anymore. Only the pair of sisters she'd somehow inherited, who were little more than strangers. Skinny, hardbitten Marie, and the insufferably sanctimonious Clare. She'd socialized with them, sure, at Rose's, on family occasions and holidays, but the concept of their actually being related to her was still utterly and completely foreign to her. Last week, when Marie, gruff as a prisoner welcoming a fellow inmate to the cell block, had invited her over for coffee, Rachel had scrambled to make up an excuse. She didn't know if she'd ever be able to see Marie as anything other than Rose's sister.

When Brian's limo arrived to take him to the airport, Rachel kissed him lightly on the cheek, fighting back her tears. She'd spare him those. "Take care," she murmured, thinking how ironic it was: all those years, she had imagined every catastrophe that might befall Brian while he was away, when the real threat to their happiness had been right here at home.

Watching from the window as Brian emerged onto the sidewalk, where a black Town Car was idling at the curb, Rachel wondered if she'd merely imagined the searching look he gave her at the door.

The way his thoughtful gray eyes had seemed to rest on her, as if waiting for an answer to the question neither of them dared ask.

As the limo pulled away, she brought her forehead to rest against the cool glass, welcoming the chill that seeped down into her hot cheeks. It numbed her, put her tears on hold, reminded her she had work to do.

Hours later, as she was plowing through the last of the folders on her desk, her private line at the clinic rang. *Brian,* Rachel thought. Reaching for the phone, she glanced at the clock on her desk, and saw that it wasn't quite nine. No. His plane might have landed, but he wouldn't be at his hotel yet.

"It's Drew," said the taut voice on the other end. He sounded upset. "I can't seem to find Iris. Have you seen her?"

"Iris?" Rachel echoed, feeling a sudden chill. "I thought she was with you. Yesterday, when I called . . . she told me you two had plans."

"We did."

"I've been trying to make a date with her—for lunch, coffee, whatever—but she always says she's too busy." Even as she said it, Rachel felt a pang of guilt for not having pursued it; for being so caught up in her own *tsuris* she didn't just march over there and demand to know what was *really* going on. "Drew, I'm worried about her. She doesn't look well. I know how distraught she is about her grandmother . . . but . . ." Rachel drew in a breath. "Drew, is something wrong?"

He hesitated a beat too long, and that's when she knew. *Oh God.* She'd been counting on Drew to act as watchdog—but where had *she* been, Iris' own mother?

A little guiltily, he replied, "I was expecting her last night . . . and she never showed up."

"Last night?" Rachel had to restrain herself to keep from shouting. "Why didn't you *call?*"

"She was at a friend's. I just figured she'd changed her mind about coming over. We . . . we haven't been getting along all that well lately. Besides . . ." He paused. "Look, I know it was wrong, but she made me promise. She didn't want to worry you. That's why she's been avoiding you."

"What mother *wouldn't* worry?" Her voice rose, edged with hysteria. *She tried to kill herself. Twice. Isn't that reason enough?*

"I should've called sooner, I know." His voice was low and ashamed. "I thought we could handle it. She even talked to her shrink about it. After that, for a little while, she really *did* seem better . . . but this thing with Sylvie, and the house, it really got to her." He exhaled raggedly.

"Drew, what happened?"

"She locked herself in the bathroom," Drew said. "She had the razor out, and . . ." His voice caught, ending in a muffled sob.

Rachel felt a lightning bolt of alarm streak through her. *Rose warned me. Mama, too . . .*

When she could trust herself to speak normally, she demanded with quiet urgency, "Tell me everything you know."

Drew cleared his throat, and his voice grew stronger. "Okay, but not now. We have to look for her. Right now, that's what we have to do."

Rachel squeezed her eyes shut. "Have you . . . Are the police involved?" she forced herself to ask.

"I haven't told anyone except my sister," he said. "She's out looking for Iris now. With my mom's boyfriend. Eric. He's taking Mandy over to some shelter for runaways that he knows of."

"Iris is . . ." Rachel stopped. She'd been about to protest that Iris was too old to be considered a runaway, and besides, she *had* a home to go to. Then she reminded herself: Iris wasn't like other girls her age. Gripping the receiver hard enough to make her knuckles pop, she told Drew, "I'll be right over."

Rachel hung up, rushed about the office, grabbed her coat and purse. She wasn't just scared—she was furious. At herself. For letting her daughter down, believing Iris was out of the woods when she should have known better.

I'm her mother. I should have done something.

Even Mama, however misguided, and however horrible the consequences in the end, had tried to protect her daughter, her Rachel—though in the end it was Rachel, not Mama, who was paying the price.

Rachel wanted to scream, throw something at the wall. Yet all she could do was stand in the doorway, struggling with a coat that seemed to have grown three sleeves since she'd last put it on. In her mind, too, everything had gotten tangled. Brian's leaving . . . Iris' running away . . . Mama's dying.

Yes, Mama, I'm angry at you, too. For taking away the only mother she'd known—not just in body, but in spirit as well. Because the woman Rachel had called Mama never could have abandoned her own baby, then, decades later, deny that child her birthright. It was monstrous. Cruel. Unforgivable.

Suddenly Rachel knew who she needed to call.

Rose.

Rose, to whom she was bound by a secret stronger than blood—one that had destroyed lives, no question, but which had to have *some* purpose as well, some thread of redemption. And, however slender that thread, however tightly woven into the tapestry of lies and deception, it might ultimately lead to her daughter.

The office was quiet. It was after nine, and Mallory had left hours ago. Rose was getting ready to pack it in herself; she'd promised Jay she would stop at Blockbuster for a movie he wanted to watch. Even the unwelcome prospect of Sly Stallone, drenched in sweat and blood, slugging it out with the baddies wasn't enough to deter her from what might be her last chance ever to curl up on the sofa with her younger son, who, for a brief shining moment, seemed to have forgotten that *she* was the bad guy.

Good. Because at the moment she felt more like the innocent bystander who'd been shot through the heart.

Less than forty-eight hours since Eric had walked out of her life . . . and already the thought of not seeing him again, *ever,* felt like a small death. She hadn't been prepared to miss him this much. Rose couldn't remember when she'd felt so desolate. Losing Max had been the worst—it had nearly killed her—but there had been no one to blame, least of all herself. And always, at the heart of her misery, had lain the knowledge that, had she been given the choice, she would have sacrificed everything to bring back her husband.

With Eric, she wouldn't have to give up anything. All she'd have to do was pick up the phone.

Rose found herself remembering a long-ago trip to Montana, a three-day trail ride through the wilderness Max had talked her into. It would be fun for the boys, he'd cajoled. As city dwellers, they knew next to nothing about roughing it, and even less about horses. Overcoming her terror, Rose had agreed—and lived to regret it. The second day, halfway up a narrow switchback, her horse had balked. Without warning, it began backing up—a wild little dance that sent a small avalanche of stones skittering down the steep slope inches away. She'd thought for sure she was going to die, from a heart attack if not a broken neck, but somehow had managed to bring the horse under control before they both went plunging over the edge. Afterwards—when she was too shaken to walk, much less ride—their trail guide said, "Ain't no such thing as a guaranteed safe horse. Even the quietest ones can spook . . . and nobody knows why."

Rose knew why. The poor animal had been scared out of its wits.

All these years later, she felt a kinship with that horse. There was no rhyme or reason to why she'd balked with Eric, at least none she could adequately put into words. But the plain fact was, she was terrified.

Seated at the desk in her office, staring sightlessly down at the string of Matchbox cars crawling along Park Avenue, Rose wondered if maybe certain people weren't meant to be lucky in love. If her true legacy, more real than any house, was the losses lined up one after another, like dominoes, starting with a mother who had left her at birth.

If only she could find a way to stop *wanting* him so much. If she could simply accept her fate, and move on.

Go home, she told herself, disgusted by her self-pity. *Go home to your son. That's where you belong. He needs you.*

Rose pulled herself heavily to her feet, and began stuffing papers into her briefcase. Minutes later, as she was making her way along the corridor to the reception area, she passed the open door to Mandy's office, and gave a little wave to Hayden Lockwood, hunched like a tall question mark over a stack of files he was placing on Mandy's desk. In his cardigan vest and tortoiseshell spectacles, he looked strangely out of sync with the rest of his generation, like a young actor poorly made up as an elder statesman. But where was Mandy? Her stepdaughter usually worked late herself; she must have had plans. Or else . . .

Don't even think it, a voice in her head warned.

Nevertheless, Rose offered up a silent little prayer that her stepdaughter wasn't off getting plastered in some bar. Since the big showdown, Mandy, as far as Rose could tell, had been sober . . . but you never knew. Did Mandy have the slightest idea how worried she was? And how dearly Rose loved her, as if Mandy were her very own daughter? Rose felt a tiny bit guilty, too, like the tickle at the back of the throat when a cold is coming on. It was as if Max had left her to watch over, not only this office, but his daughter as well, and she were somehow letting him down.

Riding down in the elevator, Rose had to suck in her breath; the glassy descent seemed sharper than usual. She was stepping into the lobby when she caught sight of someone familiar. Rachel—walking briskly toward her wearing a look of grim determination. Her raincoat was unbuttoned, one end of its belt trailing along the polished marble floor tiles. Their eyes met, and Rachel smiled, a joyless smile that melted faster than a snowflake.

"I tried to reach you at home," Rachel said, when she'd caught up to her. "But Jay said you were working late. I came straight over."

"What is it? Is something wrong?" Rose was instantly alert—another by-product of Max's death: every pale, stricken face with which she was confronted, in her mind immediately equaled disaster.

"I need your help," Rachel said in a low voice, pulling Rose to one side. "It's Iris—she's been missing since yesterday, and no one seems to know where she is. Not even Drew. He's worried she might be"—she swallowed hard—"in some kind of trouble."

"You're sure he's not just jumping the gun?" Rose felt obligated to ask. "Maybe they had a fight."

"I don't think so." Rachel looked as if she wished that were all it was. Her gaze was troubled, her mouth thin and flat as a surgical scar. "Do *you?*"

Rose's mouth went suddenly dry. "No."

Rachel leaned forward, gripping Rose's wrist. "Will you help me look for her?"

Something in Rose balked. *Enough!* What thanks had she gotten for trying to reason with Rachel, get her to see that Iris needed more than Drew could provide? Now she was supposed to drop everything and take off on some rescue mission?

But under the spotlight of Rachel's unblinking blue gaze, Rose somehow couldn't bring herself to refuse. Her burst of obstinacy faded as abruptly as it had flared. She sighed. "Where do you suggest we start?"

For once, Rachel wasn't quick to direct the operation. Except for her permanent-press posture, as crisp and upright as ever, she seemed almost defeated. "I don't know," she admitted. "According to Drew, none of her friends know where she is, or where she might have gone. Any ideas?"

"Maybe she decided to leave town without telling anyone. Has she talked about taking a trip?"

Rachel shook her head. "I looked in the drawer where she keeps her passport. It's still there, thank God."

"That only rules out other countries."

"I found her checkbook in her room, with her bank card tucked inside. It doesn't look like she's made any withdrawals this past week. Besides . . . that's not like Iris. She's always stuck pretty close to home."

"What about her therapist? Maybe he knows something."

"I called him. It seems she had an appointment with Dr. Eisenger this morning, and never showed up." Tears glimmered in Rachel's eyes. "Oh, Rose, I should have listened to you. Everything you said was true. She *does* need help—much more than we've been able to give her. I see that now."

"It's not too late," Rose reassured her. "We'll find her."

"*Where?*" Rachel's voice dropped to a fierce whisper.

Rose thought for a moment. Not like a mother, but like a lawyer. As she often did with cases involving potential witnesses who seemed to vanish into thin air when she tried to have them subpoenaed, Rose mentally put herself in Iris' shoes: where would she go? What haven would seem the safest?

A beloved aunt or uncle? Grandparents?

Suddenly it came to her: Sylvie.

Except Sylvie was gone . . . and her beloved house was empty.

Still, Iris could have her own key.

That's crazy, Rose thought. *I was there most of yesterday. If she'd been in the house, I would have seen her.*

Unless, of course, Iris had sneaked in after she'd left. Or was lying low in one of the upstairs rooms. The place was so huge. How else could Sylvie have managed to have an affair practically under her husband's nose? Rose, struck by the irony of it, nearly gave in to a bitter laugh—if it hadn't been for all those hidden corners, she herself might not have been conceived.

"Let's go." She grabbed Rachel's hand; she would call Jay on her cell phone on their way, let him know she'd be late getting home. "I have an idea where she might be."

As the taxi sped up Park Avenue, Rose said a silent Hail Mary. She hadn't been to church in years, except at Max's funeral. Whenever someone asked what religion she was, she would always joke, "I'm a recovering Catholic." She'd had both her sons baptized, of course, and as a family they'd attended services on Christmas and Easter. But whenever she knelt to pray, it always felt phony somehow, pointless. If God even existed, He would know she was merely going through the motions. And why should He listen? Prayers were just words. Dogma hammered into her brain by nuns who'd been just as thorough at smacking the backs of wrists with a ruler. What had God ever done for her? What had He given her other than lies and false promises?

But perhaps the praying she'd done at Sylvie's, when she discovered those letters, had loosened some rusted tap Rose had believed forever frozen shut. The familiar words came easily now, soothing as cool spring water. *Hail Mary, Mother of God, the Lord is with you. . . .*

Maybe you didn't actually have to believe the words, she thought. Maybe all you had to do was *say* them, wrap their familiar cadences around you like an old quilt, worn soft with many washings. In this world of bumps and bruises, maybe praying wasn't meant to solve anything, but was simply a way of smoothing the rough edges.

Lord, she found herself praying, *I know I haven't been very good at keeping in touch. You have my sister for that. The way Clare acts, you'd think she had the 800 number to Your special hot line. But, see, I figured You'd pretty much given up on me, so what was the point? This time, I'm asking for real: help Rachel find her daughter. And help me do what's right for MY children. . . .*

Rose's eyes were wide open, her hands loose in her lap. Yet her prayer was more sincere than any of the thousands she'd murmured into her steepled fingers while in church. More heartfelt, in its way, even than her you-owe-me appeals to God in the months after Max's death.

Max. She'd mourned him with all her heart, each day without him faithfully ticked off like another bead on a rosary; every light switch fumbled for in a dark room like a penny candle lit in his memory. And what had it gotten her? No more than the prayers she'd offered up merely out of duty, or self-pity.

With Eric, she'd had a shot at something real and sustaining. But she'd tossed it away. Yes, maybe she wasn't destined to be happy. Maybe, like Iris, she'd been damaged in some crippling way that wasn't visible to the naked eye, and the contentment she'd known with Max had been the exception rather than the rule . . .

"*. . . If you're tuned in right now, Iris, please, call home just to let your family know you're okay. Okay?*"

Rose snapped to attention with a little jerk of her head. The voice coming out of nowhere was Eric's. Had she conjured it up?

Then she realized—it was coming from the taxi's radio.

She turned to Rachel, whose eyes were wide with amazement. They shared a long look before Rachel, her voice hushed with gratitude, said, "Drew. He must have asked Eric to do it."

Eric had to be subbing for someone else, Rose thought. His show aired earlier in the day; he'd clearly made a special effort to trade slots with one of the other hosts.

Oh, Eric, you're a good man, with good instincts. It was just rotten luck that made you fall in love with me.

She stared out the window at the hulking prewar apartment buildings that, in the purplish October twilight, seemed to preside over the avenue like heavily decorated old generals on parade. Eric had been right about one thing, she thought. He deserved a woman who would meet him halfway. Someone who wasn't too paralyzed by her past to move forward.

The taxi was on West Seventy-ninth, nearing Riverside Drive, when Rose first heard it: the wail of approaching sirens. The taxi swerved into the far lane just as a fire engine came looming out of the deepening shadows to streak past them like a comet. Rose rocked back in her seat, her heart leaping. Farther up the block, she saw a cloud of gray, like a huge thumbprint smudging the line of rooftops sketched against the evening sky. She caught a whiff of smoke . . . and something more acrid-smelling, like burning rubber.

No. It can't be . . .

But as the taxi slowed to a stop near the row of blue police barricades closing off access to West Seventy-ninth, Rose saw with a sick, spreading horror that the house on the corner facing Riverside, the one surrounded by fire trucks and snaking hoses, was Sylvie's. *Mother of God.* Reflexively, she made the sign of the cross. This wasn't happening, she thought. It was a bad dream. No, worse, like watching Sylvie die all over again.

Beside her, she heard Rachel give a startled cry. "No! Oh no!" She gripped Rose's arm. "You don't think . . . Oh, Rose, tell me you were only guessing. *Tell me Iris isn't in there!*"

Rose stared at her. An old memory was floating to the surface. Years and years ago, being summoned to the Seventeenth Precinct one hot summer night. Her friend Lieutenant O'Neill had phoned to let her know they'd picked up the woman suspected of abandoning her three-year-old—the little girl Rose had moved bureaucratic mountains to place with Brian and Rachel.

When Rose arrived at the station, she'd feared the worst—that the woman, a *mother* no matter what she'd done, would want her child back. Hadn't Sylvie suffered such regrets, after all? But instead she'd found a drug-addicted wreck, a once-pretty woman who couldn't have been more than thirty but looked sixty—wasted, unkempt, filthy. Most of her ravings had made no sense . . . except for one that had raised the hair on the back of Rose's neck.

The woman had been burned out of her apartment, Rose learned. Rose would never forget the lunatic light in her sunken eyes, how she'd gripped Rose's hand and pulled her close to rasp, *My kid, she set it. It was no accident, either . . .*

Rose hadn't believed it, of course. What three-year-old was capable of purposely setting such a fire? That was why she hadn't said anything. What would have been the point of pushing the panic button? Brian and Rachel had enough to worry about as it was.

Two weeks later, Iris' mother was dead of an overdose. That was all Rachel and Brian needed to know, Rose had decided. Just the facts. It was enough that the little girl they'd taken into their home and hearts would bear the scars of neglect—did they have to wonder if Iris might be deranged as well?

Over the years, Rose often wondered if she should have said something about the fire. Especially when it began to grow clear that Iris' scars went much deeper than any of them had initially suspected. But whatever harm Iris had inflicted, it was mostly to herself.

Rose had never *seriously* questioned her judgment . . . until this moment.

God. Suppose that crazy woman *had* been telling the truth?

Rose, taking a deep breath, placed a steadying hand on Rachel's shoulder. "I don't know for sure, but there's a good chance Iris may have been responsible for this fire. Don't ask me why I think so, there's no time now. I promise I'll tell you later. Just trust me."

Rachel gave her a searching look, then nodded. She grabbed the door handle while Rose tossed a handful of crumpled bills at the driver.

As they shouldered their way through the small crowd gathered behind the barricade, Rose felt sickened by the awful realization that Iris must have set fire to the house out of spite. She remembered how upset Iris had been when she learned Sylvie had left it to Rose. If Iris or her family couldn't have it, she must have wanted to make sure *nobody* could. . . .

Rose was seized with panic. What if she really IS in there? Trapped?

A burly fireman in a yellow turnout was yelling at everyone to stand back. Parked at an angle on the far side of the barrier, its red lights flashing, an EMS truck was the hive around which a dozen or so cops and paramedics swarmed. Fifty feet away, a canvas hose hooked to a hydrant bucked and twisted in the hands of two straining firemen. The hiss of gallons of water turned instantly to steam filled the air like the rushing of a mighty river. As Rose watched, momentarily frozen by the spectacle, a loud explosion caused her to jerk her head up. In horror, she watched a cloud of thick black smoke pour from a shattered window on the third floor of the once-beautiful house.

Sylvie's things . . . her lovely antiques . . . her books and knick-knacks . . . the hopelessly impractical Irish linens Milagros had ironed faithfully each week. Her garden, too. Lost. All of it lost forever.

Rose heard someone scream.

She was vaguely aware that Rachel was screaming, but a moment or two passed before Rose's disengaged mind, like an oar that had slipped its oarlock, dropped back into place.

Iris. She had to think about Iris. The rest was just *things.* She scanned the nightmarish scene, but saw no sign of any rescue equipment, no ladders propped against the house's blackened façade. Instead of being reassured, she felt even more panicky. If Iris *was* in there and hadn't shouted for help, how would the firemen know to rescue her?

She turned toward Rachel . . . just in time to catch sight of her ducking under the police barricade. Rose yelled, "Rachel, no!"

Catching a glimpse of Rachel as she disappeared up the front walk, Rose thought, *Dear God, she's doing it. She's actually going in there.* And no one was stopping her.

Rose waited until the cops were all looking the other way, then darted past the police line.

With her eyes watering, and darkness closing in, it was several long moments before Rose spotted Rachel again: a slight figure in a tan Burberry vanishing into the blackness of the columned portico, from which water poured in steady streams.

No . . . Rachel . . . NO . . .

She was past the wrought-iron gates to the front entrance, usually closed but now wide open—when a hand landed on her shoulder with the jarring suddenness of a falling brick, bringing Rose to an abrupt halt. A voice, muffled by the din, bellowed, *"Hey, lady . . . whaddaya think yer doin'?"*

More precious seconds lost. Desperate, too desperate even to turn and look the guy in the face, Rose wrenched free of his grasp and stumbled down the short walkway . . . up the steps puddled in filthy water . . . and through the open front door . . .

. . . into a scene from hell.

Chapter 17

❧ Rachel wasn't aware of anyone, or anything, except the thick smoke, blanketing everything in sight. She coughed, beating at it, but her arms swung in wide, weightless arcs. At the same time, the hot gray haze felt like something solid—a rubber anesthesia mask clamped over her nose and mouth, making her woozy.

Feeling her way along one wall of the front hallway, mostly by heart, she stumbled into the small sitting room to the right of the staircase. Here and there, amid the lazily drifting gray, she caught the outline of a table, the curve of a sofa back, a glint of porcelain like a milky blind eye. No flames, though. The fire must have started on one of the upper floors, she thought. She still had time—a few minutes, maybe longer.

Iris. I have to find her. She's in here . . . somewhere.

Something huge and dark leaped out at Rachel, causing her to jump back with a strangled yelp. But it was only the Queen Anne butler's secretary, which she'd mistaken for the doorway to the dining room. Behind its glass panes, she glimpsed a neat row of spiral-bound notebooks—her mother's household accounts, neatly recorded in Mama's precise, elegant handwriting—before she was seized by a fit of coughing that bent her over nearly double. She coughed until her throat was stripped raw; the searing smoke had settled heavily into her lungs like old rags soaked in kerosene.

She could hear streams of pressurized water striking the outside of the building with a hollow drumming sound, followed by the faint tinkle of exploding glass somewhere upstairs. In the distance, sirens wailed, and voices shouted. She thought she heard someone calling her name, but it seemed to be coming from *inside* the house. She must have imagined it. No one would be crazy enough to follow her into this.

"*Iris!*" The scream tore from Rachel's raw throat. "*IRIS . . . WHERE ARE YOU?*"

She could *feel* it. Her daughter was in the house somewhere. Hurt, maybe even unconscious. *Please, God, help me find her. She didn't mean to do it. She's not responsible. I am.*

Rachel rushed blindly ahead. Something bit sharply into her shin, causing her to stumble and nearly fall. A footstool, she saw, its needlepoint design of a shepherdess staring up at her with a blank idiocy that suddenly infuriated her. She gave it a furious kick, launching it in a crippled roll across the carpet.

God . . . oh dear God . . . how, in all this madness, was she supposed to find her daughter? Rachel imagined her huddled in the corner of an upstairs room, helpless against an advancing wall of flames—and was seized by a panic so huge and mindless, she was momentarily paralyzed. Shaking with terror, she stood rooted to the carpet while the smoke pried at her with greedy, phantom fingers. Then the ghastly thought struck her:

What if Iris doesn't WANT to be rescued?

She gave herself a vicious mental shake. No, she mustn't think that way. It would only slow her down, and already she felt weak and sluggish, as if this were one of those nightmares where you run frantically but never seem to make any progress. She had to get a grip on herself. *Now.*

"*IRIS!*" Her cry, which seemed to be coming from somewhere outside of her, was like a sledgehammer smashing through a wall, freeing her to dart into the next room.

Long table. Chairs. A carved buffet. She was in the dining room, where as a child she'd sat through so many formal family meals. Something glinted at the far end, through swirling rafts of smoke— the polished brass handles of the French doors that opened onto the garden. She felt her panic subside a bit. If for some reason she couldn't get to the front door in time, she could always escape out back.

But not without Iris.

A thumping noise overhead, like a heavy piece of furniture being dragged. Or frantic footsteps. *Iris?*

With a muffled sob, she lurched forward, arms extended stiffly in front of her as she felt her way along the wall, retracing her steps. Her thoughts whirled like bits of colored glass in a kaleidoscope.

Where *was* everybody? *Where was Mama?*

A vivid picture formed in her mind: Mama, in the upstairs nursery, rocking four-year-old Iris on her lap. Mama's mouth was moving, but her words were swallowed by the roaring flames. She was trying to warn Rachel. Something awful was about to happen. Just like she'd tried to before she—

Then Rachel remembered: Mama was dead.

Her heart plummeted.

Don't think. Don't remember. Just keep moving.

Rachel staggered past the gaping socket of a marble fireplace in which a pair of logs stood perfectly stacked, complete with crumpled newspaper, all ready to be lit. The irony of it struck her, causing a hysterical giggle to erupt.

In her mind, once again, she was seeing blood. Everywhere. Smeared across the tiles over the tub. Puddled on the bathroom floor like some macabre practical joke. And Iris, in the midst of it all . . .

Dear God, what could I have been thinking all these months? How could I have ignored the signals? She *had* abandoned her family.

Another thump overhead, then a crashing noise. Hot. It was so HOT. And she couldn't breathe. Sweat dripped in rivulets down her face, stinging her eyes, making her blink hard.

Every selfish instinct screamed for her to turn back, run for safety . . . but she couldn't just leave her daughter to die.

Stairs. Go. Now. Before it's too late . . .

"Rachel? Rachel!"

Rose's voice.

"*Rachel!*"

Rachel stopped short of the staircase and swung clumsily around. Not more than a dozen feet behind her, Rose's familiar figure wavered, ghostlike, behind a gently rippling scrim of smoke. She stood near the entrance to the living room, hands clapped to her mouth, her head swiveling back and forth in wide, almost comical arcs—like a parody of someone lost at sea. Her face was smudged, her dark hair a mass of damp, skewed ringlets. One of her high heels had come off, and as Rose caught sight of her, and began limping toward her, Rachel felt a crazed impulse to laugh.

"You can't go up there!" Rose yelled, stabbing a finger in the direction of the stairs. "You won't make it. You'll be killed."

"Have to," Rachel gasped. "She's up there. I can *feel* it."

"But you don't *know* that."

"You . . . said so . . . yourself."

"I could be wrong." Rose coughed. "And even if she *did* set the fire, she wouldn't have stuck around. That would be . . ." She stopped, her face a stricken white smudge amid the gray smoke.

"Suicide?" Rachel shouted, lightheaded. Her voice rose on a shrill note of hysteria. "Maybe . . . but this time I'm going to DO something about it!" Rachel lurched toward the staircase and grasped the banister.

"No!" Rose dashed after her.

Thunder boomed overhead. At the top of the stairs, something bright and noxious bloomed. Rachel looked up as a great comber of black smoke rolled back from the landing to reveal the flames just beyond. She jumped, her heart in her throat, and for a split-second, hung back. Then, as if in a trance, she started up the stairs. She kept her eyes down, kept herself from looking at what lay ahead. There were only the polished risers, one after another, and the Oriental runner anchored with brass rods and finials that gleamed dully amid the smoke.

She was halfway to the landing when she felt a hand seize her forearm.

Rachel blinked, and looked down . . . at Rose's white-knuckled fingers on her sleeve, at the sooty smudges they'd left. Damn her. She tried to shake free, but was coughing too hard. Struggling weakly, she wheezed, "Get . . . the . . . fuck . . . OFF . . . me."

"You're crazy!" Rose shouted, holding her pinned against the banister. Rachel could feel its smooth curve digging into the small of her back.

"What the hell do you care? She's not your daughter! You *wanted* to be rid of her!" She gave a great, hacking sob.

Then, pushing against Rose as hard as she could—an effort that sent her lurching to her knees—Rachel managed to free herself. She grasped the carved rail and hauled herself upright, staggered up two more steps. Several yards above her, the solid banister shimmered behind a glassy wall of heat.

A hand clamped around her ankle. Fingers like talons that tightened the harder she tried to shake them off. Yanked off balance, she crashed onto the step below, a sheet of pain flaring up through her hip. With a cry of shocked fury, she twisted around to stare at Rose, crouched at her feet, wild-eyed, holding on to her as if for dear life. Rachel began to thrash furiously, kicking at Rose.

"Goddamn you! Let me GO!"

"No. I won't let you die!"

"What do you . . . *care?*" Rachel gasped.

"Maybe I don't," Rose snarled through gritted teeth. "But our mother didn't raise you—*I* didn't go without—just so you could throw your life away. Damnit, Rachel, it has to count for something!"

Only two words penetrated the madly whirling kaleidoscope in Rachel's head: *Our mother.*

Blindly, she began to claw at Rose. The grip on her ankle loosened. Rachel gave a hard kick that caught Rose in the stomach, and heard her grunt with pain.

Something exploded against Rachel's cheek. Her head struck the wall, and pain shot from her teeth up through the back of her skull.

A shower of red rained down behind her closed eyelids. Rachel thought with dull surprise: *She hit me.*

It was her last thought as she slipped from consciousness.

🐝 Rose thought: *Dear God, what now?*

She hadn't meant to *hurt* Rachel, only to stop her from doing something stupid. Now she was out cold. Rachel lay sprawled on her back like a rag doll, one arm outflung, in a pose that was almost ridiculously cinematic. No, not a doll, Rose thought with an oddly detached, eye-of-the-hurricane calm. If she were a doll, she'd have been easy to carry.

Rose stared down at Rachel's slack white face streaked with soot. Minus her take-no-prisoners gaze, and the determined set of her jaw, she looked young, almost unnaturally so—like a child suffering the consequences of playing where she'd been told not to. Her light-brown hair was separated into dark clumps, and one of her gold hoop earrings had come loose. It hung crookedly from its wire post, for some reason making Rose think of a phone left dangling off the hook.

In a moment of dreamlike fusion, it occurred to Rose that once upon a time it had been Sylvie in almost the exact position she was in now. She could picture it clearly, the scene she'd imagined so often—the ancient hospital linoleum hot against Sylvie's bare feet as she raced toward the nursery; the fire escape down which she'd inched, a swaddled newborn clutched to her chest; the upturned faces far below, glowing like a ring of lanterns.

Rose felt a surge of new strength, followed by a burst of clarity.

She could *drag* Rachel, couldn't she? Rachel would be bruised from head to toe, but it was better than staying here until they were *both* unconscious. And the way Rose felt—head swimming, lungs and throat burning—it wouldn't be long. Sucking in as deep a breath as she dared, she grabbed hold of Rachel's ankles . . . and pulled with all her might.

It was a moment or two before she felt Rachel's dead weight dislodge, then jerk free, to bump down several steps. Rachel stirred slightly but didn't come to.

Rose tried not to think about Iris . . . who might at this very minute be suffocating upstairs. But there was nothing more she could do. It was too late to do anything but save Rachel—and herself.

"Help!" Rose shouted.

Why didn't someone come? Where the *hell* were all those firemen she'd seen out front? So much for paying taxes. After this was over, Rose swore, she'd head straight over to City Hall. She'd demand a thorough investigation of both the police and fire depart—

Stop that. A voice cut through the madness in her head. *Stop it right now.*

She gave a hard tug, throwing all her weight into it. She thought she heard Rachel moan as she half-slid, half-bumped her way downward . . . but with the roaring in Rose's ears, and the crackle of encroaching flames, it was hard to be sure.

At the foot of the stairs, Rose paused again, gasping for air through the smoke that was like a fist rammed down her throat. She felt lightheaded, sick to her stomach.

Remembering the first-aid class all the girls at Sacred Heart had been required to take, she sank onto her belly, pressing her cheek to the floor. The smoke was a little less suffocating this close to the ground, but not much. She'd have to hurry.

Rose thought she heard voices nearby, but they might have been coming from outside.

"Help!" she cried again.

No answer. The front door, buried somewhere in all that smoke, couldn't have been more than a dozen feet away, but it might just as well have been a million miles.

An earsplitting crash shook the floor. Lifting her head, Rose watched in horror as a huge gout of smoke exploded from the sitting room, just up ahead to the left, swirling with sparks and flaming bits of wreckage.

It was just the spur Rose needed. Tightening her hold on Rachel's ankles, she began crawling in the direction of the front door. Her heart banged against her ribs like a loose shutter in a storm. Dark specks danced before her eyes. She coughed, bringing up a gob of blackened phlegm.

Lord. If only she could see where she was going.

Not that way—you're heading into the wall. Sylvie's voice, which seemed to be whispering in her ear. Rose felt her scalp tighten, as if she were wearing a cap that had suddenly shrunk two sizes. Then she heard it again. *Face forward at two o'clock. That's right. You're directly in front of the door now. You've got to move quickly, though. . . .*

Rose felt a weird calm settle over her. It was crazy, she knew, but she could actually *feel* Sylvie beside her, as if her mother were guiding her, gently *pushing* her, as she crawled toward the door, dragging Rachel with her. Not an angel, like the illustrations of winged seraphs in Catechism readers, but a real, almost solid presence that almost seemed to *lift* both her and Rachel.

Time slowed. She was acutely aware of each bruising inch of the hallway's tile floor against her knees, each labored breath. She heard the crazed tinkling of a chandelier . . . followed by a jangling crash.

You're almost there. Just a few more feet. There it was again, the nearly palpable pressure of invisible hands on her arms, actually *propelling* her. Was she dreaming this?

No. The sensation was too real. Despite her dizzying terror, she felt perfectly focused. And look . . . up ahead . . . the door.

She gave a low cry, and began to weep.

Don't worry—you'll be safe. I'll take care of you. . . .

Tears she hadn't known she was holding back flowed down Rose's cheeks.

With a last burst of strength, she jerked Rachel the last few feet to the door . . . and into the blessedly clear air on the other side.

As she collapsed onto the wet stoop, it struck her in a moment of crystalline clarity that the way her life had turned out hadn't been a mistake after all. It had all come together exactly as it was meant to.

For, had Sylvie acted differently on that long-ago night, she, the woman the world knew as Rose Santini Griffin, would not exist. However damaging her childhood, however difficult the challenges she'd overcome, they had shaped her, made her who she was: a woman who could handle almost anything.

And how could she be sorry for that?

Rose felt the weight of all that knowledge. . . . Then it was gone, the tremendous burden she'd been carrying for years lifted. The world at large came crashing in. Noise. People yelling. A clomping stampede of glistening rubber boots, and dripping yellow turnouts.

Looking up at a circle of faces blackened by smoke under the beaks of their helmets, she cracked hoarsely, "What took you guys so long?"

Chapter 18

The pigeon was an odd clay color, speckled with reddish spots like rust. When Iris put her hand out, it didn't fly away like the others. It just stood there, on the stone path in front of the park bench on which she sat, its head cocked, one odd salmon-colored eye fixed on her like some unearthly oracle's. As if it knew quite well what she was doing in this not-so-safe park on a chilly fall night when nice, normal people were safe indoors.

Good, she thought. *Because I wish you'd tell me.*

She knew two things: she was hungry, and she was lost. The park in which she'd spent the better part of the day was small—from here, she could see the streets on all four sides—but before, when she'd looked at the signs, none of them had made sense. Madison Avenue. Twenty-fifth Street. Names, just names. Like pieces of puzzle rattling loose in a box.

Her memories, too, were random, scattered. Some clearer than others, but not forming any kind of pattern that made sense, or that might point the way home. Drew, for instance. He was out there. Somewhere. She could *feel* him, as if he were here beside her—the texture of his skin, his smell, the soft hairs at the nape of his neck that formed a whorl. But, strangely, *frighteningly,* she couldn't summon the knowledge of how to reach him.

A memory of particular clarity drifted to the surface—one summer at Lake George. She and Drew had been walking back from town one day when they met up with a girl around their age, the teenaged daughter of one of the summer people renting the cottage down the road from theirs. Iris remembered only that she was pretty and blonde, with a short blue top that showed off a tanned midriff . . . and that she'd invited Drew—not *her*—to go sailing the following day. Iris had felt instantly crushed. Of course he would accept. How could he not?

When Drew politely told the girl he had other plans, Iris almost blurted, *Are you crazy?* But then as they were walking away, Drew slung an arm about her shoulders and remarked casually, "You know that berry patch up on the hill, behind Old Man Patterson's? How about we get up real early, before everybody else, and go pick a bunch for breakfast?" After a brief pause, he'd added softly, "She could've asked you, too. What would it have hurt?"

Even all these years later, Iris could feel the precise weight of his arm against her sunburned shoulders; she could see the noontime sun, high and brilliant in the washed-out blue of the sky, and their foreshortened shadows bumping together companionably over the narrow asphalt road with its dusting of fine sand, like sugar on a pair of gingerbread men.

Yet at this moment, she couldn't have found her way to safety if her life depended on it. She could picture Drew's building perfectly, down to the graffiti on the bricks by the entrance . . . but had forgotten what street it was on. And even if she could find him, she wasn't at all sure he'd want to see her.

Her parents, too. She could see them in her mind, like the miniature family in the dollhouse she'd played with when she was young: a father in a plaid shirt and trousers, with funny painted-on hair; a flaxen-haired mother in a flowered dress; a little girl in a puff-sleeved blouse and skirt. Except Iris never could seem to keep them all in one place. The father-doll would be missing for weeks, then she'd find him under the bed, or in her closet. Once, the mother-doll had turned up in the laundry basket.

And now the girl-doll was lost.

Iris shivered in the chill wind that rattled the leaves overhead. How long had she been sitting here? How long since she'd eaten? Her stomach had stopped growling; she was aware only of a pulse thumping in the hollow of her empty stomach, and a dizziness that made her head feel suspended several feet above her shoulders, like a balloon on a string.

Iris pulled her canvas jacket about her, wishing she had something warmer to wear. But she couldn't remember having put the jacket on . . . or even where she'd been going at the time.

A homeless man in a shabby coat with a grocery cart stuffed full of cans and folded shopping bags was sprawled on the bench across from hers, muttering to himself. Harmless enough. Yet she was struck by a wild, irrational fear. Was *she* like that man?

And if not, *what was wrong with her?*

Dr. Eisenger might have been able to tell her. But she wouldn't have known how to reach him, either. Though she could see him clearly in her mind. The light-blue cable-knit cardigan that rumpled in little waves over his ample belly, the little tuft between his bushy eyebrows that fascinated her so—how many accumulated minutes had she wasted fixating on those hairs, wondering why he didn't clip them? She pictured him removing his horn-rimmed glasses, and wiping the lenses with the large white handkerchief he always carried in his pocket. Polishing them with slow, ponderous strokes of his thumb, rubbing away invisible specks only he could see.

The way he'd tried to polish *her*.

But whenever he rubbed too close to the bone, something in her pulled back.

You could remember if you wanted to, she scolded herself. *You know you could. You just have to TRY.*

The voice in her head abruptly changed, growing harsher. *"Stop crying. Will you just STOP. Who the fuck can think with all that bawling . . ."*

Iris, cowering on the park bench, covered her ears. But she couldn't shut out the angry voice. And now the shouting was accompanied by a loud hissing noise—like the wave machine in her therapist's waiting room multiplied by a thousand.

Concentrate. She had to concentrate.

You're on your way over to Drew's, but first, you stop at the drugstore, for some Tampax. At the register, you realize your wallet is missing. Stolen. You remember a woman brushing up against you . . . the same woman now leaving the store. You dash after her, running to catch up. But the crowd on the sidewalk keeps swallowing her. She ducks down a side street . . . and into a building. You start to follow her inside . . . but it's a run-down building, creepy and dark, with graffiti on the walls. Something familiar about it, though. A smell you recognize. And there's a guy stumbling down the rickety stairs, glassy eyes in a sunken face. A face you've seen before . . .

The memory abruptly blinked off. Iris looked up. Streetlamps bloomed along the darkened path that wound through the park. Under one, a bronze statue was spotlit—a statesmanlike figure poised before a chair, as if to give a speech. Just beyond, above the treetops, towered a spire lit with autumn colors—green and yellow and orange. Pretty, yes, but where *was* she? And what, exactly, had brought her here?

You know. But you don't want to know. Because it was a bad thing. Scary so scary. The images came in a jumbled rush, like in her nightmares—a match flaring in a dimly lighted room, a cupped hand holding it to the stub of a candle. Then the spoon. Glinting bright in the candlelight. And now the needle . . . oh God, the *needle*.

The nightmare scene inside her head grew jerky, like an old silent film. A pale arm, against which the needle flashed. Small hands—*mine?*—tugging on that arm, trying to pull it away from the needle . . . but knocking over the candle instead. A spurt of flame . . .

. . . You're running again. And this time you know where you're going: Grandma's house. You still have the key . . . You'll be safe there. . . .

But the house isn't empty. From across the street, you see a woman letting herself out the front door. Rose. Who hates you. Who took Grandma's house away from you . . .

You start to cry. You don't know who to trust, who to call. You wait until Rose is out of sight . . . then slip in through the front door. You don't dare turn on any lights—Rose might come back and see.

Candle. Matches. Where did Grandma keep them?

There. The candlestick on the mantel. With matches in a pretty cloisonné box beside it. You carry the candle up the stairs, to the attic. It's where you always used to play, where you'll feel safe.

You're so tired. All you want to do is sleep. And there, in the corner of the attic, is the crib that used to be Mama's. You climb inside, and curl up. You're home. . . .

You wake up coughing. Smoke. There's smoke everywhere, and flames spurting from a pile of old drapes . . . next to the candle. . . .

You have to get out. Oh God. It's just like before. The fire. But what fire?—you can't remember. The only thing you know is that it was big. It blotted out everything. . . .

And now you know something else: you don't want to die. Maybe you did, those other times, but now all you can think of is getting out before it's too late . . .

Before . . .

Iris squeezed her eyes shut, drawing a heavy curtain inside her head—a trick she'd used for years—to block out the ugly pictures. She felt very afraid. She wanted Mama and Daddy. Grandma, too. Tears rolled down her cheeks, warming their chilled numbness. Mostly, she wanted somehow to stop this *hurt*.

A hurt that went even deeper than her hunger—a hurt that lay curled in the depths of her aching belly like a fat cocoon. Waiting . . . waiting. For what? *To be born.*

The blaring of a radio jerked her from her thoughts. She looked over . . . at a teenager in home-boy jeans that bagged down around his Air Jordan Nikes, seated on a bench farther down the path, a boom box propped on one knee. Its volume was turned up loud— the insistent, mind-deadening beat of rap music. But now the kid was fiddling with the dial, surfing the stations. A voice jumped out at her, one she recognized.

"Iris . . . if you're listening . . ."

She snapped upright, her heart leaping. No. Not possible. Now she was hearing voices on the radio—voices talking directly to her? God, oh God, she really *was* turning into one of those looney-tunes, like the old guy seated across from her.

"*. . . just a phone call. Your family is really worried about you.*"

It was real; she wasn't imagining it. And she knew that voice. . . . Dad's friend Eric, the guy Rose was so crazy about. He was pleading with her to call home. But how? She had no money. No phone, either.

How would she be able to give directions? And even if she could, what would be the point? Her parents were better off without her. And Drew . . . he would be . . .

Mad. So mad that this time he might REALLY leave you.

No. She couldn't take that chance.

The homeless man across from her lurched to his feet, looming huge as a shadow on a wall. His dirty, bearded face, under the glare of a sodium-arc light, was like something out of a monster movie. Iris cringed, whimpering under her breath. She'd never felt so scared, so *small.*

"*. . . Now look what you done, you little brat. I swear, soon as I get my hands on you . . .*"

"You, girl, you hungry? Want some o' m' sandwich?" The shabby, bearded man thrust something at her—a crust wrapped in wrinkled wax paper. Iris almost laughed out loud with relief. He wasn't trying to hurt her; he was merely being kind.

She began to cry instead, silent tears that slid down her cheeks like rainwater from an overflowing cistern, dripping off her chin onto her clenched hands. She shook her head, yet somehow found the courage to ask meekly, "I could use a quarter, though. You wouldn't happen to have any spare change?"

The man grinned, revealing several gaps where teeth had been. A low laugh rumbled in his throat like an approaching subway train. He laughed as if it were the funniest thing he'd ever heard in his whole life. Even Iris, as miserable as she was, couldn't help cracking a smile.

"Damn. Now I heard *everythin.'* Almos' makes me wish I *could* hep you." The man cocked a thumb in the direction of the teenager with the boom box, dropping his voice to a conspiratorial whisper. "Now, *him*—you ask real nice, pretty girl like you, and he give you jus' 'bout anything you want."

Iris rose on trembling legs. When she had spoken up just now, something huge that had been holding her pinned seemed to have lifted. She felt more in control somehow. Like someone with a voice, who could ask for what she needed. Even so, her heart was racing as she approached the kid on the next bench. Swallowing against the dryness of her throat, she said, "I need to make a phone call. It's really important. Do you have a quarter you could spare?"

The kid eyed her, smiling broadly to let her know he didn't believe her excuse but she was good looking enough to get away with it. Then, with a shrug, he dug into his pocket.

Closing her fingers around the handful of coins he dropped into her palm, Iris thanked him, and hastily walked away, before he could change his mind and ask for it back. *Now* what?

Wandering through the strange park with autumn leaves floating down around her, some sticking in her hair, she felt a rush of anxiety so great her knees began to buckle. The prospect of finding a phone booth, then trying to remember which numbers to punch, was overwhelming. A mountain to climb. And what if Drew didn't want to speak to her? What if Mom and Daddy were so sick of her they decided to send her away?

Then she heard it again. Eric's voice, drifting toward her over the riffling leaves and muttering of pigeons.

"*. . . when you're on the run, there aren't many things you can count on . . . but your family, believe me, is one. . . .*"

Iris somehow found the strength to keep walking. Toward danger or safety, she didn't know. The only thing she knew for sure was that she was at least sane enough to want to find out.

❧ Eric wrapped up the evening shift—he'd traded with Miles Joseph, who normally hosted from eight to ten—and breathed a deep sigh as he tore off his headphones. Who knew what, if anything, would come of his on-air appeal? It was a long shot at best. When someone like Iris disappeared, often it was for good.

He ought to know. At every AA meeting, there was an odds-on chance the person beside you would wind up on a slab at the county morgue. Normies, they didn't get it, he thought. For most people, suicide simply wasn't an option. They couldn't envision a life of such torment it took a will of iron just to get out of bed every morning. But for someone who was sick, or deeply depressed, even tying his shoes can seem like too much effort.

That was why, instead of sending Mandy home, he'd given her a list of other shelters to search. She probably wouldn't find Iris at any of them, but it would keep her occupied for the time being. And who knew? Maybe she'd get lucky. He had to hand it to her; for someone barely holding it together herself, it had taken a lot of guts, and more than a little grace, to take on her brother's shitstorm. After tonight, when all this was over, Eric would suggest they get together for a cup of coffee, or a bite to eat. If she wasn't yet ready for AA, at least they could talk.

One thing Eric knew how to do was talk. A corner of his mouth twisted up in a bitter smile. With Rose, hadn't he talked himself right out the door? Maybe, if he'd kept his mouth shut, and his heart tucked away instead of wearing it on his sleeve, it'd be Rose waiting for him at the end of a tough day, not just another meeting, or a fellow drunk in need of shoring up.

"Eric? Hey, this just came in from the newsroom." The evening shift's engineer, an older guy named Danny Wilkinson, stuck his head through the doorway. He was holding a faxed UPI report in one meaty hand. "Fire at West Seventy-ninth and Riverside, couple of casualties, no one seriously hurt," he reported, in the matter-of-fact tone typical of those in broadcasting. "One of the names looks familiar. Rose Griffin. Isn't she the lady you been seeing?"

Eric's heart took a flying leap and slammed into his rib cage. He sat for a moment, too stunned to say anything; then he was on his feet, snatching the sheet of paper from Wilkinson's hand. Rose? Christ Almighty. All this time he'd been sitting here working the lines, hoping to hear that Iris was okay, and *Rose* had been in jeopardy. Rose, who—despite what that damn wire report said—might be badly hurt.

A jolt of adrenaline kicked through him. He had to see her, find out for himself. Rose. *His* Rose. He scanned the three-line item. Beth Israel. She'd been taken to Beth Israel, along with a second victim, Rachel Rosenthal. Jesus. *Rachel, too?*

As he was rushing out the door, Eric was struck by the irony of it—his wanting to bring solace to a woman who'd ended their relationship, believing it would only wind up causing her pain. Rose had made it clear she didn't want him in her life, not on any kind of permanent basis. Why would this change anything?

Maybe it won't. But I have to be sure she's all right. I have to do SOMETHING.

Twenty minutes later, after a trip uptown in a cab that had been more like Mr. Toad's Wild Ride, Eric was pushing his way through the double doors of the emergency room. Thanks to AA, he knew every hospital in the city like the back of his hand. How many sponsorees had he visited here, and in other ERs? Drunks too out of it to realize they'd ruptured their guts, or cracked their skulls. Guys who were lectured by so-called professionals who didn't know what the fuck they were talking about.

He didn't bother with either of the two receptionists, who had their hands full with the family crowded in front of the desk, all of them jabbering at once in Spanish. Or the triage nurse in her Plexiglas cubicle, lifting a bloody shirttail to examine a wound on the back of a skinny, shell-shocked kid. He walked straight past the rows of glassy-eyed patients in plastic chairs, cradling a wrist or an elbow, or clutching a square of gauze to an eye in need of stitching. From years of experience, Eric had learned that, if you looked as though you knew exactly where you were going, you became virtually invisible.

Around the corner, outside the first door on his left, he found what he was looking for—a harried resident who didn't question his authority when Eric asked the whereabouts of Mrs. Griffin. The ponytailed young man, who would have been handsome if not for a complexion ravaged by acne, merely pointed toward a treatment room down the corridor before brushing past Eric on his way to another, clearly more pressing emergency.

Eric, his heart pounding with a mixture of relief and apprehension, walked slowly past a gurney parked haphazardly against the wall, and a thicket of IV poles, some of them still hung with bags of Ringer's solution. Any minute now, he thought, Rose's sons would be here, and probably her sister Marie. They wouldn't make him feel unwelcome—he was pretty sure of that. But *he* would know exactly where he stood. He'd see himself as they did: as little more than a glorified bystander.

And maybe, in the end, that's all he was. Someone who'd just happened along at a low point in Rose's life. A kindly stranger who'd given her a leg up, and a reason to go on.

Eric eased the door open. Rose lay asleep on the gurney. Other than a thick bandage covering most of her wrist, she didn't appear to be seriously injured. She was breathing with the help of an oxygen mask, but he guessed that the damage from whatever smoke she'd inhaled wasn't permanent.

Mostly, he wanted to sink to his knees beside her, just like in one of those corny TV movies. Take her hand—her capable hand, with its firm grip and pronounced bones, a map of every hard row she'd had to hoe—and press it to his heart, which was hammering hard enough to make him glad he was in a place where they would know what to do with him if it gave out.

Instead, he just stood there, staring at her. He smiled a little, even, thinking how it would embarrass her to know he was watching.

When her eyes fluttered open at one point, he started. But she wasn't seeing him. And whatever she'd murmured just then, it was just sleep-talk. She would have been annoyed at him, he knew, for listening in.

It was as if, even in her sleep, Rose was holding him at a distance, warning him without words to stand back. *Loving is too hard,* he could almost hear her say. *Even when you're loved in return, it can be snatched away from you at any moment.*

It doesn't have to be that way, he cried in silent protest. Who would know better than he—a recovering alcoholic who'd learned the hard way that, in the end, taking it one day at a time wasn't just a method of coping, *it was the whole point?* There was no pot of gold at the end of some mythical rainbow; the happiness in front of you was what you took away in your pocket.

Rose stirred, and her eyes fluttered open again. And this time she *did* see him—he could have sworn it—a brief flicker of recognition that cut through him like a scalpel. He loved her. And would go on loving her. Always. But maybe it had been prophetic in a way, that inscription in the Paris cemetery he'd carried in his head all these years—All My Love, Always. Maybe what he should have paid attention to was that it had been carved on a tombstone by a man mourning a love forever lost to him.

Eric turned away, and slipped from the room as quietly as he'd entered it. A group of doctors and nurses stood clustered in the hallway outside. One of them, a silver-haired department head, looked as if he was giving the others their marching orders. They didn't even glance at him as he walked past. For all he knew, he might truly have been invisible.

℘ Rose woke with a start, bewildered to find herself not in her own comfortable bed at home but in a hospital room. Weak sunlight spilled from an east-facing window onto a bed so white it looked pasteurized. Her head throbbed, and her arms felt as if they'd been yanked from their sockets, then shoved back in. For a disoriented moment, she wondered what on earth she was doing here . . . and then it all came rushing back. The fire. Dragging Rachel down the stairs. Being taken away in an ambulance.

"I thought *I* was supposed to be the one sleeping it off."

Rose darted a glance at the next bed, not entirely surprised to see Rachel lying beside her. She looked awful, like the victim of a barroom brawl, the left side of her face bruised, one eye swollen almost completely shut. But she hadn't lost her sense of humor. Rose made a face, and brought a hand to her own cheek in sympathy.

"I'm sorry. I shouldn't have hit you so hard."

"It's okay—I had it coming." Rachel managed a smile, which must have hurt, given the way she winced. "To tell the truth, I don't remember much. But they told me you saved my life. So I guess I'm the one who owes *you* an apology."

"Let's call it a draw, okay?" Rose found that it hurt to talk. Her throat was so sore, and her lungs felt as if they'd been stripped raw. And there was something else—something lurking in the back of her mind. . . .

It hit her with the force of a blow: Iris. What about Iris?

The dismay must have shown on her face, because Rachel picked up on it at once. She shook her head, rolling it back and forth on the pillow. "She wasn't in the house," she said hoarsely.

"How do you—?"

"That poor fireman . . . One minute I was out cold, and the next thing I knew I had him by the collar, and wouldn't let go until he told me they'd checked upstairs, and no one was there. Must have scared the shit out of him." She managed a wobbly half-smile. "I should feel relieved, I guess. But I still don't know where she is." A tear slipped from the corner of her good eye.

"Your house . . ." Rose felt her own eyes welling.

"No, *your* house," Rachel corrected. "And, either way, it's just a house. It's awful . . . but it isn't like losing a person."

"But . . ."

"No." Rachel's voice was stern. "We've got to stop this, Rose. Stop thinking about what we've lost—and start concentrating on what we still have left. I don't know where my daughter is. But when we find her . . ." She stopped, and swallowed hard.

Rose thought of Eric then. She couldn't shake the feeling that she'd seen him last night, here in this hospital . . .

Rose was flooded with a sharp sense of loss. She wouldn't miss Sylvie's house, but she would miss Eric. She would miss his face, with all its interesting, mismatched facets. She would miss his voice murmuring in her ear late at night, and his street smarts that hid an even sharper intellect. And the sex, too. But most of all, the sense of being loved for who she, Rose Santini Griffin, was . . .

But she didn't dare let herself dwell on Eric, not now. What about Drew? And Jay? Where were her sons? Had anyone called them? Dear God, Jay must have been scared out of his mind when she didn't come home last night.

The door to the room opened a crack, and a narrow figure sidled in as noiselessly as an alleycat. Marie. Rose was flooded with relief. If her sister was here, her sons couldn't be far behind.

Marie came to a halt between the beds, as if not sure in which direction to turn. She shot a wary glance at Rachel, who stared back with frank curiosity. Then Marie walked over and squeezed Rose's hand. Her fingernails were bitten to the quick, Rose saw, but her grip was as steely as ever.

"Hey, kiddo." Marie, with her usual disregard for the seasons, was wearing jeans and a midriff top that showed a slice of stomach as flat and white as a tortilla. A loose-fitting pink sweater hung over her bony frame. "Well, you did it. You finally succeeded in scaring the crap out of me—and, as you know, I don't scare too easy. When I first heard what had happened, I thought you'd bought the farm." She rubbed under one eye. "Drew and Jay are outside. I asked them to give me a minute. We visited last night, but you were out like a light."

Rose, feeling suddenly drowsy, allowed her eyes to drift shut. "They're okay?"

"They're fine . . . just a little shook up."

When she opened her eyes, Rose saw that Marie's gaze had wandered back to Rachel. "Jeez, how many rounds did *you* go?" she quipped.

"KO'ed in the third," Rachel responded with a weak laugh, not missing a beat.

Marie grinned. "Yeah, I can see it now. Around the eyes. You've got our dad's eyes." She looked back at Rose. "Not like this mutt here. I always figured Rose was some kind of throwback. Too ugly to keep, and too big to toss back." Her grin widened.

"Speak for yourself," Rose shot back. "By the way, have you told Clare what happened?"

"I called last night," Marie informed her with the face of someone biting into a lemon. Her shoe-black hair, tied back in a ponytail, made her look like an older, more hardbitten version of Veronica from the Archie comics. "Clare said to tell you she'll have Father say a mass for . . . well, whatever. If you ask me, you're lucky she lives too far away to visit. If it were me in that bed, a sick call from Our Lady of Humility would just about finish me off."

"Now I *know* we're related," Rachel said with a laugh. She eyed Marie critically, like a chess player contemplating her next move, then said, "You're pretty, you know. I never noticed that before. But you are."

Marie blushed. "Get out of here." Her voice was flat and unconvinced, but Rose could tell she was pleased. "I'm still waiting," she said gruffly. "You were supposed to let me know when would be a good time for us to get together."

"I will. As soon as I get out of here. As soon as—" Rachel's gaze was pulled away suddenly, and she gave a gasp.

It was Drew, walking into the room slightly ahead of someone Rose didn't recognize at first, a bedraggled figure who looked only vaguely familiar. A girl who reminded her a little of—

"Iris!" Rachel clapped a hand over her mouth, and let out a sob.

Rose watched her try to get up, but she was still too weak, and fell back with a strangled cry. It was Iris, poor Iris, looking as if she'd been fished out of the East River and left to dry on a subway grate, who shot across the room to fling herself into her mother's out-stretched arms.

Chapter 19

🌭 It comes in all sizes, Rachel thought. Like in supermarkets and drugstores—all those breakfast cereals, laundry detergents, headache medicines, promising better taste, whiter whites, faster relief. When you finally allow yourself to feel what you've been trying hard for a very long time *not* to feel, no one package can contain it all.

In the days and weeks following Iris' return, Rachel shed more tears than she would have thought possible. . . . In the hospital, clutching her daughter to her, she wept with relief and renewed hope. With sadness, too—for Mama, and for the house she'd never quite felt at home in, reduced now to ashes and rubble. It had hurt to cry—among her other injuries, she'd cracked a rib—but it also felt *good.* Healing, somehow. Though in many ways, she realized, the journey had just begun.

Iris wasn't hurt, as Rachel had feared. But she was far from all right, either. Yet the thing for which Rachel had been least prepared was that somehow *she* was no longer responsible for her daughter. Drew, it seemed, had taken charge, with Iris' consent, while Rachel—Mother, Healer, Saviour—had become little more than a bit player. At Eric's suggestion, Drew had been in touch with the Meadows, a residential facility in Arizona that was well known, she was told, for treating people like Iris who'd been traumatized as children. He and Iris had discussed it. And Iris had agreed it would be the best thing for her right now.

When Brian, who'd caught the first plane out of Cincinnati, arrived home, Rachel had even allowed herself to fall apart—just a little. He'd held her, stroked her, murmured all the right things.

They'd been a united front, working in tandem to do whatever needed to be done. Health-insurance forms. Travel arrangements. Long conferences over the phone, both with Dr. Eisenger, and with the psychiatrist at the Meadows who would be evaluating Iris.

Getting their daughter off to Arizona turned out to be less wrenching, in the end, than Rachel had feared. Drew and Iris had decided together that he would go with her. And though Rachel had argued that it ought to be herself and Brian, Iris' *parents*, and had wept at the airport after seeing them off, she'd nonetheless come away feeling proud of her daughter for taking a stand, however small, concerning her future.

Maybe I've done TOO much for her, Rachel had thought; *maybe that's part of the problem.*

Drew, she knew from talking to him, had reached the same conclusion—that his protectiveness, his constantly picking up the pieces, had ultimately done Iris more harm than good. He loved her and truly wanted the best for her, but he had his own life, too. Maybe someday they would get married. They'd have to wait and see. . . .

It makes sense, Rachel thought wearily. In life, she had learned, there was no such thing as Happily Ever After. Look at Brian and her. Time-out had been declared—as it had been after Mama's death—but nothing had been resolved. Not really.

Now, just two short weeks since their daughter had left, and they were back to tiptoeing around one another. Polite. Careful. Limiting their discussions mostly to Iris—the progress they'd been told she was making, what they might find when they flew out for family week. The atmosphere at home so strained that returning to work sooner than she really should have was a relief.

She'd cried out all her tears. She was like an empty bowl rinsed clean. Yet this didn't stop her from aching inside—not only for what she'd lost, but for what remained to be taken from her.

Brian was going to leave her. Soon. She was almost sure of it. She could see it even in the thoughtful way he sifted through drawers—as if cataloguing the remnants of their life—and in the gentleness with which he spoke to her, as if there was no longer any point in raising his voice, or even being angry.

Rachel had thought all her capacity for pain and anxiety had boarded that plane along with her daughter, but still, oh God, it hurt. She almost wished she could go a little crazy, as she had in the midst of that horrible fire, and grab hold of what was so clearly slipping away. But it would do her no more good than if she'd been snatching at smoke. Nothing to hold on to. Not anymore.

The best thing was to seek comfort where she could. In her work.

But that, it turned out, had lost its capacity to make her forget everything else.

When Rachel, bent over a stack of files on her desk, heard her intercom beep, she assumed it was about the budget for the computer system that was being installed, or the director of Community Health Fund, to whom she'd put in a call earlier that day.

She couldn't admit, even to herself, how desperately she hoped it would be her husband. The flimsiest excuse would do—dry-cleaning that needed to be picked up, a book or magazine at home that he couldn't find, a phone number he needed. If Brian had asked, Rachel would have dropped everything and rushed home to show him where she kept an extra supply of Band-Aids.

Instead, when she punched the blinking line button, it turned out to be the last person in the world Rachel had expected to hear from.

"Sister Alice," announced her secretary, in a hushed voice. "It sounds pretty urgent."

The principal of Holy Angels, in fact, was in a panic. When Rose's secretary put her through, it was several long moments before the old nun could get control of her labored breathing long enough to speak.

"One of my girls . . ." she gasped. "Asking for you . . . won't let anyone else near her . . ."

"What's wrong?" Rachel spoke more briskly than usual in an attempt to mask her astonishment.

"She's . . . I think . . . in labor. . . ."

Rachel, her old strength flooding back as suddenly as if a switch had been flicked on, grabbed her medical bag and dashed out the door. When she arrived at Holy Angels, the hulking old brick building was humming—clusters of uniformed girls in the hallways, speaking in hushed whispers; worried-looking nuns halfheartedly attempting to shoo them into the chapel, without much success; the poodle-haired secretary Rachel remembered from the administration office actually wringing her hands, like a bad actress in some amateur production.

Sister Alice, gliding down the corridor to greet her on invisible greased tracks, was the biggest shock of all. The old woman seemed to have shrunk since the last time Rachel had seen her, her tiny proportions no longer reminding Rachel of a plaster saint but of some unearthly gnome. Her doughy face had sunk in on itself, with only her small wintry-blue eyes as sharp as ever. In Sister Alice's tightly pursed mouth, Rachel saw that she was not at all pleased to have had to summon her, that she would not have done so except under the most dire circumstances.

"Thank you for getting here so quickly, Dr. Rosenthal. Come with me, please." She gestured for Rachel to follow her.

The old toothpaste-green linoleum crackled faintly under Rachel's shoes as she hurried after Sister Alice under the ceiling's harsh fluorescents. At the far end of the corridor, the door to one of the classrooms stood open. Rachel stepped inside, glancing about. Nothing out of the ordinary here—rows of chairs with kidney-shaped desktops attached; a blackboard on which math equations were scribbled in slanting columns; a terrarium in one corner, in which, as far as she could see, nothing but algae was being cultivated.

Then she heard it. Coming from the cloakroom in back—the sound of someone moaning in pain. Once she entered the dim space, which smelled of damp wool and lunchboxes, Rachel had to blink several times before her eyes adjusted. While Sister Alice, behind her, groped for the chain to switch on the overhead bulb, Rachel knelt before the frightened girl huddled in one corner.

She couldn't have been more than thirteen, fourteen. But unlike Elvie Rodriguez, this girl's naturally heavy build had enabled her to mask her pregnancy well into her last month. Now there was no longer any hope of hiding it. She lay on her side, clutching her belly, her pale face clenched.

Rachel touched her shoulder, asking, "When did the pains start?"

The girl shook her head, unable to speak. She was unusually pretty in a Rubenesque sort of way, with a porcelain complexion and huge brown eyes. Yet Rachel was certain she'd never seen her before; she would have remembered. So why had this perfect stranger demanded that she come?

Perhaps noting her confusion, Sister Alice supplied, "Her name is Dolores Loyola. She's one of our eighth-graders."

"Dolores. Don't be afraid. I'm here to help you." Rachel pressed a hand to Dolores' rounded belly. The girl seemed to relax slightly, but the noises coming from low in her throat were those made by nearly every woman in the last stage of labor; it meant there was no time to get this girl to the hospital. Her baby was going to be born right here in this cloakroom.

Rachel felt her years of training and experience kick in like the engine of a faithful old car that had been up on blocks for a while. She reached for her medical bag, barking over her shoulder, "Get me some clean towels. A sheet of butcher paper will do, if you have it. Hurry!"

To her credit, Sister Alice didn't flinch. By the time she returned with a roll of plain newsprint and a handful of towels, Rachel had gotten Dolores onto her back, her underwear off, a folded coat supporting her head. Her water had broken earlier, it turned out. The poor girl had been too scared to tell anyone.

Minutes later, almost before Rachel had wriggled her hands into a pair of surgical gloves, Dolores began to push. Between her trembling legs, the baby's head appeared—a half-dollar–sized crown of black hair, matted with blood and white vernix. As Rachel urged Dolores on, while at the same time gently rotating the baby's head into position, a surge of adrenaline nearly lifted her off the floor. Oh, how she'd missed this! However crude the setting, however wrong that a girl so young be wrenched from innocence as suddenly and violently as this one, the miracle of new life could not be denied. Rachel, her hands now guiding the infant's shoulders through the narrow perineal opening, was seized by a sense of primal wonder so powerful it was dizzying.

"You're doing just fine, Dolores. That's it, sweetie. Just a few more pushes," she coached, astonished at the smoothness of this birth. Usually girls this young had insufficiently developed pelvises. But Dolores' broad hips were to her advantage. "You can do it. This will all be over very soon."

Dolores, her face contracted into a scarlet fist, heaved a massive grunt, and now came the baby's torso and legs in a last, slippery rush. A girl. Rachel had to bite her lower lip to keep from uttering a joyous shout.

When Rachel rose, cradling the infant, wrapped in a clean towel, the old nun surprised her by reaching out to take it from her. An expression of grudging tenderness flitted across a face clearly unused to such emotions. Gazing down at the tiny pink face swaddled in white toweling, she observed in an odd, cracked voice, "Jesus was born in a stable."

Rachel, who'd attended Hebrew school and, when she was Dolores' age, celebrated her Bat Mitzvah, nodded solemnly. She and Sister Alice exchanged a long look—and in the nun's wintry blue eyes, Rachel, just before she kneeled to attend to her patient, caught a spark of admiration.

Later, when she thought back on this afternoon, a sense of pervading wonder would remain with her like the afterglow of a bright light that's been extinguished. Along with the baby that had arrived so unexpectedly, and unceremoniously, in this dreary cloakroom, Rachel felt as if something else had been brought to life as well—her own deep connectedness to the thing she loved most, the thing she'd been trained to do: practicing medicine.

Her heart full of gratitude for the gift she'd received as well as given, Rachel gazed down at the drawn face of the girl lying exhausted on a pallet of towels and coats. Smoothing away the strands of dark hair pasted to her sweaty forehead, Rachel soothed, "You were so brave. And your baby is fine. But, sweetie, why me? What made you insist on *me?*"

Dolores gave a wan smile, her expressive brown eyes lifting to meet Rachel's gaze. In a small, quavery voice she replied, "My mother, she told me about you. The nice lady doctor. When I was born, Mami said it was *you* who delivered me."

🍂 That evening, Rachel served a dinner she'd actually cooked. Chicken breasts marinated in white wine and rosemary, wild rice, a green salad. It wouldn't win any culinary award, she knew, but it was homemade . . . and it had kept her hands busy while her brain churned on overload.

She had made up her mind about something, a life change so vital for her—and so crucial for them—that, if Brian's reaction wasn't what she hoped it would be, it would kill her. That was why she hadn't told him sooner; too much was riding on it. If she didn't say it just right . . . if he wasn't in the mood to listen, or was simply too fed up with her to care . . .

I'll tell him after dinner, she thought, too nervous to do more than pick at her food.

She watched Brian across the table. She couldn't tell whether or not he was enjoying the meal, though he ate in respectful silence, and she saw that he'd changed out of his jeans and flannel shirt. She couldn't help noticing how unusually polite he was being, too. As if he were a guest at the table of a treasured but somewhat dotty aunt.

"I ran out of ideas by the time I got to dessert," she apologized lightly as she was clearing away their plates. "I think there's some ice cream in the freezer, though. Ben and Jerry's," she added, hoping to tempt him into sitting with her a bit longer.

Brian was leaving tomorrow, Minneapolis this time, to meet with an important independent bookseller. And she had the feeling that if she didn't say something—*do* something now—when he got back, it would be too late.

"No. Thanks. What I'd really like . . ." Brian stood up, gently removing the stacked plates from her hands and placing them on the table. ". . . is to know what's going on. All evening, you've been acting like a tiger in a cage. Is it something to do with Iris?"

Rachel hardly knew where to begin. When she told him, would he react the way she hoped he would? "It's not Iris. I spoke with her counselor today. Doug says she's making progress. We'll know more when we go out there for family week." She felt suddenly shy, but forced herself to meet Brian's cool gray gaze; he was waiting for her to continue. *Slow and steady. Deep breaths. That's it.* "I had a long talk with Kay this afternoon," she began in a calm voice, her heart rearing up in her chest. "I asked her to take over as director of the clinic. And—she said she would. It'll mean hiring someone to fill her old position . . . but with the money Mama left me, we can swing it."

Except for the momentary surprise that crossed his face like headlights flaring on a dark road late at night, Brian's flat expression didn't change. He asked, "What will you do?"

"Practice medicine," she told him. "At the clinic, of course. But no more administrative duties."

"Somehow, I can't picture it. You stepping aside just like that."

"Try me."

Brian folded his arms over his chest. "What brought on this

sudden change of heart?" Not the pleased response she'd been hoping for. Not even close.

Rachel, struggling to keep her disappointment from showing, looked down at the tablecloth, a vast Mexican shawl she'd bought in an outdoor marketplace during a trip to Mazatlán, when they were first married. Its colors had faded over the years, but she liked it even more—its former vibrance replaced by something even better: wit and character.

She lifted her eyes, feeling them blaze with sudden heat, and imagining how she must look to Brian: a woman on fire—a fire that, in the past, had excited him. In a low, taut voice, she said, "You want the truth? It was everything. You, me, Iris, Mama. But every major decision has a catalyst, and today I was given one." Rachel told him about the unexpected arrival of the baby at Holy Angels. Forcing a wan smile, she added, "Sister Alice would have called it a miracle, I suppose, if she'd been in my shoes."

Brian listened thoughtfully, but remained expressionless. Oh, her heart was going to break! She could feel it happening already.

"You're sure this is what you want?" Brian asked.

Rachel stared at him, longing to demand, *Is it still what* you *want? A real* wife, *rather than one who's too tired most of the time to do more than simply go through the motions?* But, no, she'd put it off for so long. Brian had gotten tired of waiting.

Now she stood waiting for her own heart to stop its frantic racing. When it didn't, she realized the only cure was to take the final plunge.

"I'm not sure of anything, except what I *don't* want," she said, quietly. "Mainly, I don't want to lose you. Not just because I've lost so much already. Because I love you. Brian, I want us to start over. Not from the beginning—we can never do that. But from *here.* I want us to go someplace warm where we can sleep late, and lie on the beach, and make love whenever we feel like it."

Brian was silent for so long that she became convinced that he was merely embarrassed for her, that he was working up the courage to say, *It's too late for that. It's time to move on.* . . .

But he didn't say those things. He continued to regard her with those thoughtful eyes of his, which reflected every storm they'd weathered, every gray sky since passed. Then, with an odd, almost stilted formality, he stepped forward and put out his hand—like a nineteenth-century gentleman at a ball, asking her to dance. When Rachel took it, rising to meet him, she saw that his eyes were wet. Letting out a sigh that seemed to release something tightly wound inside him, he folded her in his arms and murmured into her hair, "Did you have anywhere special in mind?"

Rachel relaxed a little, but couldn't stop trembling. "I was thinking of Maui," she managed in a small, weak voice, nothing like her normal one. "We could fly there straight from Arizona."

Brian threw his head back in a hearty laugh. "Rachel. You're incredible."

"Why is that?"

"The way you'll put a thing off practically forever, then break your neck trying to get it done all at once. Knowing you, you've probably booked our seats already."

"I only checked to see which flights are available," she informed him with mock primness. "You're under no obligation whatsoever."

"Is that so?"

"Maybe you have a better idea."

"Rachel, you idiot." Still laughing, he lifted her off the floor, twirling her around so abruptly she bumped her foot on a chair leg. "I'd be happy if we stayed home and dined on Chef Boyardee for a week, as long as we're together. But if you have your mind made up about Maui, then Maui it is."

He kissed her then, and for Rachel it was like coming home after a long, long absence. She clung to him, trying not to cry, but crying anyway, tears of happiness for a change. Sometimes, she thought, even when it seemed as if nothing would ever again turn out right, you got lucky.

A feeling she hadn't had in quite a while was stirring in her. One that had less to do with the thought of palm trees and tropical breezes than with her husband's arms around her, and his warm breath ruffling her hair. She kissed his ear and whispered, "For the time being, would you settle for just me?"

Chapter 20

❧ "Good evening everyone, and welcome to the East Midtown Plaza Group of Alcoholics Anonymous. My name is Jack, and I'm an alcoholic . . ."

Mandy studied the man at the podium, a good-looking young guy in a suit and tie, and thought, *He doesn't look like a drunk.* But, to be honest, neither did most of the people around her. In this drafty church basement, with its rows of metal folding chairs, industrial-sized coffeemaker, and bulletin board announcing a special Holy Trinity service, she didn't feel all that out of place, not really. With the exception of the few who looked as if they'd spent the night in less-than-cozy surroundings, the crowd of fifty or so was made up mostly of professionals like her, all of them nicely dressed, many with briefcases. She guessed the average age to be around thirty-five.

Quiet surprise rippled through her, along with a definite uneasiness. If these people were alcoholics, then where was the line separating them from *her?* Obviously, they hadn't just stumbled in off the streets. More like an executive boardroom, or racquetball court. What had brought them here? An ultimatum from their boss? A family sick and tired of their excuses? Or maybe the burden of leading a double life had finally become too much, the way it had for her with Robert.

Robert. She still felt bad about him . . . but he wasn't the main reason she was here tonight. It wasn't even Rose's ultimatum, or the nerve-racking tension of walking a daily tightrope. The straw that had broken the camel's back, Mandy thought, had been her brother. Drew had relied on her to help him out in an emergency, which she *had*—making calls, searching shelters—but not without a dangerously close call that had nearly caused her to drink again. And what would Drew have done then? She couldn't have lived with the knowledge that she'd let her sweet, loving brother down when he needed her most.

Mandy shot a sidelong glance at Eric, seated beside her. Tonight was a speaker's meeting, he'd explained, and it was Eric who'd been asked to address the not-so-motley crew. She thought he looked remarkably relaxed, considering. Faded jeans, kickabout loafers, denim jacket. Mandy could see why her stepmother found him so appealing—he was sexy and smart, sure, but mostly just *nice*. Not in a nerdy way, but in the best possible sense. When she'd called from the deli, he hadn't embarrassed her by making a big deal of it. He hadn't seemed put out, either. He'd just listened.

Watching him amble up to the front of the room and lean into the podium, she thought, *He'd be good for Rose. Daddy would approve.*

In a relaxed, conversational tone, as if chatting with a fellow passenger on an airplane, Eric began to speak. "Hi, I'm Eric, and I'm an alcoholic." Pause. "Five years ago, I sat in my first meeting, and there was this guy, a big, burly mother—long-distance trucker from Tallahassee, with twenty years of hard drinking under his belt. We couldn't have had less in common, but the funny thing was, he was telling my story. . . ."

Mandy listened, enthralled and more than a little taken aback by Eric's tale, which made her own seem tame by comparison. She heard how his beer-guzzling college days had slipped seamlessly from the anything-goes seventies into the high-rolling eighties, where weekend house parties in Cannes and Laurel Canyon, at which lines of blow were laid out like pretzels, were the norm. His drinking had cost him not only his high-profile job, he said, but, indirectly, the life of a female colleague.

Mandy thought about her own job, and how close she stood to losing it. And Robert, whom she'd apparently blown off one time too many. But what if something even worse were to happen? What if she were to *die* because of her drinking—or cause someone else's death? She shuddered, finding it harder than ever to maintain the pleasantly detached expression she'd put on at the door like a mask.

Truthfully, being here wasn't making it any easier. Her craving hadn't gone away; if anything, it was stronger than ever. Okay, so the AA chapter in this neighborhood wasn't just a bunch of losers with nowhere else to go. But did that necessarily mean they were all in the exact same boat? Or that she should trust them with her most private thoughts and feelings?

Nevertheless, she smiled at Eric's jokes, and applauded along with the others when he stepped down. Afterwards, she even introduced herself to the person seated next to her, as she was urged to, an older woman with immaculately coiffed silver hair who looked too respectable and dignified to have indulged in anything more than an occasional glass of sherry. When the meeting was over, and those who seemed to know one another had drifted to the coffee machine to chat, Mandy let out a surreptitious sigh of relief.

Wandering over to the door, her coat folded neatly over her arm, she waited for Eric to finish chatting with one of the Young Turks—a well-dressed young man in what looked like an Armani suit. He would probably ask what she'd thought of the meeting, so she took the opportunity to compose in her head a polite, noncommittal response.

But Eric asked none of the obvious questions. As they strolled toward Madison Avenue, he asked instead about her job, and her family. He was easy to talk to. Before she knew it, she found herself telling him about her dad, what a wonderful father he'd been— funny, affectionate, overly protective at times, yet firm when necessary. It crossed her mind briefly that Eric might feel a little threatened, given that he was Rose's boyfriend. But if he had a problem with Rose's having been married to someone as marvelous as her dad, he was keeping it to himself. That was another thing about him Mandy liked. She felt so relaxed around him; there was no need to explain or justify herself. Nothing she needed to hide, or be ashamed of.

Still, it *was* sort of weird that he wasn't preaching to her about AA. Wasn't that the whole point of her attending the meeting? If anything, it was Eric who appeared in need of comfort. Beneath his relaxed-seeming banter, she caught the tense air of a man at some sort of crossroads. Had he and Rose had a fight? Come to think of it, she hadn't noticed any sign of him when she'd visited Rose at the hospital.

Before she knew what she was doing, Mandy found herself casually offering, "Buy you a cup of coffee?"

Eric nodded. "I could use one."

They stopped at a coffee shop on the corner, one of a thousand sprinkled like fire hydrants throughout the city—Greek diners masquerading as luncheonettes until you looked closely at the menu, which featured dishes like moussaka, souvlaki, and tzaziki. Still, there was something to be said for the generic familiarity of its faded vinyl banquettes, chrome napkin-dispensers, and inedible-looking cakes and pies displayed in their revolving glass case as lovingly as Tiffany jewels.

They ordered coffee, which came in thick white mugs and smelled as if it had been poured out of an auto shop's drip pan. Eric sipped his in silence. He hardly looked at her, even though she was directly across from him. Whatever was on his mind, Mandy thought, he clearly wasn't pondering whether or not she planned to attend the next AA meeting.

She touched his elbow. "Want to talk about it?"

"Not much to say." He brought his gaze back to Mandy, the corners of his eyes—eyes the blue of faded denim and desert skies—crinkled in a wry smile over the rim of his mug. Then he grimaced. "This stuff is really awful, isn't it? They ought to sell it by the slice, like meatloaf."

"You were really brilliant at the meeting," she told him.

Eric shrugged, and went back to staring sightlessly at his ghostly reflection in the window. "I wasn't there to impress anyone. That's not what it's about."

Uh-oh, she thought, *here it comes. The big pitch.* But Eric remained lost in his thoughts. Almost in desperation, Mandy found herself volunteering, "It wasn't what I was expecting. I don't know what I thought the people would be like. Easier to catalogue, I guess. But that doesn't necessarily mean I plan to go back. I . . . Oh shit, I don't know *what* I mean." Abruptly, she shoved her mug away; some of the coffee slopped over onto the Formica tabletop.

"You still don't get it, do you?" Eric studied her carefully, seeming almost irritated with her. "It's not just about *you,* Mandy. It's about me, too. And the guy in front of you, and behind you. And the woman who stood up at the end to share. Did you notice how no one arrived late? Did it strike you as a little odd that the meeting started exactly on time? Think about it. Think about all the times we were drunk and showed up late, or not at all. Any reminder of those days, however slight, is uncomfortable, even a little scary. *That's* what brings us to meetings. Our shared experience. Our mutual fears. Knowing it's not a choice, but a matter of survival."

"How? *How* can it help to share all those memories with people you don't even know?" she demanded in a low voice, feeling attacked somehow—though, rationally, she knew he'd done no such thing.

"Why *did* you go, then?" he asked, not rudely, but with a frankness she found disconcerting.

She looked down at the table, at the coffee spill soaking into the napkin she'd tossed over it—a soggy brown mess that made her feel faintly nauseous. "I . . . I'm not exactly sure. My brother, I guess. It scared me, how close I came to letting him down."

"But you didn't."

"Thanks to you."

"Believe me, whatever I did was as much for me as it was for you," he said. "If I can help, it helps me. As simple as that. There's nothing saintly about it. I can't even explain how it works. It just does."

"You don't seem very happy right now," she said levelly.

"Who said happiness was part of the deal?" Eric gave a low, ragged laugh. Under the diner's blue-white fluorescents, he looked tired: his lids heavy and faintly bruised-looking, his shoulders bent as if he were bearing up under a tremendous weight.

"You two had a fight, didn't you? And now you miss her—Rose." Mandy cocked her head at him, feeling envious in a way. She wondered what it would be like to love someone that much, to the point where missing them was worse even than not being able to drink.

Eric nodded. He was watching a pair of heavyset cops who'd bellied up to the counter and were shooting the breeze with the hostess, a middle-aged woman with bad skin and a bulletproof beehive. But there was no animation in his gaze; he might have been staring at a brick wall.

Finally, he shrugged and said, "Yeah, I miss her."

"Why don't you call her, then?"

He smiled—a genuine smile, if a sad one. "It wouldn't do any good, that's why."

Mandy shook her head in fond commiseration. "She can be pretty stubborn, I know."

"It's not just that. She misses your father . . . a lot more than she'll miss me."

"I miss him, too. That's not going to bring him back, is it?"

"Look, the ball's in her court. There's nothing more I can do."

She covered his hand with hers. "You want to talk about it? If nothing else, you'll feel better."

Eric hesitated, then slowly nodded. He told Mandy about how, from the moment he'd laid eyes on Rose, he'd known she was the woman he'd been holding out for all these years. Corny but true, he said with the faintly amused air of a man who wouldn't have believed it himself had he not experienced it firsthand. Even so, he hadn't expected her to feel the same way, not at first. What he *had* hoped was that, in time, she would come to understand that second chances were made, not given, and that sometimes the prize was worth all the effort. But Rose, as it turned out, had had other ideas. She didn't want another husband, she'd told him. And she had no intention of risking a broken heart again. Ever.

Mandy listened without moving even the tiniest muscle. She thought about Robert. Was it possible he'd felt that way about her? Just a little? If she hadn't pushed him away, would he eventually have wanted to marry her? She would never know, and that bothered her. It bothered her a lot.

"Aren't you angry?" Mandy asked.

He thought for moment, then said, "Yeah . . . but not at her."

"I think I know what you mean." She watched an old man seated at the counter slowly spooning up soup, as if trying to make it last as long as he could. Didn't he have a family to go to? A wife, or even a grown child? What made this place preferable even to heating up a can of Campbell's at home? "It's how I feel about my drinking," she said, inexplicably on the verge of tears. "Pissed off. With no one to blame but myself."

"I wouldn't exactly put Rose in the same category, but . . . yeah." His face relaxed without brightening. "What about you? Didn't I hear something about a boyfriend?"

"Former," she told him, hoping her droll delivery would help dislodge the fishhook of regret buried in her belly.

Somehow, it was working. She felt . . . if not *better*, exactly . . . then easier somehow. As if, after a lifetime of faking it, she could finally be comfortable in her own skin. She couldn't have said why. Her life was no less screwed up than it had been an hour ago. But for the first time, Mandy felt it might just be possible to forgive herself for being less than perfect.

It occurred to her that, while she'd been listening to Eric pour his heart out, her own had been given a much-needed break.

"Want to talk about it?" Eric smiled archly, tossing the ball back to her court.

"Can't," she told him, glancing at her watch. "I should get going." Not a lie. She *did* want to talk about it—suddenly, surprisingly, as if a cloud had lifted—but not to Eric. The person who needed to hear it was Robert himself.

An hour later, Mandy called him from her apartment. She'd

waited until she was pretty sure he'd be home, but there was no answer; his machine wasn't picking up, either. Each ring sent her heart crashing into her rib cage like a wrecking ball. He was out with someone new, probably. Tired of Mandy's excuses, he'd moved on to someone who no doubt returned his interest. And who could blame him?

She'd started to hang up when Robert's voice came on the line, startling her so that she nearly dropped the receiver. He sounded out of breath, as if he'd had to dash to answer it.

"It's me—Mandy. Did you just get in?"

"I was in the shower," he told her, adding with a sigh, "Long day. I'll tell you about it sometime."

"How about over dinner tomorrow night?" She closed her eyes.

There was a pause, in which she could hear him breathing softly. *I knew it,* she thought with a thud of despair. *He's seeing another woman. I'm only making a fool of myself.* But maybe, deep down, hadn't that been the real purpose of this exercise in humiliation? Wasn't it just the excuse she needed to pour herself a nice fat bourbon and soda?

No, she told herself firmly, *that's NOT why I called.* This wasn't about Robert, or who he might be seeing. It was for *her.* She had to be honest with him, come clean about why she'd been avoiding him. Even if he thought less of her because of it, she would feel better about herself.

Mandy sank down on the sofa, amid the strewn pages of this morning's newspaper, a coffee cup she'd been in too much of a hurry to rinse sitting on the table before her; it was a welcome clutter somehow, one she could look at without feeling a vague sense of shame, wondering how it had gotten there.

"Robert?" she prodded.

"I'm still here," he said. "Just kind of surprised, is all. I figured you'd cooled off."

"Oh, Robert." She put her feet up on the coffee table, remembering that was one of the things you were supposed to do when feeling lightheaded. "I'm sorry. I should have told you sooner. It has nothing to do with *you*."

"What is it, then?"

"It's a long story," she sighed. "Are you up for it?"

"Absolutely."

Mandy brought her head to rest on the back of the sofa and, with her eyes closed, smiled. More stupefied than relieved. But certain she was doing the right thing. She didn't know if her story would have a happy ending or not, but Robert, even if he walked away for good, deserved to hear it.

She arranged to meet him at seven-thirty, at a French bistro close to her office. Robert wrote down the address, and said lightly, "If I get there first, should I order red or white?"

"Neither for me," she said, as casually as she dared, hoping her trembling voice wouldn't reveal her resolve for exactly what it was: a whisper still only on the verge of becoming a shout. "I won't be having any."

Chapter 21

🌺 It was the first thing Rose noticed as she emerged from the charred remains of the house into the cold sunlight out back. The garden—trampled by fallen debris and, in the weeks since the fire, a steady parade of fire inspectors, claims investigators, city officials, and trespassers ranging from the curious to the malicious—was showing signs of life. The grass, immune to the seasons, had started to come back in several spots. And on the few remaining branches of the poplar tree, bright-yellow leaves fluttered like the brave, tattered flag of a vanquished army.

It was here, right here in this garden, Rose decided, that she would have them place the bronze plaque in Sylvie's honor. When the house had been razed, and the new building erected on the old foundation, they would have a dedication ceremony. Sylvie would have liked that, she thought. It probably wouldn't have occurred to her to do what Rose had done—donate the land to charity—but Rose felt sure she would have understood. What sweeter justice than Faith House—a nonprofit adoption agency that would serve as temporary shelter for unwanted children as well.

Still, it was sad seeing the place like this. Knowing that what lay ahead was more than just a new chapter—it was a whole new book. She wouldn't come here again, not for a while. But she'd needed to see it just one last time.

Beside her, Jay, unusually quiet even for him, spoke at last. "Mom. Let's go. It's creepy here. Besides, there's broken glass and stuff. If you step on it and get hurt, you'll have no one to sue."

She shot him a narrow, sideways glance. "Very funny, wiseguy."

"I'm serious." Jay stuffed his hands in his pockets, squinting at what was left of the garden walls, now mostly a tumble of bricks, smoke-blackened and marred with graffiti. He seemed to have sprouted up another inch in the past month or so, but maybe she was just imagining it. One way or another, he *had* grown. It was as if everything coming to a head in their lives had matured him in a way. He didn't resist her anymore, for one thing. It wasn't that he'd run out of things to complain about, or criticize her for—but they found plenty to laugh about, too. Rose had the feeling, though she wouldn't have bet on it just yet, that Jay was on her team.

"I wonder what Dad would have said," Jay remarked calmly. In his slim-fitting jeans and nylon windbreaker, with the breeze blowing his dark hair back from his forehead, he could have been Drew's age.

"About the fire, you mean?"

"Not just that. *All* the stuff that's been going on."

Rose thought for a moment before answering firmly, "He'd have said it was time to move on."

"It's hard sometimes. I still miss him." Jay screwed his eyes up even more fiercely, making her think of someone peering into a pair of binoculars, trying to bring some distant horizon into focus.

"Me, too," she said.

She held back from saying that Max wasn't the only one she missed. Jay might get the wrong idea; he might not understand how it was possible to mourn one person . . . and, at the same time, yearn for another. It had been a month since she'd last seen or spoken with Eric. He'd kept his word, and hadn't called. But it wasn't the same as with Max. She knew exactly how to get in touch with Eric—and often did, without him knowing it.

It was her guilty little secret, one she hadn't confessed to a soul: every day, at some point between eleven and two, she locked the door to her office and, for half an hour or so, she listened on her Walkman to the *Eric Sandstrom Show*.

He was good. He knew how to draw people out, how to get them to open up without browbeating them. He seemed genuinely to *care,* and Rose knew it wasn't just an act. Even the celebrities and politicians he interviewed were disarmed.

It wasn't the same as actually *talking* to him, of course. But that would be too risky; it would be like inviting him to a party she wasn't planning to throw. They'd both be miserable.

With the toe of her high heel, Rose nudged a strip of metal bent and twisted beyond recognition. "You're right, it *is* creepy. Let's get going. We don't want to be late."

They were meeting Drew and Mandy at St. Joseph's Cemetery on Long Island. It had been over a year since she had stood at Max's freshly dug grave and watched as his coffin was lowered into it, the clouds overhead skating across its polished surface like frosty exhaled breath. Rose hadn't been back since. She didn't believe in making pilgrimages to gravesites. What was a cold granite headstone compared with a pillow still smelling of the husband you loved?

But today, the last Sunday in October, would have been Max's seventieth birthday. It had seemed important to her that his family mark the occasion with some kind of ritual. And there was something about the solemn dignity of a cemetery that appealed to her Catholic upbringing. She wouldn't be lighting a candle for Max in church, or kneeling in prayer, but she could stand at his grave and remember all the good times.

"Can I drive?" Jay asked.

He'd gotten his license last month, but trusting her younger son behind the wheel of their Volvo still felt to Rose like walking blindfolded down the middle of a busy street.

"Sure," she said with forced ease, unable to refrain from adding, "if you promise to be careful."

"Look at it this way, if we get killed in an accident, at least we'll be near a cemetery." Jay shot her an evil grin, and Rose laughed in spite of herself. He may have gotten his eyes and his math skills from his dad, but his morbid sense of humor came directly from her.

The traffic on the LIE was worse than she'd anticipated. In spite of the chilly weather, there were obviously plenty of weekenders for whom the onset of fall—with its nearly deserted beaches and empty parking lots—was more enticing than a Fourth of July picnic. Rose herself had a healthy respect for the seasons. Whatever else was going on in your life, she thought, you could always count on them to be at least one constant. And each one had its pleasures, to be doled out like Halloween candy, nobody getting more or less than anyone else. Seasons even gave you an excuse to do things you might have put off otherwise, like spring cleaning, fall tune-ups, and winterizing, not to mention getting in shape for swimsuit weather.

By the time their Volvo coasted through the pillared entrance to the cemetery, with its scrolled wrought-iron gates and lifesize marble statue that looked more like an avuncular master of ceremonies than St. Joseph, Rose wasn't surprised to see that Mandy and Drew had gotten there ahead of them. Mandy was wearing a green coat, and carrying a paper cone of flowers. She looked brighter somehow, as if, like Sylvie's garden, all her colors that had been faded were beginning to revive. Rose had heard from Drew that she was regularly attending AA meetings, though Mandy hadn't discussed it with her, and Rose hadn't asked. Right now, as Mandy kissed her cheek, leaving behind only a faint trace of perfume, nothing more, Rose was told all she needed to know.

Drew, on the other hand, looked tired. Thinner, too. Still, the haunted look in his eyes was gone, and there was a new resolve to him. He seemed more sure of himself, and of where he was headed. Whether or not Iris, still in Arizona, was going to be a part of his future remained to be seen, but either way, he'd thrown himself headlong into his first year of med school.

Together, the four of them trooped along the gravel paths, armed with a map, on which Max's plot was circled in yellow felt pen. It even had a number, C-125. For some reason, that depressed Rose even more than the sterile-looking graves with their pathetically stilted inscriptions.

"Here it is." Mandy, who'd wandered off the path onto the grass, pointed out a headstone that looked as if it had been recently installed.

Yes, Rose saw, it was the one she'd ordered. Polished black granite inscribed simply with Max's name and the dates of his birth and death. She'd resisted the impulse to include declarations about what a devoted husband he'd been, and how beloved by his children. They all knew exactly what Max had meant to them, so what would have been the point?

Drew, after a moment of reflection, remarked, "It's not what I was expecting, somehow."

"It's plain, I know," Rose said. "Daddy would have hated anything else."

He looked at her, brushing a lock of dark hair from his forehead. "That's not what I meant. I wasn't thinking it should be fancier. It just . . . it doesn't seem to have anything to *do* with Dad."

Rose thought of all the usual clichéd disclaimers. Like, *He's in our hearts.* Or *We've never been a very religious family, I know.* But she didn't say them. All she said was, "I know."

Drew was right. Wherever Max was now, it wasn't here. If he had been, there would have been more color to this place, an air of festivity instead of gloom. He'd have smiled at the picture of his family huddled around his grave, each of them struggling to come up with a heartfelt response that didn't sound as if it had been borrowed from a movie. He'd have scolded them, and sent them home. Or to the beach. If nothing else, Rose thought, freezing water makes you feel alive.

Her thoughts returned to Eric. Surprisingly, they didn't leave her feeling guilty. Max would have understood. He no more would have wanted her to bury her feelings than he would have wished her dead.

It wasn't a choice, she reminded herself. She wasn't choosing between two men she loved. It never would have come to this if Max were still alive. She wouldn't have fallen in love with Eric in the first place.

Then what are you waiting for? Permission to be excused? Max's voice, affectionately mocking, filled her head. *Rosie, you never in your life asked permission to go after anything you truly wanted. What's holding you back now?*

Rose blinked hard. Her throat felt tight, and her eyes stung as they did when staring into too bright a light. But the sky was overcast, and the grass, she suddenly noticed, wasn't as green as it had looked just moments before. Patches of brown, here and there, freckled the gentle swell of lawn, and a number of the trees had lost their leaves. Winter was just around the corner. Even the squirrels foraging a few feet away seemed bolder than usual.

As if from a distance, she heard Mandy say, "I thought it would be nice if we said a prayer."

Rose swallowed thickly, and nodded. Before she was aware of it, the words were coming to her, as naturally as if she'd planned to say them all along. *"Our Father who art in Heaven, hallowed be thy name. . . ."*

It wasn't until she was in the car, on her way home, that she began to cry. Hard enough so that she had to pull over to the side of the road and let Jay take the wheel, even though she'd insisted it was her turn. This time, however, his driving didn't make her nervous. Jay really *had* grown up, she thought. That's how you knew. Not when they stopped growing out of their clothes, or even when they stopped mouthing off at you. It was when they looked after you as you'd once looked after them.

At home, she immediately kicked off her shoes and put water on to boil for tea, ignoring Mr. Chips, who was squawking for attention in his cage. Jay had plans to go to a soccer game with his friend Curtis, but was careful to ask if she'd be okay on her own. Touched, but not wanting to embarrass him, Rose made a face and pushed him gently out the door. Then she switched off the burner under the kettle, got undressed, and climbed into bed. She wasn't tired. She wasn't even that depressed. It was just that she seemed to think more clearly when lying down.

Maybe that was her problem: she'd been thinking *too* much, intellectualizing when she should have been simply *feeling*. All her life, she'd been famous for acting on impulse. Where was that recklessness when she needed it most?

Rose reached for the phone beside the bed. This time, she wouldn't analyze or cross-examine it to death. She wouldn't get mired in heavy sentiment. She wouldn't even stop long enough to glance down at the scary plunge yawning below. She would simply dial.

Amazingly, he answered on the second ring. On a beautiful fall Sunday afternoon, while thousands were stuck in traffic on the LIE or the Sawmill, on their way home from the seashore, or countryside . . . and while many more, like Jay, stood in line for a sporting event, or shot baskets in a pickup game at a park or schoolyard . . . Eric just happened to be home. Almost as if he'd been expecting her.

"Hi," he said.

"Hi yourself."

"You sound as if you have a cold."

"I've been crying."

There was a pause before Eric—rather than ask why, as most people would have done—merely remarked, "I'm glad you told me."

"I just got back from the cemetery, but that's not why I was crying," she said. "Well, partly, maybe. It wasn't as awful as I thought it would be. I felt sort of removed, in a way."

"That's how it was with me at my dad's funeral," he confided. "Like I was going through the motions. I'd cried more as a kid watching *Lassie*. It's not that I didn't love him. It just means you can only handle so much grief at one time."

Like always, Eric understood what she was feeling without her even having to express it. There was only one part he'd left out. "It wasn't *Lassie* I was thinking about," she said with a congested little laugh. "It was *you.*"

A heavy silence fell, and this time Rose imagined she knew what *he* was feeling, and even what he looked like right now, with his sandy hair mussed from raking his fingers through it, and his blue eyes narrowed slightly in anticipation of the hidden catch he never stopped looking for.

"You picked a good time to call," he said guardedly in that low, smoky voice of his. "I was just on my way out."

"I don't want to keep you."

"It can wait."

"Well, good. Because this can't." She pulled in a breath that felt like dragging something up from the bottom of the ocean. "Eric, I've missed you. Not just sort of. I'm crazy with missing you. After the fire . . . I picked up the phone to call you at least a dozen times. But I guess I wasn't ready."

"Are you now?" The wariness hadn't left his voice. "I don't want us to go back to where we were, Rose. I want to marry you."

"I know."

"Are you willing to at least consider it?"

"Yes," she said, amazed at how easily it had slipped out.

"Well. Okay, then." Eric sounded just as dumbstruck as she did. Then, all of a sudden, he began to laugh. "Rose, I didn't think it was possible for me to run out of things to say . . . but I guess nothing that happens with you should surprise me."

She laughed, too, feeling as if she'd swallowed a thunderbolt. Its tingling heat pulsed through her in blue-white veins of electricity. "Good," she said. "I've had enough surprises to last me the rest of my life. I'll settle for what's right in front of me."

"Do you want me to come over? I could be there in twenty minutes."

"Not yet," she told him, tightening her grip on the receiver. "I'm not ready to hang up. I have so much to tell you."

"Let's talk, then."

She smiled up at the ceiling that swam overhead like the bottom of a listing boat suddenly righting itself. "So much has happened just in the past few weeks. I don't even know where to . . ." She stopped, reminding herself to take a breath. Then another. Better. "Why don't I just start at the beginning?" she finished, feeling suddenly calmer, and not at all confused. "That's always a good place."